THE

TELL TALE

MURDERS

CAROLYN DAHMAN

ACKNOWLEDGEMENTS

Most of the information for **The Tell-Tale Murders** came from three sources whom I bothered over and over and over again. I imagine that at some point they either ran screaming from the computer as soon as they saw my name on the other end of the email or buried the phone under a pile of pillows when they saw my name on their caller ID. But I persisted and succeeded in making their lives a hell from which they may never recover.

I'd like to give a warm and special thank you to the FBI's Office of Public Affairs. One of their agents took me under his wing and was invaluable as a source for all things 'FBI.' I was a thorn in his side with my myriad questions and requests for help and his assistance was as endless as his patience. Without this amazing resource, **The Tell-Tale Murders** would never have made it to the printing press.

Next, I'd like to recognize, Michelle, a local pharmacy technician, who explained the intricacies of dealing with Schedule III drugs. I will admit here and now that I 'fudged' a bit with the facts, so anyone out there who spies the inconsistencies, please blame me and not Michelle!

I want to say here and now that I don't believe the CDC would ever be as lax with their security as I've made it seem in the novel. Just chalk it up to 'literary license'.

I'd also like to thank my sister-in-law, Marian, for her insights into life in Miami. I hope I was able to bring some of the flavor of the city to the reader who's never visited that wonderful city. Any mistakes are the responsibility of the author alone.

A special thank you to Elaina, my editor from Redwing Productions. Thanks for being patient and understanding even when I needed (more than one) extension on my due date. You've been great and I couldn't ask for a better writing partner.

I'd like to thank Rob at SelfPubBookCovers.com for getting me hooked up with the artist who created the incredible cover for this book.

Finally, but most importantly, I would like to thank my husband, Doug, for his never-ceasing support and encouragement. You never stopped believing in me and made this journey bearable. Without your love, understanding, financial support and computer expertise, I would have given up after the first chapter. We've been honeymooning for 32 years and I can't wait for the next 32!

PROLOGUE

The night waned, and I worked hastily, but in silence.

'THE TELL-TALE HEART'

June 22

The old house was as silent as the grave the man sleeping within would soon occupy. It slept, blissfully unaware of the turmoil about to sever its tranquility. The gleam from the streetlights was brighter than the crescent moon above, but just barely. Shadows hid on every corner and quiet permeated the neighborhood. Only a mangy stray down the street stirred as he sniffed through the scraps of an overturned trash can.

The darkness was welcomed by the killer as he approached the crumbling tile pathway. Upon reaching the porch, he transferred the two heavy tote bags from his right hand to his left. He paused to check the area.

Good, no one is around.

His stockinged feet made no noise as they reached the newly oiled screen door. The door opened soundlessly, and his serious face cracked into a sudden smile as he remembered the precaution taken days ago in preparation for tonight's gruesome work. He relocked the deadbolt and entered the hallway.

An old-fashioned grandfather clock against the wall showed the time as just after midnight.

This hallway was as familiar to the unexpected guest as any room of his own home. Hall closet to the right, living room to the left, dining room next to that. Further down the corridor was the small kitchen with its dingy white cabinets made of cheap, pressed wood and tiny breakfast table covered in that ridiculous plastic red and white checkered tablecloth and with those horrid Elvis salt and pepper shakers.

God, how I hate this place!

He shook his head and moved on to the bedroom and the waiting victim. Deep snores testified the old man slept peacefully. Opening this second oiled door, the murderer entered the room and waited, making sure it was safe to proceed. A pillow sat at the foot of the bed, as expected. The perfect weapon.

It didn't take long. The old man was sleepy and weak and barely put up a struggle. When the leg stopped moving, another thirty seconds of pressure ensured his death. The murderer removed the pillow and closed the eyes. It was done.

Now for the hard part.

It took time to prepare. The darkness was a hindrance, but as it was impossible to light a lamp, the moonlight would have to serve. He dared not risk being seen.

The bed and nightstand had to be moved first, then a tarp laid out and the dead man placed in its center. He moved the towels and sponges to within easy reach. Finally, he readied the pièce de résistance. He brought out a set of butcher knives he'd purchased under a false name over the Internet last week, their shiny blades gleaming in the moonlight shining through the crack in the curtains. These he lovingly set down beside the cooling corpse.

The first cut was the hardest. Blood trickled from the right arm as he made a jagged incision through the skin and hit muscle. More cuts were needed to reach the tendons, and then he heard a slight noise as he scraped bone. He would need all his strength to pull the humerus from the joint.

Done! One down, four to go.

He finished the left arm the same way.

Furrowed in concentration, sweat began to bead on his forehead, and his gloves became slippery with blood.

He made his way to the lower part of the body. First the right leg, then the left.

Now for the last step. The head. Time to change knives.

He took a minute to take a breather and sip from his water bottle. Looking at his watch, he smiled. It was only 1:00.

He approached the body once again. Those damned eyes would not stay shut. They seemed to follow every move, accusing him with their lifeless stare.

Don't be fanciful. Get a move-on, you don't have all night.

The old man didn't have much hair to grab, but it would be enough. Remembering his Internet research, he pulled the head back to expose the neck. One cut, two cuts, three. Through the skin, to the trachea and the esophagus. Then sever the carotids.

Christ! Who knew there would be so much blood this long after death? It's going everywhere! Good, the tarp's catching it. Okay, deep breaths. Let's finish this.

Another cut through muscle, then between two vertebrae and through the spinal cord. A little more muscle and *DONE!*

Thank God that's over. Time to clean up.

He took one more look around the bedroom to ensure he'd missed nothing, then left the way he came in. It was 3:00 a.m. and he still had a lot to do. He had to get to the dumpsters before the early morning pickup, usually around 5:00.

He walked the three blocks to his waiting car and stowed the bags in the trunk, covered with plastic in case there was any leakage.

Soon the tote bags with the bloody clothes, shoes, gory towels and sponges in one, and knives, tarp, pillow and the bloody plastic in the other, would be gone forever.

No evidence. That is the key.

He drove off into the silent night.

CHAPTER 1

What a world of merriment their melody foretells!
'THE BELLS'

July 10

Lylyana Biddix didn't want to open her eyes. Every time she tried, the room began spinning and her head ached. She tried raising her arm, but that elephant sitting on it just wouldn't get off.

What the hell is going on?

She wasn't in bed, she knew that. Her mattress wasn't the most comfortable, to be sure, but it was too cold underneath her to be a bed. It felt more like wood or, no … concrete. She was lying on concrete! But why? How?

Lylyana opened her eyes to take stock of her surroundings but could only manage small slits. It was dark and she felt closed in, almost as if she were in an extremely small room.

Slowly, she became aware of sounds around her. She heard the unmistakable noise of traffic nearby. There were cars, an angry horn blast followed by an equally angry expletive, and a siren in the distance, its wail fading as it trailed off away from her. Straining, she thought she recognized voices, too, not close, but near enough that she could distinguish more than one.

God, my head hurts!

How did she get here? She closed her eyes again and tried to concentrate through the haze that was her current state of mind. She'd been at work like usual, left at the normal time … and that's where memory ended. What happened after she left work? She would have walked to the metro, but apparently, she never made it that far. What had happened between work and the metro?

Finally, an explanation came to her fogged-in brain and she wondered if she'd been robbed. If she'd been hit in the head or shoved to the ground, that would explain why her head hurt so much. She had to be concussed.

Where was her purse? Gingerly, Lylyana tried to move her arm again to look for it. She could only make her hand move a few inches before she had to give up. She'd have to try again later when her head cleared.

Will concussion affect my arms like this or is there some other, possibly more serious, damage?

Thank God she kept an extra twenty hidden in the lining of her jacket. Even if her purse was gone, she'd be able to call the police or get a taxi or pay someone to help her.

Maybe she could yell for help. There were people somewhere nearby, she'd heard them. If she shouted loud enough, someone might hear her and come. She tried to scream but the croak that emerged wouldn't have alerted a dog.

With a monumental effort, she tried to open her eyes all the way. This time she was successful and felt a ridiculous sense of accomplishment. She waited for her eyes to adjust to the darkness surrounding her and recognized the telltale glow of a streetlamp casting its glow into wherever she was.

Moving her head ever so slightly, Lylyana couldn't make sense of anything around her. The surface below still felt like concrete, the area still felt small and enclosed, but she smelled fresh air in the room, too. Or at least as fresh as Miami air could smell.

She concentrated on the ceiling, trying to make out anything that might tell her where she was. She squinted, but the effort was too much. A drum started beating in her head and she decided to rest a little longer before trying again. Just before her eyes closed, though, Lylyana thought she made out the shape of bells above her. But, of course, that made no sense at all.

CHAPTER 2

The discoloration of ages had been great.
'THE FALL OF THE HOUSE OF USHER'

July 15

What a fucking waste.

FBI agent Mike Donaldson shook his head as he approached the three-story apartment building in northwest Miami. Abandoned and unkempt, the crumbling structure had been ravaged by years of neglect, stripped by thieves, and tagged by gangs and street artists. Now its dilapidated shell reportedly hid Philip Atkinson, a thief who'd stolen fifteen thousand dollars from a credit union in Melbourne.

One of Mike's informants had tipped him that Atkinson was laying-low in this part of Overtown and he'd caught the first available flight and made his way directly here. He pulled out his gun as he reconnoitered the area and, seeing no one about, headed to the first-floor entryway.

As his eyes adjusted to the dim light inside, Mike quickly identified fresh sneaker tracks in the inch-thick dust on the floor that his gut told him had to be Atkinson's. Mike began to follow, clearing each deserted apartment as he went.

Finding nothing on the first floor, he proceeded to the second.

Holding nearly one hundred apartments, the three floors were laid out identically, as was each individual apartment. One bedroom, one bath, a small living room and an even smaller kitchen comprised each unit. There were no balconies for Atkinson to hide on and only one door opened into each apartment.

Securing another empty unit, Mike was reminded of his first solitary retrieval some six years before. Barely thirty, he was assigned to the Violent Crime Major Offender task force in Detroit, when his partner developed an inflamed appendix, forcing him to continue alone in their search for a murderer. He'd tracked the man to an abandoned building not unlike this one and, within minutes, Mike found him hiding behind an old freezer left to rust in the basement.

After a second successful hunt, Mike realized he liked the thrill of the chase and applied for the advanced tactics training course at Quantico. Finishing at the top of his class, he soon gained a reputation for fugitive hunting and these criminals had become his 'specialty'.

Now, Mike was considered one of the FBI's best trackers and was allowed to work alone, often assigned to aid local law enforcement around the country in finding wanted felons. In fact, he spent more time on the road than at his assigned desk. That suited him just fine.

The second floor was as empty as the first and he climbed to the last floor of the deserted building. In the distance, the rumble of thunder heralded a nearing afternoon storm, and Mike felt the oppressive air closing in. Graffiti covered the walls of the third floor; gang members and budding urban artists alike had left their mark. On the floor along the empty corridor trash lay around, stray boxes in a corner, and even an old chair, two of its spindly legs broken off. All the doors were ajar except … two apartments ahead and on the right.

That door was *closed,* not standing open. Apparently in a hurry to hide himself, Atkinson had closed it automatically, never realizing that all the others were either ajar or missing completely.

That was your first mistake, Atkinson.

Doubt suddenly stayed his hand on the rusted doorknob.

Maybe I should go back and recheck the lower floors to make sure Atkinson hasn't doubled back. Maybe I should go forward and check the rest of this floor before entering the apartment. Maybe ... No.

He'd been second-guessing himself a lot after that debacle in Milwaukee and that kind of hesitation could get you killed. He could not doubt himself. He was Michael Edward Donaldson, FBI agent and Fugitive Specialist, for fuck's sake. He'd brought in dozens of criminals over the past seven years. He was practically a fucking legend in the field. He had followed the tracks to this apartment, and he knew Atkinson was inside. He fucking needed to trust his instincts.

He pushed open the door.

Inside, he saw nothing that would lead him to believe his prey was hidden within the empty front room. The kitchen, too, was bare. Another clap of thunder sounded, closer, and Mike moved toward the bedroom. In the tiny hallway, he stopped.

Peeking out from the bathroom was the edge of what appeared to be a shelf. Why would that be there? Mike investigated the empty bathroom and, on the floor, found several shelves strewn haphazardly. Most had been pushed back into the small room in an effort to hide them from view, but one was not hidden as well as the rest. Mike noticed through the dust that all displayed fresh fingerprints.

The only place these shelves could have come from was the linen closet in the hallway. Mike had discounted it as a place of refuge given the shelves inside filled the space. But, since these four had found their way to the bathroom floor, Mike realized the shelves had to be adjustable.

Is the closet large enough for a grown man to hide in?

Mike didn't know the exact dimensions of the closet but felt that if the shelves were moved, then Atkinson was hidden within.

And now that he had him, Mike Donaldson would not let him get away. He moved quietly to the side of the closet and jerked open the door. Instead of Atkinson, however, Mike saw only a gym bag on the floor.

Keeping one eye on his surroundings and the other on the bag, he knelt and quickly riffled through it. On top was a local paper with this morning's headlines screaming **DEATH BY DECIBEL** and a picture of a church. More interesting to Mike, though, was what was hidden underneath. Atkinson's gun and the money from the robbery.

If the money's here, Atkinson can't be far away.

He put his hands on his hips and glanced around the empty apartment. He jumped when another clap of thunder shook the floor and looked outside. The toe of a shoe was visible on the ledge next to the window.

So, that's where you went.

Approaching the window, Mike pulled out his gun and angled himself, so he had a clear view - and a clear shot - of Atkinson.

"FBI. Come in and you won't get hurt."

He spoke with quiet authority so as not to startle the man; he didn't want him accidentally falling off the ledge. If the fall didn't kill him, the best he could hope for was a broken ankle or leg and Mike didn't want the hassle of extra paperwork.

"I *can't* come in." Atkinson's voice broke.

"Yeah, you can."

"No, I can't. I'm scared."

Mike tried not to sigh. "I told you, I'm not gonna hurt you. If you come in quietly, it'll be a lot easier on you. Now come on in."

"You don' understand. I got out here, but now I can't move. I'm afraid of heights."

Seriously? Was this guy pulling his leg?

Mike snapped, "Why the hell'd you go out there then?"

Atkinson winced, but finally answered, "I saw you walkin' around outside and hid in the closet. But when I heard you comin' down the hall, I climbed out here. I figured after you left, I could get back in 'cause I wouldn't be scared no more and have plenty of time."

This time, Mike did sigh. Fugitives were assumed to be armed and dangerous. He'd never been trained to handle a kid hiding on a ledge suffering from acrophobia.

What the fuck do I do now?

"Okay, I get you're scared, but you can't stay out there forever." Deciding he had no choice, Mike put his gun in his shoulder holster, leaned out the window and held out his hand. "Here, grab my hand and I'll help you in."

The passing minutes seemed like an eternity, but Mike finally succeeded in getting Atkinson to the window, grabbed him by the arm and pulled. The two tumbled backward into the room, landing on the floor in a heap. Before Mike could completely regain his balance, Atkinson unexpectedly pulled out a switchblade and lunged toward him.

Years of hand-to-hand training kicked in and Mike deflected the blow. The weapon found his arm instead of his heart.

"Fuck!"

The slash hurt like a bitch, but Mike could tell the wound wasn't deep and wouldn't be serious. It probably wouldn't bleed much. He could ignore it.

He pulled out his gun and pointed it at the fleeing Atkinson. The man went down, a bullet in his left leg.

Damn. Extra paperwork.

CHAPTER 3

Come! Let the burial rite be read–the funeral song be sung!—An anthem for the queenliest dead that ever died so young—A dirge for her the doubly dead in that she died so young.

'LENORE'

Mike finished cataloging another piece of evidence, then picked up the local paper Atkinson's gun had been wrapped in.

DEATH BY DECIBEL. The headline was intriguing, and Mike spent a few moments reading the accompanying story. It seemed a woman had been found dead in the bell tower of a local church. She had died from exposure to the ringing bells.

Not a nice way to go.

Mike sighed, put the paper in an evidence bag and moved on to Atkinson's gym bag.

There was always paperwork to finish and evidence to organize after any case. Mike hated it. Someday, someone was going to figure out a way to streamline this crap.

And when that happens, I'm gonna take that guy out for a beer.

After turning over his fugitive to local police at a nearby hospital, Mike had immediately come to the Miami FBI field office, signed in and called his supervisor to report on his success. He'd wanted to check in with the local Supervisory Special Agent but was told that Bradley Zardes was in a meeting. So, Mike had planted himself at an empty desk the secretary had assigned him and started working. He planned on completing his paperwork, organizing the evidence, then checking into his hotel and getting some much-needed rest.

His arm still hurt. He'd taken a couple of ibuprofens, but the pain had already come back. He knew he could ignore it; he'd had much worse over the past few years.

"Agent Donaldson."

Mike looked over his shoulder and saw a distinguished-looking man approaching him.

"Agent Zardes, I presume." Mike smiled as he stood and held out his hand.

"Agent Donaldson, I expect visiting agents to check in with me before they make themselves at home."

Taken aback by this abrupt greeting, Mike lowered his unshaken hand. Then, regaining his equilibrium somewhat, explained, "I did try to see you, Agent Zardes, but you were in a meeting. The secretary didn't know how long you'd be and was kind enough to find a desk and computer I could use to get started on my reports."

Instead of responding to this explanation, Zardes ordered in a clipped tone, "Let me see your orders."

Mike stared at Zardes for a moment, wondering at his abrasive tone, then pulled out the forms from one of the files on his desk. As the SSA looked them over, Mike took the opportunity to study the man he'd only heard about upon his arrival.

Bradley Zardes was in his early fifties but looked ten years younger. He appeared to be incredibly fit, since his suit jacket did little to hide well-muscled biceps. Mike suspected the supervisory agent worked out on a regular, if not obsessive basis. His hair was an almost bleached blond, and his blue eyes were deep and alert. He carried himself with a seemingly calm assurance and Mike wondered if this man had ever had his authority questioned. Mike wasn't sure why Zardes was so curt with him, but instinctively felt that he didn't want to get on his bad side.

"These seem to be in order," Zardes announced as he dropped the forms on the desk. "How much longer do you think you'll need to complete your paperwork?"

"Probably another hour and a half, two at most."

"And your plans after that?"

"I'm booked at a hotel in Olympia Heights for tonight and I've got a standby reservation back to Detroit for tomorrow morning."

"Good," said Zardes. "Have a good flight back." Zardes then walked away without even a handshake.

What was that all about?

Mentally shrugging his shoulders, Mike sat down and went back to work. It didn't really matter how Bradley Zardes treated him, given Mike was leaving in the morning and would probably never see him again.

"Excuse me, are you Mike Donaldson?"

Surprised by the unexpected question, Mike looked up to see a man approaching his desk, obviously an agent, but he seemed rather young to be working at the FBI. As he came closer, Mike upped his age to mid-twenties. His jet-black hair was parted on the left and his grey eyes were alive with curiosity.

"Yes, I'm Agent Donaldson." Mike held out a hand and added, "However, you have me at a disadvantage. You are?"

"Oh, sorry," said the man as he took Mike's hand and began pumping it.

Mike noticed a small scar on his hand, but its faded quality made Mike suspect it was from his childhood, not recent.

"I'm Jamie Smythe. But you can call me Chip, everyone does."

"'Chip'?" Mike frowned. "Where'd that come from?"

Chip laughed and answered, "People've been calling me Chip since I was a kid. The short version is that when I was four, I wouldn't eat anything but chocolate for about six months. My parents had to get really creative. Chocolate milk was easy, but they had to put chocolate chips in things like vegetable soup or chocolate syrup on mashed potatoes just to get me to eat them. My cousin started calling me 'Chip' and it stuck. Anyway, I don't mind." He shrugged. "I'm really glad to meet you, Agent Donaldson."

Chip smiled, showing large white teeth that could definitely have used braces when he was growing up. The grin was infectious, and Mike found himself smiling back. After the cold reception from Agent Zardes, Mike was glad that someone in this office was friendly.

"Nice to meet you too, Chip." Several seconds went by while Chip did nothing but stare at him. Trying to relieve his unease, Mike continued the conversation. "So, Chip, why are you so glad to meet me?"

"Oh, yeah, well you see ..." Chip trailed off and Mike realized he was debating with himself. Then, obviously making a decision of some kind, he plunged into his explanation. "Well, you're practically a legend, Agent Donaldson. I mean, you captured two Most Wanted in the same week! That is so cool. You see, I want to hunt fugitives someday and I've been studying your cases. It's great to finally meet you in person."

Although he was embarrassed by this show of adulation, Mike couldn't help but be secretly pleased. He'd worked hard to establish a reputation and was grateful he'd apparently succeeded. Adulation could be overdone, however, so Mike didn't want to encourage it either.

"Well, I appreciate the thought, but I'm just doing my job. It's as much luck sometimes as hard work, so I try not to get too cocky." Mike grinned and changed the conversation. "So, Chip, if you want to find fugitives, why haven't you taken the training? You could start by joining the local VCMO and then apply for the course at Quantico. How long have you been in the FBI anyway?"

"Two years and it's not that I haven't wanted to apply, but, well, it's personal."

When Chip seemed to falter, Mike quickly backtracked. "Hey, I didn't mean to intrude, it's none of my business ..."

"Oh no, it's not that," Chip began. Before he could explain, his cell went off. "Excuse me, I need to take this."

Chip walked off and Mike returned to his paperwork. He was tagging the last of the evidence when Chip returned a few minutes later.

"Hey, Agent Donaldson, you got much longer here? I'd love to hear about some of your cases. How about a drink after work tonight? Or do you have to leave town again right away?"

Mike hid a sigh. He really wanted to get to his hotel and rest a bit, but then again, wasn't that what he liked about his job? Meeting new agents? What could it hurt?

"Sure. Why don't you call me when you're ready to go?" Mike looked at the phone on his desk. "My extension is 432."

~~

The drinks were served, and they'd ordered appetizers before Chip asked about Mike's most famous retrieval.

Mike enjoyed retelling his capture of the infamous drug kingpin two years ago in Chicago. It had taken over a month to locate Dwight Dennison and another month of surveillance to determine the best time to take him. But he'd apprehended the drug dealer without a shot being fired and had testified against him just last month. He'd listened with satisfaction to the guilty verdict.

"That is so cool," commented Chip when Mike was finished with his story and on his second beer. "I know it must sometimes get boring on the road so much, but I still think I'd like to do it."

"Well, you won't get any argument out of me. I love what I do. It's really satisfying to know I've gotten some of these creeps off the streets and even if I spend more time sleeping in a truck than a bed, it's worth it."

Mike had enjoyed the last hour. The conversation had flowed easily, and he'd been able to completely relax. Before he could say anything else, Chip's phone rang. Excusing himself, Chip turned slightly to take his call.

Normally, Mike didn't have much in common with the younger FBI agents he met and, at twenty-six, Chip was almost ten years his junior. But during the last hour, Chip had shown himself to be thoughtful and intelligent. He obviously enjoyed his chosen profession. With some training, Mike thought he'd make a good retrieval specialist. He wondered how he could bring up the subject again without seeming to butt in.

"Sorry about that," said Chip as he put his phone back in his pocket. "That was my dad, and I really need to take it when he calls."

"No need to apologize," answered Mike as he waved away the explanation. "Do your parents live here in Miami?"

"Well, my dad does. My mom ..." Chip's attention suddenly focused on the television behind the bar and he asked the bartender, "Hey, could you turn that up for a minute?" He looked at Mike. "Hope you don't mind, but they're updating the 'Death by Decibel' story and I'm interested in it."

Both men listened when the reporter started to speak.

"Police are still at a loss to explain how Lylyana Biddix got into the bell loft of Miami's Trinity Episcopal Cathedral on Northeast 16th Street. The tower is usually locked and inaccessible by the public unless a special tour has been arranged, nevertheless Ms. Biddix was found here yesterday.

"Police released the completed autopsy report this morning, confirming prior speculation that Ms. Biddix died after prolonged exposure to the ringing bells. However, it is now confirmed that death did not occur after Saturday evening services as originally thought, but more likely Ms. Biddix died after the evening peal on Friday night.

"Church officials confirm that a special peal was performed Friday evening and the autopsy showed death occurred sometime late Friday night or in the early hours on Saturday.

"Prolonged exposure to ringing bells, especially in a confined space, can cause various symptoms, including bursting eardrums and bleeding from the ears. Some of these can even lead to death …"

Chip turned away from the television and took a long pull of his beer. "Man! What a lousy way to die. I really feel sorry for that woman."

"Yeah, that's pretty horrible," Mike agreed and took a drink of his own now-warm beer. "It would be interesting to know how she got up there in the first place. I mean, if it's normally locked, how'd she get in? And why?"

"It's a pretty weird way to commit suicide, if you ask me," answered Chip as he stood up. Taking some bills out of his pocket, he said, "This one's on me. Thanks for coming out for a drink. I really enjoyed talking to you. Hope you'll get back this way again sometime."

Mike made as if to argue over the tab, but Chip forestalled him. "Nope, I insist. I invited you and you spent all your time answering my questions about life on the road. Paying for your drinks is the least I can do." Holding out a hand, Chip said again, "Thanks. Have a good trip back to Detroit."

Mike took the proffered hand. "Whenever you decide to apply for the advanced tactical training, look me up. I'll see if I can help you out."

Chip's smile was radiant as he turned and left the bar, and Mike decided he'd actually made a new friend on this trip. Too bad he was leaving tomorrow morning.

CHAPTER 4

I have told you that I am nervous; so I am.
'THE TELL-TALE HEART'

What the fuck is the fucking holdup? All I want is a simple sandwich and I've been standing in this fuckin' line for ten fuckin' minutes!

Lousy ending to a lousy day. I'm so glad it's finally the weekend. TGIF and all that. By now, Brad has figured out I cut out early, but fuck him. He'll just use it as another excuse to get on my case again anyway, so why not?

Not that the asshole needs an excuse these days. He's been on me since I lost that Jessup loan a couple of weeks ago. It's not fair. It's not my fault the folder was misfiled. But he never got on Deanna for losing it. No, it was all my fault for not telling her it should have gone into the special projects file. Well, excuse the fuck outta me.

Oh joy, I moved up another foot! At this rate I could just order breakfast for tomorrow instead of dinner and it'd be closer to the right time.

Arggh! If this fucking phone doesn't stop going off. It better not be Brad.

Oh, for fuck's sake! Sydney again. Well, I'm not gonna answer it. One argument with her a day is about all I can take right now. All I asked is if she'd pick up my suit from the drycleaners and you'd've thought I asked her to go to the moon instead of a couple miles out of her way. What a stupid argument to have anyway. Not to mention a lousy way to start the day. I already told her I'll pick up the suit. I wish she'd just get off it, for heaven's sake.

God! I need to take a breath and relax. That's what the doctor said, right? Deep breaths, count to ten or even twenty. Okay, let's try it. One, breathe. Two, breathe. Three, breathe.

"What? Oh, sorry. Uh, I'll have a twelve-inch BLT with mayonnaise and lettuce only. Huh? To go, please. Here, keep the change. Thanks."

Number 22! They're only serving number 15 right now. I'll never get outta here. Arggh!

No, no, breathe. Four, breathe. Five, breathe.

Okay, that's a little better. I can already feel my heart rate slowing down a bit. Maybe I need to do that more often during the day like the doc said.

Maybe I was a little hard on Deanna. It really was my responsibility to tell her that it was an important file and needed special handling. She is the secretary for four loan officers, and she can't be expected to know everything about every file, after all. I should apologize to her. Maybe I'll get her a plant of some kind. She likes plants. It would be a peace offering. That's what I'll do. I'll look for something this weekend.

And I need to apologize to Sydney, too. She does work longer hours than me and I know she gets tired. She's on her feet all day while I sit at a desk. She ends up doing all the cooking since I'm hopeless in the kitchen. At least I do the dishes every night. Most husbands don't or at least that's what Sydney says. Of course, that was the deal before we got married: the cook never cleans. And after ten years of marriage, we're still sticking to the deal. Some of the guys at the bank sure give me grief for it, but I don't mind. I know it's right to help out. She shouldn't do everything around the house. Marriage is a partnership, they say. And I got lucky as hell with Sydney. Not many women would put up with my temper. But I am trying. I'll apologize as soon as she gets home from her sister's tonight. Girl's night out ... well she deserves it.

"I'm number 22. Thanks. See ya next time."

Okay, now to get through this crowd. I never realized how popular this place is. Of course, they have the best sandwiches in Hialeah, that's for sure.

"Hey, watch where you're goin'. Oh, sorry, probably my fault anyway. Huh, do I know you? Oh, of course, from the bank. Uh, have a good evening ..."

"What? Uh, your loan? Well, I haven't gotten to the paperwork yet. I'll call you if I have any questions."

"Now? Well, it's Friday night ..."

Oh, come on. I don't need to hear your whole fuckin' life story! Just spit it out already.

"I understand your concerns, but I'll need to look over the paperwork before I can give you an answer. Right now though, I really need to get going."

Just what I needed, a customer flagging me down when all I wanted was to forget my fuckin' job for a few minutes. And what a talker! Gees! Funny, I don't remember that application at all. Of course, there's so many. I'll look for it Monday ...

You have got to be kidding me! A fuckin' flat tire! On top of everything else today. At this rate, I'll never get home. It'll take forever for the automobile club to get here. I wonder if I could call Gene ...

"Oh, hello again."

"Flat tire. I was just going to call a friend to come pick me up."

"Oh, I couldn't let you ..."

"No, not too far from here, but I don't want to put you to any trouble."

"Now, you wouldn't be trying to bribe me into approving your loan, would you?"

"Oh hey, I'm sorry. It was just a little joke. I didn't mean anything by it, really. Just some bank humor, that's all. Sure, I'll take you up on the offer of a ride. It's really nice of you."

"What? Oh no, I couldn't take your coffee. Oh, you have an extra. Yeah, their roasted blend is pretty good. Well, thanks then, if you're sure. I doubt if I'll get into trouble for taking a free cup of coffee."

"That's good. Thanks. And they say people don't do nice things for each other anymore. Guess I got lucky when I bumped into you, huh?"

CHAPTER 5

He had on a tight-fitting parti-striped dress, and his head was
surmounted by the conical cap and bells.

'THE CASK OF AMONTILLADO'

July 17

"You want some more coffee, hon?"

The clink of the dishes from the kitchen nearly drowned out
the many conversations taking place around him and the smell of
bacon and eggs filled Mike's nostrils as a waiter handed out plates
at the table to his right.

Mike nodded and smiled at his waitress. "Yeah, fill me up
again. This is probably the best coffee I've ever had anywhere; I
swear."

"I hear that a lot." His waitress was in her mid-fifties and her
auburn hair was obviously dyed, but her smile was friendly as she
poured the steaming hot liquid into the white cup.

Mike took a sip and looked up. "It's Beverly, right? What's
your secret? This stuff is to die for."

"Well, I didn't actually make the coffee myself," she confided
and gave Mike a wink. "The owner does that himself every
morning. He's addicted to coffee and came up with this blend after
a lot of trial and error. He started serving it a few years ago and it

really took off. People have offered him all sorts of amounts for his secret recipe, but he won't tell anyone what it is. I don't think his wife even knows. He'll probably take the recipe to his grave."

Beverly's laugh drew looks from a nearby table and a smile from Mike. "Let me know if you need anything else," she said as she walked off to serve the next table.

Mike's smile didn't last long after she left his table. He had been in Miami for two days now and he still couldn't relax. He tried reading and then walking around the area. He'd gone to the FBI target range and practiced shooting for two hours yesterday afternoon. He'd even gone to a nearby mall and looked for a new pair of shoes. Nothing seemed to work. He just couldn't relax. Mike simply wasn't a vacation kind of guy.

When he learned his flight had been delayed two mornings ago, he'd immediately called his supervisor. Instead of being angry, however, Gabriel had ordered him to take time off. Apparently, Human Resources had advised his boss that Mike was building up too much vacation time and he needed to take some of it before he lost it. Gabriel had been adamant that he didn't want to see Mike again until the 27th.

Mike hated being told he 'had' to relax but couldn't defy a direct order from his boss. Giving in to the inevitable, Mike had decided to stay in Miami for a while instead of going anywhere else. He didn't have any family and only called a few people friends.

He'd actually considered traveling to Los Angeles and visiting Ben and Isaac Sandoval. He'd worked with Ben a couple of times and the two men had become close a few years ago when Mike had helped Ben find Isaac after the younger Sandoval was attacked by two fugitive bank robbers on the Winding Trail in the San Gabriel Mountains. The three men had become friends after that and kept in fairly regular touch. However, when he'd called Ben and couldn't reach him, he'd contacted Ben's dad and found out that the brothers had taken a vacation of their own. So, LA was out, and Mike decided to just stay put in Miami.

There had to be something to do that would keep his interest.

Mike took another sip of the coffee and went back to reading his newspaper. He always saved the front section for last and was surprised to see that the 'Death by Decibel' story wasn't the lead for the first time in days. Another alliterative headline caught his attention.

MASQUERADE MURDER MYSTIFIES MEN IN BLUE

The story was brief but intriguing. The victim, Stephen Hardison, had been chained to a wall and left to die in a sealed room. Unable to get out, Hardison had died of apparent dehydration although the autopsy was still pending. It was unclear how long he'd been in the room, or why anyone would want to kill him in such a gruesome manner. He'd been found by a homeless man late the night before.

The things people did to each other never ceased to amaze him. Mike shook his head and paid for his breakfast. He picked up his paper and left the bustling restaurant still undecided as to what he was going to do to while away the day.

~~

A veteran of numerous crime scenes, Mike was unsurprised to see the many civilians standing around craning their necks to get a better look while holding up cell phones to take pictures to show their friends and co-workers. Yellow crime scene tape stretched along the road keeping the curious onlookers across the street while seven or eight MDPD officers intoned the usual "Please step back" to the curious and "No comment" to the various representatives of the media that had descended on the scene like a biblical cloud of locusts.

This area of Hialeah was littered with commercial warehouses, packed together like the proverbial sardines in a can.

Most of the one-story buildings had iron bars on their windows and rolling doors for delivery trucks to enter. Small dumpsters dotted the area in front of each structure, most overflowing with trash. There were only a few parking spots for each establishment, so police vehicles blocked the narrow street, effectively closing it down until the investigation was done.

Parking his car further down the street, Mike walked to the caution tape and showed his FBI ID to the first Miami-Dade police officer he saw. The officer's eyes first widened then narrowed and Mike already knew what the next question would be.

"This a Fed case then?" asked the cop.

He looked to be twenty-four or five, probably only on the force a couple of years. His tone implied a rivalry between local police and federal agents. A local pissing match that Mike didn't want to get into.

"No, not a federal case, Officer Dientz," Mike replied, looking at the man's name badge on his uniform. "I'm just in Miami for another case and was curious after reading the story in the paper this morning. Could I speak to the officer in charge?"

For a moment, Mike thought he might refuse, then Dientz pushed the button on the radio mic attached to his shoulder and spoke to someone he addressed simply as 'Cap'.

Mike assessed the nearby buildings while Dientz waited for an answer and was pleasantly surprised when only a moment passed before he was waved through the cordon and pointed in the direction of the on-going crime scene.

The building was an old shoe factory that had seen better days. Obviously abandoned for some time, the original color on the outside walls was impossible to determine and the grime looked to be the only thing holding the structure up. The front door was warped, the paint cracked and peeling. The parking lot was overrun by weeds growing in every crack in the pavement.

Mike continued into the building and followed the yellow crime scene tape along the walls until he reached a beehive of activity. A room had been cordoned off and several officers were collecting evidence.

Looking around, it didn't take long to identify the man in charge. The captain's whole demeanor screamed, "I'm in charge, do what I say."

"Captain Mendez? I'm Special Agent Mike Donaldson, FBI." Mike held out a hand.

"Agent Donaldson, nice to meet you."

Mendez's smile was genuine, and Mike let out a breath he didn't know he'd been holding.

"I was a little surprised when Dientz said you were out front. Then he said you were in town for another case. Just curious or just bored?"

Mike laughed. "Since when did Miami PD hire mind readers?" His grin was sheepish. "Yeah, I admit it, I'm on a forced vacation and bored out of my skull. I read the story about the murder in the paper this morning and couldn't help myself. I was hoping just to look around. I promise not to get in anybody's way."

"Got no problem with that, Agent. Look away. And if anything comes to mind, please feel free to let me know. This one is not only strange but a bit macabre."

"Really?" Mike's curiosity was heightened again. "In what way? The newspaper didn't have many details."

"Didn't have many to give out yet," responded Mendez. "Follow me."

Mendez led the way and, as he followed, Mike realized that this was the way he had hoped to be treated by Zardes the other day.

Not everybody likes outsiders horning in, I guess.

Captain Samuel Mendez looked to be in his mid-forties but was prematurely gray. Even his mustache had turned completely gray. He walked quickly and Mike had to hurry to keep up. As he listened to the captain's explanation, Mike realized two things.

One, Mendez was well-versed in all the minutiae of the case and, two, his staccato sentences went straight to the point.

"Found him over here." Mendez pointed to a door. "This door was broken a week ago. Homeless guy sometimes squats in here, and last evening noticed that the door was suddenly welded shut. Checked it out and noticed a smell. Decided something was wrong so got a cop he knows to come and look. Cop realized something *was* wrong and called it in. Less than an hour later they got the door opened and found this."

They'd reached the formerly sealed room and Mike stopped short. The body outline was taped against the far wall and showed where the victim had been chained. One arm outline dangled down, leading to the rest of the body tape crumpled in a ball and leaning against the wall. Obviously Hardison had been left there to die, which he apparently did slowly over the course of three or four days.

On the floor, Mike saw the physical evidence of what his senses had already identified. There was dried feces and stale urine where the body had been chained. He also saw evidence markers where parts of Hardison's clothing had been ripped off as the man had writhed in agony.

"We're trying to get the Medical Examiner to expedite the post-mortem, so we'll know exactly what we're dealing with," Mendez was saying, bringing Mike back to the present. "Pretty sure he died of dehydration, but we need the official report. Maybe tomorrow, but probably the next day, the Medical Examiner says. In the meantime, we're looking into Hardison's life to see if he was targeted or just a random victim."

Mike looked around and said forlornly, "No witnesses, I suppose."

"Not a chance," Mendez agreed. "We'll ask, of course, but nobody lives on this street - it's all commercial - and no one comes down to this area at night, so I doubt we'll get lucky there."

"But he had to be here for several days before he died. Didn't anyone hear him screaming?"

Mendez shook his head. "We think he was brought here over the weekend. If that was Friday, say, in the normal course of things, no one would have been around here again until Monday. Either way, there would have been no one around for a couple of days. By that time, he was too far gone to scream loud."

Mike considered for a moment and blew out a breath. "Any chance I might look at the prelim reports?"

Mendez looked at him with slightly narrowed eyes, but answered easily enough, "Sure, no problem. Always glad of an extra pair of eyes."

Mike held out a hand and said, "Thanks for letting me look around. If I think of anything, I'll call you, but it looks like you've got it all under control."

~~~

Mike had finished his fish and chips at a pub run by some transplanted Brits when he pulled out the envelope again. He'd studied the pictures from the crime scene and the preliminary report Captain Mendez gave him on and off all day. Besides the look of fear and near-terror on the victim's face, the pictures didn't give Mike any new insight into the crime. He simply couldn't get the idea out of his head that he was missing something, though. It was in the back of his mind and Mike knew from experience that if he didn't worry it, it would eventually come to him.

~~~

"Damn!" Mike cursed as he walked into his hotel.

He always carried two or three paperbacks to read on the road, but since he hadn't planned on a vacation, he already finished the books he'd brought with him. Today he'd planned on going to a bookstore to find something to read over the next few days, but he forgot to do it. Now he faced a boring evening with garbage on TV and nothing to read.

The young desk clerk looked up at the unexpected expletive and asked solicitously, "Is there a problem, sir? Can I do anything to help you?"

Mike's tone was biting. "Only if you can find me an all-night bookstore somewhere nearby."

"I'm afraid there's nothing like that in this area, sir. However, you're welcome to look at our 'Take a Book, Leave a Book' shelf in the lobby. You may find something to interest you there."

Take a Book, Leave a Book? Mike looked at the clerk, his suspicion obvious.

Correctly interpreting her customer's look, she asked, "What have you got to lose?"

What indeed?

Mike shrugged and moved further into the lobby. His expectations were not hopeful, but you never knew. There might be *something* that could keep him busy for the night and then tomorrow he could go to a real bookstore and find something to read for the rest of his vacation.

There were actually two shelves full of books, one for children and the other for adults. As Mike ran his finger along the adult books, he realized his expectations had been too high. The titles ranged from crap ground out yearly by over-priced, 'popular' authors to no-names he'd never heard of. Nothing interested him in the least.

Just as he was about to turn away, Mike saw two books sticking out at the end of the second shelf. A thick paperback was hidden behind a couple of Jackie Collins novels.

The Complete Tales of Mystery and Imagination by Edgar Allen Poe.

Mike smiled. He'd grown up with Poe, reading and re-reading the macabre stories and scintillating poetry. He'd spent hours and hours poring over the plots and descriptions. Poe had written the first detective story *ever* and these stories instilled in Mike his love of solving mysteries. They were one of the reasons he'd decided to go into law enforcement after his time in the army.

Mike pulled the volume off the shelf. It was old and worn with stains every few pages and dog-ears scattered throughout, but he knew the stories would engross him and he'd be able to keep occupied for several days. This was just the diversion he needed.

Mike grabbed the tome and, looking forward to the evening ahead of him, practically skipped up the stairs.

~~

"In pace requiescat!"

And so ended 'The Cask of Amondtillado'. Mike leaned back against the headboard and sighed. This had always been one of his favorite Poe stories. He remembered being scared to death at the picture Poe created of a man sealed up in a crypt, chained to a wall and left to die alone …

Shit!

It couldn't be …

Steven Hardison had been chained to a wall and sealed up in a room and left to die. Just like Fortunato in Poe's story. What was more, 'The Cask of Amontillado' took place during Carnival and Fortunato was dressed up in a colorful costume. Wasn't Hardison dressed up, too?

Mike grabbed the folder on the desk in the corner and started pulling out papers. He reread the police report and then began to pore over the crime scene photos.

Yes. Hardison *had* been dressed up in a wild-looking outfit of some kind. Purple pants and a green shirt, a silk cloth tied around his neck and, to top it all off, a brown felt hat with a feather sticking out of it was found nearby. The clothes had not been described in detail in the newspaper, but there was enough information available for the headline to mention 'Masquerade' clothing.

Looking carefully at the room itself, he finally saw what he'd been looking for. That was what had been bugging him all day and tugging at the back of his mind.

In pace requiescat.

These three words had been written on a sheet of paper and taped to the wall across from where Hardison had died. Miami PD had assumed it was something left by the former occupants and hadn't associated it with their current crime.

Why would three words in Latin be taped to a wall in an old shoe factory? That hadn't made any sense and Mike realized that was what had bothered him.

This same phrase were the last words of Poe's story.

Mike didn't know Latin and the story had not explained them.

He hurried to his laptop and tapped his foot as he waited for it to boot up. He plugged into the hotel's wi-fi and typed in the words. He wasn't surprised when he read the results.

Rest in peace.

It was too much a coincidence to be coincidence.

But why? What would be the point of killing someone based on an Edgar Allan Poe story? And why Steven Hardison?

And more importantly, would anyone believe him?

CHAPTER 6

I neither expect nor solicit belief.
'THE BLACK CAT'

July 18

The next morning found Mike shaving and still trying to decide what to do with his suspicions. Last night, he'd decided the best idea was to go to the FBI. He was an agent, and it would be natural to share his thoughts with them. On reconsideration, however, he decided he needed to find proof first.

But where to get that proof?

Mike picked up the Poe anthology. The Table of Contents was divided up between the stories and the poems. Mike recognized many of the short stories as ones he'd read as a kid. 'The Murders in the Rue Morgue', 'The Tell-Tale Heart' and 'The Fall of the House of Usher' were particular favorites.

The poems were a different matter. Although he knew he'd read many, he didn't remember them as well since he'd always been more interested in the stories. He'd re-read most of those stories several times while he might have read most of the poems only once.

He'd have been teased mercilessly if the kids in his school had known that he read *any* kind of poetry on his own and not at the behest of an English teacher. So, he'd not read most of them more than once and remembered them even less.

Looking through the list of poems now, his eyes immediately found 'The Raven', probably Poe's most famous poem. He also recognized 'Annabel Lee' and 'A Dream within a Dream'.

Mike stopped short as he read the next title listed.

'The Bells' was vaguely familiar, and Mike suddenly remembered the 'Death by Decibel' story in the paper a few days ago. He immediately went to the listed page and read the poem.

'The Bells' was divided into four stanzas and each one seemed to reflect a different stage of life as represented by differing types of bells. Reading carefully, Mike recognized that the first stanza's silver bells reflected the joy of youth, the second's wedding bells mirrored harmony. Brass bells exemplified terror in the third stanza while the last movement of the poem used iron bells to announce approaching death.

> *What a tale their terror tells*
> *Of Despair!*
> *How they clang, and clash, and roar!*

Sweat beaded on Mike's forehead as the implications of what he read began to take shape in his mind.

Can it be? Can someone really ...?

No. He needed proof. That was what he'd told himself only a few minutes ago and he didn't have that yet.

Mike no longer had the newspaper of a few days ago, so he googled the 'Decibel' story. He read each successive item trying to get as many details as he could.

Lylyana Biddix, twenty-nine years old, had been found in the bell tower of Trinity Episcopal Cathedral. She had apparently died from exposure to the sound of the bells ringing during a service over the weekend and had been found a few days later. The autopsy showed ruptured eardrums and shock from proximity to the noise. As of now, the official cause of death was suicide, but no one had yet been able to explain how Biddix was able to enter the bell tower unseen or why she had chosen such a terrible way to die.

In the same way that Poe described the brass bells as 'screaming out their affright' and 'a horror they outpour', the bells at Trinity Episcopal Cathedral had rung for over fifteen minutes and killed a young woman.

This was not a suicide, Mike realized. Lylyana Biddix was murdered and the instrument of her death were the bells in that tower.

Another death by Poe …

The room seemed to spin as Mike tried to accept his discovery. The painted scenes hanging on his walls of egrets in the Everglades and manatees in the Gulf were incongruent when juxtaposed with the macabre deaths depicted in the pictures on his desk and laptop. Death had been slow and painful for Lylyana Biddix and Stephen Hardison.

Mike knew the two murders were linked. He had to tell the FBI now.

~~

"That's the craziest thing I ever heard, Donaldson. I don't know where you got this idea of yours, but I'm not buying it. You're just a tracker, not an investigator. When was the last time you investigated a case, instead of merely looking for the guys other agents' work found for you? Now, get out of my office. I don't have time for this kind of crap."

Zardes all but threw the unopened file back at Mike. He made a show of ignoring Mike while he returned to signing off on some forms on his desk.

For his part, Mike was disappointed but not surprised by the SSA's reaction to his theory. He'd known it was a long shot that Zardes would believe him, but he had hoped the man would at least listen to his reasons for believing the Biddix and Hardison murders were related.

This was too important, though, not to keep trying. Mike began again.

"Sir, if you'd give me a minute to explain what I've found ..."

"Explain what?" Zardes' tone was deadly. "Explain that you've invented some sort of link between two unrelated deaths? That you manufactured some sort of theory based on a couple of stories? That one of these deaths hasn't even been labeled a murder? That you're suddenly on vacation when you were supposed to be gone days ago? That you're bored so you made this whole thing up to give yourself something to do?" Zardes practically sneered the last question.

"Agent Zardes," Mike began. "I didn't manufacture anything, and I'm not bored. I can show you the relative passages from the Poe works and all I'm asking for is a desk and a computer. In a couple of days, I think I can prove that these murders are not only related but that there may be more deaths to come. I just need ..."

"To investigate two *local* murders, Donaldson?" Zardes interrupted. "If you were any kind of a real FBI agent, you might have remembered that we have no jurisdiction in local crimes unless we're *asked* to investigate. We can't just butt in because you have a hunch."

Zardes stood up and, leaning forward, slapped his hands on the desk. "You may not be one of my agents, but I still outrank you, Donaldson. This is still my office and if you don't get out now, I'll have you thrown out. Do I make myself clear?"

Mike had no choice, and he knew it. "As crystal, Agent Zardes." Mike picked up his file, turned and left the office with as much dignity as he could muster.

He waited until he was down the hall to exhale. He'd kept his temper, but just barely. The man was an asshole, but Mike was used to dealing with those. What angered him was Zardes' apparent close-mindedness. He wouldn't even listen to the theory or look at his information. For a man in Zardes's position, that was tantamount to a dereliction of duty in Mike's opinion.

Not an investigator?

Mike stopped in the hallway and tried to control his rising temper. Zardes' comment had stung, and not just because the man was a bastard. No, it stung because deep down, Mike was afraid Zardes was right. Over the past seven years he'd been on the road hunting fugitives more often than investigating cases. Maybe his skills weren't as sharp as they could be. Maybe he was in over his head. Maybe ...

No. He was as much an investigator as anyone else in this office. Mike wasn't going to let that bastard Zardes make him doubt himself. He knew he was right about these murders and he wouldn't sit idly by while a killer was on the loose. He had to do something before another innocent person died in some hideous manner. He needed definitive proof, not just a theory based on one poem and a story.

CHAPTER 7

Keeping time, time, time,
In a sort of Runic rhyme.
To the tintinnabulation that so musically wells
From the bells, bells, bells, bells,
Bells, bells, bells.
'THE BELLS'

Where to start?

As he drove back to his hotel, Mike realized he could do a lot on his computer and probably even some research at the library. That would only get him so far, however. At some point he'd need access to police reports, and the autopsies, things he could only get through MDPD. But he wasn't ready for that yet. He'd need more hard evidence and facts before he could request access to official information.

He'd start with his own laptop and see if he could find more information to add to what he already had on hand. He was certainly no doctor or the coroner, but he might be able to get some of the medical background he needed online. He'd begin with the Biddix murder since that was the first death, then move on to Hardison's killing. The newspaper had been rather vague about how one died by listening to bells ring - something to do with the loudness and proximity - so he'd start first with bells.

~~

150 decibels is usually considered enough to burst a person's eardrums, but the threshold for death is generally agreed to be around 185-200 decibels.

Close up, the sound of Big Ben measures about 118 decibels, and is loud enough to cause physical pain.

A bell isn't just a single tone. There are several overtones to it. Partial harmonics, inharmonic tones and subharmonic tones.
It's the reverberation. The vicar struck the bell and the effect shocked me and my entire body was vibrating from my toes up. If a person climbs into a belfry to sleep and the bell ringers don't know they're there, they could end up deaf or worse. That's why bell ringers stay on the ground and use ropes to ring the bells.

Sound level meters incorporate electronic filtering to correspond with the varying sensitivity of the ear. This filtering is called A-weighting and measured sound pressure levels are signified as dB(A).

The ringers risk hearing damage if sound levels exceed 85 dB(A), recommended levels are <80 dB(A).

Reverberation: When a bell is struck in a bell chamber, a significant amount of the radiated sound energy is reflected at the chamber surfaces, augmenting the intensity of the sound in the chamber. Only a fraction of this sound energy is absorbed at any one reflection and so the sound does not die away instantaneously, giving rise to reverberation.

~~

This shit is going to drive me crazy.

Mike knew his Internet researching skills weren't the best, but after several hours his head was swimming with information about cathedral bells, decibel levels, bursting eardrums and a ton of other minutiae. He was trying to make sense of it all, but in the end, he'd really only glimmered that church bells could indeed kill, given the right circumstances, and that proving that Lylyana Biddix's death was a murder would be even more difficult that he thought.

Mike didn't give up easily. He decided his next topic of research needed to be more targeted. He'd learned a lot about church bells in general, now he needed to learn specifically about the bells at Trinity Episcopal Cathedral.

The Cathedral's website was less detailed than he'd hoped. The only cogent paragraph was its first:

> Miami's Trinity Cathedral commissioned a ring of eight bells from the Whitechapel Bell Foundry of England, following construction of a tower adjacent to the narthex. The Patterson Memorial Bells were installed and dedicated on December 4, 1984. The largest bell weighs 2007 pounds (1700 ct), and the smallest weighs 558 pounds (303 ct).

Following this was just information about the change ringers responsible for the upkeep of the bells and change ringing in general.

Nothing here to help much.

There were directions to the cathedral and Mike wondered if an on-site visit would be worthwhile. No hours of operation were given, but a phone call might get him the name of someone he could talk to and his FBI ID was sure to elicit cooperation.

His watch, however, told him that it was probably too late to call now. It was nearly six o'clock and the cathedral offices were more than likely closed for the day.

But he'd definitely call tomorrow morning. Surely there would be someone in the office by 9:00.

What else can I do tonight?

Mike looked at his Poe book and thought he might re-read both 'The Bells' and 'The Cask of Amontillado'. He could spend the time writing up a chart comparing the appropriate passages with the information he had about the murders. That might help prove his theory.

~~

Mike put the box of leftovers in the refrigerator in his hotel room. He'd been preoccupied over dinner and hadn't eaten much, so he'd given up and come back to the hotel.

He was brooding and he knew it. Part of him was trying to decide on his next move while the other part was wondering if he'd bitten off more than he could chew. He felt as though he were floundering, going from one idea to another and not really getting anywhere. He needed a plan.

As he looked over the police report again, he realized his best bet would be to approach Captain Mendez. He was in charge of the Hardison case and the Miami PD captain seemed more open-minded. Or at least, more open-minded to Mike Donaldson. Where Zardes had been aloof and dismissive, Mendez had been friendly and approachable. Mendez would at least listen, he hoped. He might also know the officers who'd investigated the Biddix case and be able to smooth the way with them as well.

With a grin on his face, Mike picked up the remote control of his TV. He'd relax a little before turning in early.

He planned to head toward the Doral office of Captain Samuel Mendez early in the morning. He'd find a way to convince the man, then he could really get going on proving his theory and hopefully save some lives.

CHAPTER 8

Now let us be off, for we have no time to lose.
'THE GOLD BUG'

July 19

The wealth of soccer paraphernalia in his office was evidence enough that Captain Mendez was a big soccer fan. Mike looked at a picture proudly displayed on the wall of the captain surrounded by members of the Fusion, Miami's now-defunct Major League Soccer team, apparently taken on the team's home field. On a table under the picture sat a clear plastic display box within which sat a soccer ball autographed by that same Fusion team and dated some years previously.

"Do you like soccer, Agent Donaldson?" asked the captain as he entered his office and saw his visitor looking at his collection.

"I'm not really a fan," admitted Mike as he turned to look at Mendez, "but I did watch a couple of the World Cup games a couple of years ago and thought it seemed an interesting sport. But I don't watch regularly."

"Unfortunately, too many Americans are just like you," bemoaned the captain. "However, I live in hope that may change someday."

Mendez offered his hand for Mike to shake, then waved him to a chair as he himself sat down behind his desk. "Sorry I'm late, Agent," continued the captain, "Got held up at a briefing. Hope you understand."

"Of course, Captain Mendez, no problem," answered Mike with a smile, "I understand how busy you are, and I appreciate your agreeing to see me on such short notice."

"Well, your message sounded quite urgent," stated Mendez with a question in his voice.

Mike nodded and began to speak as he laid a file on the desk in front of him. "Captain Mendez, I believe there is a serial killer at work in Miami. I believe he has killed two people so far but there may be more victims I haven't been able to identify yet."

Mendez sat up straight in his chair as he exclaimed, "A serial killer? I've heard nothing about any murders that seem related in Miami lately. What is the killer's MO? Why haven't I heard anything about this?"

"If I'm right about this, Captain, and I sincerely believe I am, then it's not a 'normal' MO that you'd readily recognize. I don't think anyone at MDPD has been negligent in any way. I just happened upon the commonality by accident, as it were, and did some research to prove my theory. I have to tell you in all honesty, Captain," said Mike with a slight blush, "that I told the FBI about my theory first, but they did not agree that it warranted an investigation. I was reminded that it wasn't the FBI's place to investigate local deaths. However, I decided that I needed to bring this to your attention immediately."

Mendez sat back in his chair and considered the FBI agent. His lips set in a thin line, Mendez requested, "Tell me everything, Agent."

~~

"You really believe someone is killing people based on Edgar Allen Poe?" Mendez with upraised eyebrows looked at Mike as he flipped through the much-read volume.

"I'm still working on the theory, Captain. However, I think it's plausible." Mike noted skepticism in Mendez's tone and knew he had to convince the MDPD captain quickly. "That's why I'm here. I was hoping you'd keep an open mind and give me access to the case files and evidence in order to get the proof I need. If you'll give me a few minutes to show you the relevant passages and the evidence I've uncovered so far, I could show you what I mean."

~~

Half an hour after his meeting with Captain Mendez, Mike was settled in a borrowed desk in the MDPD's main office. He'd been given a computer to work on and a temporary login and password to access their database. Mendez wasn't exactly on board with his theory, but he hadn't thrown him out of the office either and for now that was good enough for Mike. The captain had even advised him to contact the University of Miami to ask if they had a Poe expert on the faculty who might aid Mike's research. Mike had promised to do so that same afternoon.

He started with the Hardison case since he already had some of the information in hand. A couple of hours later, Mike had copies of all the photos and evidence collected at the scene as well as copies of all the reports from the scenes of crimes officers, witness statements and, most importantly, the preliminary autopsy report.

He stood up and stretched. He decided to get something for lunch, then come back and keep working. His goal for the afternoon was to at least get a good start on compiling information for the Biddix death.

He had less official information on that murder, so he'd need to spend more time going over the investigation.

With the information he needed on both murders, he could then compile his proof that the two deaths were indeed the work of one man.

CHAPTER 9

The boundaries which divide Life from Death are at best shadowy and vague. Who shall say where the one ends, and where the other begins?

'THE PREMATURE BURIAL'

July 19

Lucy Benton's eyes opened slowly, and her head felt muddled as if she'd been woken from a deep sleep. She'd grown up hearing the phrase 'like being tossed in a blanket' but never understood it until now. When she tried to focus, everything was blurred as if she had a hangover, but of course, that wasn't possible. She hadn't gotten drunk since college. Maybe she'd been sick and was recovering. Was she at home? No, this wasn't her bed. It was hard and cold. If anything, she was on a floor. She moved her head to the right and thought she saw a sliver of light under a door but couldn't be sure. Where was she? And why was it so hard to wake up?

None of this made sense. Lucy tried to think coherently and remembered being outside where a bright afternoon sun blazed down, making the sidewalk unbearably hot. There had been traffic and people all around her. She was trying to get home. And before that ... she'd been at the bookstore looking for a gift for Jenny. She bought a coffee at the kiosk and waited in line. The person in front of her had a funny-looking book about cats and they'd gotten into a conversation about pets. It seemed normal enough, but everything between the street and here was a blur.

Where was here? She tried to sit up and felt something soft against her leg. Was that fur? It felt like it, but that didn't make sense either. Finally making it to an upright position, she looked around again. There was more light now, or maybe her eyes were adjusting to the dark. Either way, she saw shapes surrounding her. They were small and seemed to be haphazardly tossed around. It looked like most were stacked on top of each other.

That was when the smell hit her. It was fetid and rank and Lucy grabbed her stomach as a wave of nausea hit. She was suddenly ten again, watching as the drunk from the apartment next door stumbled down the hall. In his hand, a torn trash bag spilled its stinking contents onto the bare floor as he weaved his way toward the stairway. The fifty-year-old building had been a hell to grow up in and the last thing she needed right now was a trip down nightmare lane.

She breathed through her mouth to settle her nerves. Steadier now, she realized a wall stood behind her and put out her hand to brace herself. It took a couple of tries but, with many groans, she was finally able to stand upright. Focusing on the thin beam of light, she tried to move toward the door. Her sandaled foot immediately bumped into something, something that didn't feel right. It was soft and hard at the same time. Lucy attempted to move in the other direction and encountered another small obstruction.

Bending, she found the pile and her hands felt fur again. But there was something else. A sick smell filled her nose and she felt moisture, thick and sticky, and her hand came away with the metallic scent of blood on the fingers. In a flash of understanding, she realized what it was. A dead animal. She didn't want to do it, but she had to know. She felt the first clump and realized it was another animal. This one was bigger but just as dead.

Panic hit her and she moved to run for the door. She kept stumbling over the piles of fur, each one sending a waft of stink to her overwhelmed nostrils. All were dead animals. She knew that without touching the rotting corpses. God! What was this place? Who brought her here?

Mustering an inner strength she didn't know she possessed, she kicked enough of the carcasses away to make a path and after an eternity reached the door. She began to pound on it, praying that it was an outer door and someone passing by would hear her and free her from this room of horrors. She cried out for help, her tears trailing down her face and landing on her dirty and blood-stained clothes.

It seemed like hours passed, but finally there was a noise outside. She heard a key scratching in the lock and saw the door handle begin to turn. Then realization struck her. A key meant this wasn't salvation. No, a key meant it had to be her captor. She stepped back, tripping over another pile of reeking beasts, and lost her balance. She fell onto the furry heaps, but her scream was silent as her voice failed her. The door creaked as it opened and all she could see was a shadowy figure.

The shape moved just inside the doorway and stopped. The moment stretched and Lucy was finally able to make out features.

"You?" she croaked. "Why did you ...?"

The words died in her throat as she saw what was in her captor's hand. Her renewed screams ended as the first blow struck her head.

CHAPTER 10

Literature is the most noble of professions. In fact, it is about the only one fit for a man. For my own part, there is no seducing me from the path.

'LETTER TO FREDERICK W. THOMAS'

July 20

"I don't see why the FBI is interested in Edgar Allan Poe," said Jeniviere Barty for the third time in as many minutes. "I'm flabbergasted that you've even heard of him." Her voice dripped sarcasm as she squinted at her visitor. "But obviously, if there's anything I can do to aid in your investigation, I certainly will. Especially if it meant preventing the downfall of another innocent man."

"Another innocent man?" Mike's eyes widened in an attempt to make sense of this apparent non-sequitur.

"Well, of course!" said Dr. Barty matter-of-factly. "There are always stories in the paper and on the news of innocent men and women getting out of prison after *years* of unnecessary incarceration. Everyone *knows* the police just select the first likely suspect and ignore any non-incriminating evidence. It happens all the time. Oh, excuse me," Jeniviere said as she picked up her ringing phone.

Just what I need. The only Poe expert at the University of Miami and she hates cops! Ain't that just great?

Mike held his tongue and took this opportunity to look around his would-be consultant's office. One wall was floor-to-ceiling shelves crammed full of a truly impressive number of books. There were even more books, papers and files on the floor in front of another wall, while against a third was a mini kitchen complete with a small refrigerator and microwave and two open cabinets filled with food, bottled water, utensils, glasses and coffee mugs. Above this hung Dr. Barty's numerous diplomas, certificates and framed copies of published articles. Next to the door was an old-fashioned coat rack, every peg full. Two jackets, a sweater, a garment bag, and a wide-brimmed sun hat competed for space on three hooks. Looking around, Mike felt that Jeniviere Barty only needed a fold-out bed and she could probably live here.

The woman herself, however, was the polar opposite of her surroundings. While her office at the University of Miami was crowded and cluttered, Dr. Barty was tidy and nondescript. She was in her late forties or early fifties; her mousy brown hair was worn in a simple bun on the back of her head with a few stringy strands falling down her neck. She wore no makeup or nail polish, and Mike would bet a paycheck that she'd never had a pedicure in her life. While her brown dress probably looked nice on the hanger, on her it was ill-fitting and contrasted unfavorably with her pale complexion. Her flat shoes did nothing to complement the outfit.

A typical spinster. Probably still lives with her mother. Mike resisted the urge to snort out loud.

"Sorry about that," said Jeniviere as she set the receiver back down. "My mother. The dear, eighty-two and still quite spritely, you know. But, just in case, I always try to answer whenever she calls. Just in case, you know."

Mike made a sympathetic noise, then tried to get the conversation back on track. "As I said earlier, Dr. Barty, I have a copy of all of Poe's works, but what I'm looking for now is information on his life and maybe about the stories and poems themselves. Reviews, discussions, that kind of thing."

"You mean you didn't find what you wanted online?" she asked with a touch of condescension. "There is quite a lot of Poe information there, you know."

Damn! She had to ask.

Of course, there'd been reams of info about Poe online, but there was so much that Mike hadn't bothered trying to slog through it all. He'd decided to take Mendez's advice and find an expert at UM and ask her. Mike didn't want to look stupid, so decided to try to disarm her with compliments.

"Well, of course there is a lot of information about Poe online, Dr. Barty, but I was hoping for some real insight from an expert. On the Internet, you never know if you're getting information you can trust or just some crackpot spouting off. The kind of expertise I'm looking for can only come from a bona fide expert in the field. From your credentials, I understand you're one of the best in the area. This could potentially be an important case and I need someone I can rely on to give me the best information possible."

Jeniviere practically preened as she sat up a little straighter and leaned forward. "Of course, it's true that I do know more about Poe than just about anyone else at any of the universities in southern Florida, if I do say so myself." She looked away in what seemed to be an attempt at humility.

Mike felt his effort had worked even better than he'd hoped, if the blush that came to Dr. Barty's cheeks was any indication. Mike knew people and he felt silence was his best option now. He'd been flattering, now it was up to the professor to reach the obvious conclusion. He didn't have long to wait.

"Of course, I want to help if I can. It's my civic duty. What kind of information are you looking for exactly?"

~~

Well, this didn't turn out exactly as I hoped.

Mike sighed as he set aside another of the books Dr. Barty gave him. Out of six books, he'd already discounted three of them, thought one could be useful but wasn't very hopeful about the remaining two. Most were pedantic in nature, written by scholars for scholars. Mike wasn't stupid by any stretch, but his background wasn't in academia and these books were way too academic for him. He opened the next book on the stack.

"Still at it, Agent?"

Mike jumped slightly, concentrating so hard that he didn't hear anyone approach. He looked up to see Captain Mendez standing at his desk. The MDPD captain was smiling.

"Yes, sir. I'm still researching Poe trying to tie the murders with his works."

"And where did you get all these books from? Visit to the local library?"

"No, sir. I visited the University of Miami as you suggested and spoke to their resident Poe expert, Dr. Jeniviere Barty. She loaned these books to me and I've been looking through them to see which ones I might be able to use."

Captain Mendez picked up one of the books at random and, leafing through it, said, "Looks a little dense to me if you get my drift."

"Yes, sir, they are a bit. I'm having trouble myself, although I have found some good information in a couple of them. After I've decided which ones I can use, I'll take the others back to Dr. Barty."

"Good enough," said Captain Mendez as he set the book back down. "Not trying to look over your shoulder, but I would like to be kept apprised of your progress. However, I don't want you to overdo it. Make sure you take breaks when needed and get out of here at a reasonable hour." Making a show of looking at his watch, Mendez continued, "Like now. It's almost six and you should be thinking about dinner. I don't want to hear of you eating at your desk, Agent Donaldson."

Mike looked at his own watch. *Six o'clock already?* The last time he'd checked it was only three. Trying to cover his surprise, he nodded. "Of course, sir. I just wanted to get through one more of these books before I left for the evening. And thank you for your concern; I'll take it to heart, I promise."

Obviously not believing Mike for a minute, Mendez's eyes twinkled, and he answered in a dry tone, "I certainly hope so. Have a good evening." With that, the precinct captain turned and left Mike to his work.

Mike stood up and stretched. He really had lost all track of time. He needed to stop doing that if he was going to do anyone any good. Making a quick decision, Mike straightened his desk, picked up the last two books he needed to review and, as he walked down the hall toward the elevator, tried to decide where he was going for dinner tonight.

CHAPTER 11

I attacked with great resolution the editorial matter, and, reading it from beginning to end without understanding a syllable, conceived the possibility of its being Chinese, and so re-read it from the end to the beginning, but with no more satisfactory result.

'THE ANGEL OF THE ODD'

July 21

"Thank you for meeting me on such short notice, Dr. Barty," Mike said as he sat down.

"Well, luckily one of my students just cancelled her conference with me so I had some free time." Dr. Barty smiled slightly as she took a sip from her coffee.

Jeneviere was dressed in another unflattering outfit: a horizontal blue and white striped blouse that clashed horribly with her pencil skirt.

"Did the books I gave you help your investigation, Agent Donaldson? Surely you didn't read through all six that quickly?" Her tone implied her lack of expectations regarding Mike's intelligence.

"No, I didn't read all six cover to cover, Dr. Barty," Mike acknowledged, refusing to rise to the bait, "but I skimmed enough to get the general idea of each book and have chosen one I think will be useful." Mike opened the bag he'd carried the others in and began placing them on the desk.

"Only one. I see. Which one?" Jeneviere looked over his head as she spoke, a mannerism that Mike had noticed yesterday.

"The companion guide. I think the in-depth information about each work, as well as the commentary, will be beneficial in explaining the stories and poems."

"Well, certainly that work is one of the premiere titles of its kind," she agreed immediately. Pulling the other five towards herself, Jeneviere asked, "Did you have any questions about any of these?"

Mike hesitated. He actually did have a question about one of the books but didn't want to give Dr. Barty more reason to doubt his abilities. Then he thought twice. *Don't be stupid. There's a killer on the loose and if looking stupid gets you more information that will help you catch him, then that's a small price to pay.*

"Well, truthfully, I'm not quite clear on the appendix of this one," Mike said as he pointed to the book second-from-the-top of the stack. "I knew Poe wrote a lot of poems and stories, but I was amazed at all the entries in this chronology of his writings. There were multiple entries for the same month time and time again."

"Yes, well, Poe didn't just write fiction and poetry, Agent Donaldson. As a matter of fact, most of his writings were literary criticisms of works by other authors. Most of these reviews were published in monthly periodicals or newspapers, so he might have several of these articles published in the same month."

Mike thought about this for a minute. "That certainly makes more sense." After another moment, Mike asked, "So this chronology would be more detailed than the companion book regarding publication dates then?"

"Oh, yes, certainly. Also, this book has a great deal more detail regarding Poe's biography as well."

"I see. Then that would help tremendously, Dr. Barty." Mike tried his most disarming smile and asked, "Would you mind if I changed my mind and kept both the Companion book and this biography as references for my investigation?"

Dr. Barty's smile was not quite condescending. "Of course not, Agent. And if there's anything else I can do to help, please don't hesitate to contact me."

"Thank you for your help, Dr. Barty. I might take you up on that offer."

At that moment, Mike had no way of knowing just how important Dr. Barty's help would end up being.

CHAPTER 12

Hush, little baby, don't say a word,
Mama's gonna buy you a mockingbird.

And if that mockingbird don't sing,
Mama's gonna buy you a diamond ring.

And if that diamond ring turns brass,
Mama's gonna buy you a looking glass.

"Please stay asleep for more than an hour this time, little man. Could you do that for me just this once?"

Ruby James laid her five-month-old son in his crib, patted him softly on the cheek, then stood up and stretched her back. She knew motherhood was going to be hard, but she'd been unprepared for how difficult it was sometimes. She'd give her right arm for just one night of uninterrupted sleep.

She started to put the clean diapers in the drawer and smiled as she remembered her friends' surprised looks when she announced she was planning to use cloth diapers instead of the disposable ones. "Better for the environment," she'd said and, even though it was a pain sometimes, she knew it was the right thing to do to protect the environment. And her son's future.

Her son. Her and Bobby's little man. They'd waited for so many years for this little guy. They'd waited and hoped. Seen doctors and taken tests. They'd almost given up so many times. They even started talking about adoption.

Then one day she realized she was late. Really late. She'd snuck the pregnancy test into the house and said nothing to Bobby. She was so excited when she saw that color change. But just to be sure, she took a second test. And a third. Then she'd called the doctor.

Bobby's face lit up like the proverbial Christmas tree when she told him. He screamed and cried just like she knew he would. Then he'd treated her like glass until she pointed out that women had been having babies for thousands of years without special treatment and she could do it, too.

Those months had been so wonderful. They wanted to go traditional, hence the cloth diapers and breast feeding. The room was painted blue and there was wallpaper with trains, planes and automobiles. It was perfect for their little man.

After closing the nursery door, Ruby went to the living room and sat down. She still had another load of clothes to do, dishes to take out of the dishwasher and she needed to decide what to do for supper.

Bobby was working late so it was just her tonight. She didn't really want to cook, but a ham sandwich didn't sound any good at all. Did she have anything decent in the fridge?

As she was going to check, the doorbell rang.

No, no, no! Don't wake him up. Please!

She looked through the peephole and didn't see anyone. Remembering her self-defense training, she didn't unchain the door, but opened it only enough to see out.

On the welcome mat was a box with her name on it.

I haven't ordered anything lately. Maybe Mom sent something. She's always sending stuff for the baby.

Ruby brought it into the house and placed it on the kitchen table. 'Perishable' was written on the side and she grabbed a knife to open it.

Inside was a Styrofoam box with an invoice on top.

Sorry this is so last-minute, but I had trouble with the order. Give yourself a break from cooking and enjoy! P.S. There's a special jar of apples for the little one. All my love.

How sweet! But who was it from? The message wasn't signed.

She looked at the contents list and smiled. A steak, baked potato and green beans. And to top it off, a piece of apple pie.

Funny, though, it's a meal for one. Mom doesn't usually forget Bobby. Of course, the note did say for me to take a break from cooking. Must be why there's just one serving.

Ruby put the wrapped containers in the fridge and unpacked the apples for the baby.

Well, guess I don't have to worry about supper now.

CHAPTER 13

My mistress!—my mistress!—Poisoned!—poisoned!
'THE ASSIGNATION'

At his borrowed desk, Mike made more detailed notes comparing the two murders with their respective Poe works. He paused to take a drink from his water bottle when two officers passed his desk.

"It was pretty sad," the first officer said. "The baby was only five months old. I mean, what mother does that?"

"Are they absolutely sure the mother killed the kid, then herself?" asked his partner.

"Well, they're still waiting for the final autopsy results, but MacKenzie told me there were no signs of a struggle or anything."

"Damn! That's pretty bad. The mom must have been crazy, but at least it was an easy death, I guess, right? The poison acted quickly, right?"

"Yeah, that's what I heard."

The voices trailed off as they continued down the corridor and Mike went back to work. Only a few moments later, however, something registered in his mind and he sat up straight. He furiously wrote down everything he could remember from the overheard conversation, then grabbed the Poe companion book and began looking through its pages.

Ten minutes later he found what he was looking for. With a sick feeling in his stomach, Mike realized his killer had struck again.

~~

Mike's frustration level was growing. He now had three crimes he believed were part of a series when he added the death of Ruby James and her five-month-old child to the Biddix and Hardison murders. Poe had written a short story entitled 'The Assignation' in 1843 and Mike had read its synopsis last night while looking through Dr. Barty's books. The storyline fit his theory up to a point. In Poe's story the child lived, and the mother committed suicide, while in the current scenario, Ruby James apparently poisoned herself after poisoning her son. If there was a murderer on the loose, Mike thought that he might use the story as a guideline, so to speak, and killing the child as well as the mother would certainly be more macabre.

The problem was that he couldn't prove Ruby James' death was actually a murder. The coroner's report had ruled it a murder-suicide and stated Ruby probably suffered from post-partum depression. In this scenario, she had killed her son first, then herself. Her husband, family, and friends all disputed that and stated they'd seen no evidence of depression of any kind. The ten-day-old investigation was on-going, but the police didn't expect to learn anything that would change their findings.

To top it all off, the coroner's final report on the Lylyana Biddix death was inconclusive. She could not state definitively if that death was accidental or a suicide.

Mike was beginning to think he was barking up the wrong tree after all. So far, he only had one bona fide murder, one inconclusive death and a murder-suicide. And, while all three deaths had elements that tied them to the Poe works, there were inconsistencies in all three.

Mike tapped his pen against the desk as he considered his options. He could stay here and keep digging. There were still reports to look at, autopsies to review and witnesses he could interview. It was the 21st of July and he had six days until he had to report back to Detroit. Or he could admit he had bupkus and pack up now, go back home and finish his vacation there.

It wasn't even close. Mike picked up another folder and started reading.

CHAPTER 14

The most important crisis of our life calls, trumpet-tongued, for
immediate energy and action.

'The Imp of the Perverse'

July 23

He blew into the cup of coffee to cool it down and then took a long
sip and opened the newspaper.

"How's the coffee, Agent?" Mike's favorite waitress asked as
she approached his table.

"Great as usual, Beverly," he answered with a broad smile. "I
swear, I'm thinking of transferring to Miami just to have this
coffee each morning."

Beverly laughed and opened her notebook. "What'll it be
today, Agent Donaldson?"

"Two eggs over easy and bacon, thanks."

"Toast or English muffin?"

"Neither today, Beverly." Mike sighed as he said, "I'm eating
too much on this vacation with going out to eat every meal. I'll
have to go on a strict diet when I get back to Detroit."

Beverly laughed, picked up the menu and walked on to the
next table as Mike unfolded the complimentary newspaper he'd
gotten at his hotel. The front-page story had a one-inch headline

that screamed **AXE MURDER DISCOVERED IN HIALEAH**
with an accompanying picture of a cat. Mike did a double-take.

A cat?

What the hell was this all about? He quickly perused the story,
then stopped, took another drink of coffee, and began again from
the beginning. After only a minute, he took out his pen and began
marking up the newsprint.

~~

"Four murders?" Captain Mendez's voice rose as he regarded his
guest agent in anger. "Last I spoke to you, you had the same two
murders you've had since the beginning, and now you're telling
me you think there are four? Thought we had an agreement, Agent
Donaldson. I allow you to pursue your theory of a serial killer and
you keep me up to date on your findings. Now you're telling me
there's two more murders. What the hell are you playing at,
Donaldson?"

Mike took a breath and explained himself. "Sir, the James
death was officially labeled a murder-suicide and the
circumstances didn't follow the Poe story exactly. I wasn't sure
then that it was part of this series and, frankly, I'm still not. But it's
close enough that, with this new murder, I thought I should
mention it."

Mendez considered Mike for a moment before looking at the
newspaper story. "And this axe murder is which Poe story?"

"'The Black Cat', sir. I recognized it almost immediately. In
the story ..."

"Just the lite version, Donaldson," Mendez interrupted and
waved a hand.

"Yes, sir." Mike began again. "The murder is discovered
when the murderer's cat howls while the police are investigating
the disappearance of his wife. When they open the cellar, the
police find the bloated corpse of the wife and she'd been killed

with an axe. What really drew me to this new murder, sir, is that when the MDPD found Lucy Benton's body last night, she was surrounded by a bunch of dead animals including a cat and a monkey. In Poe's story, the murderer killed a bunch of animals before he got around to killing his wife and they included ..."

"Don't tell me, Agent," interrupted Mendez again. "A cat and a monkey."

"Yes, sir. The other animals ..."

"Never mind, Donaldson. I'm sold. It's too much of a coincidence to be a coincidence."

Mike let out a breath. Mendez accepted his theory. That was the best news he'd had this entire week. He'd begun to think that maybe Zardes was right, and he *was* out of his mind. He'd been working on this research for days and wasn't sure he had anything to show for it. Now, however, with this most recent murder he was sure he was on the right track and decided to inform Mendez immediately. He was gratified that the captain believed him. A real investigation could begin, and this maniac caught. Hopefully before anyone else died.

"Need to get the Violent Crime unit working on this immediately. Like to get my most experienced people on it." Mendez began to pick up his phone, then put it down again and looked at Mike thoughtfully.

Not knowing what the captain was thinking, Mike wasn't sure if he was expecting a comment or waiting for him to leave. Technically, his work was done. He proved his theory, and the Miami police would take it from here. Strangely, Mike didn't feel triumphant. He was a little disappointed that he wouldn't see out the investigation. He'd ask if he could keep in touch for updates on what was going on. Surely, Mendez wouldn't deny him after all he'd done on the case already?

Mendez cleared his throat. When he addressed Mike, there was an unusual hesitation in his voice. "Agent Donaldson, how long are you in Miami for? You told me you were here on vacation, isn't that right?"

"Yes, sir," Mike answered with a grin. "My boss said I had too much vacation time saved up and told me not to come back until the 27th. I've got a flight back for the 25th."

"I see," said Mendez. He doodled on a sheet of paper in front of him for a moment, and then, finally coming to a decision, looked up at Mike. "Agent, I've been impressed with you these last few days. You had a theory, worked on it on your own and stuck with it. Have to admit I wasn't sure at first, but you've convinced me. My people are good, but so are you. Do you think the FBI would allow you to work on our joint Violent Crimes task force? Think we could borrow you for a while?"

Mike was speechless. He'd just been wondering how he could keep tabs on the investigation, now Mendez wanted him to work it? Mike didn't hesitate.

"Sir, I'd really like to work on this case. I feel I'm invested in it, you might say. I don't have any specific assignments waiting for me in Detroit that I know of, and I think my supervisor might go for it. But, Captain Mendez, I need to be candid with you." Mike took a moment to collect his thoughts. "I worked VCMO early in my career, but I've been mostly hunting fugitives for seven years now and it's been a while since I've been involved in a true investigation. From the beginning, I mean. I spend most of my time looking for perps once other agents have already done the leg work and identified them. I'm not sure how much I can contribute to the investigation."

"Nonsense." Mendez stood up and looked Mike in the eye. "You've got good instincts and follow through. You're underestimating yourself." He held out a hand. "Like you on the team. What do you say?"

Mike took the proffered hand and smiled. "I accept."

CHAPTER 15

This functionary, however well disposed to my friend, could not altogether conceal his chagrin at the turn which affairs had taken.
'The Murders in the Rue Morgue'

"Let me get this straight, Donaldson. I told you to forget about your wild theory, but you decided you knew better. You went around me and straight to MDPD. Told them your theory and somehow convinced Captain Mendez to let you work on it there."

Bradley Zardes was in rare form. He had his hands on his hips, a pulsing vein snaked down his temple, its dark blue hue stark against its owner's pale skin, and his voice held an almost hysterical tone that Zardes was obviously trying to control. He was losing the battle.

"Now, we've got an official request from MDPD for access to the FBI database and lab facilities and a MOU requesting you specifically to help with the investigation, which the SAC has already signed. In effect, Captain Mendez wants to borrow you. Did I miss anything?"

Mike stifled a sarcastic reply. He'd known Zardes would be angry when he received the official Memorandum of Understanding with Mendez's requests but thought that his own supervisor's written okay and the fact that Mike had been proved right would have been enough to blunt the Supervisory Agent's wrath somewhat. Obviously, he'd been wrong.

It didn't matter, however. He had been right, MDPD was investigating the case and his boss had agreed to let him remain in Miami to work it. Mike didn't really care what Zardes thought.

On the other hand, if Zardes did agree to the MOU, then Mike would probably end up being the go-between between the two law enforcement agencies. He'd need to keep on Zardes's good side in order to preserve a good working relationship between MDPD and the FBI. Because, when the case was over and Mike was back in Detroit, the Miami police and the FBI still had to work together. It was his responsibility to keep the peace.

Mike tried to be diplomatic. "Sir, I realize that I went behind your back and I apologize for that. However, as you rightly pointed out last week, homicides are under the jurisdiction of the local PD, so I thought it would be better to approach Captain Mendez and try to get the information I needed from him in order to research my theory."

Mike ignored Zardes' snort of derision and ploughed on. "I've been working at the Doral office on my own time and not using any FBI resources. But when I thought I had enough to convince the captain, I spoke to him and he agreed that there seems to be something there. I had every intention of returning to Detroit once the case was in MDPD's hands, and I was just as surprised as you that Captain Mendez wanted me to work this case. But I'm glad he did. I like finishing things when I start them, and I hope to help MDPD get this guy and keep him from killing again. I wasn't trying to upstage you, sir, but if I can keep this guy from hurting anyone else, then I want to do just that."

Mike waited but Zardes said nothing. Just as Mike was getting ready to try again, the SSA finally spoke.

"Donaldson, I don't care for the way you do things. I do *not* like being made a fool of. SAC Martinez, *my boss*, had me on the carpet because I didn't listen to you in the first place. Now I've got an official reprimand in my file thanks to you and your wild theory. Which, by the way, I still don't buy for a second. I think it's crap and I'm laying odds you'll fall flat on your face, just where you belong. Now get out of my office, Donaldson. I don't want to see you again unless I have to. Go look for your serial killer and his raven."

With that, Zardes turned his back on Mike and returned to the paperwork on his desk.

CHAPTER 16

*I am actuated by an ambition which I believe to be an honourable
one — the ambition of serving the great cause of truth.*
'LETTER TO WASHINGTON POE'

July 24

Mike took a drink of his coffee as he sat down at the large table. It
was 6:50 a.m. and a large group was congregating in the
conference room at the FBI field office. Mike didn't recognize any
faces except for Captain Mendez and, unfortunately, Bradley
Zardes. Zardes certainly wasn't happy with him, first by going
behind his back to Mendez, now for being asked to stay to work on
the case. Mike instinctively felt that no good could come of Zardes
being involved in this investigation.

It had all happened in a flurry. One minute he was explaining
his theory to Captain Mendez, the next Mendez was talking to the
SAC about a task force and an MOU. He wasn't involved in those
discussions, but less than a half-hour later he was talking to his
supervisor in Detroit and getting the okay to stay in Miami for the
duration of the case. He'd seen Zardes, then gone back to MDPD's
Doral office to collect his research. He'd spent the rest of the
afternoon and most of the evening at the FBI office organizing his
notes and the evidence into a more cohesive presentation. Mendez

had asked him to prepare the information for the task force this morning, including a Power Point to show on the monitor.

Mike noticed a pile of briefing books on a table behind Captain Mendez and a laptop set up. He was glad they were ready to go. He'd been up late into the night working on that information, collating everything he'd discovered and guessed about the cases so far and was afraid that the FBI analyst/technician he'd met, Danny McKissick, wouldn't have had time to put it all together before this meeting. He hoped they'd be put to good use.

Suddenly the door opened and into the room walked Danny and Chip Smythe. Mike's shoulders relaxed slightly. If Chip was on this task force, then he knew there was someone he could count on. Chip sat next to him, but before the younger agent could speak, two more people walked into the room and made themselves comfortable.

A moment later, a middle-aged Hispanic man addressed the room. "Good morning, ladies and gentlemen. I'm Ronald Martinez, SAC for the Miami FBI office. I'm only here to get things started, then I'm going to turn this meeting over to Captain Mendez from MDPD."

The Special Agent in Charge seemed to exude confidence and control despite his nondescript appearance. Martinez was about 5'10", of medium weight, and had dark brown hair and brown eyes. There was nothing special about him that would make him stand out in a crowd or inspire confidence. Despite his seemingly bland character, it didn't take Mike long to realize that Martinez had a razor-sharp mind. In just a few words, Martinez got the entire room's attention by summing up the case succinctly.

"In a nutshell, we believe there is a serial killer on the loose. We believe that the 'Death by Decibel' death of Lylyana Biddix, the poisonings of Ruby James and her child, Stephen Hardison's murder and the death of Lucy Benton are all murders and the work of one person."

At this, everyone sat up attentively. Chip put his coffee down and stared at the SAC while someone whistled, and several people started writing in their notebooks.

"This theory was first developed by FBI agent Mike Donaldson. He brought it to the attention of Captain Mendez. Captain Mendez spoke to me about this last night. We decided to have the Violent Crime Major Offender task force investigate. We brought in Agent Donaldson and Agent Smythe," here Martinez pointed to Chip, "from the FBI, and detectives Alex Welch, Blaine Hoskins and David Scotty from MDPD to complete the task force."

Mike noticed that Martinez spoke without notes and that his speech was rather staccato. *Probably doesn't like too much extraneous detail.*

"Also with us this morning are Rhonda Sagan, from the FBI's Behavioral Analysis Unit, and Meghan Richmond from the Medical Examiner's office. This task force will meet here in the FBI offices. We have more access to databases and laboratories and we're providing the profiler. However, the MDPD detectives not previously involved with VCMO will be deputized today and have the same authority as the FBI agents. The task force will report directly to SSA Zardes and he will let me know if there are problems he or Captain Mendez can't handle. I don't anticipate that being an issue, however."

Martinez paused and Mike noticed that his smile was welcoming.

"That's it from me. Thank you for your attention. Captain Mendez, I'll leave this in your capable hands." Martinez nodded to the room in general, shook hands with Mendez and left without a backward glance.

Mendez waited for a moment before taking over the briefing. "Just a quick housekeeping detail before we get to it. As SAC Martinez mentioned, the case agent will report to Agent Zardes and he will report to Agent Martinez. Detective Welch, as senior member on the VCMO task force, I'm going to ask you to report to me each day as well. I'd like to be kept in the loop. And again, if there are any problems, I want to hear about them. The MDPD and the FBI have always worked well together and, as most of you know, the VCMO is only one of several on-going joint task forces in Miami. I don't anticipate any problems either.

"Now it seems to me the best thing to do at this point would be to turn this over to Agent Donaldson, since he was the one who first realized there was a connection between these deaths and has done most of the preliminary research. On top of that, Agent Donaldson spent a great deal of time yesterday and last night putting together these briefing books for everyone," Mendez pointed to the pile of folders on the table next to him, "and he should have the honor of showing off his work."

Mike was surprised but tried not to show it. He thought Mendez would describe the background and then hand out the books and everyone would get to work. But, he acknowledged, he knew more about this than anyone else, and could explain it best. He stood up and walked to the head of the room. It was time to make his case.

~~

"Thank you, Captain Mendez." Mike took a deep breath. "First let me introduce myself. I'm FBI Special Agent Mike Donaldson assigned to the Detroit field office. I mostly work fugitive cases and was here in Miami on such a case when I decided to stay in the area for a vacation. I heard about the deaths of Lylyana Biddix and Stephen Hardison, noticed some similarities and asked Captain Mendez for access to the case files and evidence a few days ago. After hearing about Ruby James and her son, and Lucy Benton, I realized there was a connection between the four cases. At that point ..."

"Excuse me, Agent, but I don't see any connection."

Before Mike could say anything, Detective Blaine Hoskins continued.

"I see that Hardison and Benton were murdered, but the Biddix death was inconclusive and the coroner ruled the James case a murder-suicide. Biddix died from exposure to the bells in that cathedral, Ruby James poisoned her kid, then offed herself, Hardison was chained to a wall and died from dehydration and Benton was axed to death. What could they possibly have in common?" The skepticism in Hoskins' voice was palpable.

"Yes, Detective, I understand why you'd ask that question. The connection is not in the manner of their deaths, but in how the deaths were staged. I believe the killer is murdering his victims based on deaths in the works of Edgar Allan Poe."

Everyone stared at Mike for several seconds.

Hoskins burst out, "Edgar Allan Poe? Are you out of your mind, Donaldson? That's crazy!"

"So are most serial killers, Detective," replied Mike drily. He had expected some resistance to the idea at first, of course, but he was somewhat put out by the tone of Hoskins's reaction. "Just hear me out for a few minutes."

Hoskins nodded in affirmation, but her posture was anything but inviting. She had put down her coffee, sat back in her chair and crossed her arms tightly across her chest.

Mike, however, was incredibly stubborn. He was right and given he already had Captain Mendez and SAC Martinez on his side, it didn't matter whether any of the members of the task force agreed with him or not. Still, it would make things easier if he had their acceptance.

"Okay, so let's start with the first death: Lylyana Biddix." Mike spoke to Danny at the laptop and he brought up a picture of the crime scene on the monitor. "In the Edgar Allan Poe poem entitled 'The Bells' ... Danny, could you put the poem on the screen, please?" Immediately alongside of the crime scene photo appeared a copy of the poem with several words or lines highlighted. Mike continued, "In 'The Bells' the author uses bells to describe the stages of life. In the final stanza, iron bells announce death.

"The bells at Trinity Cathedral are made of iron and I did a bit of research; it only takes 185 decibels to kill someone and a minimum time of exposure. Biddix was up in that tower plenty long enough for the bells to kill her at such proximity. What's more, the autopsy reported that she had Temazepam in her system. She was drugged, somehow left in that tower, and died from the bells' ringing."

"Excuse me, Agent Donaldson," Detective Scotty interrupted. "What is Temazepam? I've never heard of it."

Mendez spoke before Mike could answer. "Perhaps we should let Dr. Richmond answer that."

Everyone looked over to the medical examiner, awaiting her response.

Meghan Richmond had been with coroner's office for over six years, having moved to Miami from Atlanta after a difficult divorce. African American, she was thirty-seven but looked much older. She had deep wrinkles around her eyes and mouth and her black hair had numerous silver streaks running through it. Her eyes were blue, the result of contacts, and her only seeming bow to fashion were the expensive-looking gold hoop earrings she wore. She hunched over her notes and never really looked at her audience as she spoke. Her voice, however, had a melodic quality to it that surprised Mike.

"Temazepam is a psychoactive drug and is prescribed on a short-term basis for insomnia. Although it can become addictive fairly quickly, nevertheless it's very common." She looked up briefly and said, "I'm jumping the gun a bit here, but we do have evidence of Temazepam in one of the other deaths as well."

"Thank you, Dr. Richmond," Mendez said. "We will get to that in a moment. Agent Donaldson?"

"Yes, thank you, Dr. Richmond. As I was saying, I do not believe Ms. Biddix went up there willingly. She was taken up there and left to die."

"Donaldson, that's a ridiculously long stretch. And what's more, your poem doesn't say anything about drugs or anything else. Is there even an actual person mentioned in 'The Bells'?" Hoskins had again interrupted and again her tone was dismissive and condescending. "It seems to me that you're making quite a mountain out of a molehill. Lylyana Biddix committed suicide. Just because she picked a weird way to do it doesn't mean there's something sinister about it."

Blaine's short, curly black hair framed a round face that currently sported a skeptic look Mike tried not to take personally. He was quickly getting tired of these interruptions but knew a confrontation was the wrong way to go. He wanted to get his information out there and hopefully everyone would understand where he was coming from. Hoskins wasn't FBI and Mike had no authority to do anything about her intransigent attitude.

Taking a calming breath, Mike began to speak again. "I believe she was murdered, Detective Hoskins. I already said that the murderer is basing his killings on deaths in Poe's works. I never said that the stories or poems would all involve murders."

"It's still a stretch, Agent," stated Alex Welch. "I assume you have more?"

This was the first time Detective Welch had spoken and Mike took heart. "Yes, I can compare the other three murders to other Poe works as well."

Mike turned once again to Danny and spoke quietly. The tech immediately took the first pictures off the monitor and replaced them with another crime scene photo.

"This is the second murder, Ruby James and her son. She was discovered in her home on the 13th. And, as has been pointed out, her death was considered a suicide as it appeared that Ms. James had poisoned herself after killing her son. The scene reminded me of one of Edgar Allan Poe's stories called 'The Assignation', which tells the story of the Marchesa di Mentoni who accidentally drops her child into a canal. The child is recovered by a mysterious stranger and returned to the Marchesa, but her husband suspects that the child is really the stranger's. The next day, both the Marchesa and her supposed lover commit suicide to be together in the afterlife since they cannot be together in the present." In a dry voice, Mike summed up, "I think the corollaries are apparent. A young woman apparently commits suicide and when found, beside her is the body of her child. Again, just like the Poe story."

"Seriously, Donaldson?" Hoskins interrupted for the third time. "First off, you just said the kid in your story lived and do I need to remind you that the coroner's office declared this a murder-*suicide*? James probably suffered from post-partum depression, couldn't live with it anymore and killed the kid, then herself. End of story."

"Not quite, Detective."

Everyone looked in surprise at Dr. Richmond. "The ME's office stated that Ms. James' and her son *probably* died from murder-suicide, but we weren't definitive. I didn't do the autopsy myself, but I read the reports and none of Ms. James' family or friends said she showed any sign of depression. And before you ask, Agent Donaldson, I'll check this and the fourth death for traces of Temazepam. If we find that, then I think we will be able to say that Ms. James probably was murdered, as was her son."

Mike hid a sigh of relief. "Thank you, Dr. Richmond, I was going to ask you to do just that. And, Detective Hoskins, our murderer is using the Poe works as a basis for his murders; not every detail is going to match up exactly."

Before anyone said anything, Chip stuck his neck out. "Mike, I think you're making a good case. There are a lot of similarities for both deaths to be coincidence. I'm sold."

David Scotty spoke next. "I'm not so sure, but," and he continued with a sideways glance towards his friend Hoskins, "I'd like to hear more."

Mike smiled. He knew he could convince them. And he still had evidence to present. "And I have more to tell you. Let's look at murder number three, Stephen Hardison." Mike nodded to Danny, who changed the scene on the monitor to the warehouse were Hardison had died. "Last week I read about the death of Stephen Hardison in the paper. I was interested and visited the crime scene. That's where I met Captain Mendez, who was kind enough to let me look around and share some information with me. As you may remember, Hardison had been chained to a wall, then sealed in the room and left to die. The interesting part of this crime was his clothes; he was dressed in bright colors as if going to Mardi Gras.

"I found that this death corresponds to the Poe short story, 'The Cask of Amontillado', in which the narrator, Montresor, a rich Italian, kills his rival by getting him drunk, chaining him to a wall in a niche of a large crypt in his deserted villa, then sealing him in with stone and mortar, leaving him to die alone of starvation and suffocation. The victim, Fortunato, is described as dressed in 'motley' since it is carnival season. I reviewed the coroner's report and, along with alcohol, our killer used Temazepam to sedate Hardison, which made it easy for the killer to subdue him and arrange the murder to look like the one in Poe's story. And, as in 'The Cask of Amontillado', it took several days for the victim, Stephen Hardison, to die. Again, I think the parallels speak for themselves." Mike took a breath and continued, "Finally, let's look at victim number four, Lucy Benton."

This time, Danny needed no prodding, and on the monitor appeared one of the most gruesome scenes any of these experienced law enforcement officers had ever seen.

The woman was in a corner of a small room, maybe 8' wide by 12' long. Her head had been sliced open in several places and there was blood all over her body as well as the room in general.

The mutilation made it impossible to determine features. The only way the body had been identified as a woman was the presence of breasts on the chest. Also lying around the room were what appeared to be several dead animals in various stages of decay.

Mike began his explanation. "Lucy Benton was thirty-seven, unmarried and had no living relatives. She didn't show up for work last Friday and when no one had heard from her the following Monday, her supervisor contacted MDPD. They had no real leads until her body was found yesterday in an empty storeroom. Her supervisor made the identification from a tattoo on her wrist." Mike pointed at the corpses around the body. "These dead animals include two cats, a rabbit and a monkey."

"She'd been in that cellar for four days?" asked David. Although he tried to disguise it, his tone of voice couldn't hide the horror he felt.

"Yes, MDPD is positive she was killed in that room, then left there."

"With the animals?" asked Chip, a disgusted quality to his tone.

"Forensics is still working on that one, Chip, but their preliminary finding is that at least some of the animals were also killed in that room. Some were not but they were definitely there when Ms. Benton was killed, since her blood was found on all of them," responded Mike.

No one said anything for a moment, then Alex asked, "Which of Poe's works does this murder correspond to?"

Despite the seriousness of the situation, Mike couldn't help the swelling of pride in his chest. Welch had asked the question as a *given*, not as if he wanted convincing. At least he'd gotten one of the detectives on board with his theory.

"The name of the short story is 'The Black Cat'. Briefly, the narrator of the story blames alcohol for his change in personality. This manifests itself by his mistreatment of various animals including a dog, a rabbit, and a monkey. Finally, he injures his black cat by prying its eye out with a penknife. The cat recovers and the man is sorry, but it's only temporary. The narrator starts acting out again and eventually hangs the cat, but his wife gets him another. This new cat has a white splotch on its breast and for some reason that pushes the guy over the edge. He tries to kill this second cat, but his wife protects it, so he kills her with an axe. He puts her in a walled-off room in his cellar and thinks he's gotten away with the murder. Several days later, the police come to the house and they hear the howling of the cat and find the dead woman."

"Okay," announced Alex after a moment had passed, "I'm sold. This murder has to be a recreation of that story. You said there was even a dead monkey in that room, right? That *cannot* be a coincidence. I'm convinced."

"And I have more evidence to present to prove my theory," stated Mike. "Danny, could you please put the timeline up on the monitor?"

A list broken into several columns and headed 'Edgar Allan Poe: A Chronology' appeared on the monitor.

"After I realized the link between the first two murders and Edgar Allan Poe, I also realized that just reading the Poe works wasn't going to be enough. I needed information about his background and analyses of the stories and poems themselves.

"I went to the University of Miami and met with Dr. Jeniviere Barty, their Poe expert. She loaned me several books and I brought a couple of them with me this morning. I already had this one. It's the **Complete Tales and Poems** by Edgar Allan Poe," Mike said, holding up the thick black book.

Picking up a second book, he continued, "And this is one of the best reference books Dr. Barty had. It gives a synopsis of each poem and story as well as a time-line of his life." Mike picked up a third book. "This one has a terrific chronology of everything ever written by Poe and when it was published. This includes not just his poems, stories and the one novel he wrote, but also every article or review he ever penned. I was looking at the chronology for names of poems and stories when I realized something. There were dates for everything listed and some of those dates were the same as some of the dates of our murders. I expanded my search to include important dates in Poe's personal life, and found a date to correspond with the last of the four murders."

This time even Hoskins took note. Everybody knew that many serial killers killed according to some sort of schedule. If Mike had found a pattern of *time*, then it would be difficult to dismiss his theory.

"The Biddix murder occurred on July 10 and on July 10, 1845, Poe's only novel, **The Narrative of Arthur Gordon Pym**, was published in book form. Ruby James and her son died on July 12 and on July 12, 1849, Poe published an article entitled, 'How to Write a Blackwood Article'. The third murder, Stephen Hardison, occurred over a three to four-day period. He was found on July 17 but the ME estimates death on July 14 and on July 14, 1849, Poe arrived in Richmond and met with his childhood sweetheart, Elmira Royston."

As Mike spoke, he pointed to the relevant columns on the chronology.

"Finally, we come to the murder of Lucy Benton, the one based on 'The Black Cat'. The ME estimates Lucy's death occurred on July 19 and on July 19, 1844, Poe published a satirical article entitled 'Desultory Notes on Cats' in the Philadelphia Public Ledger. I think the murderer was trying to be cute with that one."

Mike turned back to the members of the task force and declared with conviction, "So not only is our killer using works written by Edgar Allan Poe as a basis for his murders, but he's also timing those deaths to coincide with dates corresponding to Edgar Allan Poe's life and literary career."

Everyone stared at Mike while they digested what they'd just heard.

Captain Mendez broke into the silence by saying, "Agent Donaldson, perhaps now would be a good time to distribute the briefing books."

Mike glanced gratefully at the Captain. "Of course, sir, thank you for reminding me." Mike picked up the thick packets and began to distribute them, explaining, "I have to thank Mr. McKissick for helping me with these last night. We put together all the information I had so you could look at it yourself. Reports concerning each of the murders, including pictures from the crime scenes, and the corresponding Poe work with the relative texts highlighted for comparison. Also a copy of the chronology with the murder dates highlighted and another timeline of important events in Edgar Allan Poe's life. This is where we got the timeline up on the monitor now. I think this is all the evidence you need to reach the same conclusion I did. There is a serial killer out there murdering people based on Edgar Allan Poe's writings and if we don't do something right away, he's just going to keep killing."

Chip and Alex began looking through the materials eagerly and nodding to themselves as they reviewed the important points. David, too, studied the papers intently and it was obvious he was paying attention to Mike's arguments. Only Blaine Hoskins wasn't looking at the thick pile of papers.

"I still think this is crazy. I mean, who are we going to look for here, a disgruntled librarian?" Hoskins demanded.

"May I remind you, Detective Hoskins, that SAC Martinez and myself have already heard Agent Donaldson's theory and we believe it." Mendez's voice grew hard. "Hoskins, I put you on this task force because of your experience with the VMCO and your outstanding record. However, I will take you off again if you can't give your full effort to this case. Unless you have something constructive to contribute to this discussion, I suggest you sit, listen and take notes."

Hoskins' face had turned a deep red as the captain spoke and when Mendez was done, she did nothing more than nod and look down at the open notebook in front of her.

Captain Mendez spoke to the room in general. "All right, everyone. It's time to get down to business. SAC Martinez and I have agreed that Agent Donaldson will be case agent. He will make the assignments and conduct the investigation. Welch, you will report your progress to me daily. This does not need to be a formal report, just a phone call will do."

Mendez rose from his chair. "At this point, I'm going to let Agent Donaldson take over. I know each of you will do your best and give Agent Donaldson your full cooperation." Here, Mendez gave Hoskins a pointed look. "Good luck to you all." With that, the MDPD captain left the room.

CHAPTER 17

Depend upon it, after all, Thomas, Literature is the most noble of professions.
'Letter to Frederick W. Thomas'

Mike looked at his team. "Let's start with Dr. Richmond; I know she needs to get back to her office. First, let me thank you for coming this morning, Doctor, I know this is a little unusual for you. What can you tell us about Temazepam?"

Meghan Richmond looked up. "I did the autopsy on Ms. James and I've reviewed the autopsy of Stephen Hardison and can confirm that Temazepam was found in both victims. And, although Temazepam is common enough, it's unlikely both would have had the drug in their system. As I said before, I'll go back to the morgue and check the other two bodies for Temazepam. I'd be surprised if it wasn't there."

"Is there any way to track our killer through this Temazepam?" asked Scotty.

"I seriously doubt it," responded Meghan with a shake of her head. "Temazepam is pretty common and can be found everywhere. It would be like looking for the proverbial needle in a haystack."

"Well, it was a good thought anyway," said Mike. "Dr. Richmond, please let me know as soon as you have your report ready. And if you think of anything else, please contact me."

Meghan nodded, gathered her notes, and left the room without comment.

"Next I'd like to get your thoughts on the case, Agent Sagan." Mike's voice took on a mischievous tone. "By the way, before we go any further, do you prefer behavioral analyst or don't you mind the more common term, profiler?"

Rhonda's laugh was deep, throaty and infectious. She was forty-one, tall and had the bluest eyes that Mike had ever seen. Her fair complexion was enhanced not only by her startling eye color but also by the beautiful shade of her auburn hair, which attested to her Irish heritage. But even if the listener were unaware of the profiler's roots, he or she would know the truth as soon as she opened her mouth. For, despite being a second-generation American, Rhonda Sagan still had the accent, a deep burr, she'd learned from her parents.

"I don't worry too much with politically correct terminology in my job, Agent Donaldson. I have no problem if you refer to me as a 'profiler'."

"Thank you, Agent Sagan," said Mike with an answering smile. "I understand you need to get back to your office in Tampa, and we appreciate you attending the meeting, so we'll get your thoughts and let you get on your way."

"Thank you. And please, call me Rhonda." She smiled again, showing bright teeth with a small gap in front. "Obviously, I haven't had time to look through this information," she began as she held up her briefing book, "but based on what I've heard so far, an educated guess would be that your killer is of an above-average intelligence, probably has his Bachelor's or possibly even a Master's degree. He's careful, thorough and meticulous and pays special attention to the little details, as shown by the inclusion of the monkey in 'The Black Cat' murder. However, he's not afraid to change those details if he can't fulfill certain requirements. For example, in the murder based on 'The Assignation', he killed the child even though in the story the child lives. This shows us that he is more concerned with his need to use Edgar Allan Poe as a basis for his killings than in recreating each story point by point."

"Rhonda," interrupted Alex, "Mike showed that the killer is using dates from Poe's life. The first two murders took place on dates pertaining to his literary career, while the third was staged on a date important to Poe's personal life. Do you think that could be significant or some sort of an escalation?"

The beautiful profiler considered a moment. "Frankly, it could go either way. Serial killers will sometimes escalate their murders if the police aren't taking them seriously enough or if they are concerned the investigation isn't going fast enough. Remember, some serial killers actually want to be caught, they want to be stopped. That's why they start communicating with the police in the first place. They subconsciously hope that by communicating with the police, they will make a mistake and lead the police to them. So, it's possible that changing to dates from Poe's life might mean an escalation the killer hopes we'll notice. Remember, since nothing has been said yet about a serial killer in the news, he doesn't even know we're looking for him. He may be trying to get our attention."

"So that's what's he's doing, then," interrupted Alex, "trying to get us to notice him?"

"No, Detective, I said he *might* want to get noticed, but that isn't what I think, actually," came the surprising response. "Frankly, the whole idea of serial killings based on Edgar Allan Poe's writings is so far out there that I don't think our killer is expecting us to put it together. Personally, I think he picked this date because it fit in with his preparations to commit this particular murder."

Agent Sagan pointed to the chronology on the monitor. "This list has hundreds of entries. It would be nearly impossible *not* to find a date if you wanted to kill someone. I think the killer got ready for the Ruby James murder, then chose the next relevant date."

Mike barely stopped himself from sighing in frustration. Taking a breath, he asked, "Then, Rhonda, do you see anything from his use of these dates to help us get a line on identifying him?"

"No, Agent Donaldson, not specifically," admitted the Irish woman. "All I can say is that it shows that your murderer is meticulous in his research. He very probably got a book similar to your reference book or spent some time researching Poe on the Internet."

"If you look at that list," began David as he planted himself next to Rhonda, "there are dates throughout the entire calendar year and there are several, for lack of a better word, 'clusters' of dates in certain months. Obviously, there are a lot in July, but there are quite a few in January, March and November, too." Scotty turned to the profiler. "Could there be significance in why he chose July to start his killing spree?"

Rhonda considered, then said, "I don't have enough information to answer, Detective Scotty. Until we know what tipped him over the edge and started him on this path, I can't say why he chose July. It's possible that something happened to him in the month of July."

Rhonda turned back to the list and pointed, "As you see, there are thirteen possible dates in July, but only eight in August: 9, 16, 19, 22, 23, 29, 30 and the 31st. He'll have to slow it down to use August dates, and since there are more days in between, at least at the beginning of the month, he'll have more time to plan. He may choose even more elaborate murders *because* he'll have more time to plan." Sagan ended as she sat back down.

"Maybe we should go back to our first victim," suggested Blaine Hoskins tentatively. "I've always heard that the first victim is the most important to a serial killer, because it's such a big step from thinking about killing to actually committing that first murder. Maybe we'll find something about Lylyana Biddix's death that could lead us to this guy."

"Good idea, Detective Hoskins," answered Mike. It had been so long since Hoskins had spoken, he'd all but forgotten she was even in the room. The fact that she was participating at all was a step in the right direction, and Mike was going to make sure he praised her idea. "What do you think, Rhonda?"

"Well, it's definitely true that the first murder is usually the most important to a serial killer. And, typically, the first killing is a little different, because the murderer hasn't perfected his MO yet. But, because the methods being used by this killer differ, I'm not certain that will help you a lot. Still worth a try."

Something Rhonda just said gave Mike an idea and he wondered if he should say anything right away or research it first. His doubts started to creep in again and he didn't want to look like a fool during the first task force meeting. He decided to wait and made a note to himself to follow up later.

"I have another question," said Blaine.

Blaine Hoskins was thirty-two but had already served with the VCMO on and off for six years. She was tall for a woman, 5'10", and could beat almost any man on the obstacle course on any given day. Her muscular build was not exactly attractive, but Mike knew that if Mendez had picked her for this task force, she had to be good at her job.

Turning to her, Rhonda smiled and asked, "And what would that be, Detective?"

"Are we sure that our murderer *is* a man? Couldn't our killer be a woman? She wouldn't need as much strength to begin with for female victims and using the Temazepam would make it even easier. What are the odds of our Poe killer being a woman?"

Before the profiler could answer, David spoke up. "I think you're forgetting Steven Hardison. He wouldn't jive with your theory."

"Oh, but it would," interrupted Welch. "Look at the picture of Hardison. He was only 5'8" and weighed one-forty, so he wasn't exactly a heavyweight. I think a woman could have moved him. And once Hardison was chained to that wall, he wasn't much of a threat to our killer. Plus, using the drug made the victims easier to handle, so strength wasn't necessary. I think Blaine has a good point. Our killer certainly could be a woman." Turning back to the front of the room, Welch asked, "What do you think, Agent Sagan?"

Rhonda replied positively. "I think it's a good point, Detective Hoskins. And yours, Detective Welch. It's entirely possible that your killer could be a woman. And what's more, in general, women are viewed, by both men and other women, as less threatening. It might be easier for a woman to secure the trust of victims in order to get close enough to administer the Temazepam. It was probably added to a drink each time and that would require some degree of intimacy with the victim. It's perfectly possible for our killer to be a woman."

Mike nodded and took over the discussion once more. "Do you have anything else to add before we let you go, Rhonda?"

"Not at the moment," Rhonda replied. "I'd like a chance to look over this briefing book and go over some research notes first. Give me a day or two and I think I might be able to give you a more refined profile."

"Good enough. I've got your card and I'll give you mine. And, of course, if anything comes up, I'll let you know."

Rhonda stood, and took Mike's card. With a general wave to the room, she left to drive back to Tampa.

It had already been a long meeting, but it wasn't over yet. Mike turned to his team and started handing out assignments.

CHAPTER 18

In fine, driven to despair, she committed the matter to me.
'THE PURLOINED LETTER'

July 25

Mike already missed his morning cup of coffee and Beverly's bright smile. He'd come into the office so early this morning that the restaurant wasn't even open yet and he'd had to make do with the sludge from the office coffee maker.

Paper steeped in tar would probably taste better, he thought as he rinsed out his cup and bought a bottle of water from the vending machine in the break area. *On the other hand, that crap will keep me awake if we start pulling all-nighters.*

He'd practically pulled an all-nighter last night anyway. He'd stayed up late reading Poe stories and poems and cross referencing with the books from Dr. Barty. Mike figured he needed to be as acquainted with Poe as he could be to recognize new murders when they came along.

Problem was, there were too many to read. Poe was prolific, Mike gave him that. He'd published more than three hundred and fifty stories, poems, essays and articles under his own name, and had apparently written more anonymously. He was considered the inventor of the detective story as well as being credited with popularizing the American short story. Editor of several periodicals, he had corresponded extensively with fellow authors. With so much to choose from, there was no way to tell what the killer might use as a basis for his next murder. Even sticking to the most gruesome of Poe's writings might not help given 'The Bells' wasn't that kind of work at all, but the murderer used it to frame the Biddix murder.

Just knowing Poe's work was only half the equation, so to speak. They still had to identify new murders when they occurred and connect them to these serial killings. That meant going through crime databases and finding potential deaths. Mike needed the members of his task force doing actual investigating, not tied to a chair reading short stories or combing the crime sheets.

Mike could not do it all alone. He was responsible for leading the team, distributing resources, reviewing paperwork, and handling a million other little things that went with the day-to-day running of a major investigation. Mike looked at the pile of folders on his desk. Already several inches high, it would only be taller by the end of the day.

With a sigh, he wondered if maybe Zardes was right, and he'd bitten off more than he could chew. If he turned the investigation over to someone more experienced now, lives might be saved.

During his last ten years with the FBI and his three-year stint in the Army before that, Mike always had a lot of self-confidence. He'd worked hard to do his job as well as he could, and he'd always risen to the top of whatever he was doing. But lately, he'd made some stupid mistakes. The Milwaukee job two months ago had been a near fuck-up and he was just lucky that his fugitive was dumber than dirt. And here in Miami, well, letting Atkinson deceive him with that crap about being afraid of heights was a rookie move that Mike should never have allowed to happen. He was lucky that the knife wound wasn't bad.

Maybe he was losing his touch. Maybe …

No. He could do this. He had to do this. He wouldn't keep doubting himself like this. He needed to come up with a plan to deal with all this crap. He needed help, but without *looking* like he needed help.

Tapping his pen on the desk, he considered his options. He needed help with the Poe side of the case as well as finding more murders. He needed a way to sift through all the extra information of this case. He needed ... *Yes!*

Mike grinned as the answer came to him. Not only could he get the help he needed but the request would be perfectly reasonable. He wrote a quick list on the pad on his desk to organize his thoughts. When he was satisfied, he picked up the phone and asked to see Bradley Zardes.

~~

"It's not time for our scheduled meeting, Agent Donaldson. Has something happened?"

"No, sir. I'd like to make a request, but since I'm not familiar with the way you do things here in this office, I'd thought I'd ask you personally. If I need to make a formal request or if there's paperwork I need to fill out, I'll be glad to do that, too."

Zardes tried to smile, but even he knew it was forced. He didn't like Mike Donaldson and didn't really care who knew it. He'd argued forcefully against putting this upstart in charge of the investigation, but he'd been overruled. He didn't know how Donaldson had ingratiated himself into Captain Mendez's good graces so quickly, but somehow, he had, and Mendez had convinced SAC Martinez to put Donaldson in charge.

Fine. When the little shit fucks up, they'll know I was right all along.

As usual, Zardes was up to his neck in paperwork and didn't have time for Donaldson, his requests or his attitude. "I see. All right, what is this request of yours?"

"I'd like to request Danny McKissick be assigned to my task force as technical support."

"Doing what exactly?" Zardes barely looked up as he rearranged the papers in front of him.

"Mostly research and support, sir. He's already been a big help in organizing the information I used at the original briefing the other day and this case will have a great deal more information that will need to be processed. Then it will need to be sorted and organized so that it's coherent for the team's use. On top of that, he would be invaluable as our own Poe expert, so to speak. He can …"

"I thought you were our Poe expert, Donaldson." Zardes's interruption and his smirk were meant to put Mike on notice that he was not convinced yet. Donaldson surprised him, however, by continuing as if he hadn't even spoken.

Cheeky bastard.

"My time will be better spent leading the team's investigation, sir, and Danny can research the Poe stories or poems and start compiling evidence for the United States Attorney. We'll also need to be on the lookout for new murders that fit our killer's MO and Danny can sort through law enforcement databases, newspapers and the Internet for those murders much faster than I ever could. I'm told he knows the computer systems better than anyone and I think having the best people on this task force makes the most sense."

Zardes watched Mike with hooded eyes as he considered the request. Having a technical assistant on a case of this kind did make sense and one was routinely assigned to important cases. But Zardes still didn't think this crazy theory had merit and hadn't even considered assigning an analyst to the task force.

He hated to use a valuable resource on such nonsense, but he might be able to turn this to his advantage. If Donaldson used McKissick on murders that should by all rights be handled by local PD, instead of concentrating on real FBI investigations, it would be another example of why Donaldson shouldn't have been encouraged in this ridiculous theory of his in the first place or put in charge of it in the second. Yes, this could be an advantage.

"Yes, I see your point, Agent Donaldson," Zardes almost purred. "I'll send McKissick an email assigning him to your team and telling him to report to you first thing tomorrow. I want to give him the rest of today to get his current work up to date and hand off anything he needs to the other analysts. Will that work for you?"

Zardes almost laughed at the look of surprise on Mike's face. *He wasn't expecting that, was he?*

"Yes, sir, that would be just fine. Thank you, Agent Zardes."

~~

Danny smiled when he looked up to see Mike entering his office but held up a hand asking for a moment. He was typing a mile a minute and needed to finish before losing his thought.

That folder there and the other here ...

"Okay, got it! Thanks for waiting, Mike." Danny expelled his held breath and sighed in the satisfaction of another job completed.

Danny made one more notation on the notepad in front of him, then turned to the matter at hand, already knowing why Mike was here. Mike had moved to the far wall and was studying a poster there.

"Before you ask, yes, that's based on 'Pinball Wizard'."

Mike turned to him and smiled. "Yeah, I recognized it right away. What I don't understand is why your face is on Elton John's body."

The picture itself was iconic. Elton John standing at the pinball machine/piano in three-foot tall shoes wearing his signature glasses and a pair of suspenders over a glittering shirt. The only incongruous thing about the picture was the face: Danny McKissick grinned at the observer, his red hair tousled as if he'd had no time to comb it, his blue eyes alive with intelligence and curiosity.

"I have a kind of reputation as a technical wizard, so they took the idea and ran with it. A couple of years ago I reached five years in this office and some of the agents got together to throw me a party. It was just cookies and sodas, but it was the thought that counted. Anyway, they gave me that picture for my wall. Obviously, you recognized Elton John, but do you know 'Pinball Wizard' at all?"

At Mike's nod, Danny continued. "Well, the words go, 'He's a pinball wizard,' something, something, something, 'he's got such a supple wrist'. I have a reputation here for being fast on the computer, so they applied those lines to me. They changed it to 'Techno wizard' and photo-shopped my picture on his body. Anyway, the name stuck, so now I'm the techno wizard of the office. I wasn't sure at first, but now I kinda like it, ya know?"

Mike's laugh was deep, and Danny liked that, too. He liked Agent Donaldson and was looking forward to getting to know him better.

"I guess I know why you're here. I got Agent Zardes's email a little while ago."

"Oh, good, then I won't have to explain myself," Mike said. "Yeah, I could use some help with the technical side of the case."

"Right up my alley," Danny said. "I have to admit I was intrigued during the briefing yesterday. I'm looking forward to working on this case."

Danny was surprised as Mike's brows furrowed and his mouth took a downward turn.

"Don't say that too quickly, you don't know what I want you to do yet. It's probably not gonna be the kind of stuff you normally do on a case."

"It's not a normal kind of case, though, is it?"

Danny was glad to see Mike smile at this quip. *Just the reaction I was hoping for.*

"No, it's definitely not a normal kind of case." Mike grabbed the only other chair in the cramped room and straddled it. "Zardes said you'd probably need the rest of the day to take care of whatever you've got going right now, so let me tell you briefly what I need first, and you tell me what you think you'll need to get it done."

Danny was ready for this. "Actually, I already started clearing my desk. I just finished up some work for Agent Montez and I handed off a couple of other projects. The only thing I have left to do is for Agent Ballentine, and I'm almost done with that assignment. Figure I'll have it ready in a couple of hours, so I can get started on your investigation right after that." Danny ran a hand through his disheveled hair and smiled. "Tell me what you need me to do."

Mike's teeth showed in his bright smile. "Great. To start, I need your help with some research I started on my own last night. I'm afraid my Internet skills aren't great, but I think what I'm looking for will be really important to the case. That's what gave me the idea to ask for you in the first place. Let me tell you what I've got."

CHAPTER 19

But the question is not yet settled, whether madness is or is not the loftiest intelligence.

'ELEAПORA'

July 27

The best thing to happen over the next two days was Mike's gift to the break room of a specialty coffee maker and a box of coffee pods. Other than that, there had been no joy for the members of the task force. They were no further along now than they had been on the first day.

Chip, Blaine Hoskins and Alex Welch had painstakingly reviewed the four deaths for anything that might have been missed in the initial investigations. Hoskins re-interviewed family and friends using the new angle of the serial killer scenario. The difficulty in that, of course, was that the MDPD officer wasn't *allowed* to tell her witnesses that a serial killer may have been responsible for their loved one's death.

Not long after Mike had given out the assignments that first day, a memo had come down from Zardes, prohibiting the investigators from telling anyone that there was a serial killer on the loose. That not only hampered the investigation, it angered everyone trying to find this maniac. Mike had not waited for his anger to abate before marching up to Zardes' office.

The opening door barely followed his distracted "Come," and Bradley Zardes's eyes narrowed when he saw who his unwanted visitor was.

"Donaldson, what are you doing here? Shouldn't you be downstairs leading your team?"

Mike couldn't fail to notice the sneer in the SSA's voice, but instead of making him more cautious, it only inflamed him further.

Brandishing a copy of the offending notice, Mike hissed, "What is this order all about?

Putting on a look of innocence, Zardes asked, "What are you talking about now, Agent?"

"This order preventing my team from mentioning the possibility of a serial killer as we conduct our investigation. You're tying my hands and you know it!"

Zardes laid aside the report he'd been reading, stood up slowly, and faced the angry agent. His voice lowered and he answered, "I thought it would be best not to panic the public by making the possibility of a serial killer widely known right now. Once we see where the investigation is headed, I'll revisit that decision."

Mike's eyes narrowed. "'Where the investigation is headed'? What's that supposed to mean?"

"Exactly what it sounds like, Agent Donaldson. If you can prove this theory of yours, then we'll decide how much to tell the public. We don't want to cause undue panic."

Mike took a deep breath. "Agent Zardes, we're gonna need all the help we can get from the public to find this maniac. His MO is so unusual that–"

"That I still don't buy this theory of yours, Donaldson, and I won't put this city in a panic because you're having delusions of grandeur." Zardes sat back down, picked up his report and pointed to the door. "You'd better get downstairs to your investigation. And don't ever come here again without an appointment."

Mike didn't slam Zardes's door as he walked out but wasn't nearly so careful with the door to the conference room.

"Don't guess I need to ask what happened, huh?" Blaine looked up from the file in her hand.

Mike huffed out a breath. "We're not to cause a public panic so we can't mention that we're investigating a serial killer."

Alex's snort was response enough. "Public panic? Are you kidding me?"

Mike chose to ignore that. "Zardes will 'revisit' the decision when he sees how the case is progressing."

"I don't suppose he understands that we need to get information from that same public. Tips are what's gonna help us solve these cases. He does understand that, doesn't he?" David asked.

"Apparently not. Not yet anyway."

"Why don't you just go to SAC Martinez, Mike?" This came from Chip, who'd said nothing since Mike had announced he was going to see Zardes some fifteen minutes before.

"Going over Zardes's head would probably not be a good idea," Alex told the young agent.

"And it might just get me kicked off this case before I even get started," Mike put in. "We're just gonna have to get to a point where they will let us tell witnesses what we're looking for. And the sooner we get there the better."

~~

Matters seemed to be at a stalemate, when two events changed the nature of the case altogether. The first came from Rhonda Sagan. After reviewing the information and consulting her textbooks, she came up with a startling new analysis.

"We've been calling these murders serial killings and the murderer a serial killer. But I'm not sure that we should be."

"What!"

"Not a serial killer?"

"What the hell's that supposed to mean?"

Mike raised his hand to calm his team. He understood their incredulity - he shared it - but wanted to give the profiler a chance to explain. She *was* the expert, after all, and if they were looking at this case the wrong way, they needed to change direction and do so quickly.

Once again gathered in the conference room, they listened to the beautiful profiler deliver her surprising evaluation. Rhonda had joined them via Skype and addressed the group as a teacher addressed her students.

"I know most of you have heard a lot of this before, but I'm going to review some basic information about serial killers before we get into the present case." Rhonda took a breath and began. "A serial killer is usually defined as someone who has killed three or more people in a period of a month or more, acts alone, and gets some kind of sexual gratification from the killings. However, serial killing for financial gain or attention seeking is not unknown.

"The FBI recognizes three main types." Rhonda held up her fingers as she explained. "The thrill seeker tries to outsmart the police; they consider the whole thing a game. Mission-oriented serial killers think they're doing society a favor by killing unwanted people, such as prostitutes, and control killers enjoy their victims' suffering, they want to hear the screams as they die.

"Most identified in the United States are white males, lower-to-middle-class and in their twenties or thirties. Often of lower intelligence and very often were abandoned by their fathers, raised by domineering mothers, or have family histories of crime or alcoholism.

"There is also a subsection, if you will, of serial killers who are of above-average intelligence, are very organized and sometimes even correspond with the police or news media in order to gain more notoriety." Rhonda smiled slightly as she stated, "Unfortunately, it is this last group that gets the most media attention and what the layman usually thinks of when they hear the term 'serial killer'."

Rhonda shrugged and sat on the edge of the nearest table. "After reading through Agent Donaldson's briefing book and reviewing information in textbooks and speaking to a colleague of mine, as I said before, I'm not sure we should treat this as a typical serial killer case."

"I'm not sure I see the problem," stated Chip. He leaned forward in his chair and punctuated his words by tapping his finger on the table. "We have a killer who has killed five people so far, including a baby, for God's sake, in three weeks, and you said yourself the other day that he was highly intelligent and meticulous. That satisfies several of your criteria right there."

"You are absolutely correct, Agent Smythe," agreed Rhonda immediately. With another smile she continued, "And I'm still entertaining the theory that this could be a serial killing in the traditional sense. It's just that there are several atypical aspects to this case that concern me."

"Like what?" asked David.

The thirty-year-old African American MDPD agent had a face like Denzel Washington, a scalp ala Samuel L Jackson, could easily be on the cover of Gentleman's Quarterly, and his deep baritone was reminiscent of Nat King Cole. Now that voice was more curious than confrontational.

"For starters," answered Rhonda, "your first three murder scenes occurred in a five-day period. Even for a highly organized serial killer, that is extremely quick. It makes me wonder if he has an accomplice. Not necessarily another murderer, but perhaps someone doing the 'legwork', so to speak. Scouting out locations, finding the victims, that kind of thing, while the killer commits the actual crimes.

"Next, I see none of the typical elements. They aren't trying to outwit the police, since they've made no attempt to contact us or the media; they're not killing a particular group of undesirable people, like prostitutes, since your victims so far have nothing in common, and they don't seem to be getting satisfaction from the deaths themselves, given they aren't waiting around to watch them die or beg for their lives. In fact, so far, your killer seems to have gone out of his or her way *not* to be there when the victims died.

"Lylyana Biddix was up in that tower alone when she died, and the killer would have died as well. Ruby James and her son were poisoned, but the coroner's report stated the type of poison was slow acting. Stephen Hardison took days to die and Lucy Benton, although killed with a direct blow from an axe, apparently lingered for some time before expiring. There are other minor points, but I think you get my drift."

Rhonda closed her file of notes and waited.

No one said anything for long moments as each digested what they'd just heard.

Mike blew out a breath and asked, "Rhonda, does any of this need to affect how we investigate these murders? Should we do something different if we aren't dealing with a serial killer than if we were?"

Tapping her folder for a moment, she looked up and finally answered. "I don't think so. You already knew that there was no commonality in the victims to help you and we already knew the killer was intelligent. You had also already realized that he or she used dates from Poe's life to kill by, so you know what dates to look for. As I said earlier, it still may be that this will turn out to be a bona fide serial killer. It just may be more atypical than normal.

"No, Agent Donaldson, I think you need to continue on as you have been. Serial killer or no, you still have an extremely disturbed individual out there that needs to be found. Sooner rather than later, before something happens that might cause them to escalate their murders."

CHAPTER 20

**Meet me at Arvida Park at 7:30. I'll chill
a bottle of champagne and we'll watch the
sunset. It won't be as beautiful as you, but
we'll make do**.

Cecilia Rogers looked at the text once more. Mitch could be so romantic at times. And thoughtful. A sunset meant a picnic on a blanket and 7:30 gave her just enough time to stop at the house and change clothes before meeting him. Her uniform would be uncomfortable sitting on the ground and Mitch realized that. So typical of him.

She tried to concentrate on the incident report she was writing. Everyone thought being a security guard meant nothing but standing around all day. They had no idea of all the paperwork the job entailed. The last hour of her shift was dedicated to updating her logs and checking the sign-in sheet. Most days she was done in plenty of time, but today there'd been that stupid dust up with that idiot from the 14th floor, so she was pressed for time.

I bet if I bribed him, Jeff would do the sheet for me.

That way, she could sneak out a little early.

She reread her notes again, but her mind kept going back to Mitch's invitation. Champagne, huh? She frowned. Was today a special occasion she'd forgotten? It wasn't the anniversary of their first date, that was in January. Not their first kiss, that had also been in January. Not when they moved in together since it hadn't been a year yet. What else … Oh my God. She sat up straight. He wanted to set the date for their wedding! He'd said before that he wanted to wait for his promotion to go through but maybe he changed his mind. Yes, that had to be it.

Cecilia saved the report and gathered her things. Excitement made her clumsy and she dropped her keys twice as she mapped out the best route to the park.

Should I take 137th Ave or 94? How will Mitch go? He usually takes … wait a minute. Didn't Mitch say he had a late meeting this afternoon and wouldn't be home for dinner? I could've sworn … She shrugged. *It must've been canceled.*

The trip home was great. She hit every green light and her favorite music blared from the radio. The rebate check she'd been waiting weeks for was in the mail and her neighbor's teenage son had cut the grass as promised. 5:45. She had plenty of time to get ready. She took a quick shower and picked out the sweater Mitch loved so much. It was lightweight and showed just enough cleavage to be suggestive without being trashy. He always said it brought out the green tint in her eyes, but she knew he really liked it because it was so easy to pull off. Her most comfortable pair of jeans and brown boots completed the outfit. She put on a little makeup and let her hair hang down. Mitch liked it that way.

~~

The sun was already beginning to fade a bit when she arrived, and she parked her car in a free space next to the entrance. Summertime in Miami meant almost daily afternoon showers, making the grass a dark green with sprouting patches of wildflowers throughout the area. She heard birds crying in the distant trees and felt a slight breeze as she searched for Mitch.

She followed the concrete pathway and spent a moment looking at the map of the park. Arvida Park wasn't large, with a small playground area and a walking path that meandered in a circle around the soccer field in the middle. A dog park on one side and a picnic area between two copses of trees completed the area. Cutler Drain Canal lay on the other side of the metal fence and, as she walked, Cecilia could see a small dock along one side of the canal.

While surprised that no one else was around on such a lovely evening, she didn't mind. Privacy was always preferable for a romantic sunset. She didn't see Mitch's red hair anywhere, but finally spied the picnic he'd set out for them. He hadn't set it up on one of the picnic tables, but instead a large gray blanket lay in a bare patch some twenty yards or so away from the nearby canal. She saw paper plates and plasticware, and a bag held bread and cheese. To add to the ambiance, a vase with a single red rose sat in the middle of their 'table'. She was surprised at that touch given Mitch knew she wasn't fond of roses.

She shrugged and sat down. Maybe the store didn't have anything else. Her face crinkled. *Well, it's the thought that counts.* Looking around, she spotted one of those ice buckets you find in hotel rooms. She saw the champagne bottle peeking out and found a note leaning against it. It was typed, which was strange, but the sentiment was not.

I have to do one more thing.
Pour yourself a drink and
I'll be back soon.

Sounded like a plan. She sipped the cool liquid and pulled off a piece of the baguette. The breeze was picking up a little and she kept pushing her hair out of her eyes. It was so peaceful here. A perfect place to relax.

The sun was beginning to fall more quickly, and she was afraid Mitch was going to miss the show. Where was he? She poured her second glass and ate a piece of cheese. Her head began to feel heavy and suddenly she couldn't seem to keep her eyes open. Cecilia lay back on the blanket and closed her eyes. She'd take a snooze until Mitch showed up. She didn't think she'd get much sleep tonight once they got back home, so she'd better rest while she could.

She felt the cool of the setting sun and grinned. This was going to be the best night of her life.

CHAPTER 21

"Villains!" I shrieked, "dissemble no more! I admit the deed! — tear up the planks! — here, here! — it is the beating of his hideous heart!"

'THE TELL-TALE HEART'

Rhonda's bombshell had been a turning point in the case. Mike now had new information that would turn the investigation on its head. He'd gotten an idea from something Blaine said during their first briefing and he immediately started pursuing it.

Blaine had suggested they delve more deeply into Lylyana Biddix's death, since the first death was usually especially significant to the murderer. Often it was also different in some way, for the killer had not yet decided on a particular MO. Hoskins, Smythe and Welch had looked closely at all the murders but particularly the Biddix one to see if anything stood out. Unfortunately, nothing had.

Meghan Richmond had found Temazepam in all the victims, so they at least had a calling card for their murderer. Given Biddix also had the drug in her system, Mike believed they didn't have their victim zero yet and that was what he'd been investigating.

He quickly realized he needed help and that was one of the reasons he put in the request for Danny McKissick to be added to the team. While Danny's computer skills would be invaluable to the ongoing investigation, for now Mike had asked Danny to help him with his research to find the first victim.

He'd decided to start two weeks before Lylyana Biddix's murder and if they didn't find what he was looking for there, they'd trace back two more weeks. One month should be enough. If what he was looking for wasn't there, Mike believed going back any further would be useless.

In the end, it only took Danny and Mike a day and a half to identify victim zero.

As the team members settled down for the briefing, Mike could see the evidence of the on-going, intensive investigation, now into its second week. All the bulletin boards were filled with information and on the tables were mountains of files and miscellaneous papers. Scattered around the room, a variety of coffee cups, mugs, and water bottles, while the trash in the wastepaper basket attested to the numerous take-out meals eaten in just the past twenty-four hours. Everyone was working 12-hour shifts but since they'd been working different aspects of the case, the entire task force had not actually been together for the past two days, until now, to hear what Mike had to say.

"Thank you all for coming in so quickly," Mike began as he stood at the head of the room in front of the wall monitor. "After our last joint briefing, I got an idea and asked Danny to help me with it. Basically, Danny has been sorting crime reports of unusual murders and deaths for the weeks prior to Lylyana Biddix's murder. We then reviewed each to find any Poe aspects. We found what we were looking for this morning."

Danny was once again in charge of the monitor and at Mike's nod he put up a picture of a crime scene none of the investigators had ever seen before. On the screen was a shot of a bedroom with a bed, dresser and one chair against a wall. There were no windows in the room, but what drew everyone's eyes immediately were several holes in the floor with what appeared to be body parts within.

"Mike, what the hell are we looking at?" Alex's tone spoke to his unease with the apparent crime scene.

"This, I believe, is victim zero," stated Mike. "On June 24, Oscar Cudney was discovered by police after his mail carrier reported a problem at his home. He had apparently been smothered, then his body dismembered, the parts hidden under the floorboards of his bedroom. The coroner's report stated that death probably occurred on the 22nd, but no one noticed anything until the mail carrier realized the mail had not been picked up for a couple of days. When he went to the door to check on Mr. Cudney, he noticed a smell and immediately called the police. They broke in and dogs led them to the body parts.

"What stood out to me was the description of Mr. Cudney. He was seventy-six years old and had a glass right eye, blue in color. He lived alone but had a second cousin in Miami who came by often to help him out. While in general good health for a man his age, he did have bad arthritis and had had both hips replaced. He couldn't drive due to his poor eyesight and couldn't do a lot for himself. His cousin bought his groceries and took him to doctors' appointments."

"Just get to the punchline, Mike," interrupted Chip. "Which Poe story is this one?"

David and Alex smiled at the attempted levity while Blaine nodded and continued to take more notes.

"Most of you have probably heard of this one," responded Mike as he gestured for Danny to put up the text copy on the monitor. 'The Tell-Tale Heart' is one of Poe's most famous short stories. In it, the narrator admits that he killed an old man he takes care of. He admits that he loved the old man and that the victim had never wronged him, stating that he didn't do it for money, but because the man's 'vulture-like pale blue eye' made his blood run cold. He goes into the old man's room one night and scares him, causing him to shriek, smothers him with his own mattress, then dismembers the body, cutting off the head, arms and legs and hiding them underneath the floorboards. When the police arrive at four in the morning, having been alerted by neighbors who heard the shriek, they search the house, but don't find anything at first. However, the narrator gives himself away in the end when he swears he can hear the beating of the old man's heart and points out where he buried it."

"And the parallel to Poe's life? What happened on June 22?" asked Detective Welch.

"1815," answered Mike promptly. "On June 22, 1815, the Allan family left America for England. Another clear date pertaining to Poe's life."

No one said anything for a long moment, until Blaine spoke up. "The parallels are pretty obvious, so you have found another victim of the Poe murderer. But why do you think he's victim zero?"

Blaine had come around during the last couple of days. She'd been holding out against his serial killer theory, but once she'd gotten on board, she fell in completely. Now she worked harder than anyone else to find their killer, even working late last night. When Mike had found out, he'd thanked her, then warned her never to do it again.

"Yeah," agreed Welch. "We thought we had victim zero, so what made you keep looking?"

"And how do you know that there isn't another even earlier than Mr. Cudney? How can you be sure he's victim zero?" asked David Scotty.

Mike nodded. "Blaine suggested going back to the first victim, Lylyana Biddix, but the first victim is usually a bit atypical given the killer is still perfecting his MO. While Rhonda said these murders use different methods and that wouldn't work here, we do have one common factor to go on: the Temazepam. I figured that the first murder might not involve Temazepam but would still have Poe elements in it. I started looking for deaths that were especially gruesome and had Danny help me. This morning Danny found Mr.

Cudney. Also, I reviewed the coroner's report and found out that there was *no* Temazepam in his system. That's why I think this is victim zero."

"I agree, Mike," said Blaine. "There are too many similarities to 'The Tell-Tale Heart' to be a coincidence. And the fact that there isn't Temazepam is definitely significant." Turning to Rhonda Sagan, who'd joined via Skype, she asked, "Would you agree, Rhonda?"

The fair-faced Irish woman immediately said, "Definitely. Mr. Cudney is more than likely our victim zero. Well done, Agent."

Mike blushed slightly. Not just because the profiler agreed with his theory, but more importantly, the entire task force was on board and becoming a real team. Yesterday morning, Alex had bought Croissants for everyone and last night David had brought in two pizzas.

"What do we know about the investigation into Cudney's death?" asked Scotty.

"I have copies of the file for all of you," began Mike as he handed a pile of papers to Chip and asked him to pass them around. "There is one problem with this case, however." Mike cleared his throat. "It seems that MDPD made an arrest."

At that unexpected announcement, everyone looked at their case agent with varying degrees of surprise.

"On June 27, MDPD arrested the cousin, Cameron Cudney, and charged him with the murder, but he was released the next week due to a lack of concrete evidence. I tried to speak to the DA on this case, but he's in court today and I couldn't reach him."

"Who's on the case at MDPD?" asked Welch.

"Officer Roll found the body and Detective Sergeant Montgomery made the arrest. I spoke to Sergeant Montgomery and he said that the main evidence against Cameron Cudney was that his alibi didn't check out and he was the main beneficiary of Oscar's will. However, he told me privately that he had his reservations about the arrest. He wasn't convinced that Cousin Cameron is guilty."

"He might not be, but if he is and MDPD let him go, he could be our murderer," stated David firmly.

"That's why we're starting with Cameron Cudney. Blaine, it was your idea to look into victim zero, so you and Welch go see Detective Montgomery. He's bound to have notes that didn't go into the official file and probably ideas about other possible suspects. If Cudney is victim zero, Montgomery's insights may give us some ideas." Mike faced the rest of the group. "David, go to the coroner's office and review the autopsy on Cudney with Meghan. Ask her to double-check for Temazepam. I want to be sure about this. Next …"

Blaine interrupted. "Mike, there's one more thing. You just pointed out that we've been operating under the wrong assumption. We were looking at Lylyana Biddix as the first case when it obviously isn't. Plus, Hardison was kidnapped before the James murder even though he died after her. We probably need to change the order of the cases according to when they were actually kidnapped and killed, not when they were found."

Mike looked over to the bulletin board with the list of victims. Mentally slapping his forehead, Mike acknowledged the point by admitting, "Yeah, Blaine, you're right."

CHAPTER 22

Coincidences, in general, are great stumbling blocks in the way of that class of thinkers who have been educated to know nothing of the theory of probabilities – that theory to which the most glorious objects of human research are indebted for the most glorious of illustration.

'THE MURDERS IN THE RUE MORGUE'

Mike stood in front of the bulletin board with the victims' names and pictures, reviewing once again the list of murders in their proper order. The list had been rearranged with the following information included: Name of the victim; Date of death; Date the victim was found; Poe work upon which the death was based and date of correlation to Poe's life.

Now the updated version looked like this:

OSCAR CUDNEY; 6/22; 6/24; *THE TELL-TALE HEART*; 6/22/1815

LYLYANA BIDDIX; 7/10; 7/12; *THE BELLS*; 7/10/1845

(STEPHEN HARDISON KIDNAPPED, 07/11)

RUBY JAMES AND CHILD; 7/12; 7/13; *THE ASSIGNATION*;
7/12/1849

STEPHEN HARDISON; 7/14; 7/17; *THE CASK OF
AMONTILLADO*; 7/14/1849

LUCY BENTON; 7/19; 7/23; *THE BLACK CAT*; 7/19/1844

Mike didn't know how far this actually got them, but he was willing to try anything if it helped find this maniac. He hoped Blaine and Welch could turn up something new.

"Hey, boss, want a coffee? I brought you a hot one."

Mike's eyes widened as he looked at the proffered Styrofoam cup in Blaine's hand.

Not waiting for an answer, Blaine spoke. "Uh, Mike, look I know we got off on the wrong foot, and that was my fault. I will admit I was hard on you because I was pissed that you just waltzed in here and all but took over. I figured you didn't know Jack about investigating such a big case or running a task force or anything else, and the idea was crazy to begin with, but ..." Blaine's face turned red and she looked away. "But I was wrong. You've really done a good job here and ... well, I just wanted to say I'm sorry."

Blaine put the cup of coffee on the table and had turned to leave when Mike put out a hand to stop her.

"Look, you weren't to blame entirely. How about we start over?" Mike held a hand out and with a serious look said, "I'm Agent Mike Donaldson."

Blaine laughed. It was an infectious laugh, a laugh that made people want to be around her. It also showed two dimples around her mouth that Mike had never noticed before.

"Hi, Mike. I'm Blaine Hoskins with MDPD. Welcome to Miami." Blaine shook his hand, and her smile was warm.

"Where's that accent from? I don't recognize it."

"I was born and raised in Nebraska. I moved here about seven years ago."

"Nebraska? You're from Nebraska? I didn't think anyone actually grew up in Nebraska." Mike's tone was serious, but his eyes danced.

"All right, *Agent* Donaldson. Now you just undid the past fifteen minutes of what was turning out to be a very nice truce. Don't you dare say such things about my home state or I'll have to retaliate by bad-mouthing Virginia."

"How'd you know I came from Virginia?"

"I did a little research on you," Blaine answered. "I wanted to know what kind of smartass I was going to be dealing with, didn't I?"

There was that laugh again. Mike was beginning to think he could get used to hearing it. "Okay, back to the truce. I'm sure Nebraska is a very nice place to live … if you're a moose or buffalo maybe." Mike gave a full-throated laugh of his own.

Blaine gave him a playful slap on the arm and was about to make an appropriate rejoinder when Alex came into the room.

During the last few days Mike had not seen the detective with a hair out of place, much less panting like he was now.

"Mike, I think we might have found the commonality!"

~~

Alex Welch held the floor as he explained what he'd found. "It was an accident really. I was cross-referencing the backgrounds of our four adult victims when I saw it."

"Saw what already?" said David. "You've been going on for five minutes and we still don't know what you found."

Alex turned a shade of red that only accented his receding hairline. He was a big man, easily 5'10" and at one-seventy was developing a tire around his middle that made him look older than his forty-two years. Now, however, he looked like the veteran detective who'd been solving cases with the VCMO for twelve years.

"Yeah, okay, sorry. It's just that I'm excited, that's all."

"We understand, Alex," said Mike kindly. "Just tell us what you found."

Alex grinned and began again. "Well, it seems that two of our victims do have a connection to one another."

The members of the task force sat up straight. Could this be the breakthrough they'd been waiting for?

"And?" asked Chip. He tapped the index finger of his left hand on the table, attesting to his growing impatience.

Alex gave the young agent a quick look, then turned to the case agent. "Both Lylyana Biddix and Lucy Benton attended Miami Dade College. However –"

"Did they have any classes together?" Chip interrupted.

Alex's eyes narrowed with irritation. "As I was getting ready to say, however, they attended years apart. Biddix was there in 2005 and Benton took a few classes in 1998."

"Just because they weren't there at the same time, doesn't mean that someone else with a connection to that college might not have found them through his connection," Blaine added.

"True." Mike nodded. He considered his next move for a moment, then ordered, "Alex, you found this, so I want you to follow up. Call the college to check if Ruby James or Stephen Hardison had any connection with Miami Dade College. I guess you should probably check on Oscar Cudney, too, though that seems like a long shot. I don't want us to get ahead of ourselves here. It could just be a coincidence."

~~

"So, is this our common factor?" asked Zardes.

The Supervisory Special Agent had once again been signing forms at his desk when Mike went up to give his evening report. Mike spent the few minutes waiting looking at Zardes's office walls decorated with various certificates and awards, and Mike noticed that none were more recent than five years ago. Mike knew from the office scuttlebutt that Zardes had been in this same position for seven years and had a chip on his shoulder because of it. He wanted to move up in the FBI hierarchy and had been unable to do that. Maybe that was why the SSA was so standoffish with Mike. Maybe he resented that Mike had found his niche and was happy in it while Zardes was still twiddling his thumbs here in Miami instead of advancing his career in another field office.

The only personal touch to the office was on the north wall where Zardes had added several pictures of tennis stars and an autographed photo of Rafael Nadal was in an honored place. Despite himself, Mike was impressed. He didn't know much about tennis but even he'd heard of the tennis superstar. Zardes must have some clout to have been able to snag such an important autograph.

Mike's ruminations ended when Zardes asked for his report. Now, the SSA went straight to the heart of the matter.

"Sir, we're not sure yet that this is our commonality. So far, only two of the victims had any connection to MDC and we can't be sure this isn't just a coincidence. I have–"

"Well, you need to get sure and get sure now, Donaldson," demanded Zardes in his clipped Scandinavian tone. "Get someone on this and do it immediately."

Mike buried the impulse to argue and simply explained, "I already have. Detective Welch is contacting Miami Dade College as we speak. Hopefully, we'll hear something back today or tomorrow at the latest. It's still possible this could be a coincidence. Biddix and Benton attended several years apart and–"

"I don't believe in coincidences in a murder investigation, Agent," interrupted Zardes again. "Especially not in serial killings. Everything is important and potentially the key to finding this maniac. Donaldson, if you can't handle this investigation and do it properly, I'll talk to Captain Mendez and we'll find someone who can."

A brief vision of Mike's fist slamming into Zardes's face went through his mind, but he squelched it. He needed tact and diplomacy, not confrontation. "I'm perfectly capable of leading this investigation, sir. Once we have the information from MDC, I'll update you on our findings."

"Be sure you do, Donaldson." Zardes went back to signing his paperwork.

As soon as the door closed behind Mike, however, Zardes put down his expensive Waterman pen and picked up his phone.

CHAPTER 23

Because I feel that, in the Heavens above, The angels, whispering
to one another, Can find, among their burning terms of love, None
so devotional as that of 'Mother.'
' To My Mother'

August 1

"You do know you're gonna owe me for this big time, don't ya,
mom?" Suzanne smiled as she took the left turn a little too quickly.

They were turning onto an immaculate street in the Bayshore
Villas where multi-million-dollar mansions hid behind palm trees
and shrubs, sidewalks held no cracks, and the dogs all wore
expensive collars. The place screamed money and Suzanne was
sure no one behind those walls had ever done an hour's worth of
real work in their lives.

Not like her mother, of course. Camille Henri had worked
hard all her adult life, cleaning this kind of outrageously
overpriced home first for a cleaning company then striking out on
her own. Suzanne had never really understood why her mom had
wanted to clean other people's houses, but she did and had until
just a year or so ago. The years of pushing her body to its limits
had resulted in a bad back, painful knees and arthritic hands. Five

years of her doctor's warnings had finally sunk in and she'd admitted it was time to quit.

Suzanne knew that her mom and dad had worked tirelessly to give her a better life than they had. Their manual-labor jobs had put her through college, and she had repaid them by graduating cum laude and getting a secretarial job at one of the best law offices in the city. She'd only been there a couple years but was already impressing her boss so much that she was being trained for an assistant's position and had even been given the title already.

So, she hadn't really minded when her mom called in a near-panic, needing an emergency ride. Someone had recommended Camille for a house cleaning gig but since her mom didn't do that anymore, she'd agreed to go out to the house, look around and make a recommendation on a cleaning company.

Now, Suzanne was spending her day off playing chauffeur to her mom and, despite her playful grumblings, enjoying the time they had together. She loved her dad dearly, but it was nice to spend some time alone with her mom.

"Oh, I'm not so sure about that, young lady," answered Camille Henri with a smile of her own. "A nice area like this, big house. Who knows? Maybe there's a son in the home who's not married and looking for a beautiful, intelligent, caring woman. You may thank me someday for asking you to drive me here."

"Mom, please." Suzanne rolled her eyes. "Please stop trying to fix me up all the time. I know you want grandkids, please don't mention it again, but I'm just not ready to settle down yet. I'm only twenty-seven, I still have plenty of time."

Seeing her mother opening her mouth to respond, Suzanne tried to head her off at the pass. "And don't start on how old you and dad are either. You're only sixty-six, you'll be around for years and years. You'll have plenty of time to take any hypothetical grandchildren to the park, to get ice cream or to Disney. Can we agree to table this discussion for a little while longer?"

Suzanne saw her mother's answering grin and wondered what was coming next. She didn't have long to wait.

"All right, sweetheart. I won't say another word about grandkids or your getting married. However, I can't speak for your dad, though. You're on your own there."

Suzanne didn't answer except to change the subject. "We're here. Why don't I wait in the car?"

"Of course you're not going to wait out here, sweetheart. You'll roast in this hot car and I don't want you wasting all your gas running the air conditioner. You're coming inside with me, and that's that."

The two women got out of the car and walked up the drive to the most pretentious front doors Suzanne had ever seen. Made of real oak, the French double doors boasted bevel glass etched with a beautiful geometric pattern that had to be custom made. Suzanne couldn't even begin to guess at the price.

Camille rang the bell and the mother and daughter waited. Would the homeowner answer or a maid? Suzanne bet on the latter.

God, I hope this doesn't take long, Suzanne thought as the doors opened and she pasted on a smile.

CHAPTER 24

There was nothing to wash out—no stain of any kind—no blood-spot whatever.

'THE TELL-TALE HEART'

August 2

Blaine sat at the table, a bottle of water in her hand as she updated the team about Oscar Cudney's murder. "MDPD did a good job on this investigation, Mike," began Blaine as she put Cudney's picture on the monitor. "They did some digging into Mr. Cudney's background before arresting the cousin. Naturally, their first suspect had to be Cameron Cudney. He took care of the old man, had a key to the house, wasn't where he said he was on the night of the murder and benefited the most by Oscar's death. Sergeant Montgomery did investigate a couple of others and was able to eliminate them as suspects and concentrate on Cudney. The most damning thing against the cousin was his alibi, or rather, lack of one.

"Cameron Cudney told Montgomery that he spent the night with his girlfriend, Janice Toledo, and she backed him up. But once they looked a little closer, they suspected that Janice lied to protect her boyfriend. Both said they watched a movie and then went to bed, but when asked, they gave the names of two different movies. Janice stuck to her story for a while but finally admitted she lied. Then Cameron said he was gambling that night. They broke up shortly afterward. Anyway, the bad alibi along with being the main beneficiary pretty much sealed it for Cameron. He was arrested on the 29th."

"So why did they release him?" asked David.

"That happened later," said Blaine Hoskins. "Even though Cameron benefited from Oscar's death, he'll only get ten thousand. Montgomery felt that that wasn't enough to result in such a gory death and he felt that Cameron really did care for his cousin. But Montgomery admitted it was just a feeling and he didn't have anything tangible to back it up with, so he had to make the arrest."

Blaine turned over to another page of her notebook. "There was no concrete evidence. No witnesses to put him at the scene. They never recovered the knife Oscar was killed with, so couldn't tie him to that. Cameron's DNA was all over the house, but that wasn't anything special given he visited the old man all the time. The coroner thinks Oscar was smothered with a pillow first, but they couldn't find it and, though they found all the body parts, there wasn't even a drop of blood on the floor. MDPD figures the killer used plastic or something and destroyed it later. Nothing pointed specifically to Cameron Cudney, so they had to let him go."

Mike nodded. "Good enough. Cameron's a good suspect in the Oscar Cudney murder, but there's no real evidence. We'll keep digging. But we also need to see if we can tie him to the other murders." He paced a moment, then continued, "We'll need to look into what Cameron's been doing since he was released. David, you and Chip start on that tomorrow. Anybody got any other ideas about Cameron before we move on?"

When no other comments were made, Mike went on to the next point. "Alex, did you hear back from MDC yet? What's their holdup about Ruby James and Stephen Hardison's possible connections to the college?"

Mike didn't mention that he'd had an unexpected call last night from SAC Martinez and he was beginning to feel some heat. Apparently, Zardes told the Special Agent in Charge that he felt Mike was in over his head and another agent should take over. Zardes had given a rather one-sided explanation of the state of the investigation and Martinez had been relatively understanding once he heard Mike's account, but Mike still felt Zardes undercut him for some reason and didn't like it. He'd never been good with office politics and being caught between Zardes and Martinez wasn't a place he especially wanted to be. Besides, Mike was still unhappy that he and his team weren't allowed to tell anyone that a serial killer was on the loose. He'd considered bringing it up to Martinez but didn't think it was the right time.

His team didn't need to know about the goings-on behind the scenes. It was his place to deal with that and let his task force take care of the investigation.

Alex tapped his hand on the table; Mike had noticed this was habitual with the veteran detective.

"I had trouble with the assistant manager of the Records Department, a Ms. Pemberley. At first, she demanded a subpoena, then she wanted her boss's written approval. Unfortunately, the manager, a Mrs. ..." Alex referred to his notes. "... McFadden, wasn't in the office that day, so I had to call back yesterday. They had to do a hand search because some of the records were lost in a data glitch a few months back and not everything's been re-entered in the system yet. Anyway, I heard back this morning and they have no record of either Ms. James or Stephen Hardison ever attending Miami Dade College. I don't think this is going to be our connection."

Alex slapped his notebook shut and the dull 'thud' reverberated around the suddenly disheartened group.

Danny then walked into the room. "Sorry to interrupt, Mike," the red-headed analyst said, "but I think our guy may have struck again."

CHAPTER 25

In the greenest of our valley
By good angels tenanted,
Once a fair and stately palace—
Radiant palace—reared its head
'The Haunted Palace'

The house was enormous, even by Miami standards. Enclosed within an immaculately trimmed shrub fence, the white, sprawling, three-story home had a balcony and contained six bedrooms, five baths, a restaurant-sized kitchen and imported Italian tile throughout. There was a swimming pool in the back and a whirlpool on the lanai. The house sat on a canal that boasted its own boat dock with a small cabin cruiser tethered to it. A weather-worn sign out front showed the house was for sale and the attached flyer listed an asking price of 2.9 million. The Bayshore Villas were home to the upper-crust and Mike, Blaine and Chip were appropriately impressed.

The scene was as gruesome as Danny's first report had made it sound and Mike stopped as he took in the first of the crime scenes in the master bedroom at the rear of the house. A pungent mattress had been placed in the middle of the room and lying on an old, rickety chair nearby was a razor blade, its bright sheen dulled by drying blood. Putting on their gloves and paper booties, the three moved into the room and near the door to the closet Mike saw several handfuls of gray hair, also soaked in blood. Scattered around the room already tagged by numerous evidence markers were samples of play money, some plastic spoons and costume jewelry. There were a couple of plastic bags in a corner and an old box stood under the window, one of its sides pulled down. He checked his gloves, then knelt to look inside the box. Moving the loose cardboard slightly, all Mike saw were blank sheets of paper.

"Make sure we have plenty of pictures of all this," Mike told the nearest member of the Evidence Response Team busy taking pictures of the scene while another videotaped nearby. The man's raised eyebrow was his only answer. Mike smiled an apology. These men and women knew their jobs and Mike was micromanaging, something he normally wouldn't do. This case was getting to him.

He saw more blood in the closet. Knowing he needed to move on, he shook his head and headed back to the hallway, Chip and Blaine not far behind.

"Where was the first body found?" Blaine asked a uniformed officer, and the three task force members followed the pointed finger to the living room.

"Agent Donaldson?"

Mike turned and saw an MDPD officer standing next to the fireplace. He wasn't young, probably in his thirties, and Mike was glad there was an experienced officer on scene.

"I'm Donaldson, officer." Mike held out his hand.

"Peters, sir. Gary Peters. I was the first officer on the scene."

"Good. What can you tell us?"

"We got an anonymous tip at 9:47 a.m. stating that someone had broken into the house. I was dispatched to check it out and arrived at 10:12. I looked in the front window and immediately saw the disarray in there, so I called for backup. The door hadn't been forced, so we called the real estate agent who met us here at 11:05

with his key. We made entry and found this." Officer Peters indicated the fireplace.

The hearth was full of soot, although it was obvious that a fire had not been made here. There were no unburnt remains of logs, branches, or wood of any kind. The grate still sparkled as if it had never been used and the soot had obviously just been thrown into the fireplace to set the scene. There was no left-over smell of smoke and the four fireplace implements also shone brightly.

"Does this fireplace even work?" he asked no one in particular. "And can anyone tell me why the hell you'd have a fireplace in Florida anyway? I mean, what's the point? It's always summer here, isn't it?"

Chip laughed. "Mike, I grew up in Miami and you'd be surprised at the number of fireplaces you'll find around here. It does actually get cold a few days a year when a fire could be nice, but mostly you see fireplaces because the snowbirds like to be reminded of home."

"'Snowbirds?" Mike placed his hands on his hips. "What the hell's a snowbird?"

It was Blaine's turn to laugh. "That's the name the natives give to the tens of thousands of northerners who come down to Florida and spend the winter every year. They get here around November and stay until April or so. Just like the birds who fly south for the winter. Hence the name 'snowbirds'".

Mike stared at her for a long moment. "I'm sorry I asked," he deadpanned. Mike shifted to Peters. "Sorry, go ahead with your report."

The look Peters gave Mike could have withered a flower, but he responded with, "When we looked in the fireplace, we found the first victim."

Mike looked closer and saw hair hanging down from inside the chimney.

"You mean she was *stuck* up the chimney?"

Chip asked the question and the horror in his voice made Mike realize just how young and inexperienced Chip Smythe really was. At twenty-six, he'd only been with the bureau for two years and spent most of that time working fraud cases. Mike had reviewed Chip's record, of course, but only now put it together. This might be the first real murder case he'd ever worked on and seeing crime scene photos was hardly the same as seeing a corpse in person. Mike wondered if he should send the young agent away to interview witnesses or let him stay. He needed to get used to this kind of thing, however, if he was going to stay with VCMO. He'd never do that sitting at a desk or looking at photos. Mike decided to let him stay.

Peters, not knowing what was going through Mike's mind, answered the question. "Yeah, you can see her head if you look at just the right angle. When I called it in, I was told to leave everything the way I found it until the FBI arrived." Peters stopped and gave Mike a penetrating look. "I know we need to take pictures and all that, but it seems a bit unseemly to leave her up there. I wanted to take her down after we took pictures but was told to wait for your guys." Peters' voice was annoyed. "I have to admit I was a little peeved. Since when does the FBI automatically get called in for a murder case?"

Mike was once again angry at Zardes. *Damn! I am not going to get every MDPD officer pissed off at me because I can't tell them what's going on.* Mike made a quick decision. "Officer Peters, I'm about to tell you something in the strictest confidence. And I'm trusting you to keep this to yourself. Can I trust you with this information?"

The MDPD officer's eyes widened slightly but all he said was, "Yes, sir."

"Very well." Mike took a breath. He knew he was possibly putting his career in jeopardy in going against expressed orders. "There is a serial killer on the loose. His MO is killing in gruesome ways and we've had some extremely macabre crime scenes. Orders from above basically state that at any such murder scene the FBI gets called in first. If we determine this is part of our case, we'll be taking over the investigation. If it's not, we'll kick it back to you guys. However, just from the description of the two deaths in this house, we're already pretty sure this is ours." Mike blew out a breath. "So, while I sympathize with your feelings on the subject, the victims had to be left where they were. We have to do this one by the book; there are more lives at stake than just the two here."

Peters swore under his breath and said in a quiet tone, "I understand, Agent Donaldson. No one will hear about this from me." He flicked a look to the chimney and back to Mike. "Do you want to look at anything else in this room or should I take you to the second crime scene now?"

Mike's eyes softened in appreciation of Peters' intuitive understanding of the situation, and he then looked at Hoskins. "Blaine, stay here and make sure everything's been done to preserve the scene, then oversee taking her out. Chip, you're with me and Officer Peters."

The three men walked across the living room, carefully stepping around Evidence Response Team members and numerous yellow evidence markers, bent low to make their way under the caution tape, and through the screened-in lanai. Passing the Jacuzzi, the screen door stood open and they followed a path of stone pavers that meandered through a small, but packed garden that rivaled any nursery. Mike was able to recognize geraniums and some rose bushes, but most of the plants appeared to be native to Florida and he couldn't put a name to them. He saw decorative birdbaths and bird feeders and Mike figured he didn't want to know how much all this cost.

The only incongruity to the idyllic scene were the ubiquitous evidence markers along the way leading further into the garden. After about a dozen more feet, there was a clearing of sorts and Mike stopped short.

If anything, the scene was the worst they'd seen yet. The corpse lay on a bed of leaves, their natural green discolored completely by the pervasive stain of red everywhere. The blood had spattered onto every plant, flower, tree, and stone in a wide radius. The scene might have been pretty if not for knowing what had caused the dappling effect.

Mike gulped when he walked around the body to where the head should have been, seeing only the torso among the leaves. The head sat nearby, once-dark eyes now staring blankly up to the sky and seeing patches of scalp, Mike realized from where the gray hair in the master bedroom had come.

Chip suddenly made a gagging sound and turned away quickly. He leaned over, hands on his legs and Mike heard him take deep, calming breaths. It took almost a full minute, but the young agent got himself under control and turned back to the gruesome scene.

Mike put a hand on his arm. "Would you rather go and interview the neighbors? I can finish up here." His tone was soothing, his concern obvious.

Chip shook his head, stood up straight. "No, I'll be okay. Let's do this."

Mike nodded and asked Officer Peters, "Was she found like this?"

Peters did a good job at ignoring Chip's reaction and answered, "No. One of the other officers turned her over to check if she was dead and the head fell off."

Mike hissed, "Why the hell did he turn her over with all this blood everywhere? It would have been obvious she was already dead."

"Sorry, sir, I know. But he's young and he only saw a woman on the ground and went to give aid. He didn't see the blood at first." He looked around and huffed. "I'll have to report it to our captain, the kid will probably get a reprimand or something."

"He deserves it. He might have contaminated the whole scene. Damn." Mike ran a hand through his brown locks and tried to take a calming breath. The smell of dried blood met his nostrils, and he blew it out through his mouth. Looking at the scene, he stated in a low tone, "It's obvious she was killed out here, but why was some of her hair found inside?"

Recognizing the question as rhetorical, Peters merely said, "We've been able to make a preliminary identification."

CHAPTER 26

With one determined sweep of its muscular arm it nearly severed
her head from her body.
'THE MURDERS IN THE RUE MORGUE'

"The victims were Camille Henri, aged sixty-six, and her daughter,
Suzanne, twenty-seven. They lived together on the south side of
Kendall. We don't have much yet, but mom used to clean houses
for a living - she retired a few years ago - and Suzanne was a
secretary in a law office. Neither have a record except for a couple
of speeding tickets for the daughter. We're still waiting on more
employment info and school records." David looked up from his
notes and announced, "And before you ask, Mike, I've already got
a call into Miami Dade College to see if either victim had any ties
there."

"I'm not sure I like you reading my mind, David. It makes me
think I'm getting predictable."

Mike's comment elicited the hoped-for smiles and chuckles
from around the room and the tension eased a little.

David, however, did not smile. "Not a mind-reader, Mike, just
good police work. It made sense to check into it especially since
the daughter's not too long out of college."

Mike tried not to sigh out loud. "I know, David, I was just
kidding. Good work."

It was 5:30 and everyone was once again gathered in the conference room. Alex handed around sandwiches from a nearby deli and Chip passed out bottles of water and sodas. A large bag of pretzels and a box of cookies added to the simple meal and the team settled in for what was expected to be a long briefing.

Mike took a second to open his sandwich and take a bite. He'd skipped lunch to report to Zardes about this most recent murder and was famished. As he ate, he considered David Scotty. The African American detective was thirty and unmarried. Mike had overheard two female agents talking about him yesterday and they'd described him as a cross between Denzel Washington and Dwyane Wade. Mike didn't recognize Wade's name, but after a Google search, was only slightly surprised to find out he was a star with the Miami Heat. Good looks and athletic build. Well, that certainly described David. He was bald and wore some of the nicest suits Mike had ever seen on a police detective. Either his family had money, or he had a real knack for finding great bargains. Knowing he was attractive to women and a good dresser didn't help Mike find a connection with the man, though.

The MDPD detectives had been hard to convince when he'd taken over the task force; Blaine had been especially vocal, but David, too, had not given his theory much credence and perhaps still didn't. He seemed to merely follow orders. There had to be a way to reach him, but Mike didn't know what to do. On the other hand, as long as David gave his best and worked the case diligently, Mike didn't really need him to accept the premise of a serial killer. He needed him to do his job. On the third hand, it would be nice if he could get along with all the members of his task force. It would certainly make things easier for what was shaping up to be a long investigation.

Alex and David had been working together for several years, Mike knew, so he decided to see if the older detective might give him more insight into what made David tick.

"David, go to the daughter's law office tomorrow and see what you can find out from her coworkers. Take Chip with you."

Concerned about Chip's reaction at the crime scene this morning, Mike thought some easy witness interviews would help. Besides, pairing him with a more experienced officer might also season him somewhat. Chip definitely had potential; he simply needed the right kind of guidance. Mike liked the younger agent and wanted to help bring him along as much as he could.

"We also need to see if we can find out why they were at the house. Did they go there on their own or were they lured there by the killer?"

"And how he lured them there," added Chip.

"See what you can learn about the mother's habits. Maybe the killer found them through her." Mike looked at Blaine. "Have we got the prelim report from the ME yet?"

"Yeah, Dr. Richmond called just before dinner got here." She put down the pretzel in her hand and picked up her notebook. "Both women had numerous abrasions and scratches on various parts of their bodies. The mother's cause of death was obvious. Her throat was slashed so deeply that the head fell off when the MDPD officer turned her over. The ME thinks the murder weapon could have been a simple kitchen knife or a butcher knife. It didn't have to be especially large, just really sharp."

"Did the killer know what he was doing or were the cuts sloppy?" This from Alex, who was unwrapping a second sandwich.

"The cuts were pretty clean, Dr. Richmond said. But she also said that anybody could do a little research on the Internet and find out how to make the right kind of cuts, so skill might not be a factor here. Also, both victims had Temazepam in their systems, so that made it easier, since the victims couldn't put up much of a struggle. The daughter did have several defensive wounds, so she clearly put up more of a fight than the mother."

"How exactly did the daughter die?" asked Alex.

"Suzanne also had cuts to the throat but that's not what killed her. Dr. Richmond can't say for certain yet, but she thinks Suzanne died from a combination of blood loss and suffocation in the chimney."

"You mean she was *alive* when he put her up there?" Chip's tone reflected his revulsion.

"It's possible, yes," answered Blaine.

Mike had seen a lot in his time, first in Bosnia during his stint in the army, then in his time with the FBI, but he wasn't sure he'd ever met up with as cold-blooded a killer as this guy was turning out to be. He wondered what kind of monster they were dealing with.

He could see his own disgust reproduced in the faces of his task force members. Chip's face had gone pale; he was obviously remembering the crime scene. Blaine had begun flipping through her notebook, but her eyes weren't focused on the pages. Alex's eyes had a steely look that bode the killer no good and while David's face was angry, it seemed more a calm of determination than the anger of outrage.

Despite personal feelings, they needed to keep their cool and stay focused. Being angry about these gruesome deaths might motivate them to work even harder to catch this maniac, but they had to be smart about it or this guy might get away with everything. Mike was determined that it wouldn't happen. It was his job to keep his people focused and put that anger to good use.

"Which victim died first, Blaine? Could Dr. Richmond tell?"

"Not yet, Mike. Her tests will hopefully give us that answer."

"Does it matter? We're still dealing with two horrible murders. We can ask the killer when we find him."

David's tone was offhand, and Mike wondered if he was being purposefully callous to cover his feelings or if he really didn't care about the details as long as the murderer was found. Mike could understand the former, but not the latter. Maybe he needed to have that talk with Alex sooner rather than later.

"It might matter to the AUSA. She has a case to prepare and it's our job to give her as complete information as we can. And the order of the deaths is usually an important piece of information."

David's eyes widened and he sat back in his chair, crossing his arms as he did so. Mike realized his tone had been harsher than he'd wanted, and he cursed himself. Just another example that maybe he was in over his head as the case agent. He didn't know how to handle people as a leader should. He should be encouraging David so that they might get along better, not alienating him.

At that moment, the door opened and into the tension entered Danny.

~~

"What can you tell us about the Poe connection?" Mike asked when Danny had his sandwich and chips and sat down next to Alex.

"This murder is definitely one of ours," he said. "Poe wrote the short story, 'The Murders in the Rue Morgue' in 1841. This was one his detective stories, by the way." He looked around the room. "For those of you who may not be aware of it, Edgar Allan Poe wrote the very first detective story ever. He invented the genre, so to speak. Anyway, in this story, the mutilated bodies of a mother and daughter are found in their four-story house. Neighbors hear a bunch of shrieks and the gate is broken down by the police and some neighbors. They find the upstairs bedroom in disarray with furniture everywhere, money and jewelry scattered all over the place and a bloody knife and human hair on the floor. There's even a safe that had old papers in it in the room. They see a bunch of soot in the fireplace and find the daughter up the chimney with a lot of scratches and marks that make them think the daughter had been strangled. They search the house but can't find the mother. Then they go outside and find her behind the building. Her throat is cut so badly that it falls off when they try to pick her up."

"Yeah, okay, that's just like ours, for sure," commented Alex as he shook his head and wrote a few lines in his notebook.

"Yeah, no doubt about that," agreed Mike. He looked at Danny. "You got anything else for us?"

"Oh, yeah, lots." He stopped to take a bite of a cookie and a sip of water before continuing. "Like I said, this is a detective story and in any good mystery the detective has to figure out whodunit. Anyway, the main character isn't a detective, just a really smart layman named Dupin. He figures out who the murderer is, and you'll never guess who."

"We're waiting with bated breath," David said in a sarcastic tone that no one missed.

Danny looked slightly abashed, and Mike understood. He'd been on the wrong side of David's sarcasm a couple of times himself. Trying to smooth the waters, Mike said, "That's okay, Danny, but I don't think anyone's up for a guessing game tonight. Can you give us the bottom line?"

"Uh, sure, Mike. No harm meant, Detective Scotty," Danny apologized. "The murderer turns out not to be a person at all, but an orangutan of all things. It belonged to a sailor and had gotten away. That's why all the money and stuff was left on the floor in the house; the orangutan didn't want any of that."

"And that's why our guy left the play money, plastic spoons, and cheap jewelry all around," Blaine put in. "He even left that box with the blank paper in it. He was setting the scene as in the story. Man, this guy is sick."

"Well, like Rhonda said, he's detail-oriented," Alex remarked.

Mike said nothing to this. "Anything further, Danny?"

"Yeah, what about the date?" Blaine put in. "Any connection with Poe's life?"

Mike cursed under his breath. *He* should have been the one to ask about that.

"Yeah, I found that connection as well. On August 1,1831, Poe's older brother died. And what's more, the brother's name was Henri, same last name as the murder victims."

"Damn. This guy is nuts," exclaimed Alex as he threw down his pen.

No one spoke for a long moment. Everyone agreed with this simple assessment and wondered how they were going to find such a madman.

CHAPTER 27

Who has not, a hundred times, found himself committing a vile or a stupid action, for no other reason than because he knows he should *not?*

'THE BLACK CAT'

"Thanks, Danny, good work. How long will it take you to update our charts?"

"I can probably have everything done by lunch tomorrow."

"Good, do that." Mike paused for a moment to make up his mind about his next step. "We need to see if we can link Cameron Cudney to this murder. If we can only connect him, that could lead us to other proof against him. Blaine," he turned to the only woman on the team, "that's gonna be your job tomorrow. See what you can dig up. For now, we'll work this as if we don't have Cameron on the radar and start from the beginning of this murder. We'll keep doing it that way until we have something concrete one way or another about Cameron."

"You know, Mike, there's something I don't understand about Cameron Cudney." Alex spoke around a bite of sandwich. "I mean, if he was cleared in his cousin's murder, why kill all these people? And in such gruesome ways? What's the point?"

"Good question," Mike nodded. "That's something for Rhonda Sagan. Make a note to remind me next time we speak with her." At Alex's nod, Mike moved on. "It's time we had another chat with Dr. Barty from UM. Danny, you've done a great job with the Poe research, but she's the real expert. Maybe she can give us more insight we can use to get a better handle on this guy. Besides, the AUSA might want to use her as an expert witness at the trial and it's a good idea to keep her somewhat in the loop. Call her tomorrow and see if she can come down here. You can talk to her in one of the interview rooms. We still can't say it's a serial killer, but let her know we're looking at motivation in a murder investigation and we thought she could help."

Danny interrupted. "Mike, you know I want to do all I can to help, but I'm an analyst, not an agent. I'm not sure I'd be any good at a witness interview."

"She's not a witness, Danny, just a consultant. Just listen to her attentively, ask relative questions and be charming. You'll be fine. Actually, let me know when she gets here, and I'll try to come in for a minute to say hi. I got the feeling she doesn't think highly of law enforcement, so let's show her some courtesy and get on her good side. It might go a long way in convincing her to help us later or get her to agree to testify if the AUSA wants her."

"Mike, I don't mean to butt in or anything," Blaine interrupted, "but shouldn't motivation be a discussion with Rhonda. Isn't that what a profiler is for?"

"Yes, and I plan to talk to her as soon as I can reach her. I tried earlier but no go. Rhonda can certainly give us a psychological view of the killer, but I want Dr. Barty for the literary point-of-view, so to speak. I think getting both sides will help. This is such a weird case that we can use all the help we can get. You think I'm barking up the wrong tree here?"

Blaine's eyes widened and red patches appeared on her clear cheeks. Obviously, she wasn't used to being asked her opinion about the course of an investigation so bluntly and was embarrassed. "No ... no, I guess not. I didn't think of it that way.

As a matter of fact, looking at it from both angles makes a lot of sense. I guess that's why you get paid the big bucks."

Everyone chuckled at this.

The door opened and into the room walked Rhonda Sagan.

After the obligatory greetings and expressions of surprise, the FBI profiler explained that she was in town for a deposition and, having gotten Mike's message, decided to drop in for the evening briefing.

"Unfortunately, there was a power outage at the courthouse and my depo ran longer. Otherwise, I'd've been here an hour ago. Sorry."

"Nothing to apologize for," Mike said, "We're glad you could make it in person. You want something to eat? We've still got a couple sandwiches left and there's chips and cookies on that table." Mike pointed to the back of the room. "We have water and sodas."

Rhonda smiled. "Practically a feast. Go raibh maith agat."

"Huh?'

"Sorry. That's 'thank you' in Gaelic. It comes out sometimes without thinking."

"No problem. And you're welcome. By the way, that's 'you're welcome' in English."

"Ha! Very funny, Mike. Just for that, I'll take the sandwich and *two* cookies."

Everybody laughed and Chip got up and brought Rhonda the requested cookies.

"While you're eating, let's catch you up."

Almost ten minutes later, the sandwich and cookies were gone, the updates were over, and it was Rhonda's turn to speak.

"This case is really bugging me. I still can't decide if you've got a typical serial killer or not. I went to a workshop last year about outliers in profiling and one of the topics was specifically about serial killers. I contacted the presenter, Dr. Wolff, and discussed the case with him. He's of the opinion that this probably is a serial killer, just an atypical one. He feels there are enough common aspects to define it as such. However, he is intrigued by the outlier points of the case. And this most recent murder is probably a mark in the serial killer column."

"Why is that?" asked Chip.

"One type of serial killer is the organized one who spends a lot of time preparing the deaths and then covering up the evidence. Often the crime is done in one place, the victim left in another. These killers know the difference between right and wrong and usually show no remorse. They know our methods and try to outsmart us.

"Your murderer might be killing the victims in the same location as they were found, but he's left you no forensic evidence at all. No hair, blood or fingerprints that could lead us to him. The fact that your killer goes so far as to recreate scenes from Poe works shows his attention to detail and how much pre-planning goes into these murders. The fact that he doesn't leave anything incriminating behind shows that's he's smart. I'm sorry, Mike, but I'm afraid you're going to have a hard time catching this guy."

"Tell me something I don't know already," Mike deadpanned.

Into the silence that followed this remark, David asked, "Rhonda, can any of this help us find potential victims?" David leaned forward and stated, "So far, there's no commonality we can find. Can your profile help us figure out how he's picking his victims?"

Rhonda shook her head. "I don't think so. This killer is more interested in *how* than in *who*. Except that your two women today were named Henri and that's Poe's brother's name, he could have picked just about anyone to murder for the previous four deaths." She shrugged an apology.

"Alex had a question about Cameron Cudney I was going to ask you. Any ideas as to why he'd start committing murders if he was free and clear in his cousin's death?"

"Not without knowing a lot more about him, I'm afraid. It's always possible that Cameron is innocent of his cousin's death and someone else did all this."

Silence met this declaration until Chip practically jumped out of his chair. "Maybe we should go about this a different way. Mike, why don't we break the murders up and treat them as separate cases for a moment? Maybe one of these deaths was the real target and the others done to muddy the waters. The Poe aspect could be a red herring. If we find a good suspect for one of the earlier murders, then we might solve all of them."

"Chip, do you really think someone's gonna kill six or seven people just to cover up one intended victim? That's even crazier than having a serial killer on the loose."

Mike's eyebrows rose at David's confrontational tone.

"Well, it's just an idea," Chip stated, suddenly on the defense. "I just meant that it's possible to kill a bunch of people and add a crazy MO on top of it to keep the police off the scent. It could happen."

"Chip, I've seen a lot of things in my time," Rhonda put in softly, "but I don't think that idea holds water."

"But, Rhonda, you said yourself this isn't a normal serial killer. Maybe he's not normal because he's not a serial killer. Like I said, maybe it's just a red herring."

Mike could see Chip deflating as he spoke and decided this was an opportunity to build up Chip's self-confidence while giving him some experience at murder investigation. "Look, I said all along I'm willing to entertain any idea to catch this guy. So, let's look at both possibilities."

He walked to the monitor with the Poe chronology on it. "Since it's the beginning of August, we have some time. There aren't as many dates this guy can kill on. The next isn't until the 9th. Chip, you work on your theory. Look at each death with new eyes and see if you can find any good suspects for any of them. If so, run with it and see if you can link that suspect to any of the other deaths. I'll give you two days. Then you can report back to us on what you learn. In the meantime, the rest of us will continue with our original serial killer theory and see what we can find."

Chip gave a grateful smile and said, "You got it, boss."

"Okay, anyone else got any ideas?"

After a moment, Alex spoke. "Yeah, maybe, Mike." He took a breath and asked, "Except for the Biddix death, all these murders took place in buildings or homes. So, how's he picking these places? Maybe he's involved in real estate somehow."

"You mean," said Mike slowly, "that the commonality may not be the victims but where the murders take place. He somehow knows these buildings already and knows they're empty." Mike smiled. "That's good, Alex, really good."

Mike looked at his watch. "Okay, it's almost seven. Let's do this. Chip, I'm giving you a partner on your red herring theory. You and David start looking into that tonight. Pull anything we or MDPD have on possible suspects and make a list of how you'll proceed. Alex, you and Blaine work on the building aspect. You won't be able to do too much tonight since everything's closed, but at least get a list together of who you'll contact tomorrow. Danny, you're updating our lists and contacting Dr. Barty tomorrow. I'm gonna go see the AUSA, then Zardes and update him. Any questions?"

No one said anything and Mike nodded. "Okay, do what you can until eight, then go home and get some rest. We're in for a long couple of days. And good work, everybody."

The task force members began pairing up while Mike turned to Rhonda. "Thanks again for coming by. We appreciate your help."

"No problem, that's what I'm here for." She shook hands with Mike and, as she walked out the door, said, "Slán agat."

~~

Mike turned off his computer but before he could grab his jacket David came up to his desk and said, "Hey, man, you got a minute?"

"Sure, what's up?" Mike hitched a hip on the side of his desk and waited to hear what the MDPD detective had to say.

David didn't say anything for a long moment. He looked at the far wall, then back at Mike. Then he looked over Mike's shoulder at the calendar on the cubicle wall and back at Mike again. Finally, he seemed to come to some sort of decision and said quickly, "I'm sorry."

Mike blinked but quickly regrouped. "Sorry for what? You didn't do anything I know of."

"Yeah, I did." David sighed. "I didn't give you enough credit. I didn't buy into this whole serial killer thing for a minute. I thought you were crazy, and I didn't understand why SSA Zardes, SAC Martinez or Captain Mendez would go for this. I was sure you'd go down in flames and we would have wasted a lot of time."

"And now?"

"Now I'm on board completely."

Mike had to ask. "What changed your mind?"

"The Henri murders. There are too many coincidences for it not to be based on Poe. So, if those are, then the others must be as well." David sighed again. "I was wrong, and you were right. So, I'm sorry."

Mike smiled. "Apology accepted."

As David walked away, Mike grinned. First Blaine, now David. His task force was finally becoming a real team.

CHAPTER 28

It was not, however, until the fourth day from the period of her disappearance that anything satisfactory was ascertained respecting her.

'The Mystery of Marie Rogêt'

August 3

"The best laid plans, as they say," commented Blaine as she and Mike entered the conference room.

"Yeah, I was really hoping to actually sit down to my breakfast this morning," said Mike.

"No, 'fraid not." Blaine pointed to the coffee maker. "Want a cup?"

"Yeah, I'll have …"

"A French Vanilla. I know."

"You been researching me again, Blaine?" Mike's tone might have seemed harsh, but the twinkle in his eye told the truth.

"Didn't need to. You drink the same thing each morning. One French vanilla, then you switch to basic black. By lunch, it's plain water for the rest of the day." Blaine was smiling as she placed a canister in the machine.

Mike barked a laugh but before he could come up with an appropriate rejoinder, the rest of the team entered and began to settle down. With a last smile at Blaine, Mike took his place at the front of the room and waited while Danny set up his laptop.

"Good morning, everyone. Sorry to call you in so early, but we've got another murder."

Mike tried to ignore the groans around the room while he turned to Danny and nodded. The monitor came alive with a picture of a seemingly idyllic scene.

The peaceful waters of the canal were surrounded by rich green vegetation. Several varieties of wildflowers could be seen growing in the brown dirt near the edge of the passage and, a few yards behind the waterway, on the other side of a metal fence, trees bordered both sides, their leaves full and thick. There were even a couple of egrets in the background, their bright white plumage stark against the dark grass beneath them, unperturbed by the disturbing scene below. The quiet was marred by the sight of the victim in the foreground, swollen face and torso jarringly opposed to the postcard image surrounding it.

After giving everyone a moment to digest the scene, Mike began the briefing. "I didn't want to wake you all, so Blaine and I went out early this morning. Danny's program got a ping when the body was found, and he called me. We went down and had a look, and I recognized the general scene as a possible Poe story.

"This is Cecilia Rogers. Her body was found in the Cutler Drain Canal next to Arvida park. She'd been strangled before being dragged and dumped there. They found her purse, but the money and phone were gone. It was staged to look like a robbery. I didn't need the ME to tell us she'd been there for several days. It looked like she might have been dragged with her own belt but the body's too bloated to determine if she was also strangled with that belt or killed some other way. It was a pretty gruesome scene."

"I'm getting sick of that word," commented David.

"I agree, but I've run out of adjectives." Mike shrugged. "Let's start with the Poe background."

Mike sat down and Danny moved to the monitor. Unused to being the center of attention, his Adam's apple moved convulsively for a moment and his nervous voice was thin. As the briefing continued, however, his voice grew stronger as his confidence rose.

"This murder is based on Poe's short story entitled 'The Mystery of Marie Rogêt', which incidentally is a sequel to 'The Murders in the Rue Morgue'. This story is based on a real-life unsolved murder which occurred right here in America. The victim's name was Mary Cecilia Rogers."

"Cecilia Rogers?" repeated Alex in surprise. "Now *that* is very interesting."

"Yes, our boy is getting creative," stated Mike in a flat voice.

"Yeah, first the Henri last names in the Rue Morgue murders, now Cecilia Rogers," agreed Chip.

"He's doing serious research to find these people," commented Blaine. "But how's he finding them?"

"When we figure that out, we'll be a lot closer to finding this nut case," said David.

Mike felt it was time to get back to the matter at hand. "It's an interesting sideline, to be sure, but for now we need to concentrate on Cecilia Rogers. Danny, if you'll continue, we'll try not to interrupt you again."

"No problem, boss. I don't mind. I don't normally get to be this involved in cases, so I like hearing you guys think out loud. I'm learning a lot." Danny's face turned almost as red as his hair as he realized he'd given himself away. He quickly turned back to the monitor and began speaking again. "Poe changed certain details from the real murder, but that's not important for our purposes. What is important is the description of the murder scene and Marie herself in Poe's story. Let me put up the text for you."

Immediately the monitor became a split screen with the right side now showing two enlarged pages from the Poe story with several sentences or paragraphs highlighted. Danny began to read from the text as he pointed to the passages.

"'A corpse had just been towed ashore by some fishermen, who had found it floating in the river ... The face was suffused with dark blood ... About the throat were bruises and impressions of fingers. On the left wrist were two circular excoriations, apparently the effect of ropes ... There were no cuts apparent, or bruises which appeared the effect of blows. A piece of lace was found tied tightly around the neck ... and was fastened by a knot which lay just under the left ear.'"

Danny shifted to his audience. "In Poe's story, the detective determines that one man committed the murder, dragged the body to a boat, sailed the boat to the middle of the river, dumped it and left again. Here are the commonalities between Poe's story and Cecilia Rogers' murder: First, both women were found in a body of water. Second, both were strangled, Marie with a piece of lace that was tied around her waist and Cecilia was probably strangled with her own belt. Both women were dragged after death and dumped in the water. Finally, both bodies had been in the water for several days, making it difficult to determine specifics. And, of course, there's the names. Cecilia Rogers - Mary Cecilia Rogers. There are too many similarities for it not to be one of our murders."

"Not to mention the fact that the killer committed back-to-back murders based on two stories that were written as sequels," Chip added.

"And what about our Poe date?" asked Alex. "I assume there is a correlation to something in Poe's life?"

Danny turned red again. "Thanks for reminding me. The Allan family moved back to the USA on July 27, 1820."

Alex looked up from his notes. "I know the body was bloated and decomposed, but can we be sure she died that many days ago?"

155

"We'll have to wait for the ME's report," Mike answered, "but I imagine it'll be close to that date. Or close enough that it won't make much of a difference."

"This guy is really getting on my nerves," said David as he all but threw his pen down on the table. "He's rubbing our noses in it. What with using real people that have the same names as Poe characters or family members, and it's not even getting us anywhere! We're no closer to finding him now than we were a week ago." David huffed as he crossed his arms and stared ahead of him.

Blaine added, "And on top of that, these last murders seem to be upping the gruesome quotient. I think it's getting worse."

Chip chimed in, "Surely by now he's made his point. It can't get much worse than this."

Unfortunately, Chip was sorely mistaken.

CHAPTER 29

I burned to say if but one word, by way of triumph, and to render
doubly sure their assurance of my guiltlessness.

'THE BLACK CAT'

August 5

This workout is gonna feel so good. Blaine smiled in anticipation
as she walked down the hall. Rooting through her purse for her car
keys, the brunette shook her close-cropped head. *Where the hell
did all this crap come from?* Stopping at the elevator, she threw
several old gum wrappers into the trash can along with a pen that
ran out of ink days ago.

"Hey, Blaine, we're gettin' out of here for a few and gettin'
some lunch at the deli. You wanna come along?"

Blaine grinned at the two men walking toward her. "No
thanks, Alex, I'm goin' to the gym. But if you'll pick me up a ham
and cheese on rye, I'd be grateful."

"Sure, no problem."

"Working out during your lunch hour again, Blaine?" David
asked. "Don't you ever take a day off?"

"Nope. Gotta stay in shape." She pushed the elevator button.
"If I have to arrest guys that weigh a hundred pounds more than
me, I'm gonna be ready for 'em."

Her MDPD colleagues laughed, but before the trio could enter the arriving car a whistle caught their attention. They turned in unison to see Chip headed for them.

Oh, this can't be good.

The young FBI agent's hair was mussed, and his face was red as if he'd run a mile to catch them instead of just down the hallway. His usually bright eyes were apologetic.

"Not another murder?" groaned David.

"You gotta be kidding me," interrupted Alex. "It's only been two days since the last one."

"No, no, guys," said Chip as he held up his hands. "There hasn't been another murder, or at least, none that we know about yet. No, this is something else entirely."

I just wanted to go to the gym, for Christ's sake.

"Okay, Chip. So, if there's not another murder, what is going on?" asked Alex.

"Mike said to tell you guys that he's been able to schedule a conference call with Rhonda for 2:00. You guys are gonna have to cut your lunches short. Sorry."

"Does she have something for us?"

"Don't know. Mike just said he was able to schedule the call."

"Okay," said David. "I'll go to the deli and bring our food back. You guys stay here and get ready for the meeting. I won't be long."

"Here's my money, David, thanks." Blaine handed over some bills and headed back down the hallway. *Good thing the gym is open all night.*

~~

"Hello, Rhonda, thanks for joining us."

"No problem, Mike, glad to help."

The profiler's auburn hair was tied back today, and Blaine could see the braid hanging down her back when she turned to pick up her notes. Blaine had never worked with Rhonda Sagan before but saw her testify in court a couple years ago. She'd been professional and never lost her cool, not even when the asshole of a defense lawyer had condescendingly called profiling 'psychobabble'. In fact, she'd put the guy in his place on more than one occasion.

Glad she's on our side.

"I got the information you sent me on the latest murder, Mike, and I'm sorry to say, I'm not sure it helped me refine my profile much. Your killer …" Rhonda paused as Mike raised a hand.

"Sorry I'm late, Mike." Chip entered the conference room. He had a sandwich in one hand and a bottle of water in the other. "It took longer at the mobile truck than I thought it would."

He sat in the first available chair. His windswept hair hung over his eyes; his breathing was shallow. He'd obviously run up the stairs to get here.

"Try not to let it happen again."

Blaine was surprised at Mike's rebuke until she remembered that this was the second or third time Chip had been late getting back from lunch.

"It's not a problem, Chip," Rhonda tried to smooth the waters, "I was just starting." Rhonda consulted her notes. "As I was saying, your killer continues to prove that the Poe aspect of these deaths is more important to him than the victims. I don't need to mention all the similarities between 'The Murder of Marie Rogét' and Cecilia Rogers' murder; I'm sure you have gone over that enough. I will say that the attention to detail further proves how organized this killer is.

"I will also say that I went back to Dr. Wolff yesterday and we had a long discussion. He still feels there are enough points of similarity to call this a typical serial killer with some atypical aspects, but I have my doubts. In the end, as I said before, I don't think it matters to how you investigate these killings. Just because you don't have a commonality, doesn't mean you wouldn't pursue the case like any other. You still have to follow all the leads and see where they take you."

Well, that's not gonna help us much.

"You're right about that, Rhonda," Mike said.

Blaine noticed he was trying not to sigh and felt for him. This had been a bad case from the start, and it hadn't helped that she and David weren't exactly supportive at the beginning. But they'd both come around and Mike had turned this group into a team pretty quickly. Now she was not only on board with the serial killer theory but was glad Mike was Case Agent.

He seems to know how to get the best out of everyone, I'll say that for him. Sure wish he realized what a good job he's doing.

"Thanks for your help anyway," Mike said.

Mike's comment pulled Blaine back to the present. Looking around surreptitiously, she hoped no one noticed she'd briefly zoned out.

"We won't keep you from your other cases. And if we get anything more, we'll–"

"I do have a couple more things to add, Mike," Rhonda interrupted.

"Oh, sorry. I thought … uh, sure what have you got? We can use anything at this point."

"I went to the bookstore for a copy of Poe's writings, and read the stories the killer's used so far. I noticed something interesting from a psychological point of view. It's a myth that all serial killers really want to be caught and that's why they sometimes contact the police. Most of the time this simply isn't true. Serial killers in general need to kill and need to keep on killing. They don't want to be caught because, if they were, they wouldn't be able to kill any more. The ones who do contact the police want to rub their noses in the fact that the police haven't been able to catch them. So, if this is a typical serial killer, we'd assume he wants to keep doing what he's doing.

"Some of the stories the killer chose have interesting psychologies. In 'The Black Cat' for instance, the man doesn't think he's going to get caught and this overconfidence is his downfall. He takes the police down to the cellar, bragging about how strong the walls are. This leads the police to discovering his dead wife. A psychologist might say he secretly wanted to get caught because he felt guilty over killing his wife.

"In 'The Tell-Tale Heart' the guilt factor is even more obvious. The murderer is talking to the police and hears the old man's beating heart in his head. He jumps up and points to where he buried him to get the sound out of his mind. Again, guilt wins out.

"The guilt in 'The Assignation' is a little different because this is derived from the hopelessness of the lovers' situation. They don't think they can ever be together, so they commit suicide rather than be apart. And finally, in 'The Murders in the Rue Morgue', the sailor feels guilty that he allowed the orangutan to get loose, leading to the deaths of the two women."

"You're losing me here," interrupted Blaine. "What exactly is your point?"

Rhonda's face turned a little red. "I admit it's a stretch, but I think your killer is subconsciously choosing stories that show guilt of some kind because he feels guilty about what he's doing. Which is atypical for a serial killer. It might help to understand his thinking processes a little better."

"Even if this guy is subconsciously feeling guilty," added David in a decidedly sarcastic tone, "and choosing stories with characters that feel guilty, where does that get us? Would that help us find him?"

Uh oh! David's getting pissy again. I've been on the end of that tone myself a couple times over the years. Bet Rhonda will put him in his place.

Before Rhonda could respond, Mike did it for her. "I said we can use any help we can get, so maybe we can use this. Danny, as our resident Poe expert, could you go back over Poe's stories and look for any where the main character feels guilt over something. Maybe if we had an idea of what stories he might use, you could concentrate on those kinds of crimes when you're trolling for new murders."

There were some grins and a few low laughs at Mike's use of the word 'trolling' and his satisfied look told Blaine he'd gotten the reaction he was hoping for.

"Actually, Mike, I think it might be easier to ask Dr. Barty. She could probably rattle the names off the top of her head, where it would take me a lot longer to do the research. I haven't been able to get with her since you asked me the other day - she's been busy with student conferences - so I could just ask her about this at the same time. You said you wanted to keep her in the loop. What better way than to ask her for specifics about the stories?"

"Yeah, Danny, good idea. And it might stroke her ego a bit and keep us on her good side." He nodded. "Do it." Mike turned back to the profiler's image on the monitor. "Thanks, Rhonda. I won't cut you off too soon anymore. You got anything else for us?"

"Not really. Just a reminder, more or less." Rhonda looked at the folder on her desk and pulled out a sheet of paper. "The other day we said that there were more dates in July for the murderer to use, but not as many in August."

"Yeah, there's only eight in August," said Danny as he split the monitor screen and put up the chronology.

"Exactly. The next possible date for a murder isn't until the 9th, giving you several days to continue the investigation." Blaine saw an uncharacteristic hesitation in Rhonda, who cleared her throat and added, "More time could also mean more spectacular murders. In July, he was bunching them together, maybe trying to get us to notice him. Given there's been no acknowledgment yet, he might use August to make a splash, so to speak."

"I really hope she's wrong this time."

Blaine heard Alex's whispered comment. She nodded her agreement.

"We'll have to use the next few days as wisely as we can," said Mike. "Anything else?"

"No, not this time. That's all I have for you today."

"Okay, thanks again. We've been working in small groups to pursue leads and I am going to get updates next. If you have time, you're welcome to listen in."

Looking at her watch, Rhonda said, "Sure. I'm free for a half hour or so. If I won't cramp anybody's style."

"Nope. The more the merrier." Mike smiled. "Let's start with the ME's reports on our last two murders." As Mike picked up a file, the door opened, and a junior agent handed him a note. "Well, speak of the devil." Mike grinned and turned to Danny. "It seems Dr. Barty is here and ready to speak to you."

"What? Now? She didn't even call first." Danny's voice dripped indignation.

"I know, but you said you've been having trouble getting her in here, so take it as a good omen." Mike tried to take the sting out of his words by saying, "Ask her about the stories and see what she says. Remember, I'd like to keep on her good side in case we need her down the road."

"But the briefing ..."

"I'll make sure someone updates you on anything you miss. Just get as much from her as you can and, when she's ready to go and if I haven't come down yet, send someone for me. I want to see her before she leaves."

"Okay, boss, I'll do my best." Danny got up but his shoulders slumped, and he took his time getting his files together and picking up his notebook.

Blaine watched him go, stifling a laugh. *He hates missing the rest of the meeting. I guess he does like working this side of a case. I hope he gets to do it again.*

Mike started speaking again and she turned her attention back to the matter at hand.

CHAPTER 30

For my own part, I have never had a thought which I could not set down in words, with even more distinctness than that with which I conceived it.

'MARGINALIA'

Interview Room Two was an anomaly. One would think it should be located in the thick of the action in the center of the office. One would be wrong. It was out of the way in a back corridor.

Not only that, but it was also one of the smallest and worst furnished of the interview rooms. While the rest were equipped with new and modern furniture, this one was home to the cast offs tossed out from offices and meeting rooms throughout the building. The table was older, made of pressed wood with numerous marks on its scarred surface. The chairs were mismatched - the powers that be refused to throw anything out. Even the blinds on the windows were ripped in places and not functioning, always stuck at half-mast, the cords hopelessly tangled, and no one had the time, energy or concern to try and fix them. Only the worst of criminal suspects were brought here, mainly because agents thought this room was the first punishment that could be meted out to them.

It was evident that Danny McKissick had never interviewed a witness, or he'd not have brought Dr. Jeniviere Barty to this all but useless room for their discussion. Looking around the room now, Danny blushed at his faux pas and wondered immediately if it were too late to find another space. Would the University of Miami professor take this as an insult?

If she does, Mike's gonna be pissed at me. We need her and he wants her to like us.

"Dr. Barty, please have a seat," Danny said as he motioned to a chair. "I must apologize up front for the room, but all the other rooms are either being used at the moment or are booked," he lied. "We weren't expecting you and ..."

"Yes, I know I dropped by unannounced, as it were," interrupted the Poe expert, "but I had some unexpected time and decided to take a chance that I could be seen. However, I thought I would be speaking to Agent Donaldson."

Danny cringed inwardly at the professor's tone, which bordered on insolent. Not only that, but as she spoke, Dr. Barty didn't look at him so much as above him, as if he were insignificant and unworthy of her notice. Danny was not intimidated, though. He would treat her with all the respect and consideration as per his instructions.

I'll show her what real courtesy is.

"Yes, Agent Donaldson is the case agent but unfortunately he's in a previously scheduled meeting and can't get away right now."

Dr. Barty's mouth turned into a near pout and she drummed her fingers on the table. "I see. Well, I guess I'll have to speak to you then. I'm sure you'll take good notes, and my statements will be reported correctly."

Danny reassured his recalcitrant consultant. "This isn't an interrogation, Dr. Barty. We just want to tap into your vast expertise and experience to help us understand Poe and his psychology. We consider you a valuable consultant."

The sudden metamorphosis was interesting to witness. Dr. Barty sat up straighter, squared her shoulders and all but preened at his blatant flattery. That told Danny everything he needed to know.

Danny took up his pen, brought the two Poe books closer and opened one of the folders in front of him. "Dr. Barty, we were hoping that you could give us more insight into Edgar Allan Poe's life and his work. We're looking for the motivation behind some of these stories and whether his personal life influenced them. For example, 'The Black Cat'. The narrator kills his wife and becomes overconfident and his crime is discovered. But before that he has killed and mutilated several animals. Do you know if Poe hated animals or maybe had a bad experience with one at some point in his life?"

In this way, Danny took Dr. Barty through several of the works the killer had used during his spree. He read passages to her or asked her to point out relevant parts to him, then asked questions as specific as he dared to see if anything in Poe's life reflected on their killer's motivation. Danny also made sure to jump around and not ask about the stories in the same order of the murders. He wasn't sure why he was doing it this way, it simply seemed important not to stress one story over another.

Half an hour later, the subject got around to 'The Tell-Tale Heart'.

Lying through his teeth, Danny stated, "This story has always intrigued me. It seems that the narrator, the killer, is very remorseful in the end. Otherwise, why confess when the police apparently don't suspect him of anything?"

Dr. Barty smiled and Danny was suddenly reminded of his high school algebra teacher after he'd finally conquered a difficult word problem. He was sure she was getting ready to give him an 'A' for effort.

"Many people have remarked on the same thing, Agent McKissick."

He'd already told her twice that he wasn't a field agent, but she called him agent anyway. Danny didn't bother to correct her this time.

"And guilt is an important theme in 'The Black Cat'. Interestingly, some scholars say the narrator isn't remorseful so much as overconfident. I don't subscribe to that viewpoint, however."

Dr. Barty's face took on the smug look of someone who wouldn't listen to anyone else's opinion anyway. Danny didn't care about Dr. Barty's disagreements with other scholars. He'd brought the conversation around to guilt and that was the other point Mike had asked him to check on.

"It seems to me that guilt is a fairly common theme in Poe's stories. 'The Tell-Tale Heart' shows guilt, so does 'The Black Cat' and even in 'The Assignation' you might think that the two suicides feel guilt over their affair."

"Yes … er, yes, that's very interesting. You're right that several of Poe's works do involve a guilt factor of some kind. I have to admit, though, I've never looked at 'The Assignation' that way."

Danny seized on the opening. "Maybe you could help me identify other Poe works, both stories and poems, where someone shows guilt or remorse of some kind." Danny pushed the Poe compilation toward her.

Dr. Barty's eyes widened and her mouth formed an 'O'. "I do want to help, of course, but I still don't understand why the FBI is interested in Edgar Allan Poe. I'm sure there's an interesting story behind it …" Dr. Barty trailed off and Danny realized she was fishing.

"I'm sorry, Dr. Barty, but I can't discuss specifics about any investigation. Rest assured; we wouldn't be asking if it weren't important." Danny started to open the Poe book.

"I'll certainly try my best, but I'm afraid I can't name them off the top of my head, I'd have to do a little research."

"I certainly didn't mean to put you on the spot, Dr. Barty." He pulled the book back towards him a bit. "Please, take some time with it. I'm sure you're incredibly busy right now with the start of the new semester and all. If you wanted, you could email me the list. I can give you my address and you can send it along whenever you like."

Dr. Barty hesitated. "Of course, I'll get to it as soon as I can." She looked above him again and seemed to be considering something. "Perhaps I should go over this with Agent Donaldson. I'm sure you're very competent, but as you said, Agent Donaldson is the main investigator, and wouldn't it be better for me to give him the information directly? Just to make sure there are no misunderstandings," she finished quickly.

Danny was framing a response when Dr. Barty's cell phone rang.

CHAPTER 31

If you wish to forget anything on the spot, make a note that this
thing is to be remembered.

'MARGINALIA'

Mike smiled to himself as Danny left the room before facing his
waiting team. "Okay, moving on. Dr. Richmond found
Temazepam in all three victims, so our boy is still sticking to what
works. She also said that Cecilia Rogers was definitely killed
before the Henri's." Mike turned to the monitor. "Actually, I'm
glad you're still here, Rhonda. If 'The Murder of Marie Rogét' was
a sequel to 'The Murders in the Rue Morgue', why was Cecilia
Rogers killed before the Henri's? Shouldn't it be the other way
around? Do you think he made a mistake?"

Rhonda stared at the case agent for a long moment. "That's a
good question. Give me a few minutes on that one, would you? Go
on with the briefing and come back to me later."

"Didn't mean to put you on the spot. If you want to think
about it, get back to me in a day or two if you need it. I'm not
goin' anywhere."

Another smile from Rhonda.

Mike turned back to the team. "Let's start with you, Alex. Did
you and Blaine find anything on the buildings where the bodies
have been found?"

Alex sighed and Blaine felt sorry for him. *He so wanted this to be the key to the whole thing.*

"No, we didn't find anything. Obviously, the church didn't meet our requirements, so we didn't really look into it. Nor did the Cutler Drain Canal where Cecilia Rogers was found, although there's something interesting about that I'll get to in a minute. The other murders took place in empty or abandoned buildings …"

"Except for Oscar Cudney and Ruby James and her son, killed in their own homes." Blaine didn't like to interrupt, but thought it was important to be precise.

Alex flicked a look at her. "Right. We thought we might be on to something at first because Stephen Hardison was found in that abandoned shoe factory in Hialeah and Lucy Benton in an empty house also located in Hialeah. But Ruby James and her son were killed in Palmetto Bay and Oscar Cudney's home was in South Miami. The Henris were killed in that multi-million-dollar home at the Bayshore Villas."

"Hang on," Mike interrupted. "Sorry, guys, but you seem to forget I'm a stranger down here. I don't know where any of these places are. It might help if I could see them on a map."

Blaine and Alex looked at each other and she could tell he was thinking the same thing as she was. Blaine spoke first.

"You're right, Mike. We forgot you didn't know the area. Unfortunately, pinpointing these places on a map isn't going to help. Bottom line: we couldn't find any commonality."

"Right." Alex took up the report. He started to tap the table. "They're all over the map. North, south, east and west, they span the entire Miami-Dade County area. Two murders did take place in Hialeah but none of the others. Bayshore Villas is on the water as is the Cutler Drain Canal, but all the others were inland. None of the abandoned or empty buildings were owned by the same group or property manager. They're different kinds of buildings. A factory, and two houses, one your run-of-the-mill house while the other one was practically a mansion. We thought we had something with Hialeah, and there is a Miami Dade College campus in Hialeah, so we thought maybe–"

"But that's great!"

Everyone turned at Chip's interruption. The young agent's eyes were as big as melons and he was leaning forward punctuating the air with his hands.

"We know two of the victims had ties to the college, so maybe we're back to MDC after all."

"I'm afraid not," answered Alex. "MDC also has campuses in Kendall, Homestead, Little Havana, there's even one in Doral. I'm afraid that's not it either."

Chip's shoulders slumped and he leaned back in his chair.

Alex turned back to Mike. "We also thought about Kendall as the common factor. The Henris lived there, the Cutler Drain Canal is in Kendall and there's an MDC campus." Alex sighed. "But none of the other victims had any ties to that area we could find. So that was another dead end."

"It was a stretch," Blaine jumped in, "but Trinity Episcopal Cathedral where Lylyana Biddix was killed is on Bayshore Drive and the Henri's were killed in Bayshore Villas. We wondered if that was a starting point. But again, none of the other victims had anything to do with that side of town."

"So, another dead end?" This from David who'd remained unusually quiet for most of the briefing.

Blaine nodded. *I'm getting sick of those words.*

"To put it bluntly, my idea was a bust. We can't find anything common." Alex dropped his notebook onto the table, where it landed with a hollow thump.

"It was a waste of time, I'm afraid," added Blaine.

"Okay, I see that's not the commonality, but that doesn't mean you've wasted your time." Mike smiled.

That smile takes five years off his age. Blaine found herself smiling back.

"What it tells us is that our killer knows the entire county pretty well. And that could be important." Mike paced a minute. "In fact, I think we might be able to use this in a different way." He focused on Blaine. "Remind me later to get with Danny about putting together a map, will you?"

Blaine nodded and wrote a line in her notebook.

"Alex, Blaine, I know you guys did a lot of work in just a couple of days and I appreciate it. And even if it's a negative, it's given us another angle to look at. Good job."

Alex sat up a bit and even Blaine felt better about things.

~~

"Sorry, Mike, but I'm gonna have to leave in a few moments. I have a meeting at three."

"Sure, Rhonda, no problem. Thanks for sticking around."

"Any time. But before I go, I was thinking about your question. Why did the killer murder Cecilia Rogers before the Henris? All I can think of to explain it is that he figured it would take a few days for Cecilia to be found and, since the Henris would be discovered first, the order of finding the bodies would conform to Poe, not the murders themselves. Remember, I've said it before: the Poe aspect of all this is the most important element, not the victims. I know it's thin, but it's all I've got. If I think of anything else, I'll let you know."

"Thanks, Rhonda, we appreciate it. Take it easy."

"You, too, Mike. Don't let all this get you down, you're doing good work."

I couldn't have said it any better myself. Blaine smiled as she gave a quick nod to the profiler as a silent thanks.

"Anybody need a quick break before we go on?" Mike asked as he grabbed his bottle and took a drink.

When no one answered, Blaine turned to a new page in her notebook and waited.

"Chip, you and David are up next. Did ya find anything to support your red herring idea ?"

Chip sat up and squared his shoulders. Blaine was reminded of an old movie where the bad guy was facing the firing squad and she could tell Chip believed Mike was going to do the shooting.

Chip cleared his throat. "David and I looked into each of our murder victims to see if any of them might have had enemies or be a target. We already know that Cameron Cudney was arrested for murdering his cousin, Oscar. We think he may have done it, but no proof. Since we know about him already, we moved on to the other murders.

"Next came Lylyana Biddix. She was twenty-nine and worked as the manager of a discount store. Everyone liked her. She didn't have any beefs with any of the employees, the owners had nothing but good things to say about her and no one knew of any problems with customers. So that didn't get us anywhere. She was unmarried and although she had been in a long-term relationship until a year ago, it seems that it ended amicably, and she and the ex are still friends. We're waiting on information from her prior employer, but she left that job three years ago, so we don't think there's anything there."

Chip looked over at David and nodded for him to continue.

The African American detective never looked at his notes as he reported, "Our next victims were Ruby James and her son. They lived in Miami Gardens. She was twenty-seven and a housewife. Ruby and her husband married right out of college, so she had no work history per se. Now normally, we'd look at the husband as a suspect, but he was the one who found her and basically suffered a breakdown afterward. He's under a doctor's care and she says the grief is genuine. Besides that, he has a solid alibi, and no one could understand why he'd kill his son. They'd been trying to conceive since they got married and his Facebook page is full of nothing but pictures of Ruby's pregnancy and their preparations for the baby. So, we don't think that she could have been the intended target."

A typical David report. He probably stays up late at night memorizing everything, so he never has to look at his notebook while he's talking. Blaine shook her head as she made a couple of notes.

David continued, "Next up is Stephen Hardison. He was thirty-two, married, and worked as a loan officer at a local savings and loan. His marriage was apparently happy, although we've only been able to talk to his wife. We plan on speaking to neighbors and members of his bowling team to confirm. Again, we'd normally look at the wife as a suspect, but she's the one with the money in the family and if they were as happy as she says, there isn't a reason for her to kill him.

"We do have a lead to follow through his work. It turns out that a few weeks ago one of the customers at the bank threatened Hardison because he was turned down for a loan. We just got that info and haven't had time to look into it yet. It's possible it may lead somewhere."

"Good," said Mike. "Keep on it."

David nodded, then waved for Chip to continue.

"Lucy Benton was thirty-five, divorced, and owned a boutique. Her ex lives out of state and has an alibi for her death. The boutique was struggling but we can't see how that would have a bearing on this. So, nothing there.

"Cecilia Rogers was twenty-eight and was engaged to a guy five years younger than her. We can't find a reason for him to have killed her. Both sets of parents said the couple was happy. Interestingly, Cecilia Rogers was a security guard at a downtown office building. She had good evaluations and no complaints from her supervisor. We're waiting on the Incident Log to see if there were any problems with anyone who came into the building, but we're not holding out a lot of hope. She'd worked there for over five years and if there'd been any problems, the supervisor would have mentioned it."

Chip turned over another page of his notebook and looked up at Mike. "The last two victims were Camille and Suzanne Henri. Camille was sixty-six and retired a year and a half ago from cleaning houses. She had been married to the same man for forty years and he's devastated that he lost both his wife and his daughter, their only child, at the same time. He has no alibi but no motive either. There was no money, and the life insurance policy was only for ten grand.

"Suzanne was single and not seeing anyone, according to her father. She worked as an administrative assistant at a law firm that specializes in corporate law. She had good evaluations and was well-liked. There was one coincidence, though. Suzanne sang in a choir and, about four months ago, the group performed at an Interfaith celebration that was held at Trinity Episcopal Cathedral. We just got that info, so we haven't been able to follow up on it.

"I guess the question is, should we bother? It's a long shot and the Hardison lead sounds more promising. But overall, I don't think my red herring idea is gonna work out. It's been a waste of time. Sorry, Mike."

That slump in Chip's shoulders was back and Blaine felt sorry for him. She wanted to say something positive to make him feel better but didn't want to come across as trite or patronizing.

Mike had the right words. "This has not been a waste of time, Chip. Getting more information is never a waste of time in any murder investigation, especially one like this. That's why we look into every aspect of the victim's life because you never know where an investigation is gonna take you. You're gonna find that murders don't come with road maps. If they did, we'd solve every case on the first day. But we don't. It's a slog and we just gotta keep goin' through all those little details until we find the right clue that will lead us to this guy.

"It's possible there's still something in what you found out that will give us that clue. That's why I want you to follow up on the concert along with the Hardison lead. It's possible there is a link there that will help us. And even if it doesn't, there's no shame in making a mistake or going down the wrong path. That's how you learn. The shame is in not speaking up when you have an idea. It might be the right one and if you didn't speak up, a murderer stays on the streets that much longer. So don't sweat it. You had an idea, you pursued it and you've learned from it. That's the most important thing right now. Learn from it."

The pep talked worked. Blaine looked at her colleagues and was amazed at the change. Chip sat up straighter and beamed at Mike. David was smiling and Alex had a grin on his face. A couple of hours ago they couldn't wait to get out of this place for an hour, but now she saw her own renewed determination reflected in the faces around her.

He's really good at this. Too bad he's not sticking around. I could get used to having him on VCMO.

"All right. It's after 5:00. I want ..."

Everyone turned as Danny came in.

"You could have sent someone to get me, Danny. What room is Dr. Barty in?" Mike stood up. "I'll go down for a minute ..."

"No need, Mike. She had to leave."

"Oh. Why?"

"She got a call from her mother. Apparently, there was an emergency at the house and Dr. Barty had to take care of it. Don't worry, she said she'll be glad to come back and see you real soon. I think she has a crush on you, Mike."

Blaine joined the chuckles around the room but had to keep from laughing out loud at Mike's beet red face.

Mike crossed his arms and ignored the jab. "Alex can update you on what you missed later, and you can tell us about your meeting with Dr. Barty tomorrow. Something came up earlier and I have another job for you. I know I've asked you to wear a lot of different hats in this investigation. Well, I've got another for you."

Danny gave Mike a cheeky grin. "Hit me, boss. I was getting bored just reading Poe all day."

Mike's lips moved slightly, and Blaine could see him fighting a smile. "Be careful what you wish for, Danny. What I want this time isn't too difficult, just time consuming. Here's what I want. A map, it'll need to be a big one, of the entire Miami-Dade area. Use Alex and Blaine's notes and everything we have on the murders already. I want you to map out each murder and victim. I want where they lived, where they were killed, where they worked and anything else you can think of. And color-code it. You know what I mean, home addresses in blue, for example, and the crime scenes in red. Maybe where they worked in green, that kind of thing. Maybe if we see everything on a map laid out, something will jump out that we won't catch by reading our notes or the files. You obviously need something else to do since you have so much extra time to matchmake."

"Back at ya, Danny!" Alex laughed.

"Good one, boss," said Chip.

David raised his bottle of water in appreciation of the jest.

Got your own back, Mike. Good job.

Apparently, Danny knew when he was beaten, giving his boss a mock salute although the smile had left his lips.

"As I was saying, it's after five and I want everyone to finish up your 302s and try to get out of here by seven. Go home, get some rest and be back here at 7:30 in the morning. We'll regroup and figure out where to go from here. I'm up for any suggestions, so don't be afraid to think outside the box. I'm meeting with Agent Zardes at 6:30 and then …"

"You'll go home and get some rest."

The interruption came from David, but he'd only said what Blaine was thinking.

Mike blushed and shrugged. "How about if I promise to try?"

"Deal."

"All right, everybody, get to it."

Blaine began to collect her notes. *Maybe I'll see if he wants to go to the gym with me tonight. With that body, he's bound to work out, bet he'd be a good challenge. Maybe dinner after ... Blaine, you know better! No dating colleagues. That's your rule. But he is leaving when all this is over. What's wrong with a little harmless flirting? Maybe I'll just see if he wants to work out, no dinner. Yeah, that's the ticket. I'll say we could talk about the case. Kick around some ideas. Yeah, that's what I'll do.*

Blaine walked over to Mike's desk. "Hey, Mike, got a question for you."

CHAPTER 32

We should bear in mind that, in general, it is the object of our newspapers rather to create a sensation—to make a point—than to further the cause of truth.

'THE MYSTERY OF MARIE ROGÊT'

August 10

Mike woke up to the ringing of his cell phone at 5:15 a.m. *This can't be good.* He grabbed the phone and answered, "Donaldson," not even bothering to pretend he'd been awake.

"This is Zardes. Get your team over here immediately. I want everyone in the conference room at 6 o'clock, no exceptions." The phone call ended with not so much as a 'goodbye' or 'see you then'.

Mike groaned as he got out of bed and started dialing. Yesterday was the 9th and Mike had been hopeful that the killer hadn't struck. That would give them more time before he potentially killed again on the next possible date, the 16th. Zardes's call probably meant there had been another murder, or that something even worse had happened.

An hour later, Mike knew he'd been too optimistic and wondered just how bad things were going to get.

~~

When Mike saw all the brass in the conference room, he wondered if he needed to start drinking coffee late into the day. SSA Zardes, SAC Martinez and Captain Mendez were clustered at the front of the room, and David, Chip and Blaine were seated at the farthest table from them. Mike recognized the media liaison, Joanie Bear, at a far table. Chip was watching the bigwigs, but when Zardes looked directly at him, he put his head down quickly.

He's so young. Mike gave his friend a warm smile and took another drink of his coffee.

Within ten minutes, Meghan Richmond had joined the group, then Danny arrived and last to enter was Alex Welch, who gave Mike a raised eyebrow. Mike merely shrugged in return and the older detective took a place at the nearest table. Suddenly the phone rang, and Danny put Rhonda on speaker phone. If he hadn't known it before, Mike was now positive that this would be no ordinary briefing.

Without preamble, Mendez began the meeting with the bad news. "Our killer has made himself known and taken credit for his work." Mendez held up a newspaper. "He sent a letter to the *Herald_*and all the major television networks. In his letter, he describes each murder, giving details that have never been released to the press, and claims that either the police have been keeping the existence of a serial killer a secret or they have been incredibly inept in not putting it all together. Either way, both departments look bad. The media has been hounding us since five this morning, when the news broke. SAC Martinez and I will be giving a news briefing at 7:30 and we want the most up-to-date information you have before we face the press."

Martinez took the floor next and announced, "For the record, Capain Mendez and I will take full responsibility for keeping this from the public. We will explain that the FBI and MDPD have been running a joint task force since July 25, but that it was our decision not to release the information about a serial killer to the public."

Mike was surprised. He knew Zardes had made the decision not to reveal anything and thought that the SSA had not told his superior. Now he wondered if he'd been wrong. Why would Martinez take responsibility if he hadn't known? But if he hadn't known, maybe he was taking the heat for one of his subordinates. If that was the case, then Mike's respect for the SAC and Captain Mendez ratcheted up a notch and he determined to find this guy as quickly as possible to minimize the fallout for both law enforcement leaders.

Mike spoke, "With your permission, sirs, we'll start with Dr. Richmond and Agent Sagan, then go on to Detectives Welch, Hoskins and Scotty. Agents Smythe and Mr. McKissick can finish up after that."

"Since the press briefing is at 7:30," Mendez said, "I'll ask each of you to keep your reports to five minutes."

Mike nodded to Meghan, and the Medical Examiner started with the Oscar Cudney murder. She went through the medical findings for each case with minimal interruptions from Mendez and Martinez.

As Meghan finished and the conversation around him continued with the next report, Mike listened with one ear as his attention shifted to the copy of the *Herald* Mendez had thrown on the table. The headline was bold and to the point: **SERIAL KILLER TERRORIZES MIAMI**. Reproduced in an adjacent column was the letter from the killer.

Mike couldn't curb his curiosity and began to surreptitiously read the long missive. He skimmed over the Poe references but read closely the descriptions of the gruesome deaths, hoping that the killer had inadvertently included something that might lead them to him. Something started to tickle at the back of his mind and Mike went back up to the beginning of the letter. He realized something important was missing.

"Excuse me, sir." Mike looked up from the paper to realize he'd interrupted Alex in mid-sentence.

"Yes, Agent Donaldson?" Although the tone was non-committal, the SAC's raised eyebrows said more than words ever could about his feelings regarding Mike's apparent rudeness.

Mike's throat went dry and he felt sweat gathering in his armpits. He swallowed hard and plowed on. "Sir, I'm going to admit upfront that I haven't been paying as much attention as I should have been to the discussion going on. Actually, I've been reading the killer's letter." Mike held up the copy of the paper. "I think I've discovered something that you need to know about before you go into your press conference."

"And what would that be, Agent?" asked Captain Mendez, his voice laced with curiosity.

"If you look at the list of murders the killer has admitted to, he began his list with Lylyana Biddix's death. He has omitted victim zero, Oscar Cudney, completely."

Everyone stared at the case agent and more than one mouth gaped opened. Danny quickly called up the article and posted it on the monitor and all the investigators began reading it to see for themselves.

Alex whistled and remarked, "You're absolutely right, Mike. He starts with the Biddix murder on July 10."

Several heads in the room nodded and Martinez looked nonplussed as he commented, "Thank you, Agent Donaldson. That is important information. What do you think that means, Agent Sagan?"

"I'm not sure, to tell you the truth," admitted the profiler. "It's unusual for a serial killer to hide one of his murders, especially when he's trying to get attention, as our killer is by writing this letter in the first place."

"There can only be one reason that makes sense," stated David. "There's something about that first murder that could lead us to him, and he doesn't want to bring our attention to it."

"Maybe not," responded Welch. "Blaine and I looked into the Cudney murder in every which way and couldn't find anything new. And, since the killer didn't use Temazepam and since MDPD made an arrest and since the killer hasn't claimed it in his letter, maybe we were wrong and Oscar Cudney isn't victim zero. Maybe he has nothing to do with these killings."

Mike bristled. It was all he could do not to remind the MDPD veteran that it was he who found the connection in all the murders in the first place and alerted the authorities to the presence of a serial killer. And it was he who did more research and found the Cudney murder and linked it to their killer in the second place. Thirdly, the odds of that death, obviously based on 'The Tell-Tale Heart' not being part of the serial deaths were impossibly long and, finally, everyone in the room had been on board with adding that death to the sequence. Taking it out at this point made no sense. But before Mike could frame a diplomatic response to Welch's suggestion, Rhonda did it for him.

"No, Detective Welch. If there's one thing I am sure of, it's that Oscar Cudney's murder is part of this. And more than that, I believe he *is* victim zero. Except for the lack of Temazepam, everything else is the same. The scene of the murder, the use of a meaningful date, even the fact that a caretaker was accused of the murder, the same as a caretaker in Poe's story, points to our killer. No, I think Agent Scotty's suggestion is more likely."

"All right then," stated SAC Martinez decisively. "For now, we're going to take the killer at his word and accept Lylyana Biddix's' death as the first victim. Only we will know that isn't true. In the meantime," and here Martinez turned to Mike and addressed him, "I want you to go back over that first murder. Look at everything every which way from Sunday, then do it all again. I understand that MDPD had to let that cousin go, but we need to find the link. There has to be something connecting Cameron Cudney with that first murder and probably all the subsequent ones. Find it. I want this guy arrested and I want it yesterday."

CHAPTER 33

The whole circuit of its walls did not exceed twenty-five yards.
'THE Pit and the Pendulum'

August 11

Jeremiah Twitchell paced the spacious area that had been his prison for the last couple of days. At least he thought it was two days based on the rise and fall of the sun he could see through the small transom door near the ceiling. His watch had been taken away, as had his phone and belt, but he had been allowed to keep his jacket. He was grateful for that; it got pretty cool in here after dark. He'd walked the length and breadth of this hellhole so many times he knew its dimensions by heart. Twenty feet long by twenty-four feet wide.

Of course, there was no furniture; his captor wasn't going to make this comfortable for him. There was a bed, if you could call it that, pushed up against the west wall. Really, it was just a metal table about the same size of the examination beds at a doctor's office. There was no mattress or pad to lay on, no pillow either, but there was a sheet and a coarse blanket. In another corner was a pail he used as a bathroom, but no toilet paper. After two days, the smell was rank.

There were no windows, and only a pass-through in the door where his food was left each morning. Only in the morning. He'd been given enough food for each day at dawn, then left to fend for himself the rest of the time. The food wasn't five-star by any stretch of the imagination, but at least it was edible. A couple of bagels or muffins for breakfast, bananas or apples for lunch, with chips and one of those pre-packaged all-in-one meals for dinner. Nothing that was hot or needed to be warmed up. Three bottles of water each day completed his sustenance. It wasn't much, but at least he wouldn't starve. His captor obviously wanted him alive for something. What that something was he had no idea.

He walked in the other direction, just for a change, keeping near the walls as always. He hadn't been here long before he realized he didn't want to walk around the middle of the room. On his first inspection of the place, he'd seen a hole cut into the concrete floor. Thinking it might be a way out, he rushed over only to draw back in horror at what he found. Six or seven large rats were caught underneath, trapped by a mesh screen over the top of the hole and attached to the floor by concrete screws. Within the aperture there was a smaller cavity that held water and that was all. They had no food, and their constant scurrying was the only sound Jeremiah could hear day and night. It seemed they never slept.

Jeremiah tried for the umpteenth time to remember what happened before he woke up here. He had walked to his favorite cafe for a cup of coffee and a croissant. With Jayne at her mother's in Connecticut, he never cooked and picked up the same thing for breakfast each morning after his early run. That morning had been like every other. He knew all the regulars and nodded to them each in turn. He nibbled on his pastry while in line. Nothing unusual had happened.

No, wait, that wasn't right. He remembered now. On the way out, his arm was jostled and most of his coffee had ended up on the floor. The other customer apologized profusely and insisted on getting him another cup. It was a minor mishap, not even his fault, so that couldn't be important. He'd walked on home, but by the time he arrived, he remembered feeling a little groggy. The next thing he knew, he'd woken up in this hell, the nightmare just beginning.

Why was he being held here at all? Each morning when his food was brought, he banged on the door and begged for answers, but there was never any response. He tried being nice, then tried threats. He'd offered money. His wallet had been taken but he'd only had twenty, maybe twenty-five dollars on him. Robbery couldn't have been the motive. He promised every cent he had in the bank, but to no avail.

He changed direction again and thought about Jayne. She must be worried sick about him. She went to her mother's every summer, but they talked or texted each day. So, when he didn't answer, his wife would be concerned. Concern would give way to worry and she'd start calling around to family and friends. By now, she would have called the police and would be on her way back to Miami. He prayed he'd see her soon.

Why was this happening to him? His mind kept going over and over possible reasons. They hadn't asked him any questions yet, so he didn't think he was being held for information. He was only a school counselor, for heaven's sake. What could he possibly know that anyone would go to all this trouble to find out?

Then a new thought hit him. Maybe it was a mistake! Maybe they'd mistaken him for someone else and once they realized they had the wrong guy, they had to figure out what to do with him. He couldn't identify anyone - he'd never seen any faces - so maybe they were trying to figure out how to get rid of him safely. That made sense and gave him hope. If he bided his time, didn't make any trouble, maybe they would just drug him or put a bag over his head, or something, then let him go.

Wait, that led to another thought. Maybe what happened at the cafe wasn't an accident. The second cup of coffee must have been drugged and that was why he was so tired when he got home.

Then, when he'd lost consciousness or fallen asleep or whatever, they'd taken him and brought him here.

That also explained why his thoughts had been so foggy when he'd woken up. The drug was wearing off.

Pacing faster, Jeremiah looked up at the window. The sun was coming up, the darkness of the night giving way to a few golden streaks. His food would be brought any minute now by his faceless, nameless kidnapper. It was day three in this hell, but Jeremiah thought it would be a better day. Better because he had hope now. All he had to do was get through these next couple of days. Soon, his captor would figure out how to get him out without compromising his or her own identity. Then Jeremiah Twitchell would be free to go home.

CHAPTER 34

The fury of a demon instantly possessed me.
'THE BLACK CAT'

"This is harassment, plain and simple. I'll have your badge for this. I'll sue you and the FBI for everything you got, I swear!" After this defiant statement, the speaker crossed his arms and sat back in the wooden chair in Interview Room Three.

Christian Mount was thirty-seven, had a scruffy beard and mustache, and was clearly spoiling for an argument. He hadn't stopped complaining from the moment Alex and Chip picked him up outside his home in Hialeah until they reached the FBI offices. This was the man who'd threatened Stephen Hardison, and Alex had grinned from ear to ear when Mike gave them the go ahead to bring him in for questioning.

So far Mount hadn't given a direct answer to anything they'd asked. He worked for a construction company, but grudgingly admitted to being fired from a previous job after an arrest for assault on a coworker with whom he'd argued.

"But it wasn't my fault. That asshole called me lazy and when I went to the boss, he wouldn't listen to me. Then the bastard had the nerve to get in my face and gloat. Naturally, I belted him. He deserved it after egging me on like that."

"You have quite the temper, don't you, Mr. Mount?" Alex asked in the same tone he'd use if he were asking about the weather.

Mount's noncommittal grunt was anything but.

"Never mind, Mr. Mount," Alex continued in that conversational tone. He looked at the file in front of him, then up at the man across from him. "I'd like to ask you about Stephen Hardison. What was your relationship to Mr. Hardison?"

Mount leaned forward and his eyebrows drew together. "Stephen who?"

"Are you saying you don't know Stephen Hardison?" This came from Chip, who had said almost nothing since the interview began.

"That's what I'm sayin'. Never heard of him."

"Maybe this'll jog your memory." With a movement reminiscent of a magician, Alex produced a picture of the man in question.

Mount looked closely at the picture. After a moment, his eyes widened, and he looked at his interrogators. "This is the guy from the bank. Fuckin' loan officer that wouldn't give me money for a new car. Said I had a bad credit history. Jackass." He threw the picture back at Alex, barely missing his arm.

"So, you recognize him now?" Chip asked.

"Yeah, I know who he is. Just didn't know his name."

"You mean who he *was*, don't you, Mr. Mount?" Alex's voice dripped sarcasm.

"Was? Whaddya mean, 'was'?" Mount's surprise didn't seem feigned.

"Mr. Stephen Hardison is dead, Mr. Mount. Are you saying you didn't know?" Alex was incredulous. "It's been in all the papers and on the news."

"Don't read papers. Don't watch news on TV. That stuff don't mean nothin' to me. All about people I don' know doin' things I don' care about. Waste of time."

"Where were you on July 11, Mr. Mount?"

"How the hell should I know where I was? That was a fuckin' month ago! Why you wanna know anyway?"

"Because that was the night Stephen Hardison was drugged, kidnapped, taken to an abandoned warehouse where he was chained to a wall and left to die three days later, Mr. Mount." Alex leaned in a bit. "You made threats against Mr. Hardison and two weeks later, Mr. Hardison was dead. It doesn't take a genius to put the pieces together."

Christian Mount's face paled with realization. He clenched his hands and looked from Alex to Chip and back at Alex again. He opened his mouth and tried to speak, but no sound emerged. Gulping audibly, he tried again, and this time succeeded in articulating one sentence.

"I want a lawyer."

~~

"He talked to his lawyer, then to us," Alex stated as he updated Mike. "Mount's got no alibi for the 11th, says he was home watching a game on TV and drinking beer. He admits to threatening Stephen Hardison but says he didn't mean it, that he was just blowing off steam. His lawyer says if we don't have any concrete evidence then we need to let him go."

"Unfortunately, he's right about that," said Mike with a shake of his head.

"He's still a good suspect, Mike," Alex argued, "even if we don't have anything definite yet. We can hold him for twenty-four hours and I think we should." In an uncharacteristic movement, Alex twisted a rubber band around his fingers for a while before finally saying, "I'd like to hit him with the dates of the other murders to see if he has an alibi for any of them."

"Do that and you show our hand, Alex," cautioned Mike. "I'm not sure that's a good idea."

"Maybe, but if he has an alibi for even one of the other murders, we can eliminate him as a suspect and cut him loose." Alex's eyes almost begged. "I think he's good for it, Mike. I'd like the chance to prove it."

Mike tapped a file against the desk a few times. "Let me run it by Zardes, then I'll let you know." He looked at his watch. "I'll call and see if I can get in to see him right away." Mike turned to pick up the phone but looked back at the MDPD detective. "You did a good job on this, Alex, no matter which way it goes."

CHAPTER 35

The eyes of the public were upon him; and there was really no
sacrifice which he would not be willing to make for the
development of the mystery.

'THE MYSTERY OF MARIE ROGÊT'

August 12

Mike was exhausted. He was getting almost no sleep given that his
mind was fixated on the case and he couldn't rest. He got to the
office by 6:30 most mornings and didn't leave until after 7:30 most
evenings. His meals consisted of take out or delivery and he
usually just inhaled his coffee.

The only bright spot was his budding friendship with Blaine.
He got along with everyone on the task force now, but his almost
daily workouts with her gave him the chance to release some of the
tension as well as kick around ideas about the direction of the
investigation. Plus, she was good for his confidence. His insecurity
was back, and he needed an occasional boost.

Mike knew that Zardes was actively lobbying to get him taken
off the case. He'd suspected as much but was unaware of just how
much the SSA wanted him off the case until he had an enlightening
conversation with Blaine a few days ago.

"That was a great workout, Blaine. I feel a hundred percent better." Mike threw his dirty towel in the nearest laundry sack and opened his locker.

The FBI building boasted a top-of-the-line fitness center that Mike and Blaine visited almost daily. It had a variety of equipment and Mike never did the same routine two days in a row. Some days, he did the running trail, but today he'd ridden an exercise bike for twenty minutes while Blaine lifted weights. Next, they'd taken turns at the punching bag. Now, Mike was dripping with sweat and looking forward to a quick shower before they headed back upstairs to the offices.

Mike had laughed at first when he found out that the Miami field office was located in nearby Broward County, but stopped laughing when he saw the imposing structure for the first time. While the outside was curtained in glass and solar panels, the inside was designed to give its thousand-plus employees a state-of-the-art working environment with what they called 'hybrid floor layouts' of open bays as well as traditional offices and meeting rooms. There was a medical suite, a commissary, and an automotive shop to keep the bureau vehicles in top condition. With an eye to conservation and local ecology, the builders had also incorporated features to conserve water and energy. This combination of futuristic architecture and ecological preservation made it arguably the nicest field office in the nation.

"You wanna grab a sandwich at that deli on Palomino?" Blaine asked as she opened her own locker.

Mike huffed. "No thanks. I'd rather not drive if I don't have to. The drivers in this town are insane! I mean, hasn't anybody down here ever heard of turn signals? Just this morning on my way here, a guy made a right turn right in front of me - no blinker of course - and when I honked at him, he had the nerve to give *me* the finger! Like it was all my fault." He slammed the door of his locker in disgust.

Blaine's laughter rang out and a couple of nearby exercisers looked over in surprise. "Mike! Nobody uses turn signals in Miami. That's how they know you're from out of town. If you want to act like a local, never signal, weave in and out of traffic and drive like a bat out of hell! Do that, and you'll drive just like the natives."

"Drive like a bat outta hell? How? Turtles go faster than the traffic on US 1. It's insane. How do you stand it every day?"

"I've learned a few shortcuts over the years." Blaine smiled. "Tell you what. Tonight we'll sit down, and I'll see if I can't find you a better way to get to your hotel."

"Do that, and I'll owe you big time."

"Take me out to dinner sometime and we'll call it even."

Mike's face went pink and he unfolded and refolded his sweatshirt. Clearing his throat, he looked at his watch. "We better get moving." His chuckle was slightly forced as he added, "It'll look really bad if the boss is late. I don't want to give Zardes another reason to yell at me."

Blaine chewed her lip and Mike knew his joke had backfired.

"What's up? What'd I say wrong?"

Blaine took a deep breath and wouldn't meet his eyes. She was obviously trying to make a decision, and Mike waited for her to compose her thoughts.

"Look, Mike, I know I wasn't supportive when you first showed up and told us about a serial killer, but now I'm completely on board. You know that, right?" Mike nodded and she continued, "I know you've had trouble with Zardes from the get-go, but I'm afraid it's worse than you think. I've worked on and off with VCMO for six years now, so I know a lot of agents and a few of them are pretty good friends. I did some checking and got the lowdown on him. Mike, Zardes is bad news. He's wanted out of Miami almost since the day he got here. He hates being an SSA and wants to move up to an SAC job somewhere, anywhere. Apparently, he's applied for that position at least twice that my sources know of and maybe more, but never gotten it, even though he's willing to move to take it.

"He thought this case would do the trick. He'd make a name for himself that the bigwigs couldn't miss. But he made a mistake by keeping a serial killer on the loose a secret, it blew up on him and Martinez had to take the heat. Martinez was pretty pissed. Now, Zardes has a chip on his shoulder big time and you're in his cross hairs. Word has it, he's pushing to get you taken off the investigation and get himself put in charge. If he can solve a big serial killer case, he thinks the brass would have to give him that promotion. He thinks the media attention alone would pressure them into it."

Mike didn't know what to say. He hated office politics but never dreamed Zardes would use the case against him like this. He had a lot of questions but blurted out the first one that came to mind.

"When did you find all this out? Why didn't you tell me before? If I'm gonna be used like some sort of pawn in a game, I think I have a right to know. How could you keep this from me? I thought we were getting to be friends. I thought ..." Mike stopped before he said too much. He was hurt more than he thought possible by Blaine's apparent betrayal.

"We are friends, Mike," Blaine protested. "And I only found most of this out late last night and today we've been so busy with the case, I haven't had two minutes alone with you. I admit I didn't want to tell you now. I was gonna see if you wanted to grab something tonight and tell you then, when you had more time to digest it. Now we've got to get back and you won't have much time to think about it. I didn't want this to interfere with the investigation today or get in the way of your meeting tonight with Zardes. You'll need a strategy to deal with him and time to plan it. You won't be able to do that now."

She was right, of course. Mike spent that entire afternoon stewing over Zardes and didn't get much done.

~~

The case was going nowhere, and the spotlight was becoming very bright indeed. After the report of the murders hit the news, the resulting media storm was of biblical proportions. The story had made national headlines and news organizations from around the country converged on Miami. The task force members began entering the building from the delivery entrance to avoid reporters' questions. Martinez and Mendez gave briefings every day but had little that was new to report. The public was up in arms and demanding an arrest.

Mike needed a confidence boost and between Blaine's calming presence and their lead into Stephen Hardison's murder, he hoped they'd get somewhere on the case today.

The twenty-four-hour deadline to either charge or release Christian Mount was originally set for this evening, but when Chip discovered half a dozen outstanding traffic fines that Mount couldn't pay, they were able to keep him longer. The pressure to find something on him was enormous, even more so after someone 'leaked' the construction worker's name to the press and his attorney was now threatening a lawsuit.

Mike suspected Zardes, since the SSA had been overruled by SAC Martinez when he'd wanted to announce Mount's impending arrest. Martinez had put his foot down in no uncertain terms and given Mike and the team permission to question the construction worker about the other murders. He agreed that an alibi for even one murder would eliminate him as a suspect. As Martinez said, "Might as well find out where we stand right away rather than drag it out."

Alex, Chip and David were working on the Mount lead while Mike and Danny tried to figure out their next move if Mount didn't pan out. A special hotline had been set up to handle tips from the public, but as with any high-profile case, most were useless. They'd all had a much-needed laugh when one caller accused an overzealous librarian who'd charged him for the late return of a movie based on 'The Masque of the Red Death' a year ago. That was the only thing they had to laugh about, though. Mike was increasingly frustrated and beginning to think that he should just save Zardes the trouble and resign from the investigation.

Now, he leafed through the book on Poe, then dropped it on the table and the dull thud was as empty as his thoughts. "Okay, I admit it. I'm totally stumped and have no idea where to look next. I'll take any suggestion you've got. Nothing's too off the wall at this point."

Danny didn't answer and the silence stretched, broken only by his dancing fingers on the keys of his computer.

Suddenly Blaine burst into the room. Her eyes were bright, and she was waving a sheet of paper in the air. "Mike! We've got a lead on the Temazepam!"

"What? How?" Mike's surprise was genuine.

After the killer's letter had been publicized, the first media briefing had been short on details. Before the next press conference, however, the three supervisors and Mike met with the FBI's Public Relations liaison, Joanie Bear, to discuss which details should be released in subsequent conferences. A long, and sometimes loud, discussion ensued when the subject of the Temazepam came up. The killer had not given the name of the drug he used, and Mike wanted to keep it to themselves. Investigators often suppressed one or two important facts from the press to identify genuine suspects from the myriad of crackpots who always claimed responsibility in high-profile cases.

Mike had been backed up by Captain Mendez with Zardes and Martinez on the other side. In the end, the SAC won the argument and released the name of the drug found in the victims' bloodstreams, since Temazepam was too common to track. This allowed the SAC and the MDPD Captain to warn the public to be on their guard and not leave a drink unattended in a public place, an admonishment that had been made many times in the past, but now had more timeliness. In the end, they had suppressed the information that the killer murdered on dates relating to Poe's works and life.

The idea that this common drug could give them a lead to their killer was something Mike had hardly considered. He called the rest of the team to the conference room to hear Blaine's report.

"Start at the beginning, Blaine. What happened?"

She sat down and took a breath. "I got a call this morning from Teresa Pinot, owner and manager of Medical Supplies, Inc. It's a small business in South Miami that deals in medical supplies and pharmaceuticals. One of the drugs they sell is Temazepam. And when I said small, I mean *small* business. There are only ten employees, total. So, every summer, Ms. Pinot closes the business down completely, gives the staff three weeks off, and then she and her husband take a European vacation somewhere."

"Let me guess," interjected Alex. "Their vacation was in July and August?"

"Right! The store closed on July 16 and reopened on August 10. On the 11[th,] the pharmacist and her assistant did an inventory of their supplies. They found a discrepancy and rechecked everything a second time. They were missing some Temazepam, reported it to Ms. Pinot, and she remembered reading about the murders in the paper and that the killer is using Temazepam and thought it might be important, so she called us as soon as she could."

Mike tried not to get too excited, although he could tell that everyone else was. Beside the Mount lead, which Mike wasn't sure would pan out, this was the first lead they'd had in days, but it was a long shot at best, and they needed to take this one step at a time.

"Okay, did she say anything about who might have taken it?"

"Not exactly," hedged Blaine. "She's on her way over now with a printout of the inventory and how much is missing. She says she's pretty sure she knows how the drug was stolen, but there's more than one person who could have done it." Blaine looked at her watch as she said, "She should be here in about fifteen minutes."

~~

Ms. Teresa Pinot turned out to be an unremarkable African American in her mid-forties, tall, and wearing an incredibly bright blue, ankle-length dress. Upon entering Interview Room One, Blaine was positive she'd never seen that shade of blue before. It was not only bright, it was *bold,* but in a good way. It took only a moment for Blaine to get used to the color and then realize that she liked it. Not every woman could have pulled it off, but Ms. Pinot made it look fashionable as well as flattering.

"Ms. Pinot," Blaine addressed the businesswoman as she held out her hand, "I'm Detective Blaine Hoskins and this is Special Agent Chip Smythe. We spoke on the phone."

"Yes, of course," agreed Teresa as she shook hands in turn.

Chip held her hand for an extra moment while blurting out, "Thanks for coming down so quickly. I'm sure you must be busy with running your business and all, so you coming in now really helps. We appreciate it. We know you're busy, so, uh, thanks again."

Once again, Blaine was reminded of just how new to law enforcement Chip was as she tried not to smile at his fumbling remarks. She'd start off the questioning and let Chip take the second half and get more experience in interviewing.

"Well, I wasn't sure if this would be important to the FBI, but I figured it couldn't hurt to tell you. I'm only sorry I didn't see the stories sooner, but we've been out of the country for vacation ..." The store's owner trailed off as she shrugged.

"We understand what happened, Ms. Pinot," Blaine assured the businesswoman. "And we appreciate that you contacted us as soon as you found a problem." Blaine gave the witness her most ingratiating smile and continued her questioning. "Could you tell us exactly how much of the Temazepam is missing?"

"Each Temazepam capsule is 30 milligrams and thirty capsules are missing, which is a total of 900 milligrams."

Blaine and Chip looked at each other.

They had kept track of how much the murderer had used in the murders. So far, each victim had received 30 milligrams. Oscar Cudney didn't have any in his system and neither did Ruby James. But her son had been given the drug as well as the poison that killed his mother. That left seven victims at 30 milligrams each. If the same person who stole this supply of Temazepam was their murderer, then subtracting 210 from the total of 900 meant the killer still had 690 milligrams, or twenty-three pills, in his possession, enough for nearly two dozen more murders. And this was supposing that their murderer only stole from Medical Supplies Inc. If he got more Temazepam from other sources, there was no telling how many lives he could end before they caught him.

Both Blaine and Chip shuddered inwardly as they considered this unsettling possibility.

"You told me that you thought you knew how the drug was taken from your business, Ms. Pinot, and we still want to hear that. But first, we will need to look at your employee records. If this was an inside job, finding who took the Temazepam could lead us to the murderer."

"Of course, but I'm not sure about handing over my employee records. Most of them have worked for me for years. I–"

Chip interrupted. "Ms. Pinot, it's vital we have all information pertinent to our investigation. You–"

Now it was Teresa's turn to interrupt. "You didn't let me finish. I was about to say, I want to help, but I feel I should talk to my attorney first. I'm sure she'll advise me to cooperate completely, but I need to be sure of my obligations here. Not only to the police, but to my employees as well. Surely you can understand that."

Blaine jumped in quickly. "Of course, we understand your concerns, Ms. Pinot, and we appreciate your position. In the meantime, can you tell us how the pills were taken?"

"I'll be glad to explain how I think it happened."

CHAPTER 36

I have absolutely no pleasure in the stimulants in which I sometimes so madly indulge. It has not been in the pursuit of pleasure that I have periled life and reputation and reason.

EdGAR ALLAN POE in A LETTER in THE LAST YEAR OF HiS LiFE.

Having secured everyone's attention, Mike began the meeting. "Okay, Blaine and Chip met with Teresa Pinot of Medical Supplies Inc. about the Temazepam stolen from her business. Blaine, start us off."

Mike sat down and Blaine turned in her chair to address the group. "Ms. Pinot was extremely helpful. She discovered that thirty capsules were missing and contacted us right away. Let's start with the theft itself." Looking at Chip, she nodded for him to explain.

"Medical Supplies Inc. is a small business with less than a dozen employees. There's the pharmacist and five licensed assistants, two clerical assistants and one office manager. Then, of course, there's Ms. Pinot herself. Most of the employees have been with her for years and almost all are cross trained in case of illness or vacations. Because of this, everyone has access to all medical supplies as well as the medicines themselves. Everyone knows where the key to the supply area is and they all know the code to get in."

Chip unconsciously rubbed the scar on his hand in a nervous gesture. He didn't really want to be in on the interview. He'd rather have continued working on the Mount lead and knew Mike put him on it to give him more experience. He appreciated the chance but had become tongue-tied and ended up letting Blaine do most of the talking. She should be giving this briefing but had indicated he take the lead. He would do the best he could.

"Temazepam is a Schedule III drug and has lesser restrictions than Schedules I and II. The company was previously owned by a guy who got into trouble with the DEA over auditing practices, so Ms. Pinot decided that she'd go above and beyond the regulations and inventory the drugs quarterly. They did an inventory in May, so the next audit was due when they got back from vacation in August. The inventory must be done by two licensed people working together and each person signs off on the log. They had one 500-count bottle of Temazepam, delivered in May and opened for dispensing that same month. After accounting for sales from May to July, they realized pills were missing. The pharmacist alerted Ms. Pinot, who personally witnessed a recount, one that still came up short. They triple-checked the sales record but that confirmed they only sold ninety pills from that bottle."

"Ms. Pinot thinks she knows how the theft was done," Blaine continued with the explanation. "She thinks somebody simply took thirty Temazepam from the 500-count bottle when no one was looking. Easy to go into the drug safe when getting another order ready, take the pills, put them in a plastic bag and stuff them in a pocket. This could have been done over a period, taking a few until he or she reached thirty pills. The thief has to be one of her employees, who'd know when the last inventory was done and when the next was scheduled, and therefore knew the theft wouldn't be discovered until August."

"But to allow everyone in the business complete access," commented Mike incredulously, and several others shook their heads in disbelief.

Blaine sighed. "Yeah, I know. It's pretty slipshod. I have to say that Ms. Pinot was really embarrassed about it. She admitted that she'd gotten too lax with her security, but she said they'd never had a theft before, she trusts her employees completely, and never considered that something like this could happen. Remember, it's a small business. There are no hidden cameras and the on-site surveillance tapes record over themselves on a three-day loop. She knows she needs to tighten up the ship, so to speak, and is already making plans to change how they handle inventory and who has access to what."

"Nothing like closing the barn door after the horses have come home," commented Alex.

"That's for sure," agreed Mike. The case agent moved the briefing along by stating, "But because all the employees had access, the thief could conceivably be any one of them."

"Or someone who left during the last few months," Blaine stated. "She said most of her employees have been with her for a long time but did admit that two people have left since January. One because she needed to help care for her elderly parents, and one quit."

"We asked for the employee files, but Ms. Pinot wants to talk to her attorney first." Chip's tone of voice reflected what he felt about that idea.

Several groans could be heard around the room and Blaine jumped in, "I think she does want to help us, but she wants to be sure her employees are protected as well."

Mike said nothing at first. In fact, he agreed completely with Chip's reaction. However, he'd come to trust Blaine's judgement and since she'd been in the interview and not him, he saw no reason to disregard her opinion.

Looking at his watch, he stated, "It's 2:30. Blaine and Chip, I want you guys to look into Medical Supplies Inc. itself. See if anything seems unusual. We must consider that Ms. Pinot could be playing us for some reason. I want to know everything there is to know about that company and I want it ASAP. We'll just have to wait for those personnel records. It might be a coincidence that there was a theft of Temazepam and that our killer is using it, or it might not. Honestly, I think it would be a miracle if we got anything out of this, but we might get lucky. And, God knows, we could use a little luck on this case."

CHAPTER 37

Melancholy is … the most legitimate of all the poetical tones.
'THE PHILOSOPHY OF COMPOSITION'

August 14

"Mike, you're not going to believe this, but we've got a guy downstairs claiming to be the Poe murderer."

Mike's eyes at first widened then narrowed as he stared at Chip for a full ten seconds before answering. "When did he get here?"

"About fifteen minutes ago," said the youngest member of the team. "It took a few minutes to find out what he wanted. Security wouldn't let him in at first because he didn't have any ID on him. Finally, he told them he had information about the Poe murders and the guard let him in. They called up here, but you weren't around, so they asked me to come down. I was getting his particulars when he just up and confessed. Just like that." Chip snapped his fingers, and his smile showed his teeth.

"Gotta be a crazy trying to get publicity," commented Alex from the other side of the conference room.

"Yeah, as soon as that story hit the paper," added David, "we knew we'd be getting every lunatic coming out of the woodwork."

"Maybe, but most people don't confess to killing ten people just for the hell of it," was Mike's comment. "Where's he now?"

Chip responded, "I got security to accompany us up here. He's in Interview Four. Johnson from Perry's team is with him right now, but I told her not to talk to the guy. That okay, Mike?"

Mike only nodded. He was almost afraid to believe it could be this easy, but if it was, he might be back in Detroit by the end of the week.

~~

"Mr. Bastyr," Mike began, "My name is Agent Mike Donaldson and I understand you have something you wish to tell me?"

"You the agent working these Poe killings?"

Mike had entered the interview room with both Chip and Alex in tow. He'd dismissed agent Johnson, and the three law enforcement officers seated themselves across the table from their suspect. Mike waited while the stenographer set up his equipment in a corner and, once he was settled, Mike began the questioning.

"Yes, I'm the Case Agent in charge of this investigation. For the record, Mr. Bastyr, I'd like to confirm that you've been read your rights. Did Agent Smythe read your rights to you?"

"That's the bit about remaining silent and all that, right? Yeah, he told me all that."

"And are you waiving your right to silence, Mr. Bastyr?"

"Yeah, I got nothin' to hide."

"And you're waiving your right to an attorney?"

"I don't need no lawyer. I don' trust 'em anyway."

"Okay, Mr. Bastyr, now that we've got that settled, will you state your name, address and age for the record?"

"I already told him all this," Bastyr complained as he pointed to Chip. "Why'd I have to go through it again?"

"Because this time, Mr. Bastyr, your statement is being transcribed for the official record. We need to do things according to the law, sir."

"Oh, alright." The man moved a bit in his chair as he changed positions. He was cuffed to a metal loop in the table and was obviously uncomfortable. "My name is Brock Bastyr. I'm thirty-seven years old. I don't have an address exactly. I usually stay with friends or at a shelter most nights."

"So, you're currently homeless?" This question came from Alex who was taking notes for Mike.

"Yeah, been out of work a couple of years now. Got no family, nowhere to go, so I stay wherever I can most nights." Bastyr looked away for a moment in apparent embarrassment.

Allowing his suspect to gather his thoughts, Mike took a moment to assess Brock Bastyr. He looked considerably older than thirty-seven, not surprising if he'd been living on the streets for a couple of years. His near shoulder-length hair was dirty blond, probably from lack of regular washing. His clothes were old and filthy, ratty jeans and a t-shirt with several small holes in it. He wore no belt and his sneakers looked too big for his feet. He wasn't wearing socks. He looked to be of mixed heritage or perhaps his skin was brown due to prolonged exposure to the sun. Mike detected a northern accent and wondered where Bastyr had been born. They'd know soon enough, once they started looking into his background.

"Thank you, Mr. Bastyr. Now what did you want to say to me?" Mike asked directly.

"I killed all those people. I'm your Poe murderer."

Seated next to him, Alex made a surprised sound while Chip merely nodded.

Mike considered his suspect for a moment, then stated, "Okay, Mr. Bastyr. What I'll need from you is a detailed description of how you committed these murders." Mike made a sign to Alex, who turned over a page in his legal pad. "Who did you kill first and how did you choose them?"

CHAPTER 38

Believe nothing you hear, and only half that you see.
'The System of Doctor Tarr and Professor Fether'

Mike, Chip and Alex walked into the conference room to find Danny, David and Blaine waiting for them. Blaine had been doodling on a scrap of paper and immediately looked up.

"Well, have we got him?" she asked before the others could speak.

Chip responded first. "It sure seems like it. Guy told us all about the murders. Gave details and everything." Chip plopped himself down in the nearest seat and gave Danny a high five.

"What a great way to finish up this case," said David with a broad smile. "Not a shot fired and a full confession. Families get closure and the guy's gonna get the needle. Good news for everybody."

Blaine didn't answer. She was watching Mike. He'd walked over to one of the bulletin boards and was looking at the list of victims. His silence concerned her.

"Mike, you don't look like a guy who just solved a big case. What's worrying you?"

Mike was startled by the question and his face turned the color of a flamingo. "Nothing. Guess I'm just underwhelmed or something. For some reason, I didn't expect it to be this easy.

Anyway, looks like I'll be able to go home sooner rather than later." He gave a lopsided grin. "God only knows if my car will still be in the parking lot at my apartment. The manager probably had it towed away already."

Blaine laughed with the others but couldn't help being sorry that Mike would be leaving soon. She'd gotten used to having him around.

"Okay, as soon as we get the transcribed interview back, I want to break it down into sections. We'll split up into teams and start checking everything Bastyr told us. Danny, you'll work with David. Alex, you and Chip will team up. Blaine, you're with me. The stenographer said he'd have it ready as soon as possible, so I want everyone to get something to eat and be back here in one hour. Then we'll go through his confession with a fine-tooth comb. Let's make sure everything's perfect for the AUSA."

"What about Medical Supplies Inc. and the Temazepam?" asked Alex. "We still gonna keep following up on that? And we're still looking into Mount's alibis. We can't reach the guy he says he played poker with for two of the murders."

Mike hesitated while considering his options. Making his decision, he answered, "We'll hold off on the Temazepam unless Ms. Pinot comes through with her records. And don't worry about those alibis for Mount unless that guy calls you back. We got a confession from Bastyr, so what would be the point? MDPD can follow up on the drug theft later and we'll let MDPD follow up on Mount's traffic fines. Right now, we need to nail down our serial killer. If all goes well, I might even be able to make plane reservations for this week."

~~

"Where've you been, Donaldson? I've been waiting for you for fifteen minutes. I told you to be up here at four o'clock."

Bradley Zardes held a rolled-up piece of paper in his hand and currently tapped it against his thigh. His desk was crowded with file folders and piles of papers along with two or three expensive-looking pens. None of this was unusual and Mike gave the mess only a cursory glance, until he spied what looked to be the handle of a mirror partially hidden under one of the piles.

What the hell is that doing there?

Realizing that Zardes was waiting for an answer, Mike quickly schooled his expression. "I'm sorry, sir, but I was waiting for Bastyr's confession to be typed up. I thought you'd want to review it." Mike offered the SSA a folder.

Zardes's face took on a satisfied look and as he held up the paper in his hand. "Already got it, Donaldson. The stenographer sent it up a half hour ago."

Mike refused to comment. He wouldn't give Zardes the satisfaction. Zardes had probably told the stenographer to send him the copy first and to purposefully make Mike wait. It was a childish move, but Mike had come to expect that kind of thing from the SSA.

What I wouldn't give to wipe that smug expression off his face.

"I've already read it through," Zardes was saying. "It seems complete enough. I'll be glad to have this case over with."

"There are a couple of points, sir …"

"I've contacted SAC Martinez and Captain Mendez," Zardes talked over Mike. "We've scheduled a news conference for 5:30 to announce the end of the case. Martinez wanted you there, but I told him I was sure you'd be too busy to attend."

Of course you did. Well, I don't want to share a podium with you anyway. "Yes, sir. We're going through the statement to verify it. There are a couple of points I'm not quite happy with …"

"Nonsense, Donaldson," Zardes interrupted again. "You've got a signed confession. What more do you want? A video tape of the guy killing someone?" Zardes snorted. "I'm sure you were hoping to dazzle us all with your detective skills, but a confession is a confession. We've got the guy and this case is over."

Mike bit his tongue. He thought of a hundred things he could say but knew not to. He only needed to get through the next couple of days, then he'd be on his way home. It would have been nice to see Zardes fall on his face, but Mike couldn't do that to Martinez and Mendez. They'd shown a lot of confidence in him and Mike wanted to repay them for it. He tried once more to explain.

"Sir, no one wants this guy more than me, but I think a press conference may be premature at this point. We need to verify the details in the confession."

Zardes tapped his thigh again. "Donaldson, you're just trying to prolong this. I'm not having any of it. The guy confessed. The case is over. You can finish up and be on your way back to wherever it is you came from in a couple of days."

Mike bit back a reply. Instead, he asked, "What about Christian Mount, Sir? We're still trying to verify–"

"Cut him loose, Donaldson. He's obviously not our Poe murderer given we've got a signed confession from someone else." With that proclamation, Zardes pointedly picked up a file and started working.

~~

As he waited for the elevator to take him back to the fourth floor, Mike fumed. He was getting tired of Zardes not listening to him. He had concerns about Bastyr's confession. A couple of things were bugging him, and he thought the SSA should know before going in front of the cameras. On the other hand, people did not usually confess to murders if they hadn't committed them.

It was my first thought. I hate to admit it, but Zardes is probably right this time. Maybe I'm overthinking this. We'll investigate the shit out of Bastyr's statement, get it all proven and be done with it once and for all.

The car arrived and Mike tried to put his worries behind him.

CHAPTER 39

Convinced myself, I seek not to convince.

'BERENICE'

August 15

The next day was remarkable more for its lack of forward movement than anything else. The VCMO task force spent most of its day tearing Bastyr's confession apart and putting it back together again, starting first with the man himself and then looking at each murder.

Brock Bastyr was a Coast Guard veteran who'd gone into landscaping after leaving the service. He had a spotless military record and no serious run-ins with the law since then. His downfall had come after being injured in a car accident a few years ago. The subsequent lawsuit had failed, and he'd been denied disability benefits. With no money and no job prospects, he'd ended up on the streets.

He was educated, however, and freely admitted to a love of reading and Edgar Allan Poe. He'd even recited the first two stanzas of 'The Raven' for Mike. He'd not given them a motive for the murders, though, and had seemed genuinely puzzled by the mention of Oscar Cudney's name. That fact notwithstanding, he did know all about the murders, although, as Alex rightly pointed out, nothing beyond what had been mentioned in the killer's letter to the *Herald*.

That was only one point that bugged Mike about Bastyr's confession, and he continued to urge his team to dig even deeper into the statement, in spite of Zardes's not-so-subtle hints about Mike's plans to leave Miami.

Despite their focus on the killer's confession, follow-up information continued to come in from prior lines of investigation.

Chip had confirmed that no one from Suzanne Henri's concert at Trinity Episcopal Cathedral had any connection to the murders in any way. It was a coincidence that she sang at the same church Lylyana Biddix was killed in.

Teresa Pinot called and asked if he still wanted her records since the Poe murderer had been caught. They no longer needed them, of course, but Mike decided to hedge his bets and asked for them anyway. When Ms. Pinot questioned why, he simply told her that the FBI could investigate the theft for her even if those pills had nothing to do with the Poe murders.

They had let Mount go with the admonition to pay his fines or end up in MDPD custody, and that night the entire team went out to dinner to celebrate the probable end of the case.

CHAPTER 40

In the meantime the investigation proceeded with vigor...

'THE MYSTERY OF MARIE ROGÊT'

August 16

The team was once again converging in the conference room to eat an early lunch and catch each other up on the investigation. There were three divergent trails to follow and Mike had divided the team into pairs.

Alex and Chip reviewed the information on Medical Supplies Inc. and the employee records from Teresa Pinot. Danny and David continued investigating Cameron Cudney, who was still under surveillance. Zardes had balked at the surveillance after Bastyr's confession, but Cameron could be on the hook for Oscar Cudney's death, so Mike had continued the tail. He and Blaine worked on Bastyr's statement, obviously the major focus of the investigation. Of course, if Bastyr's confession held water, the rest of the trails were unnecessary. Despite his initial misgivings, Mike felt reasonably confident that they did indeed have their killer in custody.

Danny and David reported first. "Cameron's still going to and from work doing nothing out of the ordinary," said David. "But there is one bit of bad news. A couple of days ago surveillance lost him for almost three hours."

Mike swore. "How'd that happen?"

"Just traffic, Mike. It happens a lot down here." Danny shrugged.

"Yeah, well, during those three hours he could have been doing anything, including destroying evidence from Oscar's murder." Mike huffed. "Okay, hopefully it won't matter if we get Bastyr for the Poe killings and he flips on the Cudney murder." He smiled. "And that leads us to Bastyr."

Mike waived at Blaine and she reported that Bastyr had no alibi so far for any of the murders. They were finding it hard to confirm this since Bastyr didn't own a watch and his statement was unbelievably vague as to specific dates and times. He could say, for example, that Lucy Benton was killed on July 13, but they'd been unable to pin him down as to when he killed the animals or even when he took Benton to that room. So far, they'd found nothing to exonerate him either, and he remained their announced killer.

Alex and Chip's report brought the entire team up short. They'd barely begun the investigation into Medical Supplies Inc. when Bastyr had confessed. Now, getting back to that, the first step had been to look into the company itself, and that's where the report began.

"Basically, Mike, we didn't find anything," stated Chip succinctly.

"There's nothing there that immediately raises any red flags," confirmed Alex.

Chip added, "I've worked in Fraud for the last two years and I know what to look for. We went through their financial records, business start-up paperwork, IRS declarations, contracts with other businesses and suppliers, and we got nothing."

"Ms. Pinot gave us copies of all the DEA Forms from the last two years," Alex said. "I called DEA and they couldn't find any problems with the company since she took it over."

"You think they're probably clean?" asked Mike.

Chip nodded. "We have more to go through, but yeah, I don't think we're going to find any smoking guns in the records of Medical Supplies Inc. They seem to be what they appear to be: A small business that has found its niche and is trying to make a living for its owners and employees."

"Having said that," Alex continued, "we did find one really surprising fact. It could just be a coincidence …"

"… or it could be something more," finished Chip.

Mike looked at the two men. "Okay, I'll bite. Whaddya find?"

"Another link." Alex's eyes narrowed and his lips formed a line. "I think we not only found our Temazepam thief but also a possible link to the Poe murders."

"What? How can that be? Unless Brock Bastyr worked for Medical Supplies Inc. in the last six months …"

"No, not Bastyr. Someone else." Alex looked apologetic. He held up one of Teresa Pinot's personnel files.

Mike took the file and read the name on top. Not recognizing it, he looked back at Alex and asked, "Who's Janice Toledo? Should I know her?"

"Janice Toledo?" echoed Danny. "Are you kidding me?"

"Okay, the rest of us give up," declared David. His tone was short, testifying to his impatience. "Who is she?"

"Janice Toledo is Cameron Cudney's ex-girlfriend. As in the same Cameron Cudney we've been looking at in the murder of Oscar Cudney, our first victim."

"But how could his ex be the Poe murderer?" asked David.

"She can't," argued Danny. "We've got our murderer locked up with a signed confession to boot."

"A confession with several inconsistencies," Mike reminded them.

"Remember what Rhonda said early on?" asked Chip. "She said there were so many murders close together that maybe there were two killers."

"So, Cameron and Janice are in this together? But why?" asked Blaine.

David threw his pen on the table. "A week ago, we didn't have even one suspect for ten murders. Now you're telling me we have *three*. Cameron Cudney, Janice Toledo and Brock Bastyr?"

"Four if you count Mr. Mount," said Blaine.

"Maybe it's all three," said Alex, obviously not counting Christian Mount.

The others stared at him, a wide range of incredulity written on their faces.

"No, just listen for a second." Alex ticked off on his fingers. "Maybe Janice Toledo stole the Temazepam and that has nothing to do with anything else. Maybe she wanted it for herself or wanted to sell the pills and make a little extra money. Cameron killed Oscar for the insurance money like we thought in the beginning, and Bastyr is the real Poe murderer." Alex smiled. "That would explain everything."

"Okay, hold on, hold on," Mike interrupted. "Let's not get ahead of ourselves."

Mike started to pace. His mind raced with this new information and what it implied.

"What we need are hard facts." He stopped in mid stride and looked at the wall. After a long moment, he said, "I've got an idea, but I want Rhonda here when we discuss it." He consulted his watch. "Danny, call Rhonda and see when she can join us via Skype. I know she's hip-deep in her other cases, but we really need her. In the meantime, I want everyone working on Bastyr's confession. We either need to confirm it or destroy it. And I want it done today."

~~

"Mike, your instincts were right on target," Alex said as he ended his call. "Bastyr has an alibi for both the Biddix and Henri murders. On the night Lylyanna Biddix was left in that bell tower, Bastyr was puking his guts out at a free clinic near Jackson Memorial, some sort of stomach bug. And we got an emergency subpoena for his VA medical records and they confirmed that he hurt his shoulder in that car accident and couldn't have stuffed Suzanne Henri up that chimney. He can't be our murderer."

"So, he really is a crazy who wanted publicity." David threw his pen down and it clattered as it rolled off the table and hit the floor.

"We always knew it was a possibility," said Chip. Although his tone was even, his shoulders slumped, and he put down his half-eaten sandwich.

"I need to call Zardes." Mike didn't look at his team as he walked out of the conference room.

~~

"You should have told us this before we had that news conference, Donaldson. You've made us look like fools on national TV. I'll have your badge for this." Zardes hissed his threat as he leaned toward Mike to intimidate him.

Mike had been summoned to Ronaldo Martinez's office where he found the SAC, Captain Mendez and Zardes waiting for him. There was a TV in a corner and although the sound was muted, Mike could see the reporter on the screen above the headline, **FBI FOOLED BY FAKE CONFESSION**. He had not been asked to sit down and Mike was sure he was going to be kicked off the investigation and out of Miami.

"Agent Zardes," Martinez interrupted, "Stand down. Confrontation is not going to help this situation. Nor are empty threats." The SAC turned toward Mike. "Agent Donaldson, Agent

Zardes stated that you reported to him after you'd finished taking the suspect's statement but made no mention of any discrepancies. Can you explain the sequence of events?"

"Sirs," Mike included Mendez in his response, "I took a copy of Bastyr's statement to Agent Zardes as soon as I got it and reviewed it. But when I arrived at his office, he already had a copy and told me he'd read it through. I did tell him we were just starting to confirm Bastyr's claims and that I felt a press conference might be premature. I mentioned there were a couple of points I wasn't satisfied with."

"What points?" asked Captain Mendez. It was the first time he'd spoken since Mike entered the room.

"Mainly that Bastyr didn't give us anything that wasn't already reported in the papers. He wouldn't say how he'd chosen his victims and was extremely vague about how he drugged them. Also, he didn't mention Oscar Cudney at all, just as the killer's letter left him out. I was uneasy about it and as soon as we got the typed confession, I ordered my team to find some concrete evidence that Bastyr was our killer."

"But you didn't raise these points with Agent Zardes?"

"As I said, Captain, I tried, but Agent Zardes overruled me. He pointed out that people don't usually confess to multiple murders if they're not guilty. I was still concerned, but since I had nothing concrete to point to, I deferred to my superior's opinion. I did order my team to continue investigating the confession, however, to be sure of our facts. And as soon as we confirmed that Bastyr had an alibi for one and was physically unable to carry out another, I reported our findings to Agent Zardes."

"I see, Agent Donaldson."

Neither Martinez nor Mendez said anything more and the silence stretched for several long moments. Mike wondered if he should offer to leave the investigation. Certainly, that would look better on his record than if he were forced out, but Mike wasn't sure that was the way to go. Maybe he should have been more forceful in his objections to Zardes, but he doubted anyone else could have done any better.

"Before Bastyr confessed, what was the status of the investigation, Agent?" asked Mendez.

Mike proceeded to summarize the main points of the case; the murders themselves, as well as the various lines of inquiry they had pursued. He mentioned that they released Mount on Zardes's order and ended with the new revelation of Janice Toledo's connection to both Oscar Cudney and the Temazepam. When he was finished, he waited patiently to hear what his fate would be.

CHAPTER 41

For my own part, I intend to believe nothing henceforward that has anything of the 'singular' about it.

'THE ANGEL OF THE ODD: AN EXTRAVAGANZA'

By three in the afternoon, Mike learned that he would be staying on the investigation as Case Agent. He assumed Zardes had pushed to have him removed, but Mike guessed that he'd been overruled by Martinez and Mendez. He was embarrassed that he'd believed Bastyr's confession at all and wanted more than ever to prove himself to Mendez and Martinez. They'd stuck their necks out for him and he wanted desperately to keep them from regretting it.

For now, the task force would continue investigating Cameron Cudney and Janice Toledo. Martinez felt Mount was insignificant and that either Cameron or Janice were the better suspects. Even if they proved both were innocent, that would still be progress, if negative. They had to keep plugging away. They'd lost time while focusing on Brock Bastyr and needed to make it up. Something was bound to give them the lead they needed. Mike refused to consider that they might never find this maniac.

Somewhile later, the entire team, including Rhonda via Skype, were assembled, discussing the latest developments. Mike began by updating Rhonda about Alex's surprising discovery, then asked the investigators to report on what they'd uncovered concerning Janice Toledo.

Alex Welch began by displaying on the monitor a picture of Cameron Cudney's ex-girlfriend. Janice Toledo had stringy blonde hair, cut in a 1980's feather-back style. Her wide-set eyes were brown with long, mascara-covered lashes, and her smile was inviting, despite the gap between her two front teeth. She seemed to be posing inside a gym or exercise facility and was dressed in a sports bra and athletic shorts while holding a hand weight.

"Janice Toledo is thirty-years-old and currently unemployed," said Alex. "She grew up in Pennsylvania, but her family moved to Miami when she was fifteen. She graduated from Florida International University where she majored in English and minored in Creative Writing. She started graduate school but didn't finish. She's never been married, has no criminal record, just a couple of tickets for speeding. Her interests are basketball and weightlifting, and she has a gym membership where she works out daily. She's not involved in any outside groups except for a membership with 'Friends of the Library', where she volunteers at book sales to benefit the library. From a personal standpoint, she's pretty boring, actually." Alex finished as he closed his notebook with a loud *slap*.

"But her job history is a little more interesting," stated Blaine as she took her place as the center of attention. "After college, Janice got a job as an editor of a free weekly. She stayed at the magazine for almost three years, editing and writing reviews of movies, books, or art shows in Miami. She left the magazine and got the job at Medical Supplies Inc., where she worked until four months ago. She started out as a receptionist/salesperson but moved up until she was Ms. Pinot's assistant, so she'd know all about the inventory."

"Why'd she leave?" asked Danny from his seat in the back.

"She told Ms. Pinot that she and Cameron were planning on getting married, even though he hadn't actually asked her yet, and she wanted to be a stay-at-home wife and mother and planned on having a big family. Ms. Pinot tried to convince Janice to stay, at least until she was formally engaged. She advised Janice not to count her chickens before they hatched, but Janice was adamant. Ms. Pinot said she wouldn't listen to anything she had to say. So, Janice quit, and Ms. Pinot hasn't seen her since."

"Any idea how Janice and Cameron met?" asked David as he took notes.

"That would be me," stated Chip as he addressed the group. "I got most of my info from Janice's Facebook page, which she hasn't changed even though she and Cameron are no more. Apparently, the two of them met in the Empower Gym where both had memberships. Cameron, by the way, worked at the *Miami Herald* as a research assistant in the Lifestyles section at that time. Anyway, from her postings, Janice and Cameron got hot and heavy pretty quickly and were all but inseparable after just a few months. There are lots of pictures of the two of them in various places, as well as working out together. A few months ago, Janice started hinting at an upcoming 'change' in their relationship and mentioned an 'important date' in her future. But nothing specific ever came of it."

"So, she wanted to get married and live the great American dream, but Cameron didn't?" guessed David.

"Probably."

Mike took over the briefing. "I didn't want to believe it at first, but the more I think about it, the more I think it's too coincidental that the girlfriend of our first murder suspect happens to have worked at a medical supplies store and has access to the drug our killer uses. Remember," Mike looked around the room at each of his investigators, "we raised the possibility of our killer being a woman. Well, Janice Toledo looks like a possible suspect to me."

The room was silent as everyone considered their boss' suggestion. After a few moments, David spoke. He hated to burst anyone's bubble, but someone had to be logical about this.

"But. Mike, we haven't found any connection for Cameron to any of our murders, except his cousin. Why would Janice leave herself open to suspicion? Remember, she gave Cameron his alibi until she got pissed at him for gambling. If she's the killer, ruining Cameron's alibi also ruined her own. And on top of that, they broke up. How can they be behind these murders if they aren't together anymore?"

Before Mike could reply, David continued, "And what motive could she have to do it alone? Killing cousin Oscar only helped Janice if she were married to Cameron when he got the insurance money. If convicted of the murder, he'd get nothing, so she wouldn't either. There was no reason to start a killing streak once Cameron was out of jail." David shook his head as he finished.

Alex responded before Mike could speak. "Let's say Janice killed Oscar Cudney, with or without Cameron's help. She wanted to get married and figured, if Cameron had the old man's money, he'd commit. Then the police discover that Cameron was gambling on the night of the murder and she reneges on her alibi to get payback." Alex stalled a minute, then admitted, "However, I don't know how we go from that to the Poe killings once Cameron's out of jail."

"If Janice and Cameron were involved with Cousin Oscar's murder together, why the breakup?" asked Blaine. "After he was cleared, he'd still get the ten thousand and at least split it, enough to keep them from ratting on each other."

Alex offered, "Remember, Cameron had the key to the old man's house, being the one who got the groceries and meds and took him to his appointments. Maybe Cameron kept her out of it so she could give him the alibi and, now he doesn't have anything to prove she was involved."

"Okay," interjected David, "the theory is that Cudney's murder is victim zero. It fits with the Poe murders, except for the Temazepam. Why use that method to kill the old man? If they were in it together, whose idea was it? If Cameron's idea, why would

Janice keep on murdering after he was cleared? If her idea, why would he go along with such a brutal crime? And, if she murdered the old man alone, she still needed him for her alibi."

"If anything," Blaine took up the discussion, "they were in it together. They conspire to kill Oscar. Janice thinks they're going to get married, but she blows the alibi. Then he gets out and they find out it's not as much money as they thought." Blaine hesitated, then shrugged. "But I admit I'm stumped after that. When did they get back together? Why the weird killing streak?"

"Our red herring," Chip joined in. His eyes were dancing, and his voice rose. "Maybe it's like I said before. One victim is the target, and all the others are red herrings. That's why the letter to the paper didn't mention Oscar Cudney. Because it brings us back to Cameron."

Mike nodded. "That's not bad, Chip, not bad at all." He looked at the group. "Maybe one's doing all the planning and the other the actual killing."

"Or they're taking turns," suggested David. "It would be easier for Janice to get close to the women while Cameron took care of the men."

No one said anything for a while, and then Rhonda spoke up. "Blaine, when you interviewed Ms. Pinot, did she have anything to say about Janice's demeanor or behavior when she discussed Cameron?"

Blaine considered for a moment. "She didn't say anything other than what I already said. But, by what she *implied*, I got the distinct impression that she felt Janice was reading too much into the relationship and counting on something that wasn't really there."

"Wasn't really there?" repeated Danny. "What do you mean by that?"

"I mean that Janice was seeing Cameron's feelings for her as stronger than what they really were."

Danny nodded as he made a note on the paper in front of him.

"Why do you ask, Rhonda?" asked David.

"Because I can see where this could go and from a psychological viewpoint, it could make sense. But before I commit myself, I'd like more information about her and her background. Would it be possible for me to interview her?"

"I'm not sure how we can arrange that right now," responded Mike. "We have no reason to interview her about anything, much less bring a profiler in. But, if we get anything actionable and I can find a way, I'll make it happen," he promised.

Mike paced a second, then said, "I understand your positions. Right now, all we have are theories. We need proof and since we don't have other suspects, I'm going with my gut. We'll look into Janice Toledo and assume she and Cameron are working together. Maybe we can tie her to one or more of the crime scenes. Maybe he's the mastermind and she does the dirty work. Or vice versa. Here's what I want …"

Danny's computer pinged and Mike saw him jump at the unexpected sound. While handing out assignments to the rest of the team, a low gagging sound made him turn back to Danny. Danny's face was ashen, and he gulped down his water.

"I guess I already know what's happened," Mike said with sympathy. "But you'd better tell us anyway."

Danny nodded. "Yeah, you're right, boss. There's been another murder." He stopped and drew in a deep breath as if trying not to gag again. "It definitely fits the bill. I don't envy you having to go to this one."

CHAPTER 42

There are certain themes of which the interest is all-absorbing, but which are too entirely horrible for the purposes of legitimate fiction.

'The Premature Burial'

August 17

Chip couldn't look at the crime scene photos for another minute. Despite knowing the scene would most likely be gruesome - Edgar Allan Poe's calling card, after all - he almost lost his lunch when confronted with the actual images from the most recent death.

Forty-two-year-old Jeremiah Twitchell was tied to a table in an abandoned building in northern Hialeah. On the floor was a truly astonishing amount of blood that had flowed freely from the victim's body when the African American man had been literally cut in half by a round blade made of steel swinging directly above him. Almost as disturbing was the hole cut into the floor to the right of the table that held a half-dozen or so large rats trapped inside by a mesh screen over its top. The rats had air to breathe and water in a puddle in the hole to drink but had been driven to near frenzy from the coppery smell of human blood, which they could not reach.

As the rest of the team entered the conference room and sat around him, Chip read through the preliminary coroner's report again. Twitchell had been strapped to the table and was fully conscious during his death. Also, unsurprisingly, Meghan Richmond had found the killer's calling card: Temazepam in his bloodstream. Apparently, the drug had been used to sedate the victim while the killer set his gruesome scene, then after the drug wore off, the murder was completed.

It was an unusually hideous death. The blade had hung above the victim and, as it swung in a downward arc, it gradually descended until it began to slice into the man's stomach, eventually slicing him in half. The ME calculated that it had taken two dozen passes before the cut was complete, but death occurred long before that. Not merely from loss of blood, for Meghan also found that Jeremiah Twitchell suffered a stroke, probably brought on from sheer terror, which contributed to his death.

"I got here as soon as I could," stated Rhonda Sagan as she entered the room. "SAC Martinez asked my supervisor if I could transfer down here while this case was going on and she agreed. I packed a few things and jumped in my car right away. So, you're stuck with me for a while."

Everyone brightened at this news, the best they'd received for several days. Having the profiler on site might give them more detailed insights quicker and help catch this nut case sooner.

The FBI profiler moved to the front of the room and sat in the first available chair. "I just got your most updated message when I hit town. I knew that he struck again, but your message said there was a problem." The Irish woman looked directly at the team leader. "What's going on?"

"The scene's pretty gruesome," Mike began as he gave a photo to the profiler. "We're sure this has to be our guy. Meghan's already confirmed the Temazepam, but our problem is with the Poe story. It's not right."

Rhonda, after studying the crime scene photo, asked, "What do you mean 'not right'?"

"Danny can explain it better than me. Guys, let's get Rhonda up to speed."

Danny nodded as he began the explanation. "It wasn't hard to figure out which Poe story this murder was recreating. 'The Pit and the Pendulum' is one of Poe's most famous stories."

"Yeah," interrupted Blaine, "even I remember reading it in school, and I hated lit class."

"I didn't even know they had literature classes in Nebraska, Blaine," grinned Mike.

Ever since he and Blaine started working out most days, the back-and-forth banter about their respective home states had been ongoing. As such, Mike enjoyed teasing her about her rural upbringing whenever possible.

There were appreciative chuckles around the room and, while Mike was glad he could release the tension a bit, he needed to get everyone back on task. "Back to 'The Pit and the Pendulum'."

Danny told Rhonda, "The thing is that in Poe's story, *no one* dies."

"I'm sorry?" asked a startled Rhonda.

"No deaths," confirmed Danny. "'The Pit and the Pendulum' takes place during the Spanish Inquisition. The narrator is arrested and tortured and then thrown into a dark room. He wanders around and finds a pit but has no idea what's in it. Later, his food is drugged and when he wakes up, he's tied to a table. Above his head he sees a pendulum that starts swinging and as it does so, it comes closer and closer to him."

Danny put the crime scene on the monitor. "So far, the scene our killer set up is the same. Mr. Twitchell was drugged, then brought to this room in an abandoned warehouse. The ME estimates he was in that room for several days before the killer apparently drugged him again and tied him to a table in the middle of the room. He even removed a section of the flooring, dug a hole and in that hole threw in some rats.

"In Poe's story, there are also rats. However, the narrator in the story takes some meat from the food he'd been given and rubs it on the straps around his wrists and waits while the rats chew through the straps so that he can get off the table just before the pendulum strikes him. Later, he is saved by the arrival of the French army and released."

Danny pointed to the monitor. "As you can see, here's the table, the straps that hold Twitchell, the hole representing the pit, the rats in the pit, but Twitchell wasn't as lucky as Poe's narrator. The rats can't get out of the hole and the pendulum cut Twitchell in half and he bled to death."

"Yes, I see your problem," nodded Sagan. "Our killer went to a lot of trouble to set the scene to recreate 'The Pit and the Pendulum' but whereas Poe let his narrator live, our killer used the pendulum to kill his victim. So, he changed the outcome of the story to make sure someone died." Waiting a beat, Rhonda stated, "I think we've gotten to the escalation we were waiting for."

"Could he be running out of stories to base his murders on?" asked Chip. "Why does it have to be an escalation?"

"No, there are plenty of Poe stories as well as poems left that have deaths in them," responded Danny. "And remember, 'The Bells' was a poem that didn't have a specific death mentioned. Our killer *made* it a murder by drugging Lylyana Biddix and leaving her in the bell tower to die from the peal. Dr. Barty and I have gone through all of Poe's stories and poems, and there are still more that have deaths of one kind or another that could meet our killer's needs. He didn't need to use 'The Pit and the Pendulum'."

"No, he didn't," repeated Mike. "So, you think this is the escalation?" he asked Rhonda.

"Yes, I do," confirmed the profiler. "And for two reasons. First, this was by far the bloodiest and most gruesome murder so far."

"I don't know that I agree with you there," interrupted Alex Welch. "I think 'The Black Cat' murder beats this one. Or even 'The Tell-Tale Heart'. Think about all the dead animals. Lucy Benton, axed to death. And in the Cudney murder, the victim was dismembered, and his body parts buried inside a house. If that's not gruesome, I don't know what is."

"I understand what you're saying, Detective," agreed Rhonda. "However, neither of those deaths had nearly as much blood as this latest one, and even though the rats were still alive in the pit, according to this report they were in such a frenzy from the smell that animal control had to be called and the rats killed anyway. That speaks of more than just torture. The killer must have gotten a perverse kind of pleasure from realizing how crazy those rats would become. If animal control hadn't been called, those rats probably would have tried to bite and attack the officers on the scene. What's more," continued Rhonda, "I think using a Poe story that doesn't have a death and changing it to include one, means the killer wants to make us notice him. The longer this goes on, the more horrific and spectacular the murders are going to get."

Unfortunately, Rhonda Sagan could not have been more correct.

CHAPTER 43

The object, Truth, or the satisfaction of the intellect, and the object, Passion, or the excitement of the heart, are, although attainable, to a certain extent, in poetry, far more readily attainable in prose.

'THE PHILOSOPHY OF COMPOSITION'

August 18

Mike was in a foul mood. He'd just gotten his ass handed to him by Zardes for releasing Christian Mount and 'letting another murder happen'. Mike didn't even bother to argue that it was Zardes who'd ordered him to release Mount; he knew it would do no good. Besides, he had confirmed Zardes's order in an email, so he had written proof of the sequence of events if Martinez or Mendez brought the subject up. He simply hated having to watch his back every minute, keeping proof of every interaction with the SAC, and the general feeling of helplessness the entire situation gave him. As he descended in the elevator, he willed himself to project a veneer of calm and poise before joining his waiting team.

Mike had handed out assignments and the team dove into the work with renewed energy. He gave them twenty-four hours before they got back together to discuss their findings.

David and Blaine oversaw the surveillance details, with Blaine following Janice and David tailing Cameron. Both MDPD detectives had a great deal of experience in surveillance and, given they would need help from the local police as well as one of the FBI's special teams to watch two separate suspects, Mike gave them a great deal of latitude in assigning teams and reporting in. For now, he only required them to update him at shift change unless something unusual came up.

Chip had drawn the job of delving even further into Janice Toledo's life. Mike wanted everything from her childhood to the present day checked out, including family, friends, and relationships. As the case agent put it, "If she cheated on a high school English test, I want to know what the answer was."

Along with this, it was decided that another interview with Cameron Cudney was in order. Chip was to take Alex along since he had more experience with this type of interview. They needed to be careful in what they said to their suspect's ex-boyfriend, but it was essential to get Cameron's view of Janice Toledo.

Alex would renew the investigation into Christian Mount's alibis. They needed to determine once and for all if Mount was the Poe murderer, involved only with Stephan Hardison's murder, or entirely innocent. Alex believed the first theory while Mike had been leaning toward the last until this latest murder. Now he wasn't sure if Mount was guilty or if it was a coincidence that the murder occurred after his release.

Finally, Danny had the hardest task of all. It was his job to reexamine each murder for anything to connect Janice Toledo with any of them. Did she know any of the victims? Could she be connected to any of the places the murders had occurred? Had she possibly been seen near the areas at some point prior to the murders? Except for the Temazepam, there was nothing to connect her with the Poe murders and *that* was tenuous at best; even Teresa Pinot said she didn't know who stole the drug, and Temazepam was so common anyone could have accessed it. They needed something more tangible if they were going to build a case against her.

While all of this was going on, Mike continued to run the day-to-day operation of a large, intense investigation. Paperwork had to be completed, resources requested and distributed, and his daily reports to Zardes written and submitted. The personal meetings got him down the most. Ever since Blaine had told him that Zardes was actively working against him behind the scenes, Mike found himself barely able to be in the same room with the SSA, and keeping his temper was proving to be a challenge. After the Bastyr debacle, Zardes's attitude toward him was even worse. He questioned almost every move Mike made and asked for explanations of every decision. Mike had enough of his own doubts without having to contend with pressure from Zardes as well. Many nights found him lying in bed, unable to sleep and wondering if he was in over his head.

Therefore, it was a tired crew that met up in the conference room. The public had not been told that the murders were occurring on dates related to Poe's life, so only the law enforcement officers were aware that the next murder might take place tomorrow. And this looming deadline weighed heavily on Mike. He agreed with Rhonda that 'The Pit and the Pendulum' death had upped the gruesome factor and the next could be worse. He was determined to do his best to prevent that from happening.

"Okay, let's get started," announced Mike as he joined his waiting team. "David, Blaine, anything interesting with the surveillance?"

"Not really," answered Blaine. "Toledo has been going about what appears to be normal business. She went out to eat twice, went to the library and did some shopping, but nothing unusual. The only thing I can see that *might* be strange, is the fact that she's staying so long at these places when there."

She picked up a report and started summarizing it. "Surveillance timed her every place she went, and for lunch she stayed at the deli for over two-and-a-half hours and, when she had dinner, she stayed at the restaurant for nearly as long. We didn't see her talk to anyone, but she had a legal pad with her and was writing something the whole time. In between those meals, that's when she went to the library. She stayed there for over three hours. One of our guys went in and reported she looked through the stacks for most of that time, taking books down here and there, but put them all back and didn't check anything out. It doesn't make sense."

"Well, maybe it does," stated Danny from his seat at one of the tables near the door. "She's unemployed, remember. She doesn't have anything else to do, so she's wandering the library and taking an inordinate amount of time over her meals. Maybe she's just trying to fill her day."

"Well, I have to admit, I didn't think of that," admitted Blaine. "I suppose it could be as simple as that."

"David, what's up with Cameron?" Mike asked.

"Nothing much, boss." David sighed. "He went back to work at the newspaper and goes to the gym regularly. What's interesting is that he changed gyms. He and Janice used to hang out at Empower, but now Cameron goes to The Ultimate Gym in South Miami. It looks like he's trying to avoid her, but that could be a ruse.

"Anyway, the only other thing is that he got a lawyer and is trying to get the money that Oscar left him. The insurance company is withholding the check because Cameron was listed as a suspect. Although he was released, they say they have the right to hold the funds if there's any doubt. And until someone else is arrested, charged and found guilty, they're refusing to pay."

"Bet he's pretty pissed about that," commented Chip.

David's only response was a nod.

"Okay, guys, keep at it," said Mike. "Let's keep up the surveillance for a couple more days and see what we get. I don't want to chance missing something." Mike turned to Chip. "What have you found out about Janice?"

"Nothing. She really is kinda boring. She pays her bills on time, doesn't seem to be too extravagant in her buying habits and just goes about her daily life. As for relationships, I'm still trying to get in touch with a few more people," reported Chip, "but the people I did talk to so far all say the same thing: She's a nice woman. They all like her. Her editor from that free weekly she worked for said that she really wanted to write. Not journalism-type articles, but original fiction. He said she was using the job at the weekly as a kind of apprenticeship so she could learn more about writing and editing. She was constantly asking the editor to look at her work, but he wouldn't do it. He didn't want to start anything or have to disappoint her if her stuff wasn't any good."

Rhonda looked up quickly from where she was taking notes and asked, "What did her editor say about the review articles she wrote for the paper? Were they any good?"

"Yeah, he said she had a good style. That's why he kept her on."

"Do you think you could get me samples of her writing?"

"Already ahead of you, Rhonda," Chip answered with a grin. "The editor is sending over some of her stuff today."

"Good job, Chip," Mike said. "You get anything else?"

"I spoke to a few people in her Friends of the Library group. They think she's a nice, normal person who likes to read and say she was an active volunteer. Apparently, she quit the group a couple of months ago without explanation and no one has seen her since. And they said the same thing - she wants to be a writer. She showed this one guy I talked to, uh ..." Chip flipped through his notes. His hands began to shake slightly, and his face got red as he turned page after page. Finally, he found what he was looking for. "Uh, Denis Jersey, and he said her stuff was pretty well-written, but not very original. It was romantic stuff about star-crossed lovers who eventually get together and live happily ever after. He said real Harlequin Romance type stuff." Chip exhaled with relief when he put the notebook down.

"That's interesting," murmured Rhonda.

Mike pounced. "Why interesting, Rhonda?"

Startled that she'd been overheard, the auburn-haired agent responded, "Ms. Pinot said that Janice wanted to get married, stay home, have kids, right? And now you're saying her stories are like classic romance novels. I think that says a lot about her emotional state. I'd really like to read some of those stories."

"We'll see what we can do," promised Mike.

Writing romance was a far cry away from being a serial killer but if his profiler thought it important, he'd do whatever he could to get her the samples she wanted.

"What about Cameron Cudney?" asked Mike. "Did he have anything of interest to say?"

"Not really," answered Alex. "He said she wanted marriage, he didn't, and that's why they broke up. He *claimed* it had nothing to do with his gambling or the alibi she took back, but I don't buy it."

"Yeah, that is a bit of a stretch," agreed Mike.

It seemed more likely that Janice broke up with Cameron when she learned his secret. Before he could move on, Alex spoke up.

"I have a question." Alex nodded at Chip. "Chip's been looking into Janice's life right now, as well as her history. But what confuses me is how is she living? I mean, like Danny said, she's been out of work for months and because she quit her job, she can't get unemployment benefits, but she's still paying her bills on time. She has a nice apartment, a car she's making payments on, the regular telephone, electric and water bills, and she hasn't been late on any of them. Not even once. And now you say she's going out to eat twice a day. How is she paying for all this? Where's her money coming from?"

Mike's smile showed his approval. "Good point, Alex. We need to look more closely at her finances. You can help Chip with that next. Now it's your turn. What have you got on Christian Mount?"

"Bad news there, Mike." Alex looked like he had drank a stale beer as he said. "Just got a call as I was coming in for the meeting. Mount's in the wind."

Mike practically jumped out of his chair and repeated, "In the wind? How? When was the last time anyone saw him?"

"He didn't show up for work the day before yesterday, or today. His boss called and texted him, but no response. He figured Mount skipped for some reason and didn't report it. This morning, I asked a couple of uniforms to go look in on him while I was checking alibis and they just called to tell me he wasn't at work and not at home either. He's not answering his phone or texts. He's AWOL." Alex's eyes spoke his apology.

"Are you telling me that we had a possible suspect in custody, let him go after a false confession, had another murder, and now that suspect is in the wind? Can this get any fuckin' worse?"

"Mike," Blaine spoke into the silence that followed this outburst, "you said yourself you didn't think Mount was guilty. And when he was released, there was no reason to have him followed. Besides all that, Zardes ordered you to release him. This isn't your fault."

Mike huffed. "Yeah, tell that to Zardes when I have to report to him." He inhaled a breath and counted to ten. With a sigh, he said to Alex, "Put a BOLO out on him and follow up on any place he might go or anyone he might hide with. Let me know the minute you hear anything." Not waiting for Alex's acknowledgement, Mike turned to Danny. "I hope you have some good news for us, Danny."

"Not yet," admitted Danny reluctantly. "I started by looking at the locations the bodies were found and asked officers from MDPD to start re-canvasing for witnesses. But so far, nothing. Along those same lines," he added, "I've contacted the building and property owners and requested lease agreements or any other paperwork they have. It's only been a day, so I'm still waiting to hear back. It's too early to tell if we'll get anything useful."

Mike sighed again. He'd known Janice Toledo was a long shot, but at this point he wasn't above trying for the Hail Mary. However, it looked as if he was barking up the wrong tree, after all. Looking at his watch, Mike made a decision.

"Okay, we'll keep at the Toledo/Cudney angle for a couple more days. They could still be meeting in secret or something and surveillance might get lucky. If we haven't made any headway by then, we'll give up on them and go at this another way."

Mike looked at his team and saw the same disappointment tinged with apprehension mirrored in their faces as had to be evident in his. He figured it was time for a pep talk, but he didn't have any new words of wisdom.

"I know you guys are disappointed. Frankly, so am I. But I've said it before and I'll say it again, even negative information is better than nothing. If all this does is rule out Janice Toledo and Cameron Cudney, then that's one less thing we need to worry about. It's still progress. We have to keep that in mind."

The blank looks that met his gaze told him his pep talk didn't work. With nothing more to add, Mike ended the meeting with a simple, "Let's get to work."

~~

Danny waited by the elevator for the car to arrive. He drummed his fingers against his thigh and looked again at his watch. 4:30.

I hope this doesn't take too long.

Finally, the familiar ping announced the car's arrival and his guest got off. Danny forced a smile. "Good afternoon, Dr. Barty. Please follow me."

Standing next to Danny's 5' 10" frame, the 5' 5" University of Miami professor seemed even smaller than Danny remembered. Her skirt was tight-fitting and showed her burgeoning belly, while her lifeless hair hung straight down her back and made her round face more prominent. Danny noticed she wore make-up today, although the mascara was too thick and the blush too red. It looked more like a teenager's first attempt at beauty than a mature woman's everyday habit. Her purse was voluminous, and Danny wondered what in the world she could be carrying in it. He did his best not to stare as he led her through the maze of cubicles to Interview Room Three.

"I had hoped to speak to Agent Donaldson today, Agent McKissick."

Danny didn't bother to correct her by explaining *again* that he wasn't an agent. If she was more comfortable thinking he was one, then that's what he'd be for now. Besides, she sounded more anxious than angry, and he wondered again why she had called and asked to see them. Dr. Barty apparently didn't have a high opinion of law enforcement, but now she looked around the office with more curiosity than distaste. Did she think someone was going to pull out a gun and start shooting? Danny tried not to roll his eyes. She probably got all her ideas about law enforcement from TV shows and thought all police officers got into shootouts every week.

The reality was just the opposite. Most of the agents he worked with had never even pulled their guns, much less had to shoot anyone. He wanted to give Dr. Barty a more realistic view of the FBI and hoped he'd have the opportunity to do so at some point. For now, he'd show her as much courtesy as he could and reassure her when necessary.

"You will, Dr. Barty. When I told him you wanted to see us, Agent Donaldson changed his schedule so he could be here to meet with you. He's waiting for us in the interview room. It's just around the corner."

Dr. Barty raised a beefy hand to smooth her hair and Danny did his best not to laugh. *Mike has an admirer alright.*

This interview room was much nicer than the one he'd used before and he was glad he could offer Dr. Barty a glass of water and a comfortable chair to sit in. Once all three were settled and the pleasantries over, Mike got right to the point.

"I understand you have information for us, Dr. Barty. Mr. McKissick will be taking notes and we can certainly use your help. I'm sure you've seen the papers and understand now why we wanted to consult with you."

"Oh yes, that's why I'm here. Unfortunately, I had a small disaster at my home, then my poor mother was ill for a few days and in the hospital. I just got her back home two days ago and started catching up on my newspapers. I read them in order, you see."

Of course you read them in order. Danny barely caught himself from rolling his eyes.

Mike, however, was much more in control. "I'm very sorry to hear about your mother, Dr. Barty, and glad to know that she's getting better. I'm sure that's a great weight off your mind." He smiled and, for the first time, Danny noticed a dimple on his chin. "So, something in the newspaper accounts stood out for you, I suppose?"

Smooth, Mike. Nice way to get back on topic.

"Yes," began Dr. Barty breathlessly. She leaned forward and lowered her voice. "I couldn't believe that anyone would use Edgar Allan Poe as a model for murders! Or maybe I should more correctly say *misuse* because that's exactly what he's doing. It's a travesty and an insult to one of the greatest American writers ever. Such nerve. Really, I don't believe in the death penalty, but this madman deserves it if anyone does. How dare he defame Edgar Allan Poe in this way? Why it's absolutely criminal. It's ..."

"Yes, Dr. Barty, it is criminal," Mike cut in quickly. "And I'm sure you want to see us catch him before he can do more damage to Poe's reputation or hurt anyone else."

Danny had to admire Mike's handling of the woman. She was more upset about possible damage to Poe's reputation than the ten people dead at this maniac's hand, but Mike was treating it as a perfectly logical concern.

He's damned good at this. I could learn a lot from him.

"I am sure whatever you have to tell us will help us do that. Just what did you see in the paper, Dr. Barty?"

"Yes, of course. It's right here."

The University of Miami professor pulled two file folders from her over-sized purse. She opened the first and Danny saw clippings from the *Miami Herald*.

Dr. Barty looked up and addressed Mike. "When I saw the headline about a serial killer, I naturally read the article first. Then I jumped to the next day's paper and read as much as I could about the murders and how they related to Edgar Allan Poe. It wasn't until that second day's story that I understood there was an actual letter from the killer, so I went back to the day before's paper and read the letter." Her face suddenly took on a reddish hue and she stated, "I'm ashamed to admit I only skimmed over the descriptions of the murders themselves; I didn't want to read such horrible details, but I read the parts about Poe most carefully." Dr. Barty's normally dull brown eyes became bright with animation. "I realized the writer of this letter is well-versed on Poe. He or she did a great deal of research and shows some interesting insight."

I don't believe this! Of course, the killer knows a lot about Poe, for heaven's sake. This is gonna be a colossal waste of our time.

"Yes, Dr. Barty," Mike responded, "we also believe the murderer is an expert on Poe. Does that ring a bell for you?"

"As a matter of fact, it does." Dr. Barty pulled out a sheet of paper from the second file. "You see, there aren't many students who study early American literature anymore and almost no one specializes in Poe, so when I read about this killer, well, I thought it was extremely unusual." She paused as if expecting something.

"And I'm sure you were right," responded Mike on cue.

Dr. Barty visibly preened. "Yes, there are so few students of Poe these days. It's very sad, of course."

Dr. Barty threw him a quick look and Danny realized she must have heard his sigh.

"But I digress," she continued. "Since I'm the only Poe expert in Southwest Florida, I end up being the thesis adviser for any graduate students studying him. Some come up through UM and some transfer over from other institutions. There haven't been many over the years, mores the pity, but on the off chance it would help, I brought a list along. I thought you might be able to contact these people and they might be able to give you information that would aid your investigation."

Dr. Barty handed Mike the paper and Danny saw it held only a handful of names.

This should be easy to check up on.

Mike took a cursory glance at the sheet and Danny heard his intake of air. He was even more surprised when the case agent wrapped the interview up quickly.

"We're very grateful to you, Dr. Barty, for bringing this to our attention." He stood up and held out a hand to her.

Dr. Barty's eyes grew wide then narrowed. She was obviously trying to frame an appropriate response, but Mike spoke first, "If we need to consult with you again, I hope we can count on your help. But since I know how busy you are, we're going to let you get back to work now and, of course, to your recovering mother. Mr. McKissick will escort you back to the elevators."

He gave her that dimpled smile and Jeniviere Barty melted again. She returned the handshake and picked up her folders and purse. Danny gave Mike a knowing grin and led their academic consultant out of the room.

~~

Mike pushed open the door to the conference room with so much force, papers throughout the room glided to the floor.

"Heads up, everybody. Give me your attention." Mike's voice held a tone of command that brooked no argument.

The members of VCMO looked up in surprise. Blaine's mouth formed an O, while both David and Alex abruptly ended phone conversations and Chip dropped the Poe Companion he was studying.

Just then the door opened again, and Danny entered at a near run. "Mike. What is it? What'd you see on that list?"

"Maybe the answer." Mike held up the paper. "Dr. Barty gave us the names of five graduate students she's worked with over the last ten years who studied Edgar Allan Poe." He turned to his analyst. "Danny, read number two."

Danny took the paper and immediately his eyes grew wide and he cursed. He looked back up, first at Mike then at the rest of the team. "Janice Toledo."

CHAPTER 44

We had birds, goldfish, a fine dog, rabbits, a small monkey, and a
cat.
'THE BLACK CAT'

August 19

The next day loomed large for the Poe Murders task force, and Dr.
Barty's bombshell of yesterday had given each of them new hope
that they were indeed on the right track with Janice Toledo and
simply needed to dig deeper to find the missing link. Janice might
be smart, but the men and women of the group investigating these
murders were determined, if Janice was their murderer, or Janice
and Cameron were working together, they would bring them to
justice.

Everyone had worked late into the night, taking only four-hour
rest breaks on the couches upstairs in turns. Now, as they were
gathering again at six o'clock, no one knew if today would bring a
much-needed breakthrough or another day of frustration.

"Who bought the donuts?" asked David as he made a beeline
for the sugary confections in their boxes on the back table.

"Me," answered Chip as he bit into his crème-filled pastry.

"You mean you're sucking up to the boss," translated Blaine
in a playful tone.

"Hey, works for me!" exclaimed Alex as he grabbed a cinnamon twist. "I have no problem with Chip trying to get on Mike's good side if I get to enjoy the benefits, too!"

Several chuckles were heard as the rest of the team grabbed some breakfast and sat down for the morning briefing.

"Okay," Mike addressed the group as he chuckled in turn, "let's start with Janice's academic background. Whaddya find out, Alex?"

Alex wiped his hands on a napkin and picked up his notebook. "Janice graduated from Florida International University with a major in Literature and a minor in Creative Writing. She seems to have concentrated her classes as much as possible on early American authors and poets. FIU doesn't have a graduate program in Literature, so she transferred to UM and worked on her Master's under Dr. Barty. She never finished, but her unfinished thesis was titled, 'The Macabre in the Short Stories of Edgar Allan Poe and its Influence on Late Nineteenth Century Literature'."

"Good work, Alex. Do we know why she didn't finish her Master's?"

"Money apparently," he answered. "She had a grant, but funding was cut, and she couldn't get another, so she had to quit. That's when she got the job at that free weekly. I guess she figured she'd try to save some money and get back to her Master's later." Alex shrugged.

"Okay, that's another tie for Janice Toledo to this case. She had access to Temazepam, was Cameron Cudney's girlfriend, so she knew Oscar, and she's well-versed in Poe and his work. That still doesn't tie her to the murders, though. But I'd like to think we're on the right track anyway."

"Gotta be, Mike," said David. "I think we're back to Janice being the mastermind and Cameron the actual killer."

"Maybe, but we still don't have a good motive, nothing that makes much sense anyway." This came from Chip, who was devouring his third donut.

"Maybe not, but motive doesn't make a case," said Mike.

"It does for most juries, we all know that," responded Blaine. Her look spoke volumes about her views on fickle juries.

Mike nodded. "True, I'll grant you that. Murder just for the fun of it doesn't often cut if for most juries. However, when we arrest her, or them, we'll ask why they did it. And if their lawyer's no good, they might just answer." Everyone snickered a bit at that and Mike decided to move on. "Let's see where we're at from yesterday. Who wants to start?"

"I think I might have something," Blaine spoke up. At Mike's acknowledging nod, the lovely agent reported to the group, "I was looking at the information on 'The Black Cat' murder again and thought of something. Remember how in the story Danny told us that one of the dead animals was a monkey? And that there was a dead monkey found in the room with Lucy Benton?" Several heads nodded. "Well, it occurred to me that monkeys aren't exactly common pets even in a big city like Miami. I thought I might get a lead on our killer through the monkey."

"That's brilliant!" said David as Alex and Chip both chimed in, "Good thinking, Blaine."

"Did you find anything?" asked Mike. His tone was calm, but his eyes were wide with hope.

"Maybe. There are only four pet stores in Miami-Dade County that sell monkeys and, because they are an unusual pet, all four stores keep records detailing who bought one. Now, I was able to reach those stores and two have already sent me their records for the past two months and I'm now waiting on the last two. I haven't got anything yet, but we won't know for sure until I get those last two stores' records."

"Good job, Blaine," complimented the case agent. "When you get those last records, let me know."

Blaine held up her hand and cautioned, "I have to tell you, though, that every one of those store owners told me the same thing. There is a big black-market business for exotic pets and it's very possible that no matter who our murderer is, he or she could just have easily gotten that monkey from one of those brokers. In that case, there won't be a trail to follow. It may end up being another dead end."

"I hear you, Blaine," agreed Mike, "but I'm gonna be optimistic and hope we get a lead from that monkey. That was a great idea."

Chip spoke up. "What about food? I mean, I never cared much for Tarzan movies, but I assume monkeys eat more than just bananas. Maybe she didn't buy the monkey at one of those shops, but maybe she bought its food at one of them."

"Now why didn't I think of that?" asked Blaine with a shake of her head. "It's inspired."

"It sure is," agreed Mike. "Good thinking, Chip." He turned to Blaine. "You'll have to call them back and ask about the food. I don't know what monkeys eat either, but it's definitely worth a shot."

Alex cleared his throat. "I hate to throw a monkey wrench into your enthusiasm, no pun intended," he said in response to the groans around the room, "but I'm not sure the food idea's gonna go anywhere either. I mean, think about it. Whoever our killer is, Janice Toledo, Cameron Cudney or someone else, they had to get that monkey for one reason and one reason only. To kill it. So why bother to buy special food or, for that matter, any food at all? I mean they probably just got it, took it to that room and killed it right away. She or he didn't need to feed it even once." Alex looked over at Chip. "Sorry. It is a good idea; I just don't think we should get our hopes up too much."

Chip nodded but Mike could see him wilt slightly. Damn. He'd worked so hard to bring Chip along, teaching him about murder investigations and trying to get him more comfortable with the more experienced team members in the group. And Chip had started to blossom, as it were. He was speaking up more at the briefings and putting forth his own ideas more often. Mike didn't want him to get discouraged.

"You're both right. Alex, you're right that the killer may not have needed any special food at all, but, Chip, it is a good idea and worth pursuing. I've said it before. We're not gonna discount any possible leads. This case is too weird, and we don't know what might lead us to our killer."

Mike was getting ready to go over the day's assignments when David's phone rang.

"Scotty here. Oh hey, Davis, what's up? … Really? When? … Okay, that is a bit weird … No, hang back and I'll get you back-up immediately. Keep me posted on this line … Good, be careful you're not seen."

After hitting the 'End' button on his phone, David immediately made a call. "Phillips, this is Scotty. I want you and Jenson to meet Davis on Cecilia Avenue in Coral Gables. Get there as fast as you can, but don't use the sirens within a mile of the place. We don't want her spooked. Call me when you get there."

David looked at Mike and reported, "That was Agent Zackery Davis on surveillance. Janice is on the move. She left her apartment at 5:30 this morning and went to a house in Coral Gables. She had a key and carried some boxes in. We've never seen her go to this place before and it could be something to check out. In the meantime, I've got Phillips and Jenson on their way to back him up and see if they can figure out what's going on."

"Is it an abandoned house?" asked Alex. "That's the killer's MO, you know."

"Yeah, I know," agreed David. "That's why I wanted to research the address. I'll see who owns it. Maybe this is our break, Mike. She could be setting up for the next murder."

~~

A short time later, David walked into the conference room with a large cardboard tube in his hand. He cleared off a table and pulled out a set of blueprints. As he unrolled and arranged them on the table he began to talk.

"This house on Cecilia Avenue is a two-story house that has been empty since the real estate bust. The owner went bankrupt and the house was foreclosed on. However, there haven't been any serious buyers and the house is just sitting there. I have Chip calling the bank manager now. They don't open for another hour-and-a-half, but we're going to ask him to go in early to get whatever information he can for us."

Mike asked, "What's the inside like?"

"Two floors with five bedrooms, three baths, kitchen, living room, dining room, breakfast nook and a screened-in lanai."

"That's one big-ass house," commented Alex Welch as he took a drink from his ever-present coffee.

Alex was a good officer, to be sure, but his need for strong, black coffee bordered on an addiction. Mike suddenly wondered if he'd ever seen the ruddy-faced man without a cup in his hand.

"It's over five thousand square feet. Who needs that kind of space?" continued the MDPD officer.

David and Blaine nodded in agreement, and before Mike could look at the plans himself, Chip ran into the room.

"Mike! I just finished talking to the bank manager. He was looking through his notes on the house and found that just last week, the real estate agent reported that a woman expressed interest in the house and did a walk-through. She asked a lot of questions about the size of each of the rooms and seemed really interested in how the house was constructed."

"Did she want to buy it?"

"Not buy, she asked about renting, but the foreclosure rules prohibit the bank from renting that particular house, so she walked away."

"Did he have the name of this woman?" asked Mike. His expression was hopeful, and his voice cracked a bit.

"He didn't, but he's going to call the real estate agent and tell her to expect a visit from us soon." Chip looked at Mike and took a breath. He cleared his throat and suggested, "I'd like to go, Mike. I thought I could take a photo of Janice Toledo along with me."

Mike started to pace and looked at his watch. Could this be the lead they needed at last? If they could tie Janice Toledo to this house and get a surreptitious warrant to search it, they might find something that could point to what the next killing was going to be or find evidence to tie her to one of the previous murders.

"Let's do this right, Chip," ordered Mike. "Take Alex with you for the interview and do a picture line-up. Take at least seven other photos and see if the real estate agent picks out Janice. Odds are pretty good she wouldn't have used her own name and I'll bet my bottom dollar that she never intended to take the house, she just wanted to scout it out to see if it would suit whatever purpose she has for it. Whatever name the agent gives you, you need to check to be sure it wasn't someone with a legitimate interest in the house. I mean, probably not, since Janice has apparently broken into the house for some reason now, but you never know. We need to be sure."

"On it, Mike." Chip turned away, but instead of heading to his desk to get his jacket and keys, he walked down the hall toward the stairway.

CHAPTER 45

I have great faith in fools—self-confidence my friends will call it.
'MARGINALIA'

This was the part of the day Mike hated most. His evening briefings with Zardes were excruciating and sometimes even humiliating. He hated the man's functional office. It had no personality, perfectly reflecting the man himself. *Unless you count hating me as personality.* He hated the way Zardes looked down on him, his snide comments and remarks always trying to bait Mike into saying something that would have him up on charges of insubordination. He hated how Zardes second-guessed every move, every decision he made. He could never relax in that office.

Mike knew from Blaine that Zardes wanted him to screw up so he, Zardes, could take over the investigation and succeed, thus putting him in a better position the next time he applied for an SAC job somewhere.

Zardes was nothing if not predictable. The meetings always followed the same pattern. Mike would review almost word for word the information from his written report, sent to Zardes a minimum of two hours before the meeting. From Zardes's questions and comments, Mike decided he never actually read the reports and only insisted on them so there would be a paper trail when he tried to get Mike taken off the case again. After, Zardes would make snide comments about his progress, or lack thereof, then Mike would be dismissed with little or no civility.

Mike waited, standing, while Zardes finished a telephone conversation. Mike never sat in this office. Zardes had never asked him to, but Mike wouldn't have anyway. The sooner he could get this over the better.

"I want that suit ready for my dinner Friday night," Zardes said into the instrument. He listened for a moment. "I don't care about the fire in your back room. You promised my suit would be ready yesterday and it's not. It better be ready tomorrow when I come to pick it up." The banging of the phone ended the conversation.

Zardes looked up at Mike as if he'd just noticed he was there instead of standing in front of his desk for the past three minutes. "Agent Donaldson," Zardes's tone was dismissive. "What do you have for me tonight? Are you anywhere closer to finding this maniac?"

Mike suppressed a sigh. "As I mentioned in my report, sir, we found out that Janice Toledo studied Edgar Allan Poe in college and her thesis project dealt with his works. We're also still surveilling her. This morning, she went to a house in Coral Gables; she apparently got a key to it from some place, and began taking some boxes in. It's a foreclosure and we've talked to the bank manager. We're trying to get in touch with the real estate agent but he's out of town until tomorrow. We'll do a photo line up to see if he recognizes Toledo. Tomorrow, Detective Hoskins and I will interview Cameron Cudney again. We want to see what he has to say about Janice Toledo. Maybe he can shed some light on her."

Mike noted Zardes's sneer when he mentioned Blaine and couldn't help but wonder why. As far as he knew, Zardes had never met her until that first briefing and, as he recalled, the two had not actually spoken. Zardes interrupted these thoughts with an unexpected question.

"Do you have an update on this monkey angle? That getting us anywhere?"

"No, sir. Detective Hoskins is contacting the four pet stores that sell monkeys, but she hasn't gotten anything concrete yet. We're still working that angle."

"What about Mount? Found him yet?"

"No Sir, he's still in the wind. However, Detective Welch finally located Mount's buddy. He gave Mount an alibi for two of the murders and we're convinced it's good. We kicked the case back to MDPD. If they want to continue the search because of those outstanding tickets, let 'em."

Zardes drummed his fingers on the desk and looked up. "Donaldson, it's no secret that I didn't think you could handle this investigation, and I still don't. You've been at this since July 24 and you got duped by a guy with a fake confession and let the only viable suspect go. Ten people are dead and you're no closer now to finding this whacko than you were twenty-six days ago. I'm giving you twenty-four hours. If you haven't made substantial progress by this time tomorrow night, I'm going to take a more hands-on approach to this investigation. Do I make myself clear?"

Mike stood up a little straighter and said simply, "Yes, sir. Perfectly."

~~

Walking back down the hall toward the elevator, Mike barely kept his temper. He had enough of his own doubts without Zardes piling more on, but at least in private meetings in his office, only he had to hear the SSA's snide comments. If Zardes took a more 'hands-on' approach, Mike had no doubt he wouldn't be diplomatic or pull his punches. He'd make his comments in front of the entire team and undermine him at every opportunity. Mike wasn't sure he'd be able to keep from hauling off and punching the asshole under those circumstances.

What did 'substantial progress' mean anyway? It wasn't his fault if the surveillance didn't have anything tangible yet or that Blaine hadn't been able to talk to all the managers at the pet stores. It'd only been this morning when they got that lead, and it might not go anywhere. It's not as if ...

Mike stopped in the middle of the hallway.

How'd Zardes know about the monkey at all?

He only mentioned the monkey lead in one sentence of his report and Mike would've bet twenty bucks Zardes never read them. He merely waited for him to report each night. So, how'd he known to ask about it? And, now that Mike thought about it, this was not the first time Zardes seemed to know something about the investigation that Mike hadn't specifically mentioned in his briefings. Was something else going on here besides Zardes wanting him out?

Or has someone else joined with Zardes to work against me?

CHAPTER 46

I was never kinder to the old man than during the whole week
before I killed him.

'THE TELL-TALE HEART'

August 20

They'd arranged to meet Cameron Cudney at a small deli down the
street from his office at the *Miami Herald*. Cudney had
understandably balked at meeting with them inside the building
where everyone could see them, but he'd agreed to during his lunch
hour. Blaine was surprised he'd agreed to do so without his lawyer
present, which would've been the smart thing to do. Especially, if
he was guilty, he'd want to be sure he said nothing incriminating.
On the other hand, he might also be overconfident and think he
didn't need an attorney to protect him.

We'll find out soon enough.

They finalized their strategy for interviewing Cameron on the
trip to Doral, knowing they had to tread carefully. The trick would
be to get the information they wanted while not letting Cudney
know they suspected him or his ex-girlfriend of being cold-
blooded serial killers. They decided to concentrate most of their
questions on Janice and hope that Cameron might somehow
incriminate her or himself by accident.

They arrived early and ordered sandwiches and chips. As they were eating, Blaine spotted Cameron enter the restaurant, but instead of acknowledging her wave, he walked up to the counter to order his own lunch.

Cameron Cudney looked older than his thirty-two years. His blond hair was flecked with gray and Blaine noticed that his hands were already slightly wrinkled. His blue eyes were bright, however, and his denim shirt did nothing to hide well-muscled arms and a flat stomach. Even if Blaine hadn't already been aware of the fact, just by looking at Cameron she'd have known the man worked out on a regular basis and took care of his body.

"What do you guys want again? I already talked to that other Fed a few days back," asked Cudney once he'd sat down. He pointedly hadn't shaken their outstretched hands.

"We're simply helping MDPD with their investigation, Mr. Cudney," Blaine answered. "We're checking some details and wrapping up some loose ends."

"What kind of loose ends?" Cameron leaned forward and Blaine got the feeling he was worried about where those loose ends might lead.

Mike fielded this one. "Let's start with your alibi. Or should I say *alibis*, Mr. Cudney? You didn't seem able to settle on just one." Mike opened the file he carried and pretended to search for something. "Yes, here it is. First you said you were home watching a movie, then you said you were out gambling. Now it appears you have no alibi at all for your cousin's murder. So," Mike leaned closer to the younger man, "which is it? Movie or gambling or neither?"

Cameron squirmed a bit. When he answered, his voice was laced with defiance. "Okay, yeah, I lied about being with Janice and watching a movie. I mean, I really was playing poker, I just didn't want Janice to know. Big deal. It's not my fault that Janice couldn't keep the story straight or that no one will admit to seeing me gamble. The game was illegal, ya know. But that doesn't mean

I killed Oscar. I liked the old guy. He took me in when I got to Miami and, ya know, didn't have any place to stay and no job. He let me stay with him until I got on my feet and I paid him back, ya know, by helping take care of him. I mean, I got his groceries, took him to his doctors, helped him with his money and bills, all that crap. Why would I kill him? I wasn't gonna get anything out of it, ya know. Ten grand. That's no reason to kill anybody and I didn't." He crossed his arms and sat back. "I didn't."

Blaine's gut told her something was wrong with that speech. It felt rehearsed somehow and if they didn't already think that Cameron Cudney was guilty, she'd be sure he was hiding something.

"I can see why you might not have wanted your girlfriend, uh, what was her name again, Mr. Cudney?" Blaine asked.

"Janice Toledo."

"Oh yes, Janice." Blaine smiled "I can understand why you didn't want Janice to know where you were that night, but surely you knew lying to the police would only make things worse. Why not just tell the police the truth, quietly, and let them investigate?"

"Yeah, a lot of good that woulda done me. They went to the place and nobody said they saw me. Now I still don't have an alibi. You guys are back here again because nobody believes me, but I didn't do it."

Blaine still felt something was wrong. Cudney was saying all the right things to protest his innocence, but the sincerity seemed forced. His speech had become less precise and Cudney's eye had started to twitch, a nervous tic that hadn't been there before.

"So tell us about Janice, Mr. Cudney," Mike asked with just the right amount of sarcasm in his voice. "How'd you two meet? How long were you dating? How'd you convince her to lie for you?"

Cameron's eyes widened, then narrowed. "Are you gonna talk to her?"

"We might, we haven't decided yet," Blaine asked. "If you think we should, answer Agent Donaldson's questions and we'll consider it."

Cameron weighed that for a moment, then he sighed. "It's simple enough. We met at the gym. We both went there almost every day at the same time, and we started talking. Then we went to a movie, then out to dinner. You know, the usual thing. After a little while, ya know, she wanted to be exclusive, so I went along with it. I didn't date any other women, ya know, I just didn't tell her about the gambling. Anyway, she started talking marriage and kids, but it was way too soon for that. We'd only been together about six months or so. She wanted to be a housewife and write her romance novels. I told her I couldn't support both of us on my salary, much less have kids, I mean, especially if she wasn't going to work. But she just didn't seem to understand reality, ya know? She really thought she was gonna be a writer and make a lot of money on that crap she wrote. I only read a couple of her stories, but they were stupid. I mean, it was just boy meets girl, they have some sort of adventure, then boy gets girl, and they live happily ever after. A bunch of crap. That's all it was."

"If you weren't happy, then why'd you stay in the relationship?"

Cameron took a minute to compose his answer. "I really did like Janice and she was a lot of fun and we both liked to work out. You know, it's not that easy to find a woman who understands working out and why it takes so much time and effort. Janice did, so ..." Cameron gave a shrug.

"That still doesn't explain why she gave you an alibi, Cudney," Mike added with an edge to his tone.

"Yeah, well, it does. You see, I told her I was innocent, and I am, by the way, but I needed an alibi. So, she believed me and wanted to help me, so we decided to say I was with her watching a movie and I stayed the night. I didn't know she was gonna forget which movie we were supposed to be watching. The stupid bitch."

Cameron didn't try to conceal the sneer in his voice, and he sat back once more crossing his arms yet again.

Blaine was almost impressed. If this was an act, it was a damned good one.

"So, you claim that the alibi from Janice was a fake, which she admitted, and your alibi of gambling in an illegal poker game is real. Is that right?"

"Yeah, Agent Donaldson, that's right. As I already said several times. Nobody's gonna admit to the gambling, but I was there long after Oscar was killed. I swear it. I didn't kill my cousin, Agent Donaldson. You have to find out who did and get me out of this. I'm innocent, I swear!"

Blaine noticed that tic was back. "So, if she loved you so much, why'd she take your alibi back? She could have found a way to get around not knowing the name of the movie. So, what happened?"

"She screwed up, that's what happened. She let the cops twist her around until she couldn't keep the story straight and she messed up everything."

"Learning you have a gambling habit was the real reason she broke up with you?"

"I suppose. I never thought she was that strait-laced, but I guess I was wrong. She just let them cops mess with her head, that's all."

"What's Janice doing now, Cameron?" asked Blaine. "Do you still see her at the gym?"

"Nah, I quit goin' to Empower. I didn't want to see her, have a scene or anything. I ain't seen her for months."

"We contacted Medical Supplies Inc. but they said she quit there a few months ago. Do you know where she is or if she got a new job?"

"Janice quit her job?" Cameron seemed genuinely surprised at that bit of news. "No, I didn't know anythin' about that." He thought for a moment. "Maybe she went back to writing. She worked for some newspaper before we met, so maybe she went back to that." He shrugged. "I don't know."

Cameron leaned forward again. "But it don't matter. I'm innocent, I tell ya. I had no reason to kill the old man." He pointed his finger at his chest. "I'm innocent. You find the real killer and get me out of this mess. I'm lucky my boss took me back, but you should see the looks I get from everybody back there. They act like I'm hiding an axe in my pocket and I'm gonna start killing everybody at any minute. I need to prove I'm innocent. I just want to go back to my life. It wasn't much, but it's a helluva lot better than this suspicion and until the cops find out who really did kill Oscar, no one's gonna believe it wasn't me."

CHAPTER 47

In our endeavors to recall to memory something long forgotten, we often find ourselves upon the verge of remembrance, without being able, in the end, to remember,

'Ligeia'

Mike was feeling the pressure on all sides. The media kept the Poe murders on the front page with analyses by so-called 'experts', stories about the backgrounds of the victims and pictures of the various murder scenes. The TV news led each evening's newscast with an 'update' on the progress - or lack thereof - of the investigation with a calendar counting how many days since the first murder. Bookstores reported a sellout of anything Poe-related and even the library announced that all Poe literature had been checked out. DVDs of movies based on Poe stories were rented at an unheard-of pace and Amazon reported sales were breaking all records.

Closer to home, Mike had to stop going to his favorite restaurant since word had gotten out that he was an FBI agent, and he couldn't enjoy a quiet meal anymore. He was constantly approached by people asking questions about the case or arm-chair quarterbacks giving him suggestions of how to find the killer. Now he sneaked around to the back entrance where Beverly kept a bag of food and a tray of coffee waiting for him every morning.

Her smile was about the only bright thing in his life right now. He had to face Zardes every day with nothing to show for his work and he spent most of his time wondering who was working with the SSA behind his back. It was bad enough that Janice and Cameron or whoever the killer was kept two steps ahead of them, but he also had to worry about his own team. Who wasn't really committed to finding this maniac? Who wanted him to fail? He couldn't rest, much less relax. Even his nightly workouts with Blaine were tainted because he couldn't be completely sure that she wasn't the traitor. That hurt more than he wanted to admit. Last night he had once again skipped it completely, sending only a short text to cancel.

It was with little rest and even less hope that Mike walked into the conference room that afternoon. Everyone was already there except for David, so Mike decided to check his emails at his desk, telling the team to let him know when his wayward detective arrived. He groaned when he saw forty-seven new messages since this morning. What was going on with the FBI? Didn't anyone out there have anything better to do than send never-ending emails? It was times like this that Mike missed being on the road and hunting down fugitives. He didn't have to read useless emails in a tent in the middle of Nebraska.

He'd just deleted email number twenty-two when Blaine appeared at his desk and announced, "Mike, David's here. You ready?"

Mike jumped, and a couple of sheets of paper fell to the floor. Before he could lean over to pick them up, Blaine had beat him to it.

"Didn't mean to startle you, Mike. Or were you just so interested in your emails?"

Mike's smile was more of a grimace and he simply nodded his thanks, not trusting himself to speak.

Blaine flushed and turned away, but suddenly turned around again. In a near whisper, she asked, "Did I do something to piss you off, Mike? You've been acting like we just met yesterday instead of working together for weeks now. And you've missed three workouts in the past five days with no explanation. What's going on?"

Mike really didn't want to have this conversation. He wanted to believe it wasn't her, but he couldn't be sure. He fell back on the job. "Just been a little busy, detective. You know, there's a lot to do in leading one of these cases and I'm trying to stay one step ahead of Zardes."

Mike watched her intently to see if she'd react to Zardes's name, but he was disappointed. Instead of giving herself away, she only said, "Don't let him get you down, Mike. You're doing a good job with a difficult case. We'll get there, I know it. You got this."

They walked in an awkward silence to the conference room and, upon their entrance, David immediately spoke.

"Sorry I'm late getting back, Mike. Traffic was a bitch. I tried a shortcut I know, and it took even longer than the usual way."

Mike only nodded. He wondered if David was late because of traffic or if he had been meeting with Zardes. Then he mentally shook his head. He was seeing conspiracies everywhere and questioning even the most mundane of incidents. He needed to get a grip. Wild speculation wasn't going to do him any good and would probably only hurt the team and the investigation.

Mike looked at the analyst and nodded. "Let's start with Danny."

Danny got up and walked over to a new bulletin board in the corner and turned it around. His smile was bright, and his chest puffed out. "It took a little longer than I expected, but I finished the map you asked for, Mike. The color scheme is exactly what you asked for, too. The victims' home addresses are in blue, their work addresses are in green, and the murder scenes are in red. I even added the relevant Poe work in yellow next to each crime scene. And because we've mentioned it a few times, I added an orange tab for all the Miami Dade College campuses. I hope this is what you wanted. By the way, I'm gonna need to requisition more colored tabs - I ran out." Danny's laugh was infectious, and everyone smiled along with him.

Mike moved to the map. "Good work, Danny. This is exactly the kind of thing I was talking about." Mike took a step back and said to the group at large, "Alright, everybody, take a good look. Does anything jump out at anyone?"

The others gathered around in a semi-circle and began to study the large map. It was easily three-by-four feet and took up the entire bulletin board. The many different colors in use made it look more like a child's fledgling artwork than a potential piece of critical evidence in a murder investigation. It was obvious even to an untrained eye that it had been painstakingly researched and was incredibly detailed.

The silence continued for some minutes when Rhonda cleared her throat. "I don't know about any actual patterns, per se, but I see a couple of clusters." She pointed at the map. "You've got four murder scenes in the northern part of the county and three more along the eastern coast, or not too far inland anyway."

"That's true," agreed Alex, "but you've also got the Rogers murder way over here at the Cutler Canal. And even though the Hardison, Benton and Twitchell murders were pretty close together in Hialeah, the James murder was in Miami Gardens, not exactly next door."

"And although the Biddix and Henri murders were in the Bayshore area, Oscar Cudney was killed in South Miami. That's not exactly in the same area either," added Blaine.

Chip chimed in as he pointed to one of the marked areas. "And we still can't show a link with the Rogers murder way out here in Kendall. It doesn't look like there's any kind of a pattern here." His voice lowered and he wouldn't look at Mike.

Everyone waited for Mike to say something and, when he did, it took them all by surprise. "I want to study this a while longer. In the meantime, Alex, tell us what you found out about Toledo's finances." Mike motioned the others back to their seats, but he stayed next to the map, studying it intently while keeping half an ear on the next report.

"Well, I got some info but not everything we wanted," Alex began as he found the relevant pages in his notepad. "Janice banks at the Miami-Dade Savings & Loan, where she's had an account for the past six years. They wouldn't give me any details without a subpoena, but they confirmed she has a checking and savings account there. I did find out that she has three credit cards because that's what's she's been paying her bills with. I was able to confirm that she's paid her rent, groceries, utilities, cell phone, everything by credit card for the past two months."

"Okay," interrupted Blaine. "She's out of a job so she's putting everything on the cards. What's so weird about that?"

"Maybe nothing," said Alex. "But what's she paying off the credit cards with? She still gets those bills each month and has to pay 'em."

"True enough, but she's probably making minimum payments. You know, using her credit cards to pay the bills and her bank account to pay just what she has to until she gets a new job and has money coming back in. Hell, half of America only pays the minimums on their cards even when they've got jobs."

Everyone nodded at this observation; most of them knew people who did just that. That was why the United States had one of the largest debt amounts in the world.

"But Janice isn't looking for a new job," David pointed out. "She's just going from place to place, restaurants, the library, that kind of thing. She's not job hunting. Why is she doing that?"

"I don't know," said Alex, "but ..."

"I've got it!"

Mike unceremoniously interrupted the conversation. He turned around to the group and began talking a mile a minute, not giving anyone a chance to get a word in edgewise.

"Clusters, you said, Rhonda. And we saw a cluster up north and another in the eastern part of the county, but we said we couldn't figure out why Cecilia Rogers was in that canal or what it had to do with the pattern, if anything. But what if we look at this a different way. Look at the map again," and Mike motioned everyone to come to the bulletin board.

As he went on, he pointed to the different areas in turn. "Oscar Cudney is the first victim, but he was killed in his own home. Just like the victim in 'The Tell-Tale Heart'. Lylyana Biddix died in a cathedral because that's where you find church bells like in the poem, 'The Bells'. Cecilia Rogers was found in a canal like Marie Roget and the Henris were found in that fancy house in Bayshore. And for that murder the killer needed a multi-story house with a large backyard like in the Poe story. Those kinds of houses can't be found just anywhere, especially one that was empty and available for use for the murders.

"Now, if you assume that the Cudney, Biddix, Rogers and Henri murders were dictated by the *where* and not by the who or what, then we drop those from the list. That leaves us with the James, Hardison, Benton and Twitchell murders, which all took place in the northern part of the county. Your 'cluster', Rhonda, and the only ones that point us to the murderer. We said before that the murderer was all over the county and had to be familiar with the entire region. But if we eliminate those other four murders from the equation, that leaves us in the northern part of the county. Our murderer, whether it's Janice Toledo, Cameron Cudney or someone else, is familiar with the Hialeah and Miami Gardens areas. The other murder locations were murders of necessity. She or he chose the area they knew best for the murders where they were in charge of location."

He turned around in triumph. "We need to see if Janice Toledo or Cameron Cudney can be linked to any of the murders that occurred in the north."

No one said anything for a while as they turned over in their minds what Mike had said.

Brilliant, thought Blaine as she turned towards Mike. Before she could congratulate him however, the door swished open and she turned to see Bradley Zardes walk into the room.

Today the SSA wore a bright blue tie and Blaine knew, if she looked down, his socks would perfectly match. Zardes's affectation of matching ties and socks had been an ongoing joke among the MDPD detectives since David noticed it weeks ago. It had almost become a game to see which of them would spot the SSA first each day and report to the others what color he wore.

It would almost be funny if I didn't dislike the bastard so much.

Knowing Zardes was trying to discredit Mike only made Blaine distrust him that much more and she wondered what he was doing here.

Probably nothing good.

"Good afternoon, everyone, am I interrupting?"

~~

Bradley Zardes entered the room self-importantly.

"Of course not, sir," Mike answered. "Is there something I can do for you?"

Blaine noticed Mike took a half step toward the SSA as if he were trying to shield the rest of them from his attention.

"No, nothing in particular, Agent Donaldson," Zardes answered. "I did mention I was going to start taking a more active role in this investigation, and I thought I'd drop down and see how things were going." He took a few steps closer to the group and David and Alex moved apart, allowing the SSA to come closer. "Ah, so here's the famous map," Zardes said as he joined the semicircle. "Very interesting."

Mike made a noise and Blaine looked at him. He seemed genuinely surprised and she wondered why. She soon found out.

"Danny just finished the map late last night, sir. How did you hear about it already?"

Zardes's tanned face turned slightly pink, but he answered quickly. "In almost every murder investigation a map of the relevant areas involved is standard. Any law enforcement official worth his salt would know that, Agent."

Blaine could only describe Zardes's tone as 'nasty'.

"And since this serial killer has been operating for weeks now, I assumed you would have such a map already in use. Are you telling me you only requested such a map recently, Donaldson?"

Mike didn't answer immediately, but Blaine could see his shoulders slump slightly and he looked away for a brief second.

Damn Zardes! Now Mike thinks he should have thought of this sooner.

She felt for him and tried to think of something to say to defend the case agent. She needn't have worried; Mike waited a moment, then looked back and when he spoke, Blaine heard a new defiance in his tone.

"I asked for the map a while back, but we've been busy, and Danny was only able to finish it last night. However, if you thought I should have done this earlier, I'm surprised you didn't mention it during our evening updates. I would certainly have followed through on any suggestion you cared to make."

Nice, Mike. Turned it back on him good. Jerk deserved it.

Zardes reddened but instead of answering, turned toward Danny, and ordered, "Explain what I'm looking at here, McKissick."

Danny gulped and stole a quick look at Mike, then immediately looked back to the SSA. The explanation lasted only a few minutes and Danny ended by relating Mike's insight about the killer's knowledge of the northern area of the county. His tone professed his pride in Mike's accomplishment and Blaine realized Danny was purposely trying to show the case agent in a good light.

Thanks, Danny.

Zardes said nothing to this. He neither praised Mike nor questioned the investigation further. After a brief, "Very well. Keep me apprised, Agent," Zardes barely acknowledged the rest of the group, turned and walked out the door.

"Whew!" said Alex and he sat down heavily in his chair.

"I hope he doesn't make that a habit," agreed David.

Rhonda added her two cents' worth. "He could've at least congratulated you on the map, Danny, and Mike on figuring out the killer's base of operations."

Mike had been quiet since Zardes left the room. He seemed to feel the scrutiny and his eyes moved to each of the team in turn. His gaze fell on David and his eyes narrowed.

"I find it strangely coincidental that Zardes decided to make his first appearance on the very day that the map was completed. And truthfully, I don't buy for a minute his bullshit that he didn't know we didn't have a map before or that every investigation should have such a map." Mike's tone suddenly became deadly as he asked pointedly, "What do you think about that, David?"

Startled, David only looked at Mike. Finally regaining his voice, he said, "I'm not sure what you're implying. But it sounds like you think I talked to Zardes about the map before the briefing." He crossed his arms. "If you've got something to say, I'd appreciate it if you'd just say it straight and get it over with." David stood up straighter and Blaine wondered if this was going to come to blows.

Mike put his hands on his hips and looked the African American detective straight in the eye. "Alright, David, if that's the way you want it, fine by me."

Instead of continuing to look at David, Mike turned to the rest of the group. "At least three times in the past couple of weeks I've noticed that during our evening briefings, Zardes seemed to already know things about the investigation before I put them in a report or reported on them in person. That happened with the Benton case. He knew about Blaine's idea of following the lead on the monkey before I told him about it. Then today with Danny's map. I never told him I'd asked Danny to create such a map. I didn't mention it in my written reports either. I wanted to wait and see if it got us anywhere before discussing it with Zardes. You all know he doesn't like me and has been trying to get me taken off this investigation for weeks now. I didn't want to give him anything he could try to use against me, so I didn't tell him about the map."

Mike paced a few moments. "I realized that someone was feeding Zardes information about the investigation. Someone on this team is working with Zardes and against me, trying to discredit me."

Christ! Now I get why he's been avoiding me and not coming to the gym. He thought it might be me. It's not, but, by God, when I find out who ...

"Now what a minute, Mike," Alex spoke up. "First off, I don't believe anyone here would do that to you. I'll admit, I think all of us thought you were a little crazy at the beginning of this, but now we all believe you and your theory. No one here would hurt the investigation by trying to discredit you. That would reflect bad on us, too. Look, I hate to say it this way, but don't you think you might be getting a bit paranoid? You know, letting Zardes get to you?"

David spoke up. "I haven't done anything to hurt you or the case, Mike, I swear it." David's tone became more belligerent and Blaine pivoted a bit in case she needed to break the two men up. "Why'd you focus in on me, anyway? What'd I do to make you think I ratted on you?"

Mike put his hands on his hips and moved a step closer to the MDPD detective. "Zardes knew we had a map. He came down here just to see it. And I didn't tell him about it, that's for sure. But you were conveniently late getting back from lunch, David. On the same day Zardes decides to come down for the first time during a briefing. You were conveniently late one day last week, too. And you blamed the traffic that time as well. If I check the dates on my reports, David, am I gonna find that that was the same day we got some sort of a lead and Zardes knew about it again?" Mike waited a moment. His tone became deadly. "Well, am I?"

When David didn't answer, Danny jumped up. "I don't believe it! How could you, David? Mike's been killing himself over this case, bending over backwards to keep ahead of Zardes and you go and help him?" Danny's face showed all the pain of the betrayal.

Blaine couldn't believe what she was hearing. That David would hurt Mike like this was unimaginable. She tried to curb her anger but couldn't. Finally, she exploded, "I cannot believe you'd do something like this, David. We've known each other for five years and worked together on and off for four. How could you do this to me" To the team? How ..."

"Blaine, stop. It wasn't David. It was me."

~~

Everyone turned in unison and looked at the speaker. The room was so silent, Mike thought he could hear the others' hearts beating. Or maybe it was just his own, pounding in his ears.

"Chip?" Mike whispered in shock.

He stared at his friend in disbelief, trying to make sense of the young agent's admission. Maybe he'd heard wrong. Or misunderstood. It couldn't be Chip. Chip had been his first friend here. Had believed in him from the very beginning. Had stuck by him no matter what anyone else had said. It didn't make sense.

He could only say one word. "Why?"

Chip hung his head and sat down heavily in the nearest chair. He suddenly looked much older than his twenty-six years as he stared at the floor. His shoulders were slumped, and he ran a hand through his jet-black hair while his grey eyes turned watery.

After a few moments and several deep breaths, Chip looked up at Mike and only said, "I'm sorry." He opened his mouth to say something else, but closed it again, shaking his head.

"You bastard." This from Blaine, who took a step closer and towered over the young agent. "Mike gave you a chance on this case. He's helped you, tried to bring you along. And you repay him like this?"

She balled her fists and leaned over as if she was going to grab Chip by the collar. Suddenly she stopped, took a few deep breaths of her own, and backed off. Her face was full of disgust but all she could do was repeat what she'd said before. "You bastard."

Mike raised a hand before anyone else could speak. "Chip, we can do this here in front of the others, or you and I can go to an interview room and talk. Your choice."

"Mike, you can't talk to this asshole alone," interrupted Alex. "He's working with Zardes. He could say anything to Zardes and without witnesses, it'd be your word against his. You can't do it, Mike. He'll have your career."

This seemed to get through to Chip and he looked up again. His eyes were wide, and Mike sensed there was something more in all this. He suddenly understood that Chip wasn't working against him. He was scared. Scared of Zardes. Mike grabbed a chair and sat down next to his fellow agent. He motioned for the others to sit and although their faces were filled with disgust and anger, they complied.

"Chip, talk to me. What's going on? What did Zardes do to you?"

There was a pause, then Chip spoke. His voice was low, and Mike leaned closer to hear. "He didn't do anything to me, Mike, but I swear I didn't realize what he was after right away. Then I was in so deep I couldn't get out."

Chip started speaking hesitantly at first, then more quickly as he told his story. A dam had broken, and he had to speak before he drowned.

"It was the night before our first team briefing. Zardes called me to his office and said my review was coming up and he wanted to know more about me. He asked what I wanted to do with the FBI in the future and I told him I wanted to take the fugitive retrieval training at Quantico. Just like you did, he said VCMO would be a good place to start and asked me if I wanted to be on a special VCMO task force. He said you'd be on the team and that I could learn a lot from you. Said he knew you and I had gone out for drinks. Well, I was really excited, so I said yes. He said to come see him the next night 'cause he wanted to see how I was doing.

"Well, the next night I went to see him, and he asked some questions about the case and the team and said for me to come back again in a day or two. He said if I did good on this case, he'd make sure I could work more with the VCMO and get more experience. Naturally I was excited, you know? It's exactly what I wanted, so I figured it was good that Zardes was taking an interest in me."

Mike didn't say anything. He could see it all in his mind. Zardes used Chip's inexperience and enthusiasm against him. He might not like office politics, but he could already see what was coming next. "I understand, Chip. You wanted to do good. That's okay. Anybody would've. Just tell us what happened next. When did you realize Zardes really wanted information about me?"

Chip turned red and his voice went flat. "A couple of nights later. I went up to see him but this time he kept asking about you and what you were doing, the orders you were giving, what kinds of things were you saying, you know, that kind of thing. Then he told me he thought maybe you needed some help, so I should tell him what you were doing every day. I told him I didn't want to go behind your back, but he said if I told him what was going on, it'd go a long way to showing how loyal I was to the FBI and he'd be able to better help me get into VCMO permanently."

Chip's shoulders slumped even more, his face turning bright red with embarrassment. "I knew then what he wanted and why, but I didn't know what to do or how to get out of it. He's my boss, you know? I'm sorry, Mike."

Surprisingly, Alex spoke next. "So, you saw Zardes every day or two and told him what was going on. That's why he seemed to know stuff before Mike told him. You thought he could help you in your career and then realized he really wanted dirt to use against Mike. You were stuck. Okay, so the question is, now that Mike knows what's going on, what does Chip do? If he stops reporting to Zardes, Zardes will know we know and might make things even harder for you, Mike. But if Chip does keep going, he's still gonna try to use whatever he can against you. We have to head him off at the pass."

"No. There's no 'we' about it." Mike stood up, crossed his arms, and looked at each of his team members in turn. His voice was deep, and his tone spoke of a finality that brooked no opposition. "This is between me and Zardes." He raised a hand to forestall the coming objections. "After this case is over, I'll be going back to Detroit and Zardes can't hurt me. But you guys, especially Chip and Danny, have to stay and continue to live and work here. I will not be responsible for messing up your careers.

"Having said that, I won't lie to you, Chip. I can't deny that this hurts. But I do understand why you did it and I appreciate you coming forward now to admit it." Mike put a hand on his friend's shoulder. "I need some time to think about this and how I want to handle it. For now, I think you look like you might be coming down with something and need to leave early. I want you to go home. I'll email Zardes and tell him you went home sick. That way, you don't have to see him tonight. We'll talk again tomorrow and figure out where we go from here."

Chip looked up. "Mike, I don't know …"

"No, don't say anything right now. Just go home and try not to worry. I'll take care of it." Mike patted his shoulder again.

Chip once again looked like he wanted to say something but thought better of it when he looked into Mike's eyes. Instead, he picked up his water bottle and files from the table and, not looking at anyone else, left the room, shoulders still slumped and his attention on the floor.

The others' eyes followed Chip as he grabbed a bag from his desk and made his way down the hall toward the elevators. When he was out of sight, on cue, everyone turned toward Mike.

David said, "Well, I don't know that I could be that forgiving. He should have come to you right away. And you should …"

"… apologize to you, David," Mike interrupted. He held out a hand and said, "I'm sorry I accused you of being the one. I was wrong and I hope you can forgive me."

David took the outstretched hand and answered, "No need, Mike. I understand. No hard feelings."

"You can't let Zardes get away with this, Mike," said Alex. "He's trying to hurt you and, by extension, the investigation. That could lead to more deaths. It's dangerous. You gotta do something."

"Mike, I get you're trying to help Chip, but what he did was wrong." Danny's eyes were solemn. "David is right, he should have come straight to you. There's no telling how much damage he's done. I mean, Chip's my friend and all that, but …"

"He's twenty-six and only two years with the Bureau. What would you have done if you had only two years under your belt and the SSA asked for information? No, I'm hurt, I admit it, but I'm not mad at him. I'm mad at Zardes. And I'll deal with Zardes. I just gotta figure out how."

Silence reigned as they considered everything that had just happened. Finally, it was Rhonda who broke the tense quiet.

"Mike, that's very generous of you. Most men would have kicked Chip off the team then and there and not given a damn about why he did what he did. I'm impressed and if I can help in any way, all you have to do is ask. I'm not based here, so I–"

"Need to stay out of it, Rhonda." Mike smiled, but it didn't reach his eyes. "All right, we've lost time with this and we have a lot to do. Let's get to it.

As Mike headed to his desk, he missed the look of sympathy in Blaine's eyes. Nor did he see the shift in her expression as it changed to one of finality in a decision made.

CHAPTER 48

That which you mistake for madness is but an over-acuteness of the senses.

'The Tell-Tale Heart'

They're starting to ask questions; that means they're getting closer. I didn't think the cops were that smart, but I guess I was wrong. It will mean having to move up the timetable, but that won't matter as long as I make my point before they take me.

I wanted more time to prepare and do this next week, but that is too far away. The cops might make their move before then and I need to be done before that happens.

It will have to be this week.

Where's that calendar?

Oh yeah, here it is. Let's see ... the 22nd doesn't give me much time, the 23rd would be better, but the Poe tie-in on the 22nd is perfect! Can I get it done by then?

Where's that list?

Damn! There's a lot still to do and I'll need to do most of it tomorrow, but I can do this. I've done everything else practically under their noses, I can do this, too.

Soon it'll be all over.

CHAPTER 49

That dream was as that night-wind—let it pass.
'DREAMS'

Had the routine of our life at this place been known to the world,
we should have been regarded as madmen —; although, perhaps,
as madmen of a harmless nature.
'THE MURDERS IN THE RUE MORGUE'

August 21

The clutter in the room was beyond words. Books and magazines
lined each wall and every pile rose chest high or more. Loose
papers wedged between an untold number of blue binders, and file
folders in between held even more papers, newsprint and maps.
Hundreds of pictures, some framed, some not, covered the walls
until you couldn't even see what lay underneath. Only a postage-
sized square here and there hinted at the faded yellow wallpaper
lying underneath the stark black and white photos that permeated
the room.

A twelve-inch shelf near the hallway held the only thing of
beauty in this godforsaken room: a large conch. The shell was
huge, its light brown surface decorated with thousands of dark
brown squiggly lines. Its smooth exterior was broken by a row of

pointed spikes and its underbelly was lined with mud-colored streaks. Near it sat an old-fashioned mantel clock, its steady ticking the only comforting thing in this unholy menagerie.

A stale stench saturated the room, filling every nook and cranny, every crack and crevice. Musty books vied with old soup and sauces, dog feces and cat urine to assail his nostrils until he didn't know if he'd be able to continue. Taking a handkerchief out of his pocket, he took a moment to tie it over his nose and mouth, bandana-style, and resolved to take a long hot shower when this was all over.

Gun in hand, Mike slowly made his way further into the basement apartment.

Where did all this shit come from? The guy must have been collecting it for decades.

Mike tried to make sense of the sights, smells and sounds bombarding him as he scanned the room once again to identify anything that would help him find this maniac. Unexpectedly he saw something in the corner that had eluded his first scan. A pile of clothes lay next to the kitchen door, shirts and pants crumpled underneath old boots. Mike walked toward it. Before he could lean down to examine them, several flies rose from the detritus, and Mike jumped back, a little surprised. His foot scraped a pile of books and they went down in a crash that was probably heard next door.

Sonuvabitch!

Mike held his breath even as he swung his Glock around in a sweeping motion trying to head off any resistance. A full two minutes later, when no sound followed and his breathing was back to normal, Mike continued his search of the apartment.

Down the hall was the kitchen and Mike saw nothing that led him to believe there was anyone in that side of the unit. He made his way through the hallway and a turtle would have earned a speeding ticket by comparison.

At long last he reached the bedroom, and he entered the room with as much caution as he'd gone through the rest of the apartment. He noted with dismay even more books, magazines, and the ubiquitous photos on the walls. He looked in the closet and, finding nothing, made his way back to the doorway.

Deciding this had been a complete waste of time, he put his gun back into its holster. He was about to leave when a click made him turn quickly.

The man was disheveled and slightly emaciated. His tow-colored hair was plastered to his head and his skin was the color of alabaster. He held the gun even with Mike's chest, but his arms shook, exposing his lack of experience.

Mike held up his hands to show he was unarmed and took a tentative step forward. A booming crack pierced the stillness and Mike looked down, sure he'd see a gaping hole in his belly. But there was none.

What the hell?

Mike swung around as he heard a scream. His heart stopped and he watched helplessly as Chip Smythe fell dead to the floor. The blood poured from a deep slit in Chip's gut and Mike looked up to see the glint of the blade as it spiraled ever downward. On the floor next to his friend, he looked up into a featureless face, save for a satisfied grin. In the background he heard the maniacal cackle of Bradley Zardes.

~~

"Chip, no!"

Mike thrashed around and sat up in the lumpy bed of his hotel room. His sheets were falling off the edge, a slash of light from the doorway illuminated a slit of the room and the bedside clock's glowing numbers turned to 4:58. His breath came in short bursts and the sweat on his forehead trickled down to his naked chest.

Fuck. Damned nightmare.

With another oath, he turned off the alarm, swung his aching legs over the side of the bed and padded his way to the bathroom.

He didn't remember shaving or cutting his chin. Didn't remember taking a shower. Didn't remember turning on the in-room coffeemaker or spilling the tepid liquid on his newspaper. Didn't remember turning on the TV and watching the nauseatingly cheerful weatherman predict another August day of ninety-plus temperatures, seventy-six percent humidity and afternoon thunderstorms. He barely remembered getting in his car and making the twelve-mile, forty-five-minute trip to the FBI offices.

All he remembered was seeing the surprised look on Chip's dead face.

It hardly took Sigmund Freud to figure this one out. He'd been haunted for three months now by his fuck up in Milwaukee. He was alive only due to a bit of good luck and the fact that the fugitive he'd been tracking was a complete idiot. By all rights he should be dead. The man had been hiding under the bed and Mike would have been shot in the back if the idiot hadn't sneezed just as he was snaking out from under it. As it was, Mike had ducked, turned, and fired in one fluid motion before his quarry could get his shot off. But, in the way of dreams, the scene changed to a frontal shot that missed and hit Chip. But even that morphed into the death scene of Jeremiah Twitchell's reenacting of 'The Pit and the Pendulum' with Bradley Zardes cast as the maniac serial killer.

He'd almost paid the ultimate price for his screwup in Milwaukee. And, now in Miami, he'd made more mistakes than he cared to count, starting with his capture of Philip Atkinson and continuing into the Poe murders case, and he was this close to giving up and getting the hell out of Dodge. Now even his sleep was haunting him. He had enough self-doubt without his subconscious piling it on and all he wanted was a cup of French Vanilla coffee and one break in this shit case. He had no idea if he was going to get either.

"Thanks for joining us, Blaine," Mike said with a little sarcasm as Blaine entered the conference room ten minutes late.

"Sorry, Mike. I stopped at the bakery to get some donuts, but they were short-staffed, and the line was taking so long, I just gave up. That's why I'm late."

"Hey, if you're gonna be late anyway, at least go ahead and bring us the food," Alex joked. "We'd be more likely to forgive if we could eat in the bargain."

Everyone laughed at that, including David, who quipped, "Yeah, Blaine. You want to make sure the boss lets it slide. You know what they say, 'The way to a man's heart is through his stomach'. Give Mike something sweet to eat and he'll let you be late every day!"

More laughter followed this, but Blaine's smile was forced. For his part, Mike felt a blush on his cheeks and decided it was time to get down to work.

"Okay, guys, let's get started. We'll begin with updates from our work yesterday." Mike looked to his right and asked, "Blaine, David, anything new from the surveillance teams?"

"Nada, boss." Blaine let out a sigh. "Toledo's still doing her thing. She went to eat and did a little shopping yesterday. As soon as she leaves a place, one of our guys goes in and asks about her. She went to a hardware store and bought a book on painting and another on antique furniture but that's it."

"But there was one unusual item from last evening's surveillance," reported David. "She ate at a fairly decent seafood place and since the place was packed, she sat at the bar until a table opened up. While she was waiting, she bought the woman sitting next to her a drink and the two of them talked for a few minutes until this other woman's date showed up. As she and the guy walked away, Janice got up and stopped the woman and gave her something. Unfortunately, when our guy talked to him afterward, the bartender said he didn't hear any of the conversation and the woman and guy left before Janice, so we couldn't find out what it was all about. Other than that, we got nothin' so far."

"What about Cameron?"

"Nothing unusual, Mike," Blaine reported. "He got off work, went to the gym, picked up Chinese take-out, then we think he spent the rest of the night at home. The tail did lose him for about an hour between the restaurant and home, but I don't know how much he could have done in that time. We don't think he went anywhere else and he didn't try to get in touch with anyone either. Not Janice or anybody else." Blaine slapped her notebook shut and let out a frustrated breath.

Mike resisted rubbing his forehead to ward off the headache he knew was coming. "Okay, thanks. If anything does come up, let me know. Alex, what about you, anything new with the follow up on Janice's early life?"

He addressed his question only to Alex since Chip had not been in the office yesterday following his 'confession'. He'd spoken to the remaining team members again last night and had asked them pointedly not to be too harsh on Chip. He reminded them that he'd only been with the FBI for two years and what would they have done if they'd been in his shoes at that age? He asked them to cut him some slack and for the sake of the team and the investigation, try to work with the young agent as if nothing had happened. Today would tell if his words had the desired effect.

The middle-aged detective started tapping his finger on the table as he spoke. "I reached Janice's college roommate and she said what everyone else has said; Janice Toledo is a nice person who wants to write romance novels for a living. She worked hard in college, hardly ever went out. She spent almost every weekend either with her parents or in the library."

"I'm guessing she didn't date much," interrupted Rhonda.

Alex let out a bark. "Good Lord, no. The roommate said she can't remember Janice ever dating the same guy more than twice.

'Fraid that dog won't hunt. She's got no old boyfriends we can look into."

Rhonda didn't answer but nodded as if that was the answer she expected.

Mike noticed Chip stiffen and Blaine's eyes look behind him before her face went blank. Before he could turn around to see what had upset them, a voice behind him told him all he needed to know.

"Good morning, everyone. Thought I'd sit in and see how things were going." Bradley Zardes walked in and took a seat at the head table.

Today his matching tie and socks were a dark lavender and his ingratiating grin made Mike want to retch. Knowing he was about to navigate a minefield, Mike plastered on a smile and quickly caught the SSA up on what had been discussed already.

At Zardes's nod, Mike continued with the briefing. "Danny, have you had any luck with tying Toledo or Cameron to any of the crime scenes?"

Danny ran a hand through his already tousled hair and began to speak. The researcher was still not used to giving reports to the group and the addition of the SSA added to his unease. "There's one good piece of news. Remember the empty shoe factory where Stephen Hardison died and the abandoned warehouse where Jeremiah Twitchell was killed?"

Mike had a quick flash of last night's dream and Chip's dead body. He suppressed a grimace and nodded.

"Well, the two buildings are listed for sale by two different real estate companies, but when I asked to talk to the real estate agents themselves, it turns out that the agent is the same guy. He's a freelance and works for several agencies. What's more, his husband is in the same Friends of the Library group that Janice Toledo is in. And to top it off, he remembers Janice asking him a lot of questions about how you go about trying to sell an abandoned building."

"That sounds like a tie-in to me," said Alex, and several heads nodded in agreement.

"What's more, both of those buildings are in Hialeah and that's the area you said our killer is familiar with, Mike," chimed in Blaine.

Zardes interrupted the general celebration by interjecting, "Before everyone gets ahead of themselves, may I remind you that you haven't proven anything? It might be a tenuous connection at best, but you can't get a warrant on it. Go into court with that and you'd be laughed right out again."

Mike tried not to make a snide comment. He counted to ten, once in English, then again in Spanish, before trusting himself to answer. "I understand, sir, and you're absolutely correct. It is a tenuous connection, but we'll try to build on it." Mike turned to Danny and said, "Good work, Danny. See if you can go that route for the other empty buildings our killer used. Maybe you'll find another connection somewhere."

Danny nodded but also gave the SSA a less than friendly glare. He turned over a page in his notebook and continued, "There is one more thing, Mike. MDPD finished re-canvasing for witnesses but didn't come up with much. One homeless guy who hangs out near the house where Lucy Benton was found made a half-hearted ID of Janice Toledo based on a photo lineup, but the officer said he was a little tipsy and he wouldn't want to take it to court. Don't know if it'll help or not."

"Hey, an ID is an ID," said David. His smile radiated as he added, "That's a tie for Janice Toledo to three of the murders, all in Hialeah. That's a good start if you ask me. Seems to me we can definitely build on that. Whaddaya you think, Mike?"

Mike was leaning toward caution and tried to frame his words accordingly but, before he could answer, Zardes interrupted again.

"It's still very tenuous, Detective." Zardes stood up and addressed Mike. "If we're looking for an ID, I'd like to know what happened with that photo lineup you were supposed to be doing with the real estate agent on this new house in Coral Gables. Why is it taking so long? Why wasn't it mentioned in your report last night, Agent Donaldson?"

"That was my assignment, Agent Zardes." Alex sat up straight as he made his report. "The real estate agent, Elliot Quinn, was out of town and didn't get back until yesterday afternoon. I saw him at his office and showed him the pictures. He identified Janice Toledo as the woman who toured the house last week. She asked a lot of questions about the house's construction but said she was interested in renting, not buying. Quinn told her that house can't be rented, and she said she'd think about it and then left. He hasn't heard back from her and doesn't expect to. So, we have a positive ID, but she hasn't done anything more than trespass at the house. It doesn't do us much good."

Alex's voice had risen as he spoke, and Mike detected the anger in it. Alex and Chip had been working together a lot over the past week or so and the veteran detective told Mike yesterday how pissed he was that Zardes used Chip in this power game of his. He was furious about it and laid the entire blame on Zardes. It was obvious he was trying to reign in that anger. Mike hoped Zardes was too preoccupied with trying to discredit him to notice it.

"I see. Thank you, Detective. However, just because she hasn't done something yet in that house doesn't mean she won't." Zardes turned back to Mike. "I want more men on this. Put a couple of guys on that house in Coral Gables. You never know …"

Blaine's phone rang and she looked at the display. "It's Monte, Mike, on the detail following Toledo. Give me a minute." She got up to take the call in the hallway.

It didn't escape Mike's notice that she'd addressed her information to him, not to Zardes. *Not very subtle, Blaine.* Once again, he hoped Zardes didn't notice.

The SSA addressed the group in general. "Who's on the financial end? Have you learned more about how Toledo is living without a steady paycheck? Is she still …?"

Zardes paused as Blaine hurried back into the room. Her face was red, and she began speaking before the door shut behind her.

"Mike, Janice Toledo is on the move."

~~

Things began to happen fast after that. Over the next three hours, their suspect went to several different stores and returned to the house in Coral Gables twice, each time carrying boxes and paint cans. As she left each store, an officer went in and got a list of her purchases. It appeared that Janice was planning on repainting the house since she obtained several colors of paint as well as tarps, rollers and brushes. At a furniture store, Janice ordered several pieces of furniture to be delivered the next day and, at her last stop, she bought an assortment of food and drinks as if she were planning a party of some sort.

None of this made sense and, except for the fact Janice Toledo was apparently moving into a house she didn't own, nothing she'd done over the last two days was illegal.

Mike had been able to obtain a surreptitious warrant based on the real estate's ID of their suspect, but the subsequent search had turned up nothing. Mike had personally led the team on the search, waiting until Janice was on one of her errands, and they looked in every room and every closet. Except for the items she had already bought, there was nothing else to see. If Janice was planning something for this house, she hadn't brought in anything incriminating yet.

More important to the case right now was the follow up on Blaine's lead of the monkey. The third pet store, Amy's Exotics, had indeed sold a monkey to a woman matching Janice Toledo's description the week before 'The Black Cat' murder. That jived with the coroner's report, which stated that the monkey had been tortured, probably over the course of two to three days, then killed some four days before the actual murder of Lucy Benton. And when shown a photo lineup, Amy had picked out Janice Toledo.

Now they were getting somewhere. In the Lucy Benton murder, they had a solid ID for Janice Toledo as the woman who bought the monkey, and a tenuous ID for Janice in the same neighborhood where the murder took place. They had the conversation Janice had with the real estate agent selling the abandoned buildings where Stephen Hardison and Jeremiah Twitchell were murdered and the fact that all three of those murders took place in Hialeah, an area with which Janice was intimate. They had the obvious connection for Janice with Oscar Cudney and a possible motive due to her wish for a marriage with Cameron and, finally, her interest in the house in Coral Gables was at the least suspicious if not an obvious red flag.

It was a start, but Mike felt they needed more. And he still wasn't sure where Cameron fit in all this. Mike believed Janice and Cudney had to be working together, but they hadn't been able to tie Cameron with any of it. It didn't make sense that Janice was responsible for everything. Zardes, however, disagreed and insisted Mike take what they had to the United States Attorney's Office to get a warrant for Janice Toledo's arrest. The ensuing argument in the conference room was acrimonious but short.

~~

"That monkey ties it," Zardes said when Blaine had finished her report. "It's time for a warrant. Go to the AUSA and get it. I want to have Toledo in custody before the press update this evening."

Mike bristled at Zardes's condescending tone. Announcing an arrest now would be a tactical mistake. Mike took the risk of arguing with the SSA.

"Sir, if I may, I'm not sure we have enough to go to the AUSA yet. Except for the monkey, everything else, as you yourself pointed out, is tenuous at best. And we still have to prove that the monkey Toledo bought is the same monkey that was at the Benton scene. If we arrest Toledo now, all we really have her on is trespassing. She'll just lawyer up and we'd have to show our evidence to her attorney, who'd realize how weak our case really is and have plenty of time to refute it. She'd be on her guard and be able to hide or destroy other incriminating evidence we may not know about. We'd never secure enough evidence to arrest her again. I think we should wait a while longer."

"Giving Toledo a chance to kill again while you dither around here." Zardes put his hands on his hips and looked up at Mike who had a good two inches on him. "Donaldson, you've dragged your feet on this entire case. I said it was a mistake to put you in charge, but I was overruled. Well, you've screwed this up enough. So, I'm giving you a direct order. Go over to the United States Attorney's office and get that warrant. Pick up Toledo and get her ass in an interview room today. This is your last chance, Donaldson. If you screw this up, I'm taking over this investigation and you can head back to Detroit. You hear me?"

Mike bit back the first hundred responses he thought of. He'd work too hard on this investigation to lose it now to a pompous, self-serving asshole like Zardes. Besides, if the Assistant United States Attorney refused to give them the warrant, he wouldn't be responsible. And Zardes's threat was an empty one since Mike felt sure he couldn't take him off the case without Martinez's approval.

Believing that, Mike took a breath and answered simply, "Yes, sir. I'll go right away."

~~

Having lost the argument with Zardes, Mike approached the USAO to request the warrant for Toledo's arrest. As he'd thought, the AUSA did not believe they had nearly enough to make any charges in the Poe murders stick. He advised Mike to continue the surveillance as well as their investigation to find more concrete proof of Janice Toledo's possible identity as the Poe murderer.

Needless to say, Zardes was livid when Mike reported back two hours later. He sputtered through his anger and all but threw Mike out of his office.

But, by the time Mike returned to his desk, he had an email giving Mike an official ultimatum: Make significant progress today, or Zardes would be taking over the case tomorrow.

CHAPTER 50

And Darkness and Decay and the Red Death held illimitable
dominion over all.

'THE MASQUE OF THE RED DEATH'

August 22

It was ten o'clock in the morning and if Janice or Cameron were
going to kill, today would probably be the day. Since Rhonda
believed the murders would only get more spectacular, the team
was collectively afraid of what their murderer had in mind this
time.

"Donaldson," Mike answered his phone as he reviewed the
surveillance reports.

He looked up in concern then anger as he listened to the
information from his agents on the scene.

"What do you mean, you lost her?" Mike almost yelled into
the phone. "Earlier this morning, you reported she was at her
apartment. How'd she get by you? There were two of you
watching! What happened?"

The rest of the task force watched in disbelief as their boss
was apparently being told that the surveillance had lost one of their
suspects.

"All right! Stay where you are in case she comes back," ordered Mike in as angry a tone as they had ever heard from him. "I'll send some guys over to the house and see if she goes there." Mike punched the end button on his phone. "I assume you heard?" the case agent asked unnecessarily.

"Yeah, I think we got the gist of it," responded David for the group. "How'd they lose her?"

Mike answered succinctly, "Not sure, and right now, I don't care." Mike began barking orders. "Chip, you go to Janice's apartment and find out what happened and help out with the surveillance. David, Blaine, you guys go to the house in Coral Gables and start watching there. Maybe she's just out shopping and will show up sooner rather than later. Keep me posted."

"On our way," responded David and Blaine together as all three rose, grabbed their cell phones and headed out the door.

Mike looked at his remaining investigators. "Okay, guys, here's what I want to do next. We need to come up with a detailed timeline of what Janice Toledo has been doing these past few days. We'll go through the surveillance reports with a fine-tooth comb and see if we can find something we've missed before. And I want to put a detailed list of the items she bought at each of those stores with the timeline as well. All this will be vital to the AUSA if we arrest her."

~~

With no small amount of relief David and Blaine reported that Janice showed up at the Coral Gables house only minutes after their arrival. And, from that time on, Mike ordered a member of the task force to join each surveillance team, making a total of three watchers on each shift. And since she was already there, Blaine remained with the early morning shift once Pennington and Delvecchio arrived at the house. Later, David would join the next shift, then Blaine again, followed by Chip, Alex and David. Each member of the task force was responsible for submitting the written report from their shift and reporting to Mike personally.

Despite the fact that the entire team expected a murder today, the surveillance turned out to be one of the most boring days yet.

From the time she arrived at her 'appropriated' house until almost 3:30 p.m., Janice stayed in the home. Closer scrutiny was able to report that their suspect apparently painted all the rooms inside, each room a different color, then, once the paint dried, she finished up by rearranging the furniture she had bought. For what purpose, no one knew yet. The surveillance teams also reported that Cameron was at work and never left the building, not even for lunch. There was no proof that the two had spoken or were working together in any way, although Mike continued to believe they were.

Zardes was hovering, ordering hourly reports, and coming down to the conference room at odd times throughout the day. The SSA was furious that surveillance had lost Janice in the first place and not at all appeased when she had been located again. He made it clear that he blamed Mike's incompetence and planned to add it to the list he was writing to give to SAC Martinez. Frankly, he was driving Mike crazy and if Mike didn't know his career would be over, he would have punched the man then and there. As it was, it was a near thing.

Finally, at 4:30 the report he'd been waiting for came through.

CHAPTER 51

He summoned to his presence a thousand hale and light-hearted
friends…and with these retired to the deep seclusion of one of his
castellated abbeys.

'THE MASQUE OF THE RED DEATH'

Alex called to report that several people had suddenly arrived at the
house, all dressed up and in apparently good spirits. It seemed as if
Janice Toledo was hosting a party. Knowing this was probably a
set up for the next murder, Zardes ordered the entire task force to
the house. He also requested MDPD be placed on standby. Being
careful to park several homes away on each side of the street, by
5:30 all five members of the team as well as Zardes had arrived and
crowded in or around the surveillance van. The van was disguised
as a cable/telephone repair truck and parked two houses away from
their target. Not the most original disguise, thought Mike, but good
enough for now.

"Okay what have we got?"

"Three males, two females so far, Mike," replied Alex. "They
arrived in two groups: one couple, and the other three in the same
car. We were able to get shots of three of them and facial
recognition is already working on it. So far, though, nothing's
popped up."

"What about Cameron? He show up yet?" asked Mike.

"No, he's apparently still at work."

Alex stopped updating the team as another car drove up to Janice Toledo's house and two more women tumbled out. Both appeared to be in their mid-twenties, dressed in short skirts and tight blouses, looking as if they were going to a night club instead of a house in the suburbs. One was blonde, and painfully thin, while her companion was tall, of medium-build and had auburn hair. Both women seemed to be sporting tattoos and facial piercings.

Mike made a quick decision and signaled to Blaine to try to accost the girls before they got to the front door of the house to ask why they were going in. Unfortunately, he was too late; Blaine had barely made it across the street when the two women disappeared behind the opening door. Apologizing with her eyes, she returned to the van and waited for the next orders.

"Do we have eyes inside?" asked Zardes as he checked his watch once again.

"Surveillance tried to get a camera and bug inside yesterday, sir, but they couldn't get a signal. Since then, Janice has been in the house almost the entire time, so we haven't been able to try again," answered David.

Mike's eyes became hard. "I'm positive she's up to something and we need to stop it before she kills again. Let's do this the old-fashioned way." Mike pulled out a drawer of equipment inside the van and started handing out long-range cameras. "Each of you take one of these. David, you take the south side of the house. Blaine, the north, Alex, go east and, Chip, you take the west. I'll stay with Pennington and watch from here. Get as many pictures as you can through the windows and see if you can figure out what's happening. If you think something's going down, call me and we'll go in if we have to. We also need to be on the lookout for Cameron. If he doesn't show up soon, I'll be very surprised. We'll need–"

"Belay that order," Zardes interrupted. "I'm not gonna take the chance that Toledo could see us and rabbit. We'll wait here until we see what happens."

Mike barely stifled a scream of frustration. *Of all the stupid ...* "Sir, if we wait until something happens, then people will die while we're out here twiddling our thumbs!"

"I will not lose this collar because of your recklessness, Donaldson," Zardes snarled. "Do I make myself understood?"

Yesterday I was moving too slow, now today I'm reckless?

Mike suppressed the urge to roll his eyes and tried again. "Agent Zardes, we know that Janice Toledo is using this house illegally. We could send MDPD in to break up the party by saying there were complaints from the neighbors. We wouldn't tip our hand and we might stop a murder tonight. What harm could that do?"

"The *harm*, Agent Donaldson, is that she'd then know the police have her in their sights. She'd go into hiding or leave town altogether. Then we'd have nothing and no chance to find her again. If you were any kind of an investigator, you'd think these things through before opening your mouth. Therefore, Agent, as of now, I'm taking situational command of this operation. From now on, everyone will follow my orders. Is that clear?"

Zardes's eyes raked over the task force members as he waited for each of them to nod their understanding.

~~

Hours later, Zardes was nodding off in a chair and Blaine signaled she was going to take a look around outside. Mike shook his head in warning, but Blaine paid no attention and left the van anyway. She'd been waiting since six for this opportunity and she wasn't going to let it slip through her fingers. Zardes was an idiot, and he was making everything worse. Blaine was positive Mike was right and they needed to go in soon if they were going to keep people from dying.

Luckily, there was no fence and a gravel pathway guided her to the back of the house. She was careful not to walk on the path, however, lest her footsteps be heard. Nor did she dare turn on her flashlight, so only the light of the quarter moon illuminated her way. Every chirp of a frog or meow of a neighborhood cat on the prowl caused her to stop and wait until all was serene once again. Even the staccato scraping of a solitary leaf blowing along the walkway halted her progress momentarily. In this way, she painstakingly inched her way closer to the building.

Getting as close as she dared, Blaine peered through a window. The lighting was low, but the dull glow outlined a man. He was laying on the settee, slumped against the pillow. From the way his body lay, Blaine guessed he was ill. Looking around the room, she realized he was alone. It was nearly midnight and she went back to the van as quickly as she dared to report her findings to Mike and a now awake Zardes.

While Zardes blustered his anger at Blaine, Mike sent David and Alex to look through the other windows and report back.

Barely three minutes later, David reported a similar occurrence with one of the female guests; she had been alone in the room during her collapse and no one was trying to help her.

Alex moved closer to the window on the east side of the house and immediately reported a similar scene from his vantage point.

Mike decided it was time to take action. Without waiting for Zardes, he ordered David and Alex to storm the house from the back while he and Chip went in through the front.

~~

Soon, all that could be heard was the breaking of doors and the announcing of "FBI!" and "MDPD!" from a variety of voices throughout the house. What the FBI and MDPD agents discovered there would haunt many of them for the rest of their lives.

CHAPTER 52

And the whole seizure, progress, and termination of the disease,
were the incidents of half-an-hour.
'THE MASQUE OF THE RED DEATH'

And one by one dropped the revellers in the blood-bedewed halls
of their revel, and died each in the despairing posture of his fall.
And the life of the ebony clock went out with that of the last of the
gay.
'THE MASQUE OF THE RED DEATH'

The house was a psychedelic dream, turned into a nightmare of
color and death. Each room was painted a different color, with
matching curtains and settees. The first room, the living room, was
a bright blue and had sheer curtains and a blue oval carpet upon
which sat a blue settee. There was no other furniture or decoration
within and the only fixture casting its light into the room was an
electric brazier standing in the hallway.

What drew Blaine's immediate attention, however, was the
body on the small couch. A woman dressed in her Sunday best lay
unmoving and silent in the middle of the room. Her hair had
originally been pulled back behind her head, but now large
segments of strands escaped the brightly colored band holding it.
Her clothes were ripped and torn in places and one of her arms was

bound to the settee by heavy ropes, unsurprisingly of the same blue that pervaded the rest of the room. Her appearance, though, would plague Blaine's dreams for months to come.

The skin of her arms and legs were covered with red and black patches. They resembled a rash of some kind, but within these spots of color there occasionally appeared smaller bumps of red with small circles of white in their centers. If she hadn't known better, the veteran detective would have thought that the woman had been a victim of numerous bug bites she had not been able to stop herself from scratching. Belying this conclusion was the presence of the unmistakable odor of vomit and drying blood, much of which could be seen on the young woman's clothing. Her face had not escaped this horrendous proof of illness and death. Her once bright blue eyes were now dulled with death, but Blaine could still see the shade of the terror that must have consumed her as she lay dying and helpless alone in this chamber of horrors.

Putting on her latex gloves, she gently closed the once-beautiful girl's eyelids although she knew it was against standard procedure. The horror-struck agent couldn't have cared less about procedure at that moment. She felt only sadness for the girl and wanted to give her at least a modicum of respect.

Across the hallway, with only the brazier for illumination, David found a similar macabre scene in what was supposed to be the dining room. Arranged the same way as the living room had been, this time in purple. Walls, couch, rug and ropes were colored a dark purple, and on the settee lay the body of a second victim. A man this time, approximately thirty years old and with a well-groomed mustache and beard. To David's untrained eyes, this man's death seemed to have been quicker; although he had the rash-like patches of the woman across the hall, his eyes were calmer, and his clothes were not rent and torn. While just as horrible, his death appeared to have been more peaceful.

~~

Throughout the house, this same scene was discovered repeatedly in the five remaining bedrooms. The only difference lay in the color of each room. Following the blue and purple of the first two crime scenes, the two rooms on the first floor and the three above were painted green, orange, white, violet and in the last room, black.

The last room broke the pattern. Along with the sheer curtains, oval rug and settee, there stood in a far corner a large clock made of an elegant, dark wood with a gold-tinted pendulum that swung loudly as it counted off the seconds.

Within these five rooms also lay five more bodies. When added to the first two victims, the pattern to the deaths became clear as one moved from room to room. Female-Male-Female-Male-Female-Male-Female accounted for the seven guests who had arrived at the house only short hours ago. Each victim was covered with the same rash-like patches on their faces and bodies, and the blood and vomit scattered around testified to the horror of their deaths.

~~

As the task force members spread throughout the house, Mike ignored the horrific scenes around him and single-mindedly fixed his sights on one purpose: to find Janice Toledo and Cameron Cudney and bring them to justice. It was not that the veteran agent didn't notice the dead in every room or that he didn't care about the victims' suffering, but Mike Donaldson had learned many years ago that to do his job effectively he had to put aside his anger, revulsion, or sometimes even sympathy, in order to protect the civilians who counted on him. Now the only way he could do that and end this madness was to find the perpetrators of these horrendous crimes.

If Mike thought his search was going to take time or that Janice and Cameron were going to resist arrest, he was mistaken. For, in the last room - the black room - Mike found Janice Toldeo, alone. She stood near the clock calmly and serenely as if simply waiting for just this moment.

She was dressed in a long, white skirt and rainbow-colored peasant blouse. Her ponytail hairdo had come undone and blonde strands fell in clumps around her face. Despite the low light of the brazier, Mike could see that her makeup was too heavy. Bright blush matched the red of her lipstick-lined mouth while thick mascara, eyeliner and shadow framed the brown eyes. Those eyes were bright, but it wasn't the brightness of happiness or intelligence. Instead, Mike saw a fierceness in those orbs and suddenly realized he was looking at the ferocity of mania.

"FBI! You're under arrest! Put your hands in the air and don't move!" Mike ordered as he pointed his Glock at the murderess and began to make his way slowly toward her.

"Do I look like I'm going anywhere?" asked the woman.

Janice Toledo actually *smiled* as the veteran FBI agent drew near, his weapon never wavering. She seemed calm, serene almost, as she awaited her fate at the hands of the law enforcement agencies that had invaded the scene of her crime.

Mike edged closer. "Where's Cameron?"

"Cameron?" asked Janice. She seemed genuinely confused. "He's not here. Why should he be?"

Mike let his anger get the best of him. "Because you're working together! Now, where is he?"

Janice's face turned dark. "He has nothing to do with this. It was all me."

Mike didn't believe her for a second, but for now, he'd take her and go after Cudney later.

As Mike reached the thirty-year-old suspect and began to place the handcuffs around her wrists, the loud chiming of the massive clock made him jump. Striking midnight, the ebony timepiece boomed out its song twelve times to commemorate the hour. And with each successive toll, Janice Toledo grew more and more calm as if the clock had some magical power to control its listeners.

Although a seasoned agent who had faced down some of the most wanted fugitives in recent FBI history, Mike couldn't help but be discomfited by the unusual calm of his suspect.

As a result, Mike uncharacteristically lost his cool as he got into the woman's face, pointed to the dead female on the couch and demanded, "What did you do to them?"

In response, Janice merely smiled again and replied, "I delivered them from their own fear."

"Fear of what?" asked Mike. His fingers were balled into a fist and his face had turned an uncharacteristic shade of red.

"Fear of death, of course," came the unexpected response. "You must realize that the only way to conquer death is to die. So, I helped them all conquer death. They need have no more fear now."

Mike had no idea how to respond to such circular logic, so he said nothing. He only nodded to Blaine Hoskins and David Scotty to take their suspect away.

Janice Toledo put up no opposition and without another word allowed herself to be led out of that chamber of horrors and into the waiting car outside.

~~

"'The Masque of the Red Death', Mike," stated Danny before Mike had even finished describing the second horrific room in the house. "The story was written by Poe in 1842 and tells the story of Prince Prospero. He gathered a thousand of the upper class, to use today's jargon, and barricaded himself and them in his palace."

"Why?" asked Chip from his vantage point on the other side of the room.

"To protect themselves from the plague that was killing hundreds of people around the countryside."

"And what's with all the painted rooms?" asked Alex as he jotted in his notebook.

"As the story goes," continued Danny, "Prospero throws a masquerade ball and each of the rooms is decorated in a different color. Janice painted her rooms in the same order of blue, purple, green, orange, white, violet and black just as Prospero painted his. Also, since there was no electricity during Prospero's time, only fire braziers illuminated the rooms and Janice did the same in her house, except her braziers were replicas that had to use electricity. Anyway," Danny sighed as he recounted the ending of the story, "during the ball a stranger enters the hall, and his costume upsets the prince, who orders him stopped. When Prospero himself takes off the stranger's mask, he realizes that the uninvited guest is Death, who has brought the plague to the palace, and one by one all Prospero's guests start to die. No one survives."

There was silence for a moment as each member of the task force considered the analyst's words.

It was now some three hours after the raid resulting in Janice Toledo's arrest and while their suspect waited for her attorney, most of the law enforcement officers were gathered in the conference room to review what had happened earlier in the evening.

"She painted the rooms like in the Poe story and since she couldn't invite a thousand people, she picked one person for each room." This came from Rhonda Sagan who had arrived just before the briefing began. It didn't take her long to go into profiler mode. "She then lured them to the house and somehow infected them with something that mimicked plague-like symptoms and waited for them to die."

David rushed in as Rhonda finished her analysis and interrupted, "Not just 'mimicked' plague-like symptoms, Rhonda. I just got the preliminary report back from the ME." David tried not to let the horror he felt show through in his tone as he reported, "Claudia says the victims actually died of a form of plague."

"What!?"

"That's impossible!"

"How could she get hold of plague? Claudia made a mistake."

Everyone began to react at once to the African American agent's report and no one hesitated to let their disbelief show.

"Hold on! Give me a chance!" barked David as he held his hands up. "Claudia says there's no doubt. This is definitely a type of plague. It's called Septicemic Plague, and in this case, Janice Toledo apparently injected it directly into the bloodstreams of the victims. It causes tiny clots which result in bleeding into the skin and that caused the red rashes we saw on the victims'. Sometimes there's coughing or vomiting but not always. If untreated, the victims usually die on the same day they show symptoms, but since Janice injected them directly, they died even quicker than usual."

David lowered his voice as he ended his report, remembering the horrible deaths their seven victims experienced a few short hours ago.

"But how did a woman like Janice Toledo get hold of plague?" cried out Danny. His voice had risen, and his tone couldn't hide his horror.

"I don't know," answered Mike grimly, "But I'm damn well going to find out."

CHAPTER 53

But to-morrow I die, and to-day I would unburthen my soul.
'THE BLACK CAT'

August 23

Janice Toledo's attorney arrived a short time later and, after conferring with her for about fifteen minutes, confirmed that her client was ready to talk to the investigators.

Mike had no doubt that the lawyer wouldn't let their prime suspect answer a single question, but he knew the formalities had to be gone through. This, along with the several more interrogations that were sure to come, might glean some relevant information and would also give his team opportunity to gather more evidence and give the AUSA time to decide what and how to charge Janice Toledo for these horrific crimes.

"I want it understood up front that my client is willing to answer your questions, Agent, but only as long as I am here for any and all questioning. If I discover that the FBI has interrogated Ms. Toledo without my presence, I guarantee she will stop talking immediately. Do I make myself clear?"

"Certainly, Ms. Goncalves," responded Mike with a slight smile. "The FBI will appreciate any help your client can give us with this case."

Mike had taken a moment to do a little research about the local attorney before entering the interview room. The young Hispanic woman had risen above her lower-class roots to earn her degree and return to her home state to practice law. During the last nine years, she had earned her reputation as a hard-nosed, no-nonsense criminal lawyer who had an excellent success record and was known for getting the best deals for any of her clients found guilty.

Despite the ungodly early hour - only 4:30 in the morning - Selena Goncalves looked as though she'd been awake for hours and was ready to appear in court. She had long, brown hair that currently sat on her head in a becoming bun, dark black eyes that shone with awareness and intelligence, light red lipstick and painted-on eyebrows. She was tastefully dressed in a blue business suit and reasonably comfortable two-inch heels.

Mike quickly decided he could not take Selena Goncalves lightly and her first words had confirmed this assessment. Mike looked over to Rhonda Sagan, who was assisting him with this interview, and saw that she seemed to agree with his opinion. Behind the two-way mirror, David, Chip, SAC Martinez, Captain Mendez and AUSA Robin McMurphy were watching the interview, while Blaine and Alex oversaw the crime scene.

"Let's start with the house in Coral Gables," began Mike. "What can you tell me about it?"

Janice was dressed in jailhouse orange. Her ponytail was fixed and her becoming dress shoes had been traded in for a pair of sneakers. With her makeup gone, her face was decidedly plain but not unattractive. Her cuffed hands rested quietly in her lap. She had even smiled at Mike and Rhonda as they entered the room.

She took a moment to look at her attorney and upon seeing that lady's nod, responded calmly, "I don't own it if that's what you mean."

"But you contacted the real estate agent on August 10 and made an appointment to view the house on the 11th. Why?"

"You already know why, Agent Donaldson," answered the blonde woman. "I knew that the house was perfect for my plan, but I needed to get inside and verify it. And I'll save you the trouble and just admit that I stole one of the house keys from that stupid agent and used it to get in later when I was ready."

"Ready for what?"

This question came from Rhonda. She was leaning forward as she asked the question and seemed fascinated by the seeming unconcern Janice Toledo revealed. Apparently, Rhonda had never seen a murderer so calm and in control in her ten-year FBI career. Mike agreed and was convinced that this was going to be one of the most unusual interrogations with which either of them had ever been involved.

"Ready for my last murders, of course."

Rhonda and Mike simply stared at their suspect in a mixture of surprise and disbelief.

Did she really just admit to being our killer?

Immediately, Mike looked at Goncalves and wondered why she wasn't objecting or trying to silence her client. Selena Goncalves, however, seemed unperturbed by her client's revelation and sat calmly taking notes of the continuing interview.

Janice, for her part, actually smiled at the effect her words had on the two FBI agents. Mike got the feeling she had always known what the end game would be and had been prepared for this day since she first devised her plans. She leaned back in her chair and began her unbelievable confession.

"You see, I knew it was just a matter of time before the police would start looking at me. I wanted to be prepared so that my last murder would be my greatest achievement. I mean, really, I killed seven people all at the same time! What could be greater? But I thought I'd have a little more time than I did. I was surprised when I realized you were watching me already and I needed to get everything in place so I could do what I needed to do at the right time. I was pretty sure that Teresa would figure out that I had taken the Temazepam and report me, and I spotted your people watching me on the 19th, and that was my cue to get started. I knew I didn't have much time; I had to be ready by the 22nd."

No one said anything for a moment. Mike was considering his options, then realized that Janice had specifically mentioned the date of August 22. That was a Poe date.

Taking a chance, Mike asked, "Ms. Toledo, are you admitting to being the Poe murderer?"

"Well, of course I'm the Poe murderer!" admitted Toledo with unfeigned pride in her voice. "Isn't that why I'm here?" Janice waited a beat, then with sudden venom, "Didn't you think I was capable of it? I led the police on a chase for nearly seven weeks before you were able to catch me! I gave you plenty of time to find me, but when it was obvious you didn't have a clue, I had to help you along by sending that letter to the paper. That's when Teresa Pinot came to you and told you about me. I did that! Not you! You were too stupid to figure it out on your own. I'm smarter than all of you put together!"

As she voiced this tirade against the authorities and their handling of the investigation, Janice's voice grew shriller and her demeanor became more upset. Finally, Selena Goncalves put a hand on her client's arm. It had the desired effect and Janice calmed down immediately.

"Oh, we believe you are the Poe murderer, Ms. Toledo," assured Rhonda. "It's just that there are still some details we're unclear of and it would help us if you could walk us through it. I'm sure we can learn a lot from the way you planned these deaths."

"Well, of course you can," agreed an appeased Janice immediately. She was the calm and accommodating witness once again. "Please tell me what you want to know."

Mike almost couldn't believe that it was going to be this easy. Before Janice or her attorney could change their minds, he quickly asked, "I'd like your statement to be taken down, Ms. Toledo.

Would you mind if I called a stenographer in here while we talked?"

Surprisingly, it was Janice's attorney who responded, "As I said earlier, Agent Donaldson, my client wishes to cooperate fully. We do not mind her interview being recorded at this time."

~~

The statement had gone well. There were no objections from Selena Goncalves on behalf of her client on any point and Janice herself was more than ready to admit to all her murders. In fact, she was angry when Mike suggested she'd had help from Cameron. She flatly denied this and seemed quite proud of what she'd done.

She readily admitted to stealing the Temazepam from Medical Supplies Inc. When she'd resigned, Theresa Pinot had forgotten to take back Janice's key or change the security alarm code, so she'd crept in late one night, removed pills from an open bottle of Temazepam and left with no one the wiser. She even told Mike where the rest of the drug was hidden so it could be reclaimed.

She explained how she found and identified her victims and described how she became friendly with them in order to drug their drinks before taking each one to the murder scenes. She befriended Lylyana Biddix and Lucy Benton at their stores and pretended to be a customer so she could engage each one in lengthy conversations, eventually inviting each out for lunch. Since Stephen Hardison was a loan officer, she 'accidentally' ran into him while he waited for a sandwich, pretended to be a customer of his bank and offered him a lift when he discovered a flat tire. She asked Camille Henri to advise her on a cleaning service for her supposed home in Bayshore and sabotaged her car, so she'd have to ask Suzanne to drive her there. She'd gotten lucky with Cecilia Rogers. She found out that the security guard worked out regularly, so she made sure she met her at her victim's gym.

After some two hours of questioning and a short half-hour break for a breakfast of donuts and orange juice, Mike was ready to discuss the most horrific of the murders, the ones based on 'The Masque of the Red Death'. Mike learned that the murderess had picked her victims from her hours of sitting at different restaurants. That was why she had carried the legal pad with her; she was making notes of the people she planned to target.

"But we were watching you the entire time," commented Mike, "We never saw you talk to anyone except for the servers. How did you approach them?"

"I went to the bathroom several times, Agent Donaldson," smiled the murderess. "You'd be surprised how much you can learn about someone while waiting in line or washing hands over a sink. I chose the younger ones because I knew they'd be stupid enough to give me information. I got names, phone numbers, Facebook addresses or emails whenever I could. Then later, I'd call or email them and secure their confidence. All that was left was to invite them to a 'party' with free food and drink and tell them to bring along a date. I even got lucky. One of the women asked to bring both her boyfriend and his brother. It was perfect!"

Mike made a note on the pad in front of him, then asked the question they had all had since they'd first gotten the ME's report several hours ago. "Ms. Toledo, the medical examiner has determined that the seven people in the house in Coral Gables died of Septicemic Plague. We would like to know how you got hold of such a deadly disease and is there any more of it and where can we find it?"

Under other circumstances, Mike would have expected an objection from the suspect's attorney or the suspect herself to deny everything or to ask for something in return for divulging such information, such as a shorter sentence or another consideration. However, this interrogation had been so unusual that, by now, Mike would have bet that Janice Toledo would not only tell him all about the deadly pathogen she had used but would probably do so proudly. He would not have lost that bet.

"That was actually the easiest thing I had to do, Agent Donaldson," explained the suspect. "You see, when I first decided on my Poe murders, I had to decide which stories I would use. 'The Masque of the Red Death' had always been one of my favorite Poe stories and I just knew I had to use it as my pièce de résistance. I thought that finding an illness that mimicked the plague would be difficult, but I started my research and what do you think I discovered?"

Janice smiled as if she were the proverbial cat that ate the canary as she answered the rhetorical question. "Back in April of 2006 there was actually a case of plague in Los Angeles. I found out that the CDC in Atlanta still had some samples. I drove to Atlanta and took a tour of the building. You know, they give them to the public every day. I showed my credentials from Medical Supplies Inc. to get a behind the scenes look. I got close enough to see the technician enter his security code and then, later, was able to steal an ID and a set of keys. I went back later that same week and stole two samples. The pathogen is so virulent that that was all I needed. I kept it in a protective case until I needed it tonight. Or rather last night," laughed Janice as she looked at her watch.

During the interview, it had been difficult for Mike to keep his cool in the face of Janice's obvious lack of remorse and self-congratulation. Listening to Janice brag about using such a deadly disease to kill, Mike began to feel that she had to be one of the most dangerous criminals he had ever questioned. He believed that this woman had no moral scruples whatsoever and had to be truly insane.

Looking over his notes regarding the case, Mike realized there were only two remaining points to discuss. Mentally flipping a coin, he began the next subject of his questioning. He opened another file on the table and pulled out a copy of the letter Janice had written to the media detailing the Poe murders.

"All right, Ms. Toledo, I have here a copy of your letter to the editor of the *Herald*. Would you like to look at it before I discuss it with you?"

"No need, Agent Donaldson. I remember what I wrote," came the smug reply.

"Very well," replied the case agent. "Ms. Toledo, in this letter you detail all your murders up until that time. But I'm curious. Why didn't you include the murder of Oscar Cudney, which occurred on June 22?"

Janice looked almost affronted by the question as she sat upright and declared, "But I didn't kill Oscar! That was Cameron. If I had killed that old man, I would have admitted it, to be sure."

Mike was nonplussed as he considered Janice's answer.

Are we wrong about Oscar Cudney? But that doesn't make sense! It fits the pattern of the murders. Cudney has to be victim zero.

Mike leaned forward and insisted, "Ms. Toledo, Oscar Cudney was your first victim. His death was obviously based on 'The Tell-Tale Heart'. You can't deny that you did it."

"I don't deny that Oscar's death was based on 'The Tell-Tale Heart', but I certainly deny that I did it. Cameron killed Oscar. That's how I got the idea for all the others."

"I'm afraid you're going to have to explain that to us, Ms. Toledo," stated Rhonda.

The profiler had not participated much in the questioning except to give Mike a break or get more detail on a psychological point. However, now that they were apparently getting to the heart of why Janice had started her killing spree, Rhonda decided it was time to take a more active role.

"Cameron wanted to marry me," declared Janice. "I was sure of it. I was sure it was just the money that was holding him back. I mean, I didn't make much at Medical Supplies Inc. and Cameron was just a research assistant at the *Herald*, so he didn't make much either. And in this economy, well, you know how expensive Miami is, we couldn't have managed it. I know he was worried about giving me the best he could, but there wasn't enough money. So, one day we were talking, and he said that Oscar left him insurance money, but Oscar could live for years so we'd have to wait.

"Around that time, I'd introduced Cameron to Edgar Allan Poe, and he was reading some of his stories and mentioned that Poe sure had an imagination for killing people. I had already told him that 'The Tell-Tale Heart' was my favorite Poe story and he mentioned that one specifically for how gruesome it was. Just for fun we started thinking about how you'd kill someone like that, and Cameron even got on the Internet and researched about the easiest way to dismember a body.

"Naturally I thought it was just a joke or something. Or maybe Cameron was working out his frustrations by working out the problem. You know, how the psychologists tell you to write out what you'd like to do to someone you hate so that you get it out of your system?" Here Janice gave a condescending smile to Rhonda. "Really, I forgot all about it until Oscar turned up dead a few weeks later. Then I realized that Cameron had really done it. He'd killed Oscar so that he'd get the money and the two of us could get married and have a family. It was so sweet of him to do that for me. But, of course, it was dangerous.

"So, when Cameron asked me to tell the police he was with me during that night, of course I was willing to do it. I mean, Oscar wanted Cameron to have the money anyway, so what if Cameron made it happen a bit sooner than expected? He was an old man anyway! We would have been so happy together." Janice sighed quietly, seemingly remembering her prior relationship with Cameron Cudney.

Mike and Rhonda looked at each other. This was obviously not what they had expected. It seemed that Cameron Cudney *had* killed his cousin and belonged in jail. But Janice's recollection of her courtship with Cameron was vastly different from what Cameron had described during their interview with him a week before. At that time, Cameron said that Janice had wanted more from the relationship than he had - she wanted marriage, a house, kids, the works - while he was content with the way things were. He needed her for his alibi but when she reneged, he broke up with her.

Mike mentally shook his head and asked, "So why did you take back the alibi you gave him? You stated he had been with you that night, then later recanted."

Janice almost yelled as she answered, "Because he lied to me! He made me think he wanted the money so we could be together after Oscar died, then afterwards he said he didn't want to get married anymore! You see, Cameron thought he was going to get one hundred thousand dollars from Oscar's life insurance policy, but then he found out it was only ten. Apparently, Cameron saw an old policy at Oscar's house, and thought that was the right amount. He didn't know that Oscar cashed in that policy to pay off his house and some other bills, then took out a new policy for just ten thousand. So, Cameron used that as his excuse, that it wasn't enough to get married on. But when I realized he didn't really want to marry me, I told the police the truth, that he wasn't with me that night at all."

"So, you and Cameron had been engaged when Oscar Cudney died?" inquired Rhonda with a sympathetic tone to her voice.

Janice hesitated a bit, then reluctantly admitted, "Well, no, not officially engaged. We had an ... an ... understanding."

"But Cameron didn't understand the same thing you did." This came from Mike and was more a statement than a question.

"He lied to me!" Janice reiterated angrily. "He used me. We were lovers but he didn't want to get married. He wanted Oscar's money but when he found out it was only ten thousand, he changed his mind. He used me and then just discarded me! Like an old sheet or something!" Janice had tears in her eyes as she voiced this indictment against her ex-boyfriend.

"But I thought you said you broke up with him," stated Rhonda.

"Well, of course I did!" clarified Janice. "But if he had really loved me, he would have asked me to come back, but he didn't, so he discarded me. Just like I said."

"You mean you didn't break up with him because of his gambling?" asked Mike with an edge to his voice.

"Of course not," replied Janice as if she were speaking to a child. "Cameron isn't addicted to gambling or anything. Once we were married, he'd have gotten over all that. All he needed was a good woman. All he needed was me. I'd have made him the perfect wife."

Janice smiled at Mike as if she'd just explained the most obvious statement ever spoken. It was clear now to everyone listening that Janice Toledo had been living a fantasy from one of her Harlequin-type romances where the man and woman lived happily ever after. If Mike hadn't been so angry over the many deaths this woman had committed, he might almost feel sorry for her.

Almost.

CHAPTER 54

Years of love have been forgot in the hatred of a minute.
'To M---'

Fifteen-sixteen-seventeen …

Cameron hefted the twenty-pound hand weight as if he were lifting a paperback book. He was still sweating from the dumb bells workout and had started the hand weights at a lower poundage than usual. It was only six a.m. and he had plenty of time to add more later if he wanted.

"Hey, Cameron. I'm surprised to see you here this mornin'."

Cameron looked up into the brown eyes of Mickey Martin. Built like a tank, Mickey was a writer's stereotypic dumb jock. Cameron was sure he'd sell his own mother for a state-of-the-art home gym if he had the chance.

"Hey, Mick. Why're you surprised to see me? I work out every morning before work."

"Yeah, sure, but I figured you wouldn't want to see anybody today, or not leastways until after you talked to your lawyer." Mickey barked a laugh and picked up a set of fifty-pound hand weights.

Perspiration again broke out on Cameron's forehead and he struggled to keep his voice calm. "What are you on about, man? What's a lawyer got to do with anything?"

"You ain't heard the news? It's all over the TV, on every station. They even broke into the replay of last night's game, man. Just as Fernandez was getting ready to bat. He was a triple away from the Cycle! Man, I ..."

Cameron sat up and huffed. "Mick, what are you talking about? What was on the News?"

"They caught the Poe murderer, man. And you'll never guess who it was."

In the ensuing silence, Mickey grinned at him, but Cameron didn't think it was a good grin. Mickey was baiting him, he was almost sure of it.

"Well, you gonna tell me or keep me in suspense?"

"I can't believe you really don't know, man. It's your ex. Janice! They arrested her last night, right after she killed a bunch more people. Caught her red-handed, like."

Cameron went white and sweat rolled from his forehead.

Janice is the Poe murderer? How the hell ... shit! She's bound to tell them about me killin' Oscar. What the fuck do I do now?

Cameron decided to brazen it out. "I don't believe it, man. There's no way Janice killed all those people. It's a mistake, gotta be."

Mickey was working the weights again and answered between grunts. "If you say so ... man. Guess you'd ... know her better ... than most. But ... if I was you, I'd ... be calling a ... lawyer. Cops'll wanna ... talk to you prob'ly ... and you know the media's ... gonna come callin' ... when they find out ... you're her ... ex. They always do."

Cameron had stopped listening. Without a word of goodbye, he grabbed his gym bag and practically ran out of the building.

~~

This can not be happening. Janice's gonna spill everything and I'll be up shit creek. I gotta figure out what to do. I need to think, dammit. Think!

Cameron barely paid attention to the traffic around him as he wound his way to his apartment. He drove by rote and allowed his mind to turn over the same information again and again.

I should never have asked that bitch to give me an alibi. Should've known I couldn't trust her to keep the story straight. She really screwed me up.

Maybe it's not too late to get one of the guys at the game to alibi me. They could just say they were worried about getting into trouble too, then realized it was right to admit to the game. I could offer some money after I get the insurance pay off ... no! That won't work. I already owe a couple thou. They'll never cover my ass now.

A horn beeped behind him and he quickly hit the gas and went through the green light. Thankfully at this hour of the morning, there weren't a lot of cars on the roads, but the streets of Miami were never completely empty.

Cameron knew he was panicking but didn't know how to stop. His thoughts were all over the place, moving at warp speed and he had no idea what to do next.

That's why those Feds came to talk to me so much. They weren't looking at me, they were looking at Janice. But even if she does finger me for Oscar's murder, they won't believe her now. She killed all those people ... man, she's gotta be off her rocker.

Knew I shouldn't have trusted her for my alibi. All she had to do was remember the name of the fricking movie, for Pete's sake! But no, she couldn't even do that ...

Wait a minute, that means she doesn't have an alibi either. I can use that to get off the hook. I'll just finger her for Oscar's death. That lawyer they gave me said they found her hair in Oscar's house, and she knew about the insurance money. If I can make them think she did Oscar to get that money ...

But what've I got to incriminate her with? I'll have to make up something, then give it to the cops. I can say I was going through old boxes of stuff and found it. That I was gonna give it back to Janice but never got the chance and now that she's been arrested, I realized it might be important.

I can say how upset I am and … shocked. Yeah, that's the word I'll use. Shocked. I'm shocked that a woman I knew could have killed so many people, including my dear old cousin who wouldn't have hurt a fly.

Cameron turned into his street and as he neared his apartment building, a new thought came to mind and he panicked once again.

But the cops could be here any minute. What if they're on their way right now? I don't have time to do it and I don't even know what I'm gonna give 'em yet.

No, no, no. Calm down. There hasn't been enough time for them to think about you yet. They just arrested her a few hours ago. They're probably gonna be questioning her all day, maybe tomorrow too. I just gotta calm down. I'll look around the apartment. There's gotta be something I can use against her.

I'll text Ron and say I'm sick. Even if he doesn't believe I'm really sick, he'll probably think I want to keep away from people, just like Mick said. Fuck, it's a newspaper, for fuck's sake. They'll probably want to interview me or something. Not going in would make perfect sense today.

Cameron pulled into his normal parking spot and hopped out of his car. He picked up his pace as he made his way to the stairwell and his third-floor apartment. He smiled as he convinced himself his worries were almost over.

I have all day to get something together to implicate Janice and get me off the hook. Then I can get the insurance money. I'll pay off the guys and go from there. Maybe I'll have enough left over for that exercise bike I've had my eye on.

Yeah, yeah. This'll work.

"Fuck." Cameron cursed out loud as he realized he'd left his gym bag in the car.

He turned around and headed back. As he developed, then discarded, ideas in his mind, he was almost to his parking space before he noticed two men standing by the old Ford. One had his hand on the hood.

The men turned and Cameron's blood ran cold as he recognized them. Cameron knew he couldn't run.

"Good morning, Mr. Cudney. You're quite the early bird, aren't you?"

The two men walked closer, and the older man began to speak.

"You may not remember us, Mr. Cudney. I'm Detective Alex Welch and this is Special Agent Smythe of the FBI. We'd like to ask you a few questions. Do you mind if we invite ourselves to your apartment?"

CHAPTER 55

And this maiden she lived with no other thought
Than to love and be loved by me.
'Annabel Lee'

It was now nearly nine in the morning and, after a short break, the time had finally come for the most important part of the interview. Even more important than the how of the murders was the *why*. Why had Janice Toledo killed over a dozen people in such a gruesome manner? What had motivated her to take such a step? Why had a woman with a good job, friends and no criminal record suddenly decided to go on a killing binge that had terrorized the entire city for weeks?

Mike and Rhonda had discussed their strategy for this portion of the questioning and Mike had decided that the profiler was better equipped to lead this part of the interview. She had studied psychology in general and serial killers in particular, and she had conducted more such interviews than he had. It might be sexist, but Mike believed that as a woman, Rhonda had a better chance to extract the real reason behind these murders. She was better suited for this interview and he had no trouble admitting it.

In some ways Mike was relieved to hand this thankless task over to her. He wasn't sure he could be objective or professional enough to conduct the interview without becoming emotional about it. It had been a long few weeks and he was having trouble keeping his anger in check. He was disgusted by Janice Toledo's seeming indifference to the pain she'd caused and didn't know if he could keep from reaching across the table and taking matters into his own hands. No, having Rhonda interview Janice was for the best.

Janice and her attorney had their heads close together as Mike and Rhonda entered the interview room. As they sat down, Janice leaned back and gave the FBI agents one of her supercilious smiles and Ms. Goncalves turned to a new page in her legal pad.

"Before we get started, Ms. Toledo," asked Rhonda, "Do either of you need anything to drink or eat? I think there's still some donuts left in the break room."

"No, thank you, Agent, we're fine," Selena answered for both of them. "We're ready to continue."

"Fine, then let's get to it." Rhonda looked at her own legal pad, made a note and asked, "How did you decide to make Lylyana Biddix your first victim?"

Mike looked at Rhonda with respect. By her tone, she could have been asking why Janice went for a walk yesterday instead of why she had committed a cold-blooded murder. He could never have pulled it off. If he hadn't known it before, he was now positive that he'd made the smart move by having Rhonda question Janice about her motives.

In this way, Rhonda took Janice through each murder once again, getting more details about how she chose her victims or what she did to secure their confidence. Subtly, Rhonda's questions gave Janice the chance to explain her reasons behind each choice. There wasn't much need to explain why she chose Cecilia Rogers or the Henris, but Mike was shocked to hear that the only reason Lucy Benton was killed was because she had mentioned to Janice that she didn't like pets. Janice had decided it would be fitting for her to be found surrounded by animals.

An hour later, Rhonda got to the crux of the matter. This was what Mike had been waiting for, for five weeks. He leaned forward and put his elbows on the table.

"Janice, why kill people based on the stories and poems of Edgar Allan Poe? What was the point of that?"

"Oh that. I was just following Cameron's lead. He killed Oscar based on 'The Tell-Tale Heart' so I killed my people based on Poe, too. It was *poe*tic justice!" Janice laughed at her own pun. No one joined her.

After a long moment, Rhonda continued the interview with, "Janice, will you tell me why you wanted to kill all these people in the first place? What made you do it?"

Janice leaned closer to Rhonda as her eyes grew wide. "Why, isn't it obvious? I did it for Cameron, of course!" Her face was open, and Mike realized that she truly believed they should already know this.

"But Cameron was in jail for killing his cousin," Rhonda countered. "You took back your alibi and gave the DA what he needed to charge Cameron. Although he was released due to lack of evidence, didn't it occur to you that he might remain a suspect? How would killing all these people help him?" Rhonda's tone suggested that she wasn't setting a trap, she really didn't understand that logic.

"Don't be silly," Janice answered. She waved a hand as if swatting a fly away and went on. "I didn't say I was helping Cameron, I said I did it *for* him."

Rhonda and Mike said nothing, and their blank expressions seemed to aggravate the murderess. Janice's tone was condescending as she explained, "Don't you see? I knew that when Cameron found out I killed those people he'd realize how much I loved him. He'd forgive me for taking back his alibi and then he'd come back to me. We'd be together again. We could get married and everything would be just like it was before."

Rhonda blinked at this circular logic, then found her voice. "But Cameron was under suspicion for killing Oscar. How could he come back to you and marry you if rearrested and sent to prison?"

"Oh, that wasn't going to happen," Janice responded with another dismissive wave. "I knew his attorney would find a way to get him off. And he did. That was just a minor technicality."

Another pause and then Rhonda countered with, "But what about you? You've admitted to killing sixteen people. You're going to prison for a long time. How do you expect to marry Cameron?"

"Oh, he'll wait for me. After he's vindicated completely, he'll get Oscar's money. He might even be able to sell his story to a magazine or something. He could make money off it and put that aside and it'll be waiting for us after we're married. And I might write a book. I'm a good writer, you know. I could write a book about my experiences and make a lot of money. Then Cameron and I can get married even sooner."

She's off her rocker! If he hadn't known it before, Mike would have been certain of it now.

"I want to be sure I have the sequence straight, Janice," said Rhonda. "You believed that Cameron wanted to marry you but couldn't because he didn't have enough money. So, he killed his cousin Oscar because he was the beneficiary of Oscar's life insurance policy. And he based the murder on 'The Tell-Tale Heart' after you introduced him to Edgar Allen Poe. Then you gave him an alibi for the murder but took it back when he reneged on marrying you. After you broke up, you decided to kill others, also using Poe, in order to prove your love for Cameron. You believed he'd take you back when he realized what you'd done and, after you got out of prison, the two of you would get married and be together."

"There's no 'would' about it," declared Janice as she pounded her fist against the table. "We will get married and we'll be happy for the rest of our lives."

CHAPTER 56

I was never really insane except upon occasions where my heart
was touched.

'Letter to Maria Clemm'

Later that day, everyone was back in the conference room - the
entire task force, SAC Martinez, SSA Zardes and Captain Mendez
- listening intently to Rhonda Sagan's professional opinion
regarding Janice Toledo's mental state.

Mike was content to let Rhonda take the spotlight and sat in
the back of the room saying nothing while watching the others
carefully.

He especially watched Bradley Zardes. Since he'd learned that
the SSA recruited Chip to undermine him, Mike had made it clear
to Zardes that he wouldn't report to him in person anymore. He'd
merely sent in his reports and left it at that. Mike had learned from
Chip that Zardes had not ordered him to report to him either.
Zardes apparently decided he didn't need an informant anymore
and had simply resorted to taking over the investigation.

And botching it up, he thought.

Zardes's mishandling of the stake out had led to seven deaths
and Mike was trying to decide what to do about it. But that was a
decision for a later time. Right now, Mike brought his mind back to
the matter at hand and listened to the FBI profiler.

Rhonda didn't look like she'd been in the office since 3 a.m. She was wide awake, animated, and apparently anxious to give her opinion on this unusual case.

"While her statement was being typed up, I spoke to Janice once again. This time, I concentrated on her early life growing up and her young adulthood. Apparently, her parents had an exceptionally good marriage that lasted almost thirty years before they were both killed in a car accident about five years ago. She stated they never fought, got along great and were each other's best friends. Whether that is true or not," remarked the profiler, "or just a young woman's viewpoint of it, I don't know."

"Children don't always know when their parents are having problems or fighting," commented Blaine Hoskins. "Especially if the parents try to hide it from them."

Rhonda responded, "You're absolutely correct, but for our purposes it means a great deal. Janice had a great upbringing with strong parental support and an example of the 'perfect marriage'. She thought that was what life should be like for her as well. So, when she met and became involved with Cameron Cudney, she believed that her life would end up just like her parents' lives had."

Rhonda held up a thick folder and stated, "These are some of Janice's stories that the agents found when they executed the search warrant for her apartment while we were questioning her. I've read some of it and it's as her library group friends said. She writes like life is a Harlequin romance. There are damsels in distress, knight-like heroes, and evil outsiders trying to keep the lovers apart. The protagonists have to fight to be together, but in the end, they always live happily ever after." Rhonda put down the folder again as she continued her explanation to her captivated listeners.

"Janice confirmed what her college roommate told you. Before she became involved with Cameron Cudney, she never had a steady boyfriend. She had no experience of breaking up or playing the field. In many ways she was as sheltered as one of the heroines in her stories. So, when she did meet Cameron and they began sleeping together not long thereafter, she thought she had found Mr. Right and didn't think for a minute that he wouldn't feel the same. She rationalized his lack of commitment as a problem with money - an obstacle to be overcome for the star-crossed lovers - so once Oscar was dead, she truly believed Cameron would marry her as soon as he got his inheritance. When Cameron still wouldn't commit, she became furious and took back her alibi as revenge."

"So, you believe Cameron's version of events - that he broke up with her, not the other way around?" asked David.

"Oh, absolutely," replied the profiler emphatically. "No matter how angry she may have been with Cameron, she would never have been the one to break it off. She saw all this in her mind as merely another obstacle to overcome. And despite the fact that she'd made Cameron 'Suspect Number One' by going back on her alibi, she was sure Cameron would return to her in the end and they would have that wonderful life she felt she deserved."

"Why'd she tell you that she broke off the relationship?" asked Captain Mendez.

"I believe she was trying to save face," explained the profiler.

"Then why start murdering people?" asked Alex in exasperation. "And why in such a gruesome manner?"

Although he recognized the need for profilers in his line of work, he had little use for psychology in general and hated it when killers got away with their murders on an insanity defense. And in this case, the writing was definitely on the wall. Even Janice Toledo's attorney had made it clear that she had allowed her client to admit to everything and explain her reasoning because she was going to use the statement as her first exhibit in her client's plea of temporary insanity.

"She was trying to impress Cameron, Alex," replied Rhonda.

"Impress him how?" asked Martinez.

It was the first time the SAC had spoken since he'd come into the room and Mike had almost forgotten he was there.

"Well, it's a bit complicated, but in essence, Janice believed that Cameron had killed his cousin by using one of Poe's stories as his guide to impress *her*. So, while he was waiting to be cleared of suspicion, she decided to prove to him she was worthy of his love by using the same method."

"Seriously?" asked Danny.

The look on his face spoke volumes and Mike sympathized with the analyst's suspicions. Mike had spent hours interviewing Janice Toledo and even he couldn't believe her reasoning.

"Seriously," responded Rhonda with a grim smile. "Remember, Danny, we are not dealing with a rational woman. Janice believes that her reasoning makes sense and that we should understand and accept it. Even the date of yesterday's murders was a part of her romantic fantasy."

"Huh?" asked Chip less than eloquently. "Romantic fantasy?"

"Yes. Believe it or not, romance was part of her plan." Rhonda took a breath as she explained to her audience, "Yesterday was August 22. And on August 22, 1822, Virginia Clemm was born."

"Who was Virginia Clemm?" asked Chip.

"Virginia Clemm was Edgar Allan Poe's cousin and his future wife. They were married in 1836 but she died of tuberculosis in 1847. She was truly the love of Poe's life, so Janice thought it was fitting that she committed her most spectacular murders on that date to prove to Cameron that he was the love of her life."

The assembled investigators stared in disbelief at the profiler's explanation of Janice Toledo's thought processes.

After a long moment, David broke the silence by saying, "Let me get this straight. Janice Toledo murdered sixteen people to *impress* Cameron Cudney. The same man she had previously been so mad at that she took back an alibi in a murder that he committed. And she committed these murders because she believed he'd forgive her, marry her and they'd live happily ever after on his inheritance. Have I got all that right?"

"You do, David," the profiler assured him.

"Well, whether it was ten thousand or a hundred thousand, did it never even occur to her that Cameron couldn't inherit if he was convicted of murdering Oscar Cudney?" asked Blaine, showing as much disbelief as David a moment ago.

"No, it didn't," confirmed Rhonda. "Janice said she was sure Cameron would get off and she'd be waiting for him when he did."

"Okay, I'm sold," stated Alex. "She's got a few ingredients missing from her cupboard! She'll never see the inside of a federal prison. I'd give you odds on it."

"I'm afraid you might be right, Alex," agreed Mendez. "I think her attorney has a very good case."

No one responded to that since each of them agreed with him.

CHAPTER 57

Words have no power to impress the mind without the exquisite
horror of their reality.
'THE NARRATIVE OF ARTHUR GORDON PYM'

August 24

Dr. Barty was late. Mike was scheduled to meet with the Poe
expert at nine. He'd arrived at her office a little early, but she
wasn't in yet. Mike leaned against the wall and rested his eyes.
He'd actually gotten close to seven hours sleep last night, but as
exhausted as he'd been these last few weeks, it would take several
more nights of peaceful rest for him to feel caught up.

Yesterday had seemed never-ending. After the interviews with
Janice and her attorney, there had been meetings with the FBI and
MDPD brass, the AUSA, as well as tons of paperwork to be
completed. The most difficult part, however, had been contacting
the families of the victims and informing them of their loved ones'
deaths. Both Martinez and Mendez had offered to complete the
difficult task for him, but Mike felt it was his responsibility. He
actually believed it was Zardes's job, but Mike hadn't seen hide
nor hair of the SSA since the meeting yesterday morning.

*Fine, I don't want to see him anyway. He's probably hiding in
his office calling his tailor about a new suit!*

Mike shook his head and looked at his watch. 9:10. He'd told Blaine and the others he'd be in around ten, but it was obvious he was going to be late. Today was set aside to catalog the evidence, finish reports and in general close down the case as much as possible. They might need another day, but he hoped they could get it all done today. He still needed to contact his supervisor in Detroit and make a flight reservation. He sent a quick text to Blaine to tell her he'd be late and, just as he was wondering if there was a coffee vending machine nearby, he heard the click, click, click of a pair of high heels coming towards him.

Mike turned toward the sound and blinked. Dr. Barty was headed his way, but this was not the same woman he'd met five weeks ago. Her normally straight, mousy hair held gentle curls which framed her made-up face. She was wearing a soft blue dress in a becoming style and her one-inch heels were tasteful. The effect was ruined by the garish nail polish she sported, and Mike had to wonder if she'd pulled the polish from the back of a drawer at home or if the store had a sale. Mike suddenly remembered Danny's teasing a couple of weeks ago and hoped he was wrong about what this change in their consultant's appearance might signify.

He pasted on a smile and called a cheery, "Good morning, Dr. Barty."

"Good morning, Agent Donaldson," she said as she pulled out her keys, opened her office door and ushered Mike inside. "I do apologize for my tardiness, but you know Miami traffic; most mornings I'm lucky to get here on time without leaving my house at the crack of dawn."

"That's all right, Dr. Barty, this won't take long and then I'll be able to let you get to your work." Mike gave her his most disarming smile. "I'm sure you heard that we've arrested Janice Toledo for the Poe murders?"

"Oh yes. It was the only story on the news this morning." Jeniviere almost gushed and Mike saw her hands tremble slightly as she continued, "I was shocked, of course. I mean, I knew she studied Poe, but to do something like this, it's almost incomprehensible."

While the words were a statement, the tone held a question to it. It seemed to Mike that Dr. Barty was either fishing for information or settling down for a long chat. That was not something he wanted to get roped into, so Mike decided to move the conversation along as quickly as he could.

"Of course, your help was invaluable to our case, Dr. Barty, so I wanted to bring this to you personally." Mike reached into his jacket and drew out a long envelope. As he handed it across the desk, Mike explained, "This is a letter signed jointly by the Special Agent in Charge of the Miami FBI Field office and Captain Mendez of the Miami-Dade Police Department in gratitude of your help in our investigation. We hope that you will allow us to recognize your contribution to the case in this manner."

Mike failed to say that he'd asked Martinez and Mendez to sign the unusual letter since he really wanted to show Dr. Barty the good side of law enforcement, not just the bad part she seemed to believe in. It might not be part of his job, but even Mike could recognize that good public relations were essential to all branches of law enforcement.

Dr. Barty was speechless as she fingered the official seal of the FBI on the letterhead and read its contents. Almost thirty seconds passed before she found her voice.

"I really don't know what to say, Agent." She looked at the letter once more. "I am at once honored and ashamed. I must admit that I didn't think much of the FBI when you first approached me, but as I've read and heard so much about the case over the last few weeks, I've come to realize how difficult your job must be. That's why, when I realized the murderer must be well acquainted with Edgar Allen Poe, I had to come forward and tell you what I knew. I was hoping I was wrong and that no one I had once advised could be involved in these horrific crimes, but I felt it was my duty to help. I have been extremely impressed with you and Agent McKissick and I've come to realize that I was wrong about law enforcement officers in general. You all put your lives at risk every day to protect people like me and we should be more grateful."

She tapped the paper with her finger, "I think I'll have this letter framed and put it on my wall side by side with my diplomas. In fact, it means just as much as any of them," she finished in almost a whisper.

Mike was surprised. He was glad he'd come in person instead of simply sending the letter in the mail as he'd originally planned.

He stood up and, holding out a hand, said, "Dr. Barty, it's been a pleasure. Perhaps we'll meet again the next time I'm in Miami."

Jeniviere's eyes widened. "Oh, I didn't realize that you weren't from here. That is to say, I just assumed ..." Dr. Barty trailed off as she suddenly blushed.

Mike knew then that Danny had been correct and apparently Dr. Jeniviere Barty had a crush on him. And although he was a bit flattered, the UM professor was not his type. Mike was glad to be leaving town before anything could get weird.

"It was a natural assumption, I'm sure," Mike glossed over the awkward moment. "Thanks again, Dr. Barty, and take care of yourself."

Without waiting for further comment, Mike turned and quickly left the office.

~~

"Okay, where'd Mike say he was going again?" asked Alex as he bagged another item from one of the crime scenes. "Wherever he went, it's pretty convenient that he's been gone most of the morning while we're stuck bagging and tagging all this stuff."

"He went to see his girlfriend," snickered Danny as he pecked at his computer.

"Girlfriend?" Blaine repeated as her head snapped up.

"Yeah, Dr. Barty. You know, from UM? I swear she's got a crush on him. He'd better be careful, you know. All alone in her office with no one around? There's no telling what could happen …"

A clearing of a throat caused them all to look around and Danny's face went red as he spied Mike in the doorway.

"You have something to say, *Agent* McKissick?" Mike's tone could have picked up spilled water, it was so dry.

"Agent McKissick?" echoed Chip as he looked from Mike to Danny. "Since when?"

"I'd be interested to know that myself," said Mike as he walked further into the room. "Dr. Barty spoke of you as an agent, Danny." Mike nonchalantly hitched a hip onto the edge of the table Danny sat at. "What's that all about?"

"Yeah, Danny, don't you know it's against the law to impersonate a law enforcement officer?" Alex said with a chuckle. "Just because you work for the FBI …"

"No, no! You've got it all wrong," Danny held up his hands in defense. "I told her more than once that I wasn't an agent, but she just wouldn't listen. Honestly, Mike, I didn't try to mislead her, ever. I swear."

Mike couldn't hold it in anymore. The sound began as a chuckle, then exploded into a full-bodied belly-laugh, which everyone in the room joined. Danny realized he was being teased and added his laughter to the cacophony around him. It felt good to laugh out loud again after the almost constant pressure of the last few weeks. Mike needed that.

~~

A few hours later, it was just Blaine and Mike while the others took a late lunch. Mike labeled another box while Blaine added the contents list before taping it shut.

Mike added the box to the growing collection in the corner and, when he turned back, Blaine was absentmindedly rubbing a hand along her pants leg and staring into space. She'd been like this all day, he'd noticed. Quiet and aloof, she wasn't laughing at Alex's jokes or adding to the teasing of Danny. She'd barely said two words to him, and Mike couldn't help but wonder if he'd done something to anger her. With the others gone, now would be the perfect time to ask her.

"Mike, I need to tell you something."

"Like you're a mind reader?" Mike quipped as he tried not to let his concern show.

"A mind reader? What?" Blaine's face reflected her confusion and she looked at Mike expectantly.

"I was just thinking that I should ask why you've been so quiet and so distant today. Are you pissed at me or something?"

He didn't know what to expect but Blaine's unladylike snort wasn't it. "No, I'm not pissed at you, Mike, but after I tell you what I have to say, you might be pissed at me."

"I very much doubt that," Mike said as he waved Blaine to continue. He had come to realize that very little Blaine could do would make him angry.

"It's about Zardes and what he tried to do to you." Blaine didn't look at Mike and continued to speak before he could interrupt. "I did something you probably won't like." Blaine got up and started pacing along the wall.

Mike didn't know exactly what was going on, but he could guess. He'd asked them not to interfere; this was between Zardes and himself. Besides, complaining to Zardes wouldn't have done any good since Blaine was MDPD and Zardes wouldn't care what she had to say anyway. But if Zardes got pissed enough, he could hurt her career with just a phone call to Mendez - that's why Mike told them not to get involved in the first place. He hoped that wasn't what Blaine was trying to tell him.

"I know you told us not to interfere," Blaine finally went on, "but I couldn't let it go. Zardes was targeting you unfairly and using Chip was just cruel if you ask me, so ..." She suddenly turned around, took a deep breath, and announced, "IwenttoMendez."

She'd run her words together and it took Mike a moment to figure out what she'd said. "Mendez?" Mike all but yelled, "But why? This was an internal FBI matter. Going to Mendez doesn't make any sense! What were you thinking?"

Mike was genuinely confused but more than that, embarrassed. The MDPD captain had believed in him when Zardes dismissed his theory and Mike didn't want Mendez to know he was having problems. It was unreasonable, he knew, but Mike really wanted to prove Mendez's faith in him had been well placed. He suddenly felt more hurt than he thought possible. He turned away from Blaine.

"Mike, I knew you'd be mad, but I also understood that this was an FBI matter. Going to Zardes was a non-starter, but I knew Mendez could go to Martinez. If Mendez knew what Zardes was doing to you and that it was hurting the case, I was sure he'd tell Martinez and the SAC would take care of it. Everyone wanted the same thing - find the murderer and stop him. The case was more important than anything else. So, I went to my supervisor, not yours. I figured that Mendez and Martinez could handle it at that level."

Blaine stopped talking and Mike turned back around. He could see it in her eyes; she was begging for understanding. She knew she had hurt him and all she wanted was his forgiveness. Mike wasn't sure he could give that yet, but he could at least make her feel somewhat better.

He took a breath and let it out slowly. "I understand you were trying to help and I'm glad you knew enough to go to Mendez and not to Zardes directly. We both know that wouldn't have done any good. But I'm not gonna lie to you, it does hurt that you went behind my back after I'd asked you all to stay out of it. I appreciate that you were trying to help. That does mean a lot to me." Mike's mouth sketched a wry smile. "Unfortunately, it didn't work. Zardes still took over the investigation and screwed up the stake out in Coral Gables. Seven people died and I blame him. I've been trying to figure out how I'm gonna put it in my report. It's gonna be tricky."

"Not really," Blaine answered a little too quickly. At Mike's puzzled look, she said, "Just tell it like it was. The facts will explain everything. You won't have to do a thing."

~~

"Mike, you got a minute?"

Mike looked up from his desk to see Chip standing nearby. He thought everyone had gone home a couple of hours ago. They'd argued with him when he told them to leave. They wanted to work through and get everything finished tonight, but Mike had effectively pulled rank and sent them home. He knew there were still several hours of work ahead of them and it would probably go faster if they were fresh and attacked it after a good night's sleep. Besides, he had a ton of paperwork of his own still to do and wanted to work on it in solitude.

"Chip, what are you still doing here? I thought I told you to go home and get some rest."

"You did and I did," he conceded. "But I came back. I had to talk to you without the others here and I didn't know if you'd be leaving as soon as we're finished here tomorrow. So, I went home, ate dinner with my dad, then came back."

"Okay ..." Mike drawled the word out.

It hadn't escaped his notice that Chip had not really spoken directly to him since he'd admitted to being Zardes's accomplice. He'd pretty much kept his head down and tried to stay out of everyone's way. Mike knew the other members of the task force had taken his request to heart and hadn't blamed Chip for what had happened. In fact, Alex had gone out of his way to show there were no hard feelings and Mike had taken the older man aside and thanked him for it. Now, he had a pretty good idea what his young friend needed to talk about but decided it would be better for Chip to take it at his own speed.

"What's up?"

Chip stood up straighter, squared his shoulders and looked straight ahead as if he was at military attention.

Or standing in front of a firing squad, Mike thought.

Under different circumstances, he'd be laughing at the rank fear he saw in Chip's eyes. As it was, Mike found himself angry all over again at how much damage Zardes had done to Chip's delicate self-confidence. He tried to project as welcoming and understanding a demeanor as he could and patiently waited for what was to come.

"I want to apologize again for what happened before. I want you to know that I understand what I did was wrong, and I'm prepared to take my punishment. I'll be turning in my resignation next week. I ..."

"You will do no such thing." Mike stood up quickly, spilling a couple of files onto the floor.

All his good intentions threatened to go out the door and he took a deep breath lest Chip think his anger was directed at him. He had to do this right or the FBI would lose a potentially good, but impressionable, agent. Mike was not going to let Zardes win this one as well.

"Chip, none of this was your fault. Zardes instigated this situation and he's to blame. To put it bluntly, he used your youth and inexperience against you like a pawn on a chess board. He wanted to get to me, and he went through you to do it. He mired you in office politics and used your aspirations to his advantage. You wanted to get into VCMO and he dangled that carrot in front of you."

Mike put a hand on the young agent's shoulder. "I get that you were in too deep before you even knew what was going on and that you didn't feel there was anyone you could turn to. I'm not mad at you, Chip, I'm mad at him. I will not let you carry the blame for this. And I certainly won't let you resign over it. Consider it a learning experience and let it make you a better agent. Chip, I really believe you could be a good agent with a little seasoning. Don't let Zardes and his machinations take that away from you. You're better than him. Prove it to yourself and stick around. Give yourself a break. You're a great asset to the FBI. Stay here where you belong."

Chip took an audible gulp. He looked Mike in the eye for the first time in days. "I want to stay, Mike, I really do. I just figured that if I got duped into this kind of a situation once, it could happen again. You're a great agent, Mike, and I've learned a ton from you these last few weeks. I just don't want to make the same mistake again and hurt anyone else the way I've hurt you, that's all." His shoulders sagged slightly.

"It won't happen again because you'll know what to look out for next time," stated Mike emphatically. "Like I said, learn from this experience and no one will be able to put you in that position again. Do that, and you'll be fine, I promise." Mike looked at his watch. "Now, get out of here. It's already nine and we've still got a lot of work ahead of us tomorrow. I don't want you falling asleep over your computer!"

Chip grinned at the quip and gratefully nodded at his friend. As he turned to make his way down the hall toward the elevators, Mike noticed his step was a bit lighter and his shoulders held up a mite higher.

CHAPTER 58

I remained too much inside my head and ended up losing my mind.
Attributed to Edgar Allan Poe

August 25

The case was officially over. Everyone had finished and turned in their reports, the evidence was all tagged, bagged, boxed, labeled, and headed to the evidence locker. Martinez and Mendez had given their last official briefing to the press and just this afternoon, Mike had finished going over the case with AUSA Robin McMurphy, tying up loose ends and discussing prosecution strategies.

Now back at his temporary desk, Mike was finishing up his last report. He was dog-tired, exhausted really. The emotional strain of the case had played hell with his psyche and at this point all he wanted was to go back to his hotel room and relax with a movie on the TV and a bottle of whiskey in his hand. Or maybe he really didn't want to be alone. Maybe he should text Blaine and see if she wanted to work out and then grab a bite. Maybe it was company he needed after all.

Mike was brought out of his introspection by the ping of the elevator followed by staccato heels against the polished floor. He saw a figure move into his peripheral view and looked up to see Rhonda Sagan at his side. She looked as tired as he felt.

"Hey! How'd your turn with the AUSA go?" Mike asked as he minimized the report on his computer screen.

"Okay, I guess," Rhonda said with a notable lack of enthusiasm. "I don't think Ms. McMurphy was particularly happy with me though."

Mike was startled. "Why not? You did a great job during the investigation. What's McMurphy's problem?"

"Oh, it's not my job during the case she's unhappy with. It's my 'shilly-shallying' - that was the phrase she used - on whether Janice is a true serial killer or not. I told her that I now think Janice doesn't fit the pattern and to call her that could misrepresent her mental state. McMurphy's already pissed enough that Janice will probably end up in a hospital instead of a jail cell, so my changing my mind - again - doesn't help. Even though the public generally believes that serial killers are insane, they don't usually fit the definition of legal insanity. So, if Janice Toledo could be declared a serial killer, McMurphy believes she'd have a better case for conviction. As it is, if the FBI's own profiler doesn't think she's a serial killer, then ..."

"The case isn't as strong," Mike finished for her.

"Right." Rhonda sighed. "So, for the moment at least, I'm the bad guy."

"Nonsense. You did a good job and telling the AUSA the truth is part of that. McMurphy knows that. She's just frustrated with this case like the rest of us. She'll get over it and by the time you're needed in court, it'll all be water under the bridge. Don't sweat it."

Rhonda smiled. "Go raibh maith agat."

A moment went by while Mike drew random circles on his notepad.

Finally, she said, "You know, you're really good at this. You did a great job, too." Mike snapped his pen in two and Rhonda jumped. "Mike, what's wrong? Are you okay? Did I say something wrong?"

Rhonda's tone reflected her concern and Mike felt bad. Trying to reassure her, he said, "No Rhonda, I'm just fine. Don't worry about me."

Apparently not buying it for a second, Rhonda grabbed a nearby chair and sat next to his desk. "Did something else happen with the case?" she asked cautiously.

Mike sighed as he replied "No, nothing happened with the case."

"Was it something about the way the evidence was presented that's a problem? Do you need me to go over anything again?"

Mike knew that Rhonda wouldn't quit until she'd either hit on the right question or somehow wheedled the answer from him. Mike tried to find a way tell her just enough to satisfy her without having to give away too much.

"No, Rhonda, nothing's wrong with the evidence. I'm just tired, that's all."

Rhonda seemed to consider. "Okay, Mike," the profiler began, "I certainly can understand that. But I can't help feeling there's something else behind this. Would you like to talk to me about it? Maybe I can help."

"Nothing's wrong, Rhonda!" exploded Mike suddenly. "Just leave it be!"

Mike pushed his chair out and Rhonda flinched as it hit the back wall.

"Now I know I'm right," responded Rhonda. In juxtaposition to Mike's outburst, Rhonda spoke quietly and calmly. "What happened today? Did someone say something about the case that upset you somehow?"

"No, dammit! No one had to say anything! I can do that all by myself, thank you very much!" Mike started pacing. "Do you have any idea what it was like for me to go over the timeline with the AUSA today and to know that it was my fault that so many people died while I did nothing!"

"Whoa!" responded Rhonda as she gestured with her hands. "Where the hell did that come from? Mike, you are not responsible ..."

"Yes, I am, dammit! We sat on our asses outside that house for *hours* while Janice Toledo was inside murdering *seven* people! She did it right under our noses and I let her get away with it!"

"Mike, you could not have saved those seven people and you know it. Zardes was in operational command and he wouldn't let you go in. You went to the AUSA because Zardes told you to. McMurphy said you didn't have enough evidence for a warrant, so you did everything you could to get that evidence. The surveillance, questioning of witnesses, all the sleep you lost. You couldn't find any evidence because there wasn't any to find. You did your best, Mike. You are not to blame for this."

"If not me, then who?" Mike continued to pace as he castigated himself. "At the beginning of all this, I approached Zardes and he ignored me. And while I sat on my hands, two more people died. I had to go to MDPD to get anyone to do anything. I got distracted by Bastyr's confession and Mount's relationship to Stephen Hardison. That lost us valuable time. Then, even when we had a suspect, I didn't move fast enough to get what we needed. I let even more people die while I took my time trying to decide if Janice or Cameron was guilty. Cameron didn't crack when we talked to him yesterday and since we still don't have anything concrete on him he's probably gonna get away with killing Oscar. Janice'll end up in a crazy ward somewhere. Seventeen people dead and no one's gonna spend even one day in jail. Great way to solve a case. I should turn in my badge now and save everybody a lot of trouble ..."

"That's enough!" Rhonda walked up to Mike, grabbed him by both arms and turned him around until they were face to face.

"Mike! You are not responsible for any of this! You did everything you could. You followed your boss's orders and the advice of the AUSA."

Rhonda took a breath and continued, "If you want to cast blame, then why not start with Zardes? Like you said, you went to him and he ignored you. You could have argued with him about it more strongly or gone over his head directly to Martinez. Why didn't you?"

"You know why. Chain of Command. Zardes made his decision and that was that. It wasn't my place to go over his head."

"But you went to Mendez anyway. You stuck to your guns until you could convince someone that there was a case there, didn't you?"

Mike nodded reluctantly. He wasn't ready to give in that easily, however. "I was still in over my head. I didn't get the evidence we needed quick enough or McMurphy would have been able to issue that warrant sooner."

Rhonda smiled. "The AUSA is there to interpret the law and instruct us how to proceed so she can get a conviction. You knew you didn't have enough when Zardes told you to go to her and you were proved right, *again.* It's her call on warrants and what evidence will stand up in Court or not. We have no choice but to follow her advice."

Mike shook his head. "It's not that simple, Rhonda." He blew out a breath. "I oversaw the investigation. I determined how to proceed, and I screwed it up."

"Well, then," asked Rhonda reasonably, "maybe you should be angry at me. I couldn't make up my mind about what is a serial killer or not. If I had given you the right information at the beginning, you could have altered the way you investigated the case. You might have caught Janice earlier. Why aren't you blaming me?"

Mike stared at the profiler. "That's ridiculous, Rhonda. You told us up front you weren't sure and that it didn't matter as to how we pursued the investigation. You spent hours researching serial killers, were involved in countless briefings. Hell, you even moved down here to be on the scene. You went above and beyond on this one. You're not to blame for Janice Toledo's murder spree. You did everything you could to help us. You ..."

Mike halted as he realized what Rhonda had done. She had turned his argument against him. Everything Mike had blamed himself for were the same things Rhonda had just proved no one else was to blame for either. Mike sat back down in his chair slowly and sighed for the third time.

"Okay, okay, Rhonda," Mike capitulated. "You made your point. I wasn't to blame for Janice Toledo's killing spree any more than you, David, Alex, Chip or Blaine. We all followed our procedures and did what we could. She was really smart and there wasn't enough evidence to bring her in before her final murders. It's just ..." Mike trailed off and looked away for a moment. He opened his mouth as if to say something else, but closed it again shaking his head.

"The system isn't perfect, Mike. We all followed procedure and did the best we could. And yes, more people died while we followed the clues we had, but in the end, we got her and no one else will die." Rhonda repeated, *"No one else* will die at Janice Toledo's hands because you did your job. You did good, Agent Donaldson."

Mike looked at the profiler and asked, "Then why don't I feel good?"

Rhonda smiled as she replied, "Because you have a heart, Mike. You *care* too much. I can tell you like to present the façade of the in-control agent, but that's just the face you show to the world. I can see what's really inside. And it's not a bad thing, you just need to learn to take a step back a bit. You're a *good* agent. You need to keep being a good agent."

Several moments went by before Mike gave her a small smile and nodded wearily. "I know all this inside, you know. I think I needed someone to say it to me." Now a real smile came to his face as he said, "Thanks, Rhonda. I think that's just what I needed to hear."

"Good, then my work here is done." Rhonda got up and moved her borrowed chair back to its original spot. She held out a hand and said, "I'm on my way back to Tampa late tonight so I'll say goodbye now. Good luck, Mike."

Mike shook the proffered hand and his teeth showed as he said, "Thanks for everything, Rhonda. We couldn't have done it without you. Have a safe trip back."

As he heard Rhonda's footsteps retreating, Mike brought up his report once again. He typed a word or two, then sighed.

Screw it. I'm not leaving until tomorrow afternoon. I'll finish it in the morning.

As he retrieved his jacket, he saw his phone and picked it up. The screen said 5:30. *Not late. I wonder...* Mike nodded and dialed. "Hey, Blaine. What are you up to? I was wondering if you had time for a workout at the gym? Maybe a quick dinner afterwards?"

EPILOGUE

What a world of happiness their harmony foretells!
'THE BELLS'

August 26

Done. Finally!

Mike hit 'save' on his computer and sent the report on to the higher ups. He closed his eyes with a feeling of satisfaction for a moment, then began to clean up his desk. He was used to leaving everything as he found it since he worked at borrowed desks more often than not.

It was only 10 a.m. and his flight didn't leave until late in the afternoon, so he had plenty of time. He'd already checked out of the hotel and had one last breakfast at his favorite cafe with his favorite waitress. It was kind of weird knowing he wouldn't see Beverly's bright smile in the mornings or start his day off with that incredible coffee. He'd even considered trying to bribe the recipe out of the restaurant owner, then thought better of it.

He'd said goodbye to David and Alex yesterday afternoon and spent a pleasant evening with Blaine last night. After their longer than usual workout, they ate at a quaint Italian place owned by a couple Blaine knew and had a really nice time. Without the stress of the case or deadlines to meet, the conversation had flowed easily, and Mike felt more relaxed than he had for many months. He was going to miss the beautiful brunette and planned on keeping in touch. That was something else he almost never did on his travels. He stopped at a place, finished the job then never looked back. Not this time, though. There was a lot about Miami he was going to miss, and Blaine's companionship was at the top of the list.

"Agent Donaldson."

Mike looked up and was surprised to see SAC Martinez at his desk. He stood up quickly and almost coming to attention, said, "Good morning, sir. I didn't expect to see you again before I left."

"No reason you should have, Donaldson. Have a minute to talk? When are you leaving?"

"I have plenty of time, sir. My plane doesn't leave until 4:15. How can I help you this morning?"

"Actually ..." Martinez trailed off and took a quick look around. Seeming to come to a decision, he asked, "Could we speak someplace more private? How about an interview room?"

"Certainly, sir. I believe number one is open. Please, follow me."

Mike led the way down the corridor and wondered what this was all about. He didn't think anything had gone wrong with the case already. Probably Zardes had made good on his threat and complained to the SAC about him. In his report, Mike had been as diplomatic as he could, but he'd made it clear that Zardes had taken over the stake out and, he felt, waited too long before going in. Perhaps he wasn't as diplomatic as he thought or possibly Martinez and Zardes were golfing buddies and he'd just slit his own throat.

Well, it doesn't matter, I'm outta here in a few hours anyway. I just need to get through this conversation, and it'll all be over. Too bad, though, I like Miami.

Mike shut the door and took a seat. He waited for the SAC to start the conversation.

"I don't believe in beating around the bush, Agent, so I'll get right to the point. I'm impressed with you, Donaldson. You did a great job on this case and I'd like you to consider a transfer down here. We could use someone with your experience and background in Miami. So, what do you say? Think you could consider a move down south?"

Mike was flabbergasted. Two minutes ago, he was sure Martinez was going to rip his guts out, now he was being offered a transfer? Will wonders never cease!

"Sir, I'm flattered that you'd even ask me, and I have to admit, I'm beginning to really like Miami, but I don't think I can commit to anything right away. I'd need to speak to my supervisor in Detroit and I'm not sure I'm ready to stop working fugitive cases. It's sort of become my specialty and, frankly, I'm good at it. It's been a while since I investigated cases on a daily basis and I'm not sure ..."

"Nonsense, Donaldson," interrupted the SAC. "Didn't I just tell you I was impressed with your work on the Poe murders case? I wouldn't have invited you to transfer down here if I didn't think you could do it. If you want, we could even arrange to allow you to take on some fugitive cases occasionally. Your problem is that you don't have enough self-confidence, Donaldson. You're too worried about not making a mistake to realize that *everyone* makes mistakes in this job. You were smart enough to tell Agent Smythe that, now you have to accept it for yourself."

Mike's mouth opened in surprise. "How'd you know about that, sir?"

He remembered his pep talk to Chip but had no idea how Martinez could have found out about it unless someone in the room told him.

Martinez started to chuckle, and Mike was even more confused.

"I got a blow-by-blow description of all the good things you've done on this case, Donaldson, not only from Smythe but also from Detective Hoskins."

Blaine!? She'd told him she spoke to Mendez, but when did she talk to Martinez? And why?

"Don't look so shocked, Donaldson. Detective Hoskins made a report to Captain Mendez detailing what Bradley Zardes had done, and of course, Mendez came to me. I know she told you. What I want to know is, why did I have to hear about this from a Captain in the MDPD and not from you personally? You should have come to me as soon as Zardes started giving you trouble. Why didn't you?"

Mike floundered a bit before deciding on the most diplomatic way to answer. "Sir, I didn't want to make waves. I'm only here for a short time and thought I could handle your SSA. I was more concerned about keeping the focus on the case than on any personality conflicts with Zardes. Frankly, sir, I'm lousy at behind-the-scenes politics, so I just didn't worry about it."

"And you didn't think that Zardes undercutting you wasn't going to hurt the investigation?" Martinez's voice had an ironic tone that wasn't there before.

Mike's face flushed. His reasoning at the time had made sense to him, but now saying it out loud, not so much. Mike struggled for an explanation, but nothing came out.

Finally, he went back to the original topic and asked, "I know Blaine went to Mendez and I understand he reported to you, but that doesn't explain ..."

"No, Donaldson, apparently you don't understand how things work around here." Martinez's face broke into a grin and he continued, "Mendez came to me, told me about Zardes's arrangement with agent Smythe and about Hoskins. Now, I'm not going to get a report like that and not investigate it myself. I contacted Hoskins and met with her. We spoke at length. I asked her to tell me about the task force, how everyone got along and how she thought you were doing. I have to say," Martinez's grin turned into a full-blown smile, "she sang your praises, Agent Donaldson. I'd say you have at least one fan in the MDPD. She not only told me how Zardes had used Smythe but how you were trying to bring the boy along during the investigation. Then I talked to Smythe. He confirmed the whole story and somewhere in there told me about your little pep talk. He's also a big fan of yours, by the way. That's what I was talking about earlier, Donaldson. You have an instinct about this job, but you need more faith in yourself. I think moving to Miami could be good for you. Will you consider it?"

"Yes" was on the tip of his tongue when he realized why he could never transfer to Miami.

His eyes showed his regret when he answered, "Sir, I do appreciate the offer, but I don't see how I could work in Miami permanently. You said you don't like beating around the bush, sir, so I hope you'll accept my bluntness. I can't transfer down here since I'd have to work with and report to SSA Zardes. Maybe it's paranoia, but I'd always be looking over my shoulder wondering what he was going to try next. I don't know why he's taken such a dislike to me, but I know myself enough to know that I couldn't work like that, sir. Thanks, but I'm afraid I'll have to decline."

Martinez's face held genuine confusion as he said, "Haven't you heard, Donaldson? Agent Zardes has been invited to take an early retirement. I put a formal reprimand in his file after Smythe confirmed everything that happened. Frankly, I thought about requesting a formal review, but Smythe asked me not to. But when I found out how the stake out went down, that was the last straw. Zardes took over and screwed it up. Now maybe all those people would've died anyway, but maybe not. Everybody's reports said the same thing. As a matter of fact, your version was the least damning. All the others crucified him. If it ever got out, the Bureau would probably be sued by the victims' families. To tell the truth, getting rid of Zardes now gives me cover for later.

"And as for why he acted the way he did with you, well, that was coming for a while, I'm afraid. You just happened to be the most convenient target." It was the SAC's turn to blow out a breath. "Zardes has been itching to move up since the day he took the SSA job. He applied a couple of times for open SAC positions but was passed over. You see, Zardes's record shows he was a good agent, but he never had a lot of imagination. He didn't have the kind of open mind he'd need in this position.

"Take this case, for example. He didn't listen to you when he should have. He could have taken your preliminary findings and contacted MDPD himself. But he didn't. Because of that, we lost valuable time. Then when he realized what an important case this was going to be, he decided to use it to position himself for a promotion. Truthfully, it would have been anyone in that spot, you just happened to be the unfortunate agent appointed to lead the investigation. It wasn't anything personal, Agent Donaldson. He'd've made the attempt no matter who was in charge." Martinez smiled, "Anyway, he's gone, so you don't have to worry about that. Now, what do you say? Will you think about coming down here?"

This time, Mike didn't hesitate. With a huge grin, he held out his hand and answered, "Yes, sir. I'll think about it very carefully. And thank you, sir."

~~

An elderly man dozed in his chair. His snoring seemed to annoy the young mother in the opposite chair almost as much as his bobbing head seemed to fascinate the three-year-old on her lap. Next to them, a middle-aged businessman checked stock market prices on his laptop while his trophy wife yawned over the most recent edition of a popular gossip magazine. At the check-in counter, the harassed attendant tried in vain to explain the carry-on policy to a Millennial whose purple nail polish matched her braided hair.

This snapshot of humanity and the bustle of passengers up and down the concourse would normally be enough of a distraction to entertain Mike until boarding was announced.

But not today.

He checked his watch again and began to pace around the uncomfortable plastic chairs at the gate. He still had an hour before his plane left but he felt as though time was passing too quickly. Mike pulled out his phone and checked for texts. He'd sent the message around 11:00 but he still didn't have an answer.

"Mike."

His neck popped as his head snapped up and he found himself looking into Blaine's dark eyes. He almost dropped the phone as he twice tried to tuck it into his carry-on, then with a curse just slid it into his jacket pocket.

"Uh, hi. I didn't expect you to come down here. I thought I just asked you to call." He made as if he were going to check his phone again, but a hand on his arm forestalled the effort.

"You did ask me to call, but your text was so mysterious that I was afraid something bad had happened." Her eyes apologized as she shrugged and explained, "I didn't get the message until lunch, then I had to ask for some time off from my supervisor, then traffic was a bitch, and then I went to the wrong terminal, then I ..." she trailed off, uncertainty written all over her face.

"I'm sorry you went to all that trouble. I didn't mean to worry you." Mike smiled. "But I'm glad you did. It's just that I didn't exactly know how to say it in a text, that's why I wanted to talk to you." He put his hand on her arm and gently pulled her to a more secluded area near the far wall. "Nothing happened exactly, but ... well, yeah, I guess something did happen."

He looked out the window at a plane taxiing down the runway and back to the opposite gate. He picked up his bag, put it on his shoulder, then put it back down again. He shuffled his weight from one foot to the other, then back again. Finally, he looked back at Blaine. She'd said nothing while he fidgeted but, between the piercing look she gave him and the slight drumming of her fingers on her thigh, Mike could tell she was bursting with curiosity. He decided he better get to the point before her mood changed from concern to annoyance.

"SAC Martinez came to see me this morning. He asked me to transfer down here permanently. Said we could work something out if I wanted to keep tracking fugitives occasionally." Mike stopped abruptly and waited for her reaction. He didn't have to wait long.

"Mike, that's amazing. What did you tell him?"

Blaine's pleasure was evident in her voice and Mike took heart. "I haven't yet …"

"Flight 7554 to Detroit is now boarding from Gate 53. Passengers with special requirements, parents with small children and guests in Zone 1 may now approach the gate. Please have your boarding pass out. Flight 7554 …"

As the announcement was repeated Blaine looked at Mike. "When do you have to board?"

"I'm in Zone 3, so I've got a little time." *But not much.* He decided it was time to cut to the chase. "Look, I like the idea of coming down here. I like the weather; I've liked what I've seen of the town; I like the people. I know Miami has a lot to offer. But I'd like to know if there's anything else that might give me a reason to move down here. Or maybe I should say *anyone* else." He opened his mouth to add something, then thought better of it.

Now it was Blaine's turn to look out the window, then around the concourse. His face fell as the silence dragged on.

I knew this was a bad idea.

Was it too late to save the situation with a joke? No, she wouldn't buy it and it wouldn't be fair. He'd meant the question. And at least now he figured he knew the answer. As he was about to give her a way out, she finally spoke.

"I know what you mean, and I'm flattered. But I need to explain something to you."

She paused and Mike could see she was getting her thoughts in order. He gave her the time she needed.

"You know, I didn't think much of you at the beginning of the case. I wasn't sure your idea made sense, but before that first briefing was even over, I realized you were right and I tried to help as much as I could. I was also afraid you were out of your league and you'd botch the investigation. I was wrong on both counts. Then we started working out most days and I got to know you better. I got to like you and respect you.

"I have to admit, I was furious when I realized how far Zardes went to try to discredit you. And you didn't want to call him on it. I didn't get it. After we found out that Chip was ratting to him and why, well, that just pissed me off even more. I mean, what kind of supervisor uses a green kid like that? It wasn't fair to Chip or you on any level. I knew you'd be pissed when I went to Captain Mendez behind your back, but I figured it was best for the team, so I did it anyway. But, deep down inside, I knew I was doing it for you more than for the team. I realized I'd started to like you and I wanted to, for lack of a better word, protect you from Zardes. So, I meant what I said, I am flattered. But it's not that simple."

She stopped again and Mike heard them calling Zone 2 for boarding.

"You have to go soon, so I better get this out. Without getting too Freudian on you, let's just say that my parents divorced when I was twelve. I was a lot older before I found out why. They were both health care workers and they opened a practice together. It was a disaster. They ended up fighting a lot, then my mom had an affair. It wasn't an amicable parting, though they never dragged me into it like some couples do. But I remember a lot of arguing when they thought I was asleep. Anyway, I decided I would never make that mistake. I swore I'd never get involved with a colleague no matter what. I didn't want to go through what my parents went through."

She suddenly smiled. "Having said that, I have to tell the truth here. If there was ever a guy I'd break that promise for, it'd be you. You're smart, good-looking and frankly, sexy as hell. I could easily see myself developing feelings for you. I just don't know if I should and I'd hate for you to move all the way down here just for me to decide it's a no go. That wouldn't be fair to you."

Mike felt it was time to interrupt to lighten the mood a little. "Hey, don't flatter yourself. I don't want to take a weekend trip to a chapel in Vegas or anything. I just wanted to know if you might want to go out once in a while, you know, dinners and the like. I'm hardly looking for the love of my life. Besides, I snore like a train and most women get off after the first stop."

Blaine started to laugh and soon there were tears in her eyes. She heaved to catch her breath. Finally, she shook her head and said without rancor, "You bastard. That was lousy. I'm being serious here, wearing my heart on my sleeve, no less, and you have to make me laugh. Damn you." She punched him good-naturedly on the arm. "Just for that, if you do move down here, I'm not going to help you unpack boxes."

He smiled back. "Damn, and that was going to be my next question."

Blaine returned to the matter at hand. "But really, when do you have to give Martinez an answer?"

"We didn't get that detailed, he simply wants me to think about it. I think it's a pretty open-ended offer."

"So, forget the last few minutes. What do you think you'll tell him?"

"I still need to talk to my SSA in Detroit and do some research into practical matters like the cost of living in Miami and so forth. But, since I just worked through my supposed vacation, I have more time coming, so I'll probably take some of it when I get back and look into it. I don't want to let it go too long; I'll probably make a decision within the next month or so."

"Well, whatever you decide, I want to hear from you. And if you do decide to transfer, I'll be glad to help you find a place to live and I'll probably even move a box or two. If you say please, that is."

"I always say please," he answered with as much solemnity as he could. "As a matter of fact …"

"*Zone 3 now boarding at Gate 53.*"

"That's me," Mike said.

"I know." The regret in her voice was genuine.

Mike leaned down and placed a gentle kiss on her lips. As much a goodbye as a promise, it held possibilities, and Blaine smiled in response. He picked up his bag and with a slight wave, made his way to the gate.

GLOSSARY OF ABBREVIATIONS

AUSA—Assistant United States Attorney

BOLO—Be On the Look-Out

CDC—Centers for Disease Control and Prevention

DEA—Drug Enforcement Administration

ERT—Evidence Response Team

FBI—Federal Bureau of Investigation

MDC—Miami Dade College

MDPD—Miami-Dade Police Department

ME—Medical Examiner

MO—Modus operandi

MOU—Memorandum of Understanding

SAC—Special Agent in Charge

SSA—Supervisory Special Agent

UM—University of Miami

USAO—United States Attorney's Office

VCMO—Violent Crime Major Offender (task force)

302 Forms—FBI's report of investigative activity

Did you enjoy reading **The Tell-Tale Murders**?

Don't miss Carolyn's previous novel, **Winding Trail**, published in January 2020.

Easter Sunday should be a quiet day, perfect to hike up Mount Sycamore's Winding Trail.

Shaken by several recent events, including almost losing his policeman brother in a shooting, Isaac feels the time is right to deal with his feelings in the silence of the mountain.

His reflective trek is interrupted when he encounters two bank robbers hiding from the law and is captured.

Isaac escapes his captors, but now, injured and alone, must fight for his life and make his way back to civilization.

Can he make it to safety before he succumbs to the cold of the mountain or will the bullet of a fugitive find him first?

Winding Trail is available through Amazon.com!

ABOUT THE AUTHOR

Carolyn Dahman was born in Louisville, Kentucky and moved to Florida in 2000. Carolyn's twin loves of science fiction and mysteries led her to write hundreds of fan fiction stories before taking the plunge with her first novel, **Winding Trail**, published in 2020 and currently available at Amazon.com.

Carolyn has been active in the community for many years and in the past was a Poll worker for the elections board, served on the Board of Directors for the Deaf and Hard of Hearing Center of Southwest Florida and as a board member for the Friends of the Library.

When not writing, Carolyn likes to spend time cycling, reading and watching soccer, the 'real' football.

Carolyn currently works for a non-profit agency in Fort Myers where she lives with her husband of thirty-two years, Doug.

Have comments about **The Tell-Tale Murders**?
Please contact Carolyn at cdahman@embarqmail.com

Or

Visit her Facebook page: Carolyn Dahman Writes

Or

Visit her website: www.carolyndahmanwrites.com